INTERNET FAMOUS

danika stone

Swoon READS

Swoon Reads • New York

For @MarkDoesStuff, who is just as cool in person.

A SWOON READS BOOK

An imprint of Feiwel and Friends and Macmillan Publishing Group, LLC

INTERNET FAMOUS. Copyright © 2017 by Danika Stone. All rights reserved.

Printed in the United States of America by LSC Communications, Harrisonburg, Virginia.

For information, address Feiwel and Friends, 175 Fifth Avenue, New York, N.Y. 10010.

Our books may be purchased in bulk for promotional, educational, or business use. Please contact your local bookseller or the Macmillan Corporate and Premium Sales Department at (800) 221-7945 ext. 5442 or by e-mail at MacmillanSpecialMarkets@macmillan.com.

"Tumblr Tags" meta post by Porpentine Charity Heartscape (porpentine.tumblr.com) included by express permission of the author.

Royalty-free emojis by permission of Emoji One: http://emojione.com

The majority of the New York and Paris images are from Pixabay and used under a Creative Commons CCO license. Selected images of Millburn, NJ, have been used with the express permission of the photographer: Lauren Scobell. The image of the Penn Station interior is by Joe Shlabotnik via Flickr, and used in accordance with Creative Commons Licensing, 2.0: https://www.flickr.com/photos/joeshlabotnik/2622091998. Please note, selective cropping and additional text have been added to Mr. Shlabotnik's original photograph.

Library of Congress Cataloging-in-Publication Data is available.

ISBN 978-1-250-11437-2 (trade paperback) / ISBN 978-1-250-11436-5 (ebook)

Book design by Eileen Savage

Feiwel and Friends logo designed by Filomena Tuosto

First Edition—2017

10 9 8 7 6 5 4 3 2 1

swoonreads.com

*"One of my favorite things is how
people talk to themselves in tumblr tags,
taking this space designed for metadata classification
and using it as a form of parenthetical speech.
Those grey little tags feel so cozy,
a whispered dimension to the flat
communication of the net."*

—Porpentine Charity Heartscape
(porpentine.tumblr.com)

The MadLibbers Dictionary

Anon: Anonymous.

App: An application or program designed for use on a cell phone, e.g.: a gaming app, a messaging app, etc.

ATM: At the moment.

bc: Because.

Blog: A series of posts, in written form, located online.

Cinnamon roll: A sweet, gentle character in fiction who elicits an "Aww . . ." response in viewers/readers.

Dashboard: The main, scrollable section of a website or blog.

DNW: Do not want.

Doxing: To publicly expose documents or details of someone's real life.

Fanmail: Messages, letters, e-mails, and posts sent to a celebrity by their fans, praising them.

Fake geek girl: The claim that certain females in fandom are "fake" fans, somehow not equal to "real" fans.

Flaming: Purposefully causing trouble through posting, i.e.: burning down a post.

Flist/friends list: The friends or connections in a social media site.

FML: Fuck my life.

Fridging: The unpleasant trope of killing off a character in a piece of fiction for the purpose of extending a story line (i.e.: to put a character in the morgue's fridge).

Friends-fic: An imagined story about the real life of a person you only know online.

Funemployment: Monetizing personal interests so that they provide you with the necessities of life (e.g.: a blogger such as Mark Does Stuff, who makes money off his website).

Gaslighting: A form of emotional manipulation/abuse where the victim is convinced he or she is the cause of the conflict.

GF: Girlfriend.

Halp: Help [sic].

IKR: I know, right?

IMO: In my opinion.

IMHO: In my humble opinion.

IP address: (Internet protocol address.) The numeric label assigned to each device connected on a computer network (e.g.: a computer, laptop, phone, printer). This label can be used to identify individual devices and where they originate.

LOL: Laugh out loud/laughing out loud.

Long-fic: A long fanfic.

Mary Sue: A female character, often in fanfic, who is too perfect to be believable. She's primarily tasked with teaching other characters an important message.

Obv: Obviously.

OC: Original character.

OTC: One true character.

OMG: Oh my God.

Parental units: The parents/guardians in a family.

Pls: Please.

Pwned: A variation on the term "owned," which gained popularity in its own right after many people accidentally typed "pwned" [sic].

RE: Regarding or in reference to.

RL: Real life.

Rly: Really.

SJW: Social justice warrior. A derogatory term used to describe a person (usually female) who is hyperaware of social justice issues and argues to correct them.

Srsly: Seriously.

TMI: Too much information (i.e.: oversharing).

Tor: A program designed to hide the IP address of the computer using it.

Troll: A person online who acts with the purpose of causing stress to another.

Trolling: The act of purposefully attacking or provoking someone online in order to upset them.

Vlog: A video blog, i.e.: a series of video posts on a topic.

Wi-Fi: Wireless Internet access technology.

WTH: What the hell.

WTF: What the fuck.

1

The message arrived as Madison Nakama slid into the passenger seat of her mother's sedan. She pulled the phone from her pocket with one hand and tugged the seat belt across her lap with the other.

NEW Message, *anonymous*: 3:59 p.m. EST
Subject: I Love, LOVE, LOOOOOOOOOOOVE YOUR BLOG!

Madi grinned. Fanmail was the very best kind of e-mail! The messages had been coming in more frequently the last few weeks, sometimes two or three a day and many more after a rewatch. Each note of happiness she received gave Madi a thrill of excitement. People loved what she blogged!

The voice of Madi's sister, Sarah, echoed from the backseat. "What're you reading, Madi?"

Madi hit OPEN, waiting as the message loaded on her phone. "Just a message."

"Is it Aunt Lisa again?" Sarah asked. "She texted Dad seven times today. Mom told Dad to turn off his phone since he was at home, and Dad said he was waiting for a message from his editor. But then Mom said the editor could e-mail and Aunt Lisa was interrupting their personal time, but he told Mom that she was his little sister, and if she wanted to talk, he'd talk. So is"—her sister took a quick breath—"this Aunt Lisa again?"

"Not Lisa," Madi said absently. "Someone else."

"Is it about your blog?"

Madi glanced toward the front door of the house, but their mother had yet to arrive. Madi still had time. "Uh-huh," she mumbled.

> Dear MadLib,
>
> I've never written to anyone famous before, so I hope this is okay! I recently joined the MadLibbers, and I had to tell you how much I ABSOLUTELY LOVE your blog! I'd heard about your rewatches once or twice, but hadn't checked them out before this month. When a fandom friend of mine told you'd started a rewatch of the SV series, I decided to pop by. I am SO GLAD that I did! I've never laughed so hard at—

"So who is the message from?" Sarah asked, interrupting the flow of Madi's thoughts. She groaned, scanning to find her place again.

> —the inside jokes and all those fandom FEELS. I honestly just wanted to call you up and say: "IKR???!!!" You totally GET it! And I know you were never a SV fangirl before you started the rewatch, but if you ever—

"Madi!" Sarah shouted. "Who's the message from?!"

Madi jerked. "I don't know who," she said. "It was sent anonymously."

"But why would someone send you an anonymous e-mail?"

"Because they don't want me to know who they are."

"Why would they e-mail you at all, if they didn't want you to know that? Why send anything? They could just *not* e-mail and then you'd never know anything about them. It doesn't make sense."

Madi glanced over the back of the seat to find her younger sister watching.

Sarah was small for fifteen years old, but the severity of her expression made her seem older.

"I'll explain the whole anon thing later, okay?" Madi said. "I just need a minute to finish."

"Finish what?"

"I want to reply to this message before we go to the park."

"But—"

"Please, Sarah. Just a minute."

Her sister crossed her arms and looked out the window. "Fine," she sighed. Madi hit REPLY, her thumbs blurring over the screen as she typed.

Reply to Message from *anonymous*: 4:03 p.m. EST
Subject: RE: I Love, LOVE, LOOOOOOOOOOOVE YOUR BLOG!

Hi, Anon!

   I'm so glad you're enjoying the blog! Don't feel you have to hide. Feel free to jump into the liveblog on Twitter when we start *Starveil V: Ghosts of the Rebellion.* That rewatch starts tonight at 7:30 p.m. EST. Just search up the MadLibs tag and—

Before Madi could finish, the door to the house opened and Madi's mother appeared. She took a step outside then turned back around, pausing half in and half out of the doorway. Madi figured her father must have called out to her to do some last-second errand. (Her father was always doing that.) With Olympic-level thumb-typing abilities, Madi sped through the last bit of her message.

—join in! I'd love to see you there.
   Thanks for the fanmail. Got to go!
—MadLib

With a grin, she hit SEND. The door to the car opened with a *screech* and Madi looked up to see her mother, white-faced, as she slid behind the wheel.

Madi's smile faltered. "Everything okay, Mom? You look—"

"Everything's fine," she said, then pulled the car onto the street without another word.

Madi glanced into the backseat, hoping to catch Sarah's eyes, but her sister was engrossed in something on her phone. After a moment, Madi turned back around. She slid her phone back in her pocket and frowned, the fleeting joy from her fanmail already gone.

Madi stared at her mother, the seconds ticking by.

"You're kidding, right?"

Around them, the May afternoon continued on like nothing had happened. The spring air hummed with the rumble of lawn mowers and motor vehicles. Children laughed on the playground. A bee buzzed. Madi was oblivious to all of it. Her chest ached like the time she'd fallen off the top of the monkey bars and her body had forgotten how to breathe. This time she'd been pushed by her mother.

"Mom," Madi pleaded, "please tell me this is a joke."

"No joke. I'm leaving."

Madi's eyes darted to the playground and the brick-fronted buildings behind it, seeking out her sister. Spring had arrived in Millburn, New Jersey. Around the park, crab-apple trees hung heavy with pink blossoms, the blue sky dotted with perfect silver clouds. Her fingers clenched, clawlike, around the cell phone in her hand. *This is so bad! So freaking bad!*

"It's been in the works for a while," her mother said, the nervous tapping of her foot the only hint of her emotions, "but I got the confirmation yesterday."

"Confirmation. Right."

"I'm . . ." Her mother shifted uneasily on the bench. "I'm leaving at the end of the week."

Madi jerked. "As in *this* week?!"

"Oxford has an undergrad summer course they'd like me to coteach. It starts June first. I want to have the paperwork done and be settled in the apartment before—"

"You've got to be kidding me!" Madi's shock rolled into sudden anger. "This is like some—some kind of awful joke."

Her mother gave a long-suffering sigh. "For goodness' sake, Madison, you're a senior in high school, not a child, so please start acting like one."

"But you're running away."

"No one's running anywhere."

"Driving. Flying. Whatever!"

Madi glared at children laughing on the equipment. Over on the swing set, her sister, Sarah—looking younger than her age would suggest—swung back and forth. Her lips were pursed in focus, eyes half closed. The swing's chains screeched in time to her motion. Watching her, Madi had the unsettling realization that while the pin had been pulled, the grenade had yet to go off.

But when it did . . .

"Look, it just sort of happened." Julia Nakama's voice was barely audible above the happy din of children. "And while I know this must be hard for you—"

"You know *nothing* about how hard it is."

"I know what it must seem like," her mother said, undeterred. "But my fellowship was only approved by the committee yesterday. As soon as your father and I talked about the move, I—"

"Dad knew about this?!"

Squeak . . . squeak . . .

Her mother leaned closer. "I understand you're upset, but please lower your voice or—"

"Or what? You'll leave?"

"Madi, please."

Squeak . . . squeak . . .

Madi stared at her sister, willing her angry tears to disappear. This couldn't be happening to them. Not now! Not when Sarah was finally settled into a good routine.

"I know this is hard to hear," her mother said. "But opportunities like this don't come along every day. When you're older and you're building your own career, you'll understand." *Squeak . . . squeak . . .* "Madi, are you even listening to me?"

"Listening to what? You're leaving." Her eyes narrowed. *"Again."*

Her mother's concern faded into frosty annoyance. "Calm down. People are staring at us."

Squeak . . . squeak . . .

"Calm down? How am I supposed to 'calm down' when you're taking off?!" Madi's voice grew shrill and she stumbled to her feet. A nearby mother turned in surprise. "You said you wouldn't do that. You promised us—you promised Sarah! And now you're doing it all over again."

"Madison, please!" Her mother's fingers clamped around her wrist and she tugged her back down to the park bench. She smiled apologetically at the onlookers, shrugging as if to say: *Sorry about this. My teen's just being a teen. You know how it is.* Madi could almost hear the laughter.

Squeak . . . The repetitive pattern slowed, and Madi caught her sister's eyes across the playground. *Squeak . . .* Sarah frowned. *Squeak . . .* Madi looked away.

"You need to keep your voice down."

Madi jerked her hand back and crossed her arms. "Yeah, well, you need to keep your promises."

"You'll understand when you're older. Families and careers are never easy to balance. . . ." Her mother's voice faltered. "Especially with our challenges. But I can't keep putting this off. Teaching at Oxford is an opportunity I'll never get again." She stood from the bench, brushing invisible crumbs from her slacks. "Now get your sister. We need to leave."

Madi grabbed her pack and stood. "Why don't you get her yourself since you're so certain about everything?"

A nearby woman gasped and Julia's face drained of color. She stepped in front of Madi, blocking her from onlookers. "We'll talk later. Go get Sarah."

Madi lifted her chin. "No."

Her mother let out a hissing breath as her fingers snaked around her daughter's wrist. "Now I don't know what you think you're playing at, Madison, but you *will* go get your sister or—"

"Why is Mom hurting your arm, Madi?"

6

Julia released her daughter and stumbled back. Sarah stood behind them, watching the interaction with an unwavering gaze.

"I-I'm not."

"Yes, you were. I saw you," Sarah announced. "You were talking to Madi, and then Madi started frowning, and she yelled at you, and then you yelled at her, and then you grabbed her arm, and—"

"I'll be in the car! Hurry up, girls. We're already late." Julia bolted away, dodging wayward children. She didn't look back.

Madi threw her arms around Sarah, hugging her younger sister. Sarah tolerated it for the count of three, then began to squirm.

"Thanks for saving me," Madi said as she released her.

Sarah didn't smile. (She rarely did.) "Why is Mom mad at you?"

"She isn't."

"Yes, she is."

"No."

"But I saw her, Madi." Sarah spoke with certainty. "You were talking, and then you started frowning, and—"

"I dunno, Sarah. Mom's just . . ."

Madi's shoulders slumped. It wasn't in her heart to tell her sister the truth: Everything in their lives had just changed yet again, and Sarah would be the one to suffer for it. Instead, she forced a brave smile. "Mom was just ready to go. She asked me to get you, and I said no."

Her sister seemed to consider that for a moment, and Madi wondered if she'd now have to explain *why* she'd refused to get her. Questions, with Sarah, continued until she was satisfied.

"Okay." Sarah looked up the street where their mother had disappeared. "So Mom's ready to go home?"

"Yeah. You ready to leave?"

"Uh-huh," she said, and looked back at the swing. "It was a good day."

Madi didn't answer. Couldn't. In seconds, Sarah was down the street, leaving her to follow. Madi glanced down at her phone, forgotten in her hand. In the last stressful minutes, a new post had appeared on her dashboard. Her throat ached as she read it.

That moment when your parents mess up

and suddenly you're the 'go-to' adult in the family.

15 minutes ago | 15 notes
#Parental Units #TMI #Adventures in RL #WHY????

■ laurentabelard likes this

■ museonfire likes this

■ shakespeargirlz likes this

■ artwithattitude likes this

With a sigh, Madi hit REBLOG.

This was the worst possible day in a long string of them, and her sister, Sarah, didn't know the half of it.

2

*"I don't understand. All my life I've been waiting
for someone, and when I find her, she's ... she's a fish."*

(*Splash*, 1984)

The Nakama house was unnervingly quiet. The moment they'd walked inside, Madi's mother had stormed upstairs and slammed the bedroom door. *Discussion over.*

It made Madi want to scream.

She slumped at the kitchen table, phone in hand. The view of her father, sitting across from her, was partially blocked by the screen of his laptop and the long swath of black hair that hung limp in her eyes. *Dad won't say anything,* she thought irritably. *He never does.*

She spun her thumb and a series of messages rolled up the screen. Several tweets had been posted in the last few minutes. They echoed shock at Madi's solitary message, shouted to the universe at large:

@MadLib: The parental units have really done it this time. Why do they pull shit like this and LEAVE ME TO HANDLE THE FALLOUT?!? #WTF #ParentalFail

She smiled sadly as she read the replies.

@fandometric: @MadLib Saw your post. Anything I can do?
@ModernDayWitch: @MadLib Family emergencies are rough. Take

a moment and breathe. (Or get a voodoo doll. ;) Sending good vibes.

@laurentabelard: @MadLib Just heading home. I'm only a text or Skype away. I can't fix it but I can listen.

Madi sighed and tapped in a quick reply to the group of online friends:

@MadLib: @fandometric @ModernDayWitch @laurentabelard Thanks for the replies. Things are going to get worse before better. #DNW

She belatedly added a second, personal reply to Lauren, wishing, as she so often did, that her online friends lived nearby. She needed someone to talk to tonight. Her chest felt like it was caught in a vise.

@MadLib: @laurentabelard I know. I might text you later.

She looked back up to find her father still typing. The silence of the house was as upsetting as the news. Madi had expected something—*anything*!

"I wish you'd told me before, Dad," Madi said.

He didn't look up or respond, though his mustache twitched.

"If you ask me," she added, "this whole thing's going to be just as hard as Sarah's first day of high school. There's going to be fallout from this."

Her father lifted his gaze from the screen for a fleeting second. "Then we'll manage." His eyes dropped. "Just like we always have."

Madi's phone buzzed and she read the notification.

@laurentabelard: @MadLib Msg me anytime. I'm up late. (Always.) You know I'm here for you.

Madi smiled at the sentiment. Lauren was a good friend.

From the far room, a musical swell of intergalactic proportions began.

"It's starting, Madi!" Sarah called.

Madi leaned sideways, balancing the wooden chair on two legs. "Just a sec! I'm talking to Dad."

His typing slowed. "Could you get your sister to keep it down? I have a bunch of articles to finish. Editor needs them by tomorrow morning."

"But we can't put off telling her. She deserves to—"

"These aren't going to write themselves," he interrupted. "And your mother and I *are* going to tell Sarah. We're just waiting for the right moment. We don't want to upset her unnecessarily."

Madi's phone buzzed again, but she ignored it. "Mom's leaving Saturday morning. If you ask me—"

"Friday night, actually."

"Friday?!"

"Mm-hmm."

"Then the sooner you tell Sarah, the better."

"It's not that simple, and you know that," he sighed.

"What I *know* is Mom's running off, and I'm stuck picking up the pieces."

"That's hardly fair."

"This is exactly what happened when she took the research grant."

Her father lifted his hands from the keyboard and steepled his fingers. He didn't quite make eye contact, just looked over Madi's shoulder. She hated when he did that. "That was two years ago," he said.

"And Sarah *still* freaks out when we drive by the airport." Madi leaned forward, trying unsuccessfully to catch his eyes. "You need to talk to Mom. She can't keep doing this. Every time it happens, it's harder to—"

"Madi!" Sarah shrieked. "The movie's on NOW!"

Charles shrank at the sound of his daughter's screams.

Madi craned sideways. "Just a second, Sarah! I'm about to—"

"But it's ON! The movie's starting! It's starting right NOW! Hurry, Madi! HURRY!" Her sister's words faded into sharp-pitched cries.

Charles closed his laptop with a *snap*. For the first time, he met Madi's gaze and her breath caught. Her father didn't look annoyed, nor did he look angry. He looked utterly *exhausted*.

"You'd better go," he said, cringing as the screams rose to earsplitting levels. "Sarah sounds upset. I'm going to work in the office."

"MADI! MADI, COME ONNNN!!!"

Her father tucked the laptop under his arm and walked away.

In the living room, a sci-fi sound track roared, the deep bass shuddering the windows. Sarah's panicked shouting faded into excited cries as Madi appeared.

"It's starting! It's starting! Hurry!"

"Sorry I'm late," Madi said.

"Sit down!"

Slumping down on the cushion at her side, Madi took a surreptitious glance at her sister. Sarah was rapt. She didn't smile or look over, but she leaned against Madi. This was the closest personal contact Sarah ever initiated, and the little gesture was the thing that finally tipped the balance. Madi's vision blurred with tears as the worry that had been eating away at her came rushing back. *Oh my God. When Sarah finds out about Mom, she's gonna freak!* She pulled out her phone and flipped through the contacts she knew well enough to text.

@ModernDayWitch worked night shifts. @fandometric was cool, but kept to himself. And @StarveilBrian1981 didn't commiserate unless the discussion involved science fiction or the military.

Her finger spun one last time and paused. @laurentabelard was an exchange student and relatively new to the MadLibs community, Madi's blog. The only reason Madi had even noticed Lauren in the first place was that when she got active in the MadLibs fandom, she'd begun posting her comments in French.

Curious, Madi had pasted Lauren's first, tentative comment into Google Translate, and the answer appeared: *"I love the MadLibs blog. It's fantastic! Very interesting. Can't wait to read more!"* In the months since, Madi had watched Lauren's name rise up the ranks of the most active MadLibbers. They'd even texted a few times.

Madi had launched the MadLibs website two years before in hopes of sharing her love of popular culture. For Madi, her fans were a benevolent mass of unknowns, cheering her on from behind an array of usernames. The blog had succeeded far beyond her wildest dreams: More than sixty thousand readers followed her posts directly, with twice that many popping in to read on a daily basis. The MadLibs site had nearly half a million hits each month, and that number was rising! Her followers called themselves "MadLibbers," and there were offshoot fan sites that boosted the signal to the Internet at large. According to Lauren, there was a fan collective based in Paris who painstakingly translated each of her posts.

Madi loved this connection to the world! Her readers voted topics and Madi covered them. The rewatches she hosted included everything from video games to Old Hollywood movies. In addition to her posts, Madi tweeted a running commentary, liveblogging the experience with her global followers.

Lauren was one of Madi's countless fans, and though Madi had never met her, they regularly chatted online. Lauren seemed supportive. Madi popped open her contacts and thumbed in a brief message.

> u around, l?

On-screen, an epic battle began. Madi watched from under half-closed lids. Combat scenes weren't really her thing. She saw the use of them, but she was too good at guessing the outcome. The hero, for one, always made it through with seconds to spare. (Spartan would be no different.) A pulsing trio of dots appeared on her phone's screen, letting her know a reply was about to arrive.

> salut, madi! feeling better? ☺

> hardly. i rly need someone to talk to. u up for a bitchfest? 😈

> absolument! is this about the "parental unit" tweet?

yes and no. it's a looooooooong story

the subway ride will be longer. (still not used to that word. i typed metro three times before I remembered what it was)

use metro—it sounds cool—like a steampunk novel 😜

nice! 😄 now, you said you had a story for me . . . ?

my mother's leaving

☹️ like forever? a divorce?

not a divorce (though I wonder if that's coming) she got a fellowship

hold on. i need my translator

it's like an exchange but for grown-ups— like what u r doing! only she's not attending a school, she's teaching

??? 😕

she's a prof at princeton. fellowship is to oxford (uk)

ah! and you're sad because she's leaving?

sort of but that's not really the issue

14

it's not?

it's my sister

sorry, i don't follow.

all right, long text ahead & TMI warning: i'm telling u MAJOR family drama now. u r SWORN TO SECRECY. no sharing. u promise?

promise 😊

my sister has some challenges

?

special needs

i'm sorry to hear that. what's wrong?

she's on the spectrum. she needs routine & if she has it, she does really well. she's brilliant, actually. (she'll probably end up going to harvard or something.) but whenever her schedule gets messed up, everything goes to hell . . . FAST.

oh no 🙁

exactly

do you have anyone you can talk to? someone who can visit (what's the american saying?) to talk to you head-to-head?

(the saying is face-to-face). no. not really. i help a lot with Sarah, but otherwise i don't have a lot of outside contact. i mean i do have friends and all, but they're online mostly. 😕 i sound like a creepy shut-in. i'm not, i promise! it's just complicated.

you don't sound creepy. 😜 you sound angry and sad.

YES

it's normal.

rly?

i hid in my room every night for the first month after i left france.

ugh! it would be horrible to be so far away from home 🤔

it's all right now. nyc is quite spectacular. very distracting. bright and interesting. 😆

OMG i never knew you were in ny! (my aunt lisa lives there.) i'm in nj. THAT'S ONLY FORTY MINUTES AWAY FROM YOU!!! 😃

really? that's crazy!

ikr? here i have these friends around the world & one is right in my backyard

16

> **i have an idea! COME TO NY THIS FRIDAY!**
> **we're going to a movie!!!!!!!!!!!**

Madi's hand hovered over the screen, considering how to reply. Friday was the day her mother left. If Madi went out, she'd avoid the drama with Sarah, and would return only after her sister had settled down. She glanced guiltily at Sarah. Real life was already in a nosedive; a night out couldn't make it any worse.

But . . .

The anxious side of Madi's mind began a slide show of late-night TV horror stories: young women lured to an untimely death by Internet predators. She only knew Lauren online. Her user pic was an old camera, nothing else. Madi cursed herself for not finding @laurentabelard on Snapsed. What did she *really* know about her friend? Nothing at all. *This is stupid. I hardly know her. I should just say no.* But the truth was, Madi didn't want to.

She typed a question.

> **where in ny?**

> **an old movie house called the metrograph (lower east side). ny is the midway point for a lot of us. (though we meet in other places, too.) the madlibbers from ny and nj and pennsylvania get together a couple times a month to do a rewatch.**

> **madlibbers like—my readers???**

> **YES!**

> **but . . . why? 😕**

> **why what?**

17

why do you get together?

because we are REAL friends. come along with us! it'll be marvelous! i've gone to three of these events already and I'd love to meet you!

i don't know . . . that sounds a bit weird. i mean I don't rly know any of u. 😕

why would it be weird? come meet your fans!

LOL fans???

YES! we are all your fans. you're madlib herself! you're internet famous, don't you know?

hardly 😆

please, madi. i've SEEN your follower count. you really are internet famous! think about it.

could we talk first?

??? we are talking.

no, i mean like skype or something—just so i know who u r

oh, yes! yes, of course!

"Madi," Sarah whined, elbowing her. "You're not even watching the movie!"

The smile slid from Madi's face and she sat up, focusing her attention on the technicolor explosions filling the television. Her phone buzzed.

> are you online?
> we could talk right now if you want.

i'm doing a rewatch ATM, but how about afterward?

> great! i'll wait for you to ping me.

cool

Madi dropped her phone back into her pocket. She had a movie to watch, a blog to write, and a family meltdown to avert. Maybe, just maybe, she deserved a night on the town after all of that.

She turned to Sarah: "So, what'd I miss? Give me a recap."

Her sister gave her an intense half frown. Anyone who *didn't* know her would assume she was annoyed, but Madi knew better. Sarah was enthralled.

"The movie started with a scene of Tekla on the Star Freighter *Hyperion*— leading the rebels and giving a bit of backstory," Sarah whispered. "Then the action cut to the rebel base on Earth. Darthku's troops just showed up at the space station on the moon. Right now they're getting ready to attack. But don't worry. Captain Spartan has already alerted the ground troops." She turned her attention back to the ongoing movie. "He's going to stop them. Tekla knows they're trapped, and if Spartan can contact the *Hyperion*, then they'll have the reinforcements they need. . . ."

Madi's emotions rose alongside the music, the space opera drawing her into an epic battle of flashing explosions and decadent visuals. She let out a satisfied sigh, her anxiety receding into a dull hum. This was why she loved rewatches. They were an escape—*her escape!*—and everything seemed easier to deal with once she was immersed. The weight of worries that had filled the week lifted. She'd meet Lauren tonight, albeit via Skype, and if all went well, she'd be going into New York to meet the rest of the MadLibbers on Friday.

It was past ten when the movie ended and Madi retreated to her bedroom. She paused in front of her mirror, smoothing her hair and straightening her latest TeeFury shirt, an homage to *The X-Files: I Want to Believe.* She peered at herself. While her sister Sarah's expression could be described as "intense," Madi's was pure mischief. Almond-shaped eyes sparkled in an elfin face framed by black hair. Smiling or scowling, happy or sad, her dimpled cheeks and impish grin made Madi look like she was about to tell a joke. She stuck out her tongue and her reflection did the same. Much as she might wish it otherwise, she'd always be "cute" rather than a classic beauty. It bugged her.

With a sigh, she opened the video-chat program and typed in Lauren's e-mail address. A thrill of excitement danced the length of her spine. She always got nerves when meeting people for the first time and preferred the neutral distance of online interactions to face-to-face meetings. Skype hovered in the no-man's-land between the two approaches.

"Here goes nothing."

Madi clicked CONNECT.

There was the requisite dance of image and sound, bouncing merrily from Madi's laptop in Millburn to a satellite, and from there back down to Lauren's computer in New York. The video flickered and Madi leaned into the screen.

A man appeared.

"Whoa, Nellie!"

Her hand was halfway to the laptop's touch pad, intending to hang up the video-chat connection, when she froze. Her mouth fell open. She had seen good-looking guys before—*every movie she ever watched was full of them!*—but someone with features so chiseled they could have been borrowed from a movie poster was another thing entirely. The stranger's clothes were an eclectic mix of pop culture and high fashion—a retro comic book tee mixed with jeans and a faded leather jacket that sported a TARDIS pin on its collar. The look separated him from every boy Madi knew.

"Oh . . . wow!" The words were out before she could think better of them.

He was a gorgeously realistic anime character come to life . . . and that face. *OMG that face!* He caught her eyes on-screen and she stopped breathing.

"Hello?"

"I—you—" Madi struggled to make sounds come out of her mouth, but with no air in her lungs it was a useless proposition. Lauren wasn't home alone, she realized. And her boyfriend was damned hot!

Madi took a wheezing breath. "Jesus, take the wheel."

"*Pardonnez-moi?*"

She blinked. "I, um—Did you just talk to me in French?"

"*Bien sûr,*" he said, then shook his head. "Yes, yes. Bad habit."

He grinned, and the need to sigh hit Madi right in the center of her chest. (She didn't. Swooning was for romantics, not bloggers.)

"Y-you must be Lauren's boyfriend," she said. *Her hot French boyfriend!* "Is she around?"

"Sorry, who? I thought you were Madi." The French accent cloaked his words like expensive cologne. Subtle but distinct. Madi's uncertainty grew. Hadn't Lauren said she was an exchange student when they'd texted the other day? Madi looked at the e-mail address. Every letter was correct.

"I—yeah, I am. But I thought . . ."

This guy looked more like a college student than high school senior, but there were too many other clues to ignore. Madi's stomach twisted. *Oh God— there's no way this is happening.*

"You're Madi," he repeated. "From the MadLibs blog, right?"

"I am," she said, then forced a smile. "I know this sounds weird, but how do you pronounce your name?"

"It's Laurent." The way he said his name tipped her off: *Luh-Ron.* It rhymed with LeBron—the accent on the second part of the name—clearly masculine. *Laurent Abelard, not Lauren Tabelard!* she realized. Madi fought the urge to face-palm.

"I didn't realize it was you," she said. "I thought you were a girl."

"I didn't, either. I thought you were . . ." He laughed. "I don't know. Someone else. I expected someone . . . different."

"Different?"

"I don't know. You just look like—like—"

Madi's wanton perusal came to a screeching halt. *What. The. HELL.*

"Like what?" she snapped.

"Like a blogger."

"A blogger? What's *that* supposed to mean?!"

He shrugged "I . . . I don't know. You're just not what I expected."

Madi drew herself up to her full height, vibrating with anger. "Sorry to disappoint you, but there are lots of people who look lots of ways—"

"But I only meant—"

"—and bloggers come in all shapes and sizes—"

"Yes, I know, but—"

"—and MadLibs has a HUGE fan base! Hundreds of thousands of visitors come to my site each month. I'm eighteen years old. I'm an entrepreneur. I'm not some—some kid, or something!"

Laurent recoiled from the screen, his face blanching. "*Ah, non! Ce n'est pas le cas!* I—I'm so very sorry. I didn't mean it like that. I just—I messed up. I didn't think—I—I—*Pardonnez-moi, s'il vous plaît. Je ne veux pas vous ennuyer. . . .*" His words tumbled out faster and faster, disappearing into a blur of anxiety-ridden French.

And that was the moment when Madi knew she was going to fall, and fall hard, because nothing was more romantic than a language you couldn't understand and a young man who was anything but American who was spouting apologies and wringing his hands. (That doing it on-screen made him look like a matinee idol from some brooding French film was an added bonus.)

"It's fine," Madi said. "And it's good to actually meet you, Laurent." The masculine version of his name sounded strange. "It really is. No problem."

"I'm sorry about what I said before. When I get flustered, I tend to say whatever pops to mind. That's not always a good policy. I had a picture in my mind and you weren't that, and I spoke without thinking." He covered his heart with his hand. "I'm so very sorry, Madi. That was awful of me."

"I have the same problem with saying whatever pops to mind."

"You do?"

The corners of her mouth curled mischievously. "It's gotten me in serious trouble more than once, I promise."

"Oh-ho! This sounds good."

"It is. But it's a story for another time."

Laurent's smile changed. Madi couldn't exactly say *how*, only that she suddenly felt warmer. His eyes were intense—gold-green darkening to hazel at the edges—and she had the sudden urge to look away. *She couldn't.*

"I want to hear your story," he said. "Please tell me."

Madi bit the inside of her cheeks to try to control the grin that seemed determined to flash back again. The heat of her bedroom jumped ten degrees.

"Oh, I'm sure I'll tell you eventually. I can't seem to keep a secret for the life of me." She rolled her eyes. "That's another issue."

"Any way I can lure the story out?"

"I'm sure at some point I'll spill the beans."

The smolder in Laurent's expression winked out, replaced by confusion. "Spill the . . . beans?" The heartthrob was gone, awkward tourist in his place. Madi watched as he pulled out his phone, the long-sleeved tee he was wearing pulling back slightly as he lifted it. A complex Japanese-style tattoo of fish and water appeared on his right forearm. Madi stealthily leaned across her keyboard and tapped PRINT SCREEN. (She'd check that out later!)

As if sensing her waiting, his gaze flicked up. Another jolt of awareness hit Madi, a spark of electricity arcing from his computer to hers. "I just need a minute to look that up: Spill. The. B—"

"It means I *will* tell you," she said with a nervous giggle. "But not right now, Laurent. Okay?"

"Okay." He set the phone down and the sleeve dropped, fish disappearing. "But if you're not spilling the beans now, then I'll expect you to spill the beans later." He waggled his eyebrows. "I'll be wanting *all* the beans at that point. No holding back your beans. All right, Madi? I will want *all* the beans."

The wide smile she'd been holding in popped back. Laurent's non-American earnestness was so endearing she didn't have the heart to tell him how dumb he sounded.

"All the beans." Madi laughed. "You got it."

23

3

"I'm making this up as I go."

(*Raiders of the Lost Ark*, 1981)

adi grimaced at the laptop screen, her eyes gritty from glare. Too excited after chatting with Laurent to sleep, she'd tossed and turned, wondering if the click she felt with him online would translate into a real-life connection. Only one way to find out: *talk to him in person*. Blushing at the imagined meeting, she returned her attention to her newest blog post.

Madi loved writing and she knew what she *wanted* to say, but with the mixture of bone-deep exhaustion and hormonal excitement, the words simply would not flow. She closed her eyes as Laurent's laughing face appeared in her mind's eye. Tired or not, she wouldn't have given up their late-night chat for anything. Laurent was amazing! Any anxiety she'd had about going to New York on Friday to meet the MadLibbers was gone. She couldn't wait!

With a happy sigh, she looked back to the laptop screen. Her smile faded. It was the ending of the *Starveil* rewatch that was throwing her. She twirled a long strand of black hair around her finger as she reread. She deleted two sentences and switched a third.

"Better," she muttered, then scrolled to the stats screen.

Would I rewatch this? Not a chance. Too much angst.

She deleted her original answer, and typed in a new reply.

Would I rewatch this? YES, but only after a break.

No use provoking the die-hard fans if you didn't have to. There were far too many *Starveil* minions in the world. She turned her attention to the final paragraph.

And with a final blare of John Williams–esque trumpets, *Starveil V* came to a rather dismal ending. I expected—I don't know—something else, I guess? A hint of closure? Instead, the millions of viewers who worshipped the series were left to absorb the fact that their favorite character was dead. There was no reason for the sacrifice (except maybe for the little kid he saved, but I still think they both could have fit into the escape pod). Leaving Spartan to die was a rip-off. I didn't cry when he died—sorry, MadLibbers! You always get the truth here—but I definitely choked up. And I'm certain if I were a true *Starveil* fan—not a blogger moonlighting as one—the ending would have broken me.

Here are my final stats.

Series Rating: 8/10 Mad!Cows, with definite Mad!Love going out to the early B-movie stylings of SV1 and SV2. Loved those films!

Movie Rating (for SV5 specifically): 6.5/10 with a side of disappointment for obvious fridging. No reason for that!

Would I rewatch it? YES, but only after a break.

And thus ends the MadLibs for the *Starveil* saga, which means . . . *drumroll, please* . . . the comment box is open for suggestions for my NEXT MadLib. Remember: It's your job to keep me funemployed. (And on that note, the more you clickety-click on those ads, the more likely I'll get to order pizza for dinner, so thanks for that!)

musical accompaniment rises

exeunt

MadLib

Comments enabled.

Tags: #MadLibs #StarveilV #Madi watches things and then blogs about them #Funemployment

Madi grinned as she reached the end. "And there we go."

A rush of excitement filled her as she clicked POST. Attending online school allowed her the freedom to write whenever she wanted, and today she wanted to write! When she was doing other things—schoolwork, chores, exercising—Madi had to work to keep herself interested. Writing was the opposite. Finishing a blog always left her more "full" than empty. She leaned back in her rolling chair and pushed, feeling the telltale *pop* of released vertebrae from the hours of typing. She checked the time on her phone.

"Twenty minutes to the bell," she muttered, climbing from the chair. "Time to go."

These were the last hours of "normal" before her parents told Sarah about her mother's departure. After that, it was anyone's guess as to what would happen. *If only they'd told her already. . . .* But wishing changed nothing.

Delay tactics were well known in the Nakama household, and Madi wondered if they'd wait to tell Sarah until the very last second. If anything threw off Sarah's schedule, then her whole day was off, and if her whole day was off, then school—even with support—wasn't going to happen.

She flicked the laptop into sleep mode and slid her feet into flip-flops, heading for the stairs. A guilty smile crossed Madi's face. Friday afternoon was D-day, but she'd be on the train into New York long before the bomb dropped.

In ten minutes, Madi had walked the six blocks to Millburn Academy, the private high school Sarah attended. She waited outside her sister's classroom. The hall was mostly deserted, but Madi didn't dare leave her post until Sarah arrived, another structure to her sister's timetable that kept everyone's life on an even keel. Madi leaned her head against the wall, eyes fluttering closed as she remembered Laurent on-screen the night before.

They'd been laughing about something she could no longer remember, when Laurent sighed and said: *"I should go. It sucks, but it's late."*

"You probably should. . . ." Madi smirked. *"I mean, if it's your bedtime and all."*

He snorted. *"Not my bedtime, no, but I have school in the morning. Have to do homework, too. What time is it, anyhow?"* He glanced at his phone. *"Shit! Have we been talking that long? Forget homework. I need sleep."*

"Not sure you've heard, but I'm kind of a bad influence."

"Don't believe it."

"My squeaky-clean looks are the perfect cover." She giggled. "I'm the last person you'd ever suspect."

He lifted an eyebrow. "Still don't believe you. "

"Is that a challenge, Laurent?"

"Maybe." He flashed her a sucker-punch smile she couldn't help but return.

"Then challenge accepted. Forget this nice-guy-exchange-student thing you've got going. I'm bringing you down!"

"Bring me down? Down to what?"

"Complete and utter reputation destruction!"

And for some reason that had sent the two of them into gales of laughter so loud Madi had had to muffle her face in her pillow to keep from waking her parents and sister.

At the end of the hallway a door squeaked and Madi's lashes opened. She smothered a yawn behind her hand as a teen with short red hair and a wide smile appeared. He was a classmate Madi remembered from her freshman year of high school, and though they'd been in several classes together, Madi could no longer remember his name. His parents owned the Colonial Inn.

"Hey, Madi," he said. "Nice to see you around again."

"Mmph," she mumbled in agreement. What was his name? *Ron? Rob? Rupert? No, that's the kid from the* Harry Potter *movies.* Madi's sluggish brain wouldn't provide the answer other than "Gingersnap," and she was certain he wouldn't appreciate a reminder of the schoolyard taunt.

"You here to pick up your sister?"

"As always."

"Thought maybe you decided to rejoin the rest of us drones." His voice dropped into a robotic monotone. "We are the borg. You will be assimilated."

"Not a chance."

"Resistance is futile."

"Unless you do online school."

His smile drooped at the edges. "Wish my parents were as cool as yours. I begged them for weeks after you took off."

"Er . . . yeah." He seemed to be waiting for her to say something else, but she wasn't sure what. A few uncomfortable seconds passed.

"Well, it was good seeing you again," he said.

The nameless boy waved as he disappeared into a nearby classroom, and Madi felt herself relax. Interactions were so much easier online.

A minute passed.

Then two.

At the five-minute mark, Madi was once again dozing against the wall, eyes closed, when the sound of clicking heels warned her of an adult's arrival. She opened her eyes to discover a steely-haired teacher making a beeline to her side. The woman peered at Madi from behind thick rectangular glasses.

"Hallway pass?"

"Oh, I'm not in a class," Madi said sleepily. "I'm just here to—"

"I know you're not in class," she interrupted. "That's why you need a pass. All students are provided passes for rest breaks. Where is yours?"

Madi pulled herself up to her full height (barely reaching the woman's shoulders), trying to look alert. "But you see, ma'am, I'm only—"

"I need your pass," she said irritably. "Hurry, please. I have a meeting and don't want to be late."

"But I don't *need* a pass," Madi insisted. "I'm here as one of the guardians for my sister, Sarah."

The woman's eyebrows rose until they almost met her tightly curled gray hair. "*You're* her guardian?" she said uncertainly.

"I am."

"But Mr. Wattley teaches an Advanced Sciences class."

"Yes, he does."

The woman's eyes narrowed behind thick glasses. She pulled a pen from one jacket pocket, a small pad of paper from the other. "What's the name of your sister? I need to check into this. There's a protocol for pickups, you know. The school can't just have *anyone* wandering in off the street."

The way she said *anyone* riled Madi. "It's Sarah," she said. "Now may I ask *your name*, ma'am? Because every teacher in this school *knows* I pick up Sarah from school. I've done it every day for the last two years."

The woman's heels clattered as she stumbled back a step. "Well, I never!" She sucked in a breath through pursed lips. "There's absolutely no call for rudeness. There are rules to pickups. Now, if you'll come with me—"

"Oh, I can't go anywhere! Sarah will be out in two minutes and—"

At that moment the door opened and Mr. Wattley appeared in his usual bedraggled state. Hair sprang from his head in tufts; his white lab coat was misbuttoned. "Oh my! Mrs. Preet. You're . . ." He glanced at Madi. "You're here early."

"Mr. Wattley," she said stiffly, her double chin rising in authority. "I was just having a discussion with Miss . . ." She glowered down at Madi.

"Nakama," Mr. Wattley said. "Sarah's sister. She picks her up a few minutes before the bell goes."

"Nakama?" the woman repeated. "As in Charles Nakama?"

Madi winced. Millburn was a small town where everyone knew everyone else's business. Since Charles Nakama's popular "Down Home" column headed the *Tri-State Herald*, the largest-distributed paper in New Jersey, Madi's father was practically a celebrity. His photograph accompanied each post. "Down Home" included topics that highlighted family values and traditional beliefs. It was serialized in papers across the US. Everyone who read it knew and recognized Madi's father. By proxy, everyone knew *her*. She hated that.

"Yes," Mr. Wattley said. "Madi's a senior here, but her sister, Sarah—"

Mrs. Preet's attention swiveled back like a hawk on a mouse. "I thought you said you weren't in classes."

Madi's phone buzzed, but she forced herself not to look. "I'm not. I mean, I *am*—but only online." She crossed her arms, wishing she were anywhere but here. She was too tired for verbal gymnastics. "I'm not a regular student. I do Millburn's off-campus program."

"The online high school?"

"Yes."

Mrs. Preet nodded and scribbled a note into her book. "I'll have to check into that."

Madi let out a frustrated sound somewhere between a laugh and cough. "Check into *what*? I'm just here to pick up my sister." In her exhaustion, all the annoyance at her parents came surging back. She pointed into the classroom to where Sarah was engrossed in organizing her backpack. "It's part of Sarah's program. I do this literally every day."

"I'm sure you do," Mrs. Preet said matter-of-factly. "I just hadn't been told. I pride myself on knowing what's going on at my school." Her attention turned to Mr. Wattley. "I assume you're ready for our discussion."

"Of course. Just let me send Sarah off."

She strutted into the classroom, leaving Madi and Mr. Wattley staring after her.

"I, er, I should have warned you," he said. Sarah arrived and headed down the hallway without pause. (Schedules were schedules, and Sarah's didn't vary.)

"Warned me about what?"

Mr. Wattley gave a nervous smile. "That is Mrs. Preet. She's taken over for Mr. Palmer as the new assistant principal. She's very interested in efficiency and organization." He coughed. "And rules."

Madi wilted. "Thanks for the warning, Mr. Wattley," she said as she shouldered her pack. "I'll keep that in mind."

Phone in hand, Madi scrolled through her dashboard as she and Sarah walked home. Sarah had launched into a rehash of today's topic from physics class, and as much as Madi wanted to be interested in string theory, there was no way she was going to keep up with her sister's train of thought. Sarah's monologue continued, unabated, street by street.

Madi rolled her thumb up the screen and a new post appeared. She giggled. Sarah's speech fumbled, and she glanced over at Madi. "What?"

"It's nothing."

"It's not nothing. You laughed at something."

"I didn't."

"You did."

"Fine," Madi said. "It's this post. See?" She turned her phone's screen so her sister could see. "It's about *Starveil*."

Sarah frowned. "I don't get it."

"The *Starveil* series is about a rebellion."

"I know that."

"And Captain Spartan's the 'OTC' in 'CJOTC.' Like, the one true character."

"Yeah."

"Well, the song's by Arcade Fire," Madi explained. "And there was the big explosion on Io when the rebels were betrayed."

"So what?"

"The title is 'Rebellion Lies.'"

"I still don't get it."

"It's just that . . ." Madi let out a tired sigh and put her phone away. She patted Sarah's arm. "So, what were you saying about superstrings?"

Her sister nodded and continued.

The rest of the week passed in a heartbeat. There were simply too many things to do and never enough time to do them. More than once, Madi thought her parents were going to tell Sarah that her mother was leaving, but in every case the moment passed and the announcement was delayed yet again. Sarah had no idea.

As Friday morning and afternoon dragged by, Madi threw herself back into blogging. Writing was a distraction. And if she needed one thing, it was a way to not think about meeting her fans. She shuddered. The line she so carefully followed—keeping online and real life separated—was going to be breached, if only for tonight. Panicked, she did the one thing that she knew would solve it: She focused entirely on her blog.

By late afternoon, she'd finished her latest MadLib rewatch, and she posted it as she headed out the door.

Blog Post 208, Friday 3:48 p.m.:

Mad, Mad Choices!

Keep those votes coming in, MadLibbers, because the race is a close one! The four main options at this point are:

Star Wars saga. Thank you to @StarveilBrian1981 for nominating it and also for suggesting the _Starveil_ series. That was a blast!

Supernatural, seasons one to infinity. Thank you to @WinchesterForLife for the suggestion. I'm definitely open to this one (and I'm actually not sure why I haven't seen this yet). So much fandom potential here.

Buffy series. OMG OMG OMG OMG This would be SPECTACULAR! *puppy-dog eyes* I definitely would be open to a rewatch for this 'verse. But the MadLibbers are always right—so make your own choice. *cough* Vote Buffy. *cough* PLEASE. *cough*

'80s movies. This one's the dark horse at this point, but I think there's a chance it could happen. (I'm actually named because of an '80s film, but I'm not sharing that story unless your votes demand it.) If '80s movies are a go, we'll do a second round of voting for the actual films.

Happy voting, everyone!

confetti canon

MadLib

PS: I'll respond to comments as soon as I can—I'm off for a bit of R&R tonight.

Comments enabled.

Tags: #MadLibs #Round Two MadLibbing #Madi watches things and then blogs about them #Funemployment

Madi walked through the Penn Station arrivals area, her backpack clutched tight against her chest. She scanned the crowd. There were no screaming teens wearing her recently sold-out MadLibs shirts, no signs with WELCOME MADI! to signal her online-to-real-life arrival.

"This was a terrible idea," she muttered as she forded the crowd. "What in the world was I thinking?"

It wasn't that Madi was *against* meeting new people, she just wasn't used to it. Her role at home was to keep things calm and help out with Sarah. Here—alone and on her own in New York—she wasn't quite sure what to do. She thought of herself as independent: The MadLibs blog had been a source of income for well over a year. But the difference between her online life and reality overwhelmed her.

Seeing no one waiting to meet her, Madi headed to the chairs in the waiting area. A young woman with blue hair glanced up as Madi neared.

"Are you a MadLibber?" Madi asked with a quick wave. The woman stood from the chairs and Madi smiled in relief.

The teen pushed past her, launching herself into the arms of an older woman who was approaching from the same direction as Madi. "Mom! You made it!"

People in the chairs around Madi smirked. A teen boy snickered and leaned toward his friend, whispering. Horrified at her gaffe, Madi waved at an indeterminate person in the distance.

"Coming!" she said, bustling past the onlookers and disappearing around the next knot of people. "Just a second!"

She dropped her hand as the crowd closed behind her. "Shouldn't have come," she grumbled. "Dumb. Dumb. Dumb."

Someone *should* be here to meet her. Laurent had promised her that. But in her excitement to come, Madi had totally forgotten to find out *who*.

"This is why the Internet was invented." She sighed as she peered into the sea of faces.

Tonight the group of online friends would be heading to the newly renovated Metrograph theater on the Lower East Side to see a rerelease of *Blade Runner*. It had seemed like a good idea when Laurent mentioned it, but with the moment nearing, she'd lost her excitement.

Stumbling past burdened travelers and wearied mothers, Madi felt her cheeks prickling, imagining every eye attuned to her. *What if the MadLibbers don't like me?* Before the thought could take hold, she found the farthest chair from the crowd and sat down, pulling out her phone.

Wi-Fi!

She was here. There was no way out except through. She slumped down in the seat, phone in front of her face to block her from strangers. Worst-case scenario, she had the return ticket in her wallet. She'd hang out here all night and play on her phone, then return home no worse for wear. It wasn't a fun evening by any means, but she'd manage. She peeked over the top of the screen, spying a nearby snack shack and, farther down, a sign for bathroom facilities. Food, Wi-Fi, a bathroom within walking distance. Yes, she'd survive.

With a sigh, she opened the MadLibs site, scrolling through the comments section. As expected, Brian was campaigning for another space epic. She shook her head as she read through his commentary.

Comments on Blog Post 208: Mad, Mad Choices!
Comment 12.1, @StarveilBrian1981: Thanks for MadLibbing the *Starveil* series, @MadLib. I knew you'd be a fan! It was great to see it through your eyes. Very cathartic. If you ever want to talk about it, I'm always open. There's a great fandom online. And I'm excited to see *Star Wars* got shortlisted for your next rewatch.

Madi typed in a reply, careful to keep her tone neutral. Her years of blogging had taught her the skill of fan management, and Brian seemed to be pricklier than most.

@MadLib: Thank YOU, @StarveilBrian1981, for the *Starveil* suggestion AND for the *Star Wars* suggestion for the upcoming MadLibs vote. Good luck with the campaign! Voting's open until Saturday. I'll try to tabulate the votes by the end of this weekend (if not sooner).

His answer appeared seconds after she posted her reply and refreshed the page.

> **@StarveilBrian1981:** To quote Spartan—"Trying is for fools. Rebels just do!" I really think *Star Wars* would be a great choice. I mean, it's no *Starveil*, but you can see which canon elements are linked. I wrote a big meta post on that last week. I can't post a link here, but if you search my username, you'll find it.

She slumped lower, typing another reply to Brian.

> **@MadLib:** That's really awesome, @StarveilBrian1981, but I've gotta run now. Talk to you later.
>> **@StarveilBrian1981:** Run where? I have more ideas I want to talk about.
>>> **@MadLib:** Heading for a *Blade Runner* rerelease, but I PROMISE I'll be replying to comments later tonight. Bye!
>>>> **@StarveilBrian1981:** I love *Blade Runner*! You should post as you watch it. DO IT! I think there are LOADS of MadLibbers who'd be up for an impromptu liveblog! What do you say, @MadLib?
>>>>> **@MadLib:** Um, great idea, @StarveilBrian1981, but I really can't. Gotta go.
>>>>>> **@StarveilBrian1981:** Okay, then, I'll just be waiting here. Reply when you get back. Okay?

A message from her father appeared on the phone's screen before she could type in her answer. Seeing it, a flicker of worry rose inside her—imagining Sarah getting tonight's news—but it turned out to be a list of reminders.

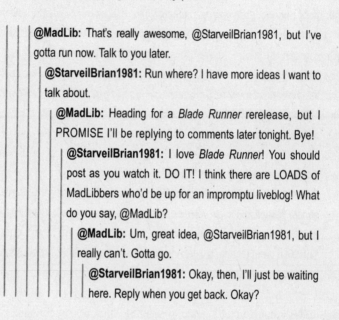

> Madi. Don't forget to be waiting for the train at least fifteen minutes early. Be safe. Walk in groups. I know you've been to New York before, but—

Another text appeared on-screen before Madi could finish her father's message. This one was from Laurent, saying he had arrived.

Madi glanced up. She had seen Laurent on-screen and knew what to expect—the flawless face and perfect physique—but having attended a couple of comic conventions, Madi realized that small-screen perceptions didn't always align. The actors she'd met at conventions seemed smaller in real life. More approachable. Laurent in real life was something else entirely. If anything, he seemed bigger. Not just tall, but *huge*. Like some Asgardian god on a humble Earth-bound errand, he loomed over the crowd, searching for her. Details sprang into focus like the close-up of a made-for-TV movie star: tanned skin that hinted at Latin roots, a straight jaw dotted with dark stubble, longish hair that varied from caramel at the tips to brownish black at the roots, and a physique that made Madi think of every teen heartthrob she'd ever spent hours dreaming about. He literally could have been torn from the pop-music poster on her bedroom door. He lifted his phone and began to type one-handed.

Oh. My. God. That can't be Laurent. I'm going to puke. Or die. Or puke and THEN die. That would be worse. He CAN'T be this hot in person. No freaking way—Their eyes met. . . . *Yes way.*

"Madi!" He laughed. "I didn't see you there."

"It happens when you're only five feet . . ." Her breath caught as Laurent wrapped her in a sudden hug.

She was in his arms. *Laurent's arms!* He spun her around and set her back down again in the space of three seconds, then stepped back and slid his hands into his pockets. His face looked flushed under his tan, but she was still reeling from being touched, her mind pulling in a hundred different directions at once. Laurent smelled good. He felt good. He was so unbelievably beyond her level.

Oh my God . . . I'm totally falling for him.

"So are you ready?" he asked.

"R-ready . . . ?"

"To go to the movie?"

"Oh—yeah, of course," Madi said. "You?"

He grinned. "Wouldn't miss a MadLibbers get-together for anything!"

4

"That's why they call them *crushes*. If they were easy, they'd call 'em something else."
(*Sixteen Candles*, 1984)

Madi followed Laurent out of Penn Station and onto the street. It felt like surfacing; the sounds and smells of the city hit her in a wave of sensory overload. A taxi peeled by. A horn blared. People milled past, on their way to countless destinations. Madi squinted into the late-afternoon glare and smiled. The hum of millions of separate lives, woven together, gave her a buzz she couldn't explain. Here in New York, she was faceless, unknown. *Herself.*

"You like the city?" Laurent asked.

She turned to find him watching. "Do I ever," she said with a nervous laugh. "You?"

He grinned and started walking. "Wouldn't be here otherwise. It's amazing. So busy. So full of . . . of . . ."

"Life?"

He nodded, and Madi fell into step at his side. "So are we walking to the Metrograph? The Lower East Side seems a long way."

"Oh no." He laughed. "We're just heading over to the Thirty-Fourth Street station. I grabbed you a ticket."

"Thanks."

"The metr—subway," he corrected, "is so convenient. Just another block."

Madi found herself puffing. Laurent's long-legged stride was nearly twice hers. A single person took position between them. Then two. Five. "Hold on," she called, fearful of losing him in the crowds. "Can't keep up."

"Ah! Sorry." He dropped his pace to match hers. "I should have waited. I'm just excited to get to the theater."

The anxiety that had only just faded, tightened once more. "We're not going to grab a coffee or something first?"

"No time," he said. "I want a good seat."

"But it won't be busy," Madi said. "I mean, it's an early show of an old movie, right? I don't think there'll be a line or anything."

"But there will! Everyone's coming!"

Madi's eyes widened. "Everyone . . . ?"

"The New York MadLibbers group has hundreds of regulars. They're thrilled you're coming tonight."

"Y-you told them?"

He grinned. "Of course I did! And they'll all want to talk to you. People started texting me as soon as I said you'd agreed. . . ." Laurent chattered on, but Madi couldn't follow his words. This *wasn't* what she'd imagined. A few people, yes, but an entire theater full of them?

". . . and I want to make sure that my close friends get to meet you," Laurent said. "Ava and Kelly and Morag." In his excitement to explain, Laurent's pace had returned to its previous speed, and Madi soon found herself lagging.

"Laurent, I really need you to slow down."

He turned to discover her two steps behind. "Ah! *Je suis désolé!* Sorry, Madi."

"It's fine. Just short legs."

"Your legs are perfectly sized."

"That should be a compliment," she said, "but it's not. Short is short."

"Petite. Tiny. Wee. Delicate." Laurent glanced at his phone, apparently checking the dictionary. "Aha! Miniature," he announced.

"That is *not* a compliment." She snorted.

"No? Fitting, though." He gave her a once-over. "Mini Madi sounds like a candy bar or—" Laurent yelped as Madi poked him in the ribs.

"Not funny!" She giggled.

"Then how about *minette* instead?"

She bit her cheeks to keep from smiling. "What does *minette* mean?"

Laurent slowed his steps as the stairwell entrance to the subway appeared.

"I'll give you a hint: small, cute, but deadly, with . . ." He poked her and she lurched sideways, laughing, nearly colliding with a businessman emerging from the Thirty-Fourth Street entrance. "Claws."

"You're calling me a cat?" She was breathing hard, and not just from trying to keep up with him.

"Not any old cat," Laurent said, grinning. "A kitten."

"Kitten, hmmm?"

"Yes, *minette*."

She couldn't help noticing his hand hovering near her elbow, guiding her toward the entrance.

"Unless you prefer Mini Madi."

"*Minette* is fine." She laughed.

The crowd outside the Metrograph was visible a block away. Knots of people milled around the entrance, most of them wearing T-shirts that Madi herself had designed. *MadLibbing for the PEOPLE!* one announced. *It Madders because YOU say it does!* quipped another. *MadLIBERATION!*

"Oh my God," Madi moaned. "Who *are* all these people?"

Laurent bumped her with his elbow. "Your fans, of course."

"My fans?" Madi's feet slowed. There were too many—far too many!—and she had no idea how she was supposed to act. This was completely different from online chatter. And any skills she'd once had with face-to-face interaction had long since faded. Dread filled her gut.

"C'mon," Laurent said. "I have a few people I want you to meet. The friends I hang out with."

"I guess that sounds all right."

"Great! Come on!"

He walked toward a small group lounging near the alley on the far side of the street, half a block down. One girl had messy blond hair and an angry scowl, the kind of person Madi would avoid on any other day. Beside her stood a beaming teen, braces flashing. Her pink T-shirt announced, *Mad for MadLibs.* She reminded Madi of an extra from the Disney channel.

The angry-looking girl glanced up, catching Madi's eyes. She scowled for the count of three, then her gaze shifted upward. Her expression backflipped into joy.

"Laurent!" she shouted. "You came!"

He strode forward, leaving Madi struggling to keep up. "I told you I'd be here."

"So what happened to MadLib? I thought you were heading to Penn Station to get her."

"I was—I did!" Laurent reached out, touching Madi's shoulder. "She's here. *This* is Madi!"

Madi waved nervously as all eyes turned on her. "Hiiiiiii . . ."

The Disney girl's eyes were so big they looked like they were going to pop. "You're her! You're Madi. Like the actual, real-to-life, in-the-flesh—"

The other girl stared at Madi with a look that reminded her all too much of the popular crowd at Millburn Academy. After a long moment she reached out a hand. "So we finally get to meet the infamous MadLib."

"Just Madi, thanks."

"I'm Ava."

Laurent nodded to the other teen. "And this is Chantal," he said smoothly. "She was going to pick you up, but I beat her to it."

"It's so weird to actually meet you," Chantal gasped, her hand to her chest. "I have so many questions! I just—I can't . . ." She let out a high-pitched giggle. "I've been wanting to talk to you forever."

"Thanks," Madi said. "It's good to be here." She peeked over at Laurent, who hadn't stopped grinning since they'd arrived.

Ava shook her head. "I still can't believe you're actually *here.* I mean, it just seems . . . weird or something."

"Why?"

She shrugged. "Aren't you, like, a bona fide recluse or something? I mean, no one's actually met you before today."

"I'm not—"

Chantal grabbed Madi's hand. "But you're MadLib—Madi! And you're here—with us—for real!" She laughed aloud. "That's crazy!"

Madi smiled. "Thanks."

"I'm so glad you came," Chantal said. "I have so much to ask you."

"Like what?"

"Like you write the MadLibs blog for a living, right?"

"Gainfully funemployed," Madi said. Laurent chuckled at the joke, and she felt her cheeks warm. *Play it cool, Nakama!* She forced herself to focus on the two young women. "So how about you two?"

"What *about* us?" Ava asked.

"What do you guys do?"

"Art program." Ava glanced at Laurent as if sharing some secret and then back to Madi. "Though I prefer painting. Not mainstream crap. *Real* art."

"And I'm in high school," Chantal added, still grinning.

"I hated high school," Madi said. "Absolutely *loathed* it!"

"God, me, too," Ava said. "So glad to be in college now."

"I haven't graduated yet," Madi admitted. "I take online classes."

Laurent laughed. "I don't think I'd be able to focus long enough to finish anything. Way too many distractions on the Internet."

"That's how regular classes were for me," Madi said. "I just kind of zoned out."

"I can't believe your parents let you do online school," Chantal said with a wistful sigh. "So does it work the same as a regular high school?"

"Well, yes and no." Madi grinned. Now that the shock had passed, she was starting to feel like herself again. Perhaps real-life interactions weren't so bad. "Millburn Academy is a private school," Madi said. "It has both regular classes and online courses. Taking my whole diploma through OMA—the online track of Millburn Academy—was sort of my idea."

"It was?"

"My parents are pretty busy most nights, so I convinced them I'd help out more with my younger sister if I could do online classes." She shrugged. "I drop her off and pick her up after school, stuff like that. Seemed like a good trade."

Ava looked skeptical. "And your parents were okay with that?"

"Eventually. They told me I could do OMA, but only for one semester, and only if I *proved* I could keep my grades up. So I spent all my time studying that first semester and . . . BAM!" She clapped her hands. "I was on the honor roll."

"I barely slide by at the best of times." Ava snorted.

"Ah, but you're a badass," Laurent said. "And that makes up for it." Madi wasn't sure why his comment to Ava irked her, but she soon forgot when he turned his attention back to her. "The honor roll is really cool, Madi. That takes a lot of work. Kudos to you."

"It's not as awesome as you'd think," she said. "I've had to keep up those grades ever since." She dropped her voice in imitation of her father. "'You've got potential, Madi. You can't waste that. I expect As from now on.'"

"Oh no," Chantal groaned. "Like for every class? And you've got to write your MadLibs blog, too?"

"Yup."

"How do you manage?"

"I dunno," Madi said with a laugh. "I just do. The blog is fun. School is work."

One corner of Laurent's lips curled up into a lopsided grin. "Aha! You set the bar," he said. "Now you're dealing with the consequences. You're a victim of your own success."

"Something like that," Madi said. "But that's not the half of it. My dad's a journalist and my mom's a professor of microbiology, so there's all this pressure to follow in their footsteps. . . ."

If Madi had been worried before meeting Laurent's friends when she arrived, those fears were gone. Even Ava seemed to have toned back the attitude. The MadLibbers were the perfect reflection of why she loved online friendships. Chantal, aka @WrittenInChantalics, was the ingénue of the group. Ava, aka @ArtWithAttitude, the rebel. And Laurent, aka @laurentabelard, was everyone's leading man. Madi peeked over at him: the unkempt hair brushing his collar, his aesthetic balanced between European fashion and grad-student poverty. *Damnit! Some people have all the cards.* It was like he'd been plucked right out of a romantic comedy.

As if sensing her watching, Laurent looked up and smiled, green eyes sparkling. Madi looked away. *Too perfect,* she thought. *There's got to be a chink in the armor.* But if there was, she had yet to find it.

"We should probably head to the Metrograph," Laurent said. "It's going to be busy, and I want seats together." Across the street, the crowds were starting to disappear through the entrance. "You ready to go?"

A twinge of fear flickered in Madi's stomach, but she ignored it. "Sure."

Chantal moved in next to Madi as the group headed down the street. "Have you decided yet?" she asked breathlessly.

"Decided what?"

"What your next MadLib topic is! I could hardly sleep last night, I was so excited about it!"

Madi peeked over to find Chantal grinning. "I, um . . . I kind of—"

"Is it hard to choose?"

"Sometimes, I guess. Especially if I have two I really like."

"So how do you decide?" Chantal asked as they reached an intersection and stopped, waiting for the WALK signal. "How do you make the call?"

"Mostly it's based on votes," Madi said.

Ava smirked. "Do you ever cheat?" she teased.

"I swear we won't tell," Chantal added.

"Never needed to," Madi said. "I'm pretty good at guessing what people will choose."

"Do you know what this one will be?" Laurent asked.

"I'm hoping for *Star Wars* myself," Chantal said. "That or *Buffy.*"

"*Buffy* is fantastic," Ava said fiercely. "I'm fighting for that one. You've got to choose it. All right, Madi?"

"It's up to the fans."

"But we're fans!" Chantal pleaded. "That counts for something, doesn't it?!"

Madi grinned.

"Can't we, like, bribe you or something?" Ava said drily. "*Buffy* needs a rewatch."

"*Star Wars* would be better!" Chantal argued.

"Would not!"

43

"Would, too."

"You haven't even SEEN *Buffy* yet!" Ava snapped. "How would you even know?"

Madi giggled.

"I'll read whatever Madi blogs about," Laurent said. "I'm all about the experience."

"The experience?" Ava scoffed. "That sounds dirty, you naughty boy." Madi fought the urge to defend him as Laurent's cheeks flushed and he looked away.

"Not at all!" he said. "I came to America to be immersed—and popular culture is part of it."

"I know, I know," Ava said.

"But I do like eighties movies. They're very . . . optimistic."

Everyone laughed. Up ahead, the entrance to the Metrograph theater was nearly clear of people. Madi sighed in relief. By the time they arrived, she would be able to come inside unseen. Irritated, Ava paced back and forth on the sidewalk, waiting for the light to change.

"I'm so excited for this new MadLib," Chantal said. "And that you're here with us!"

"Only if we get seats in time," Ava grumbled.

"It'll be fine," Laurent said. "Relax."

Ava swore under her breath.

"The light's going to change. Just give it a minute to—"

Ava darted out into traffic without warning. Chantal shrieked.

"Metrograph's going to be packed," Ava shouted as horns blared. "I'll grab us places to sit. You catch up!"

They watched as she sprinted down the street and disappeared through the theater's entrance.

"Only Ava." Chantal giggled.

A minute later, the light changed and they crossed. Laurent dropped back, coming around behind them to fall into step at Madi's side. She bit the inside of her cheeks to keep from grinning.

"You know, Laurent," Madi said, "if eighties movies are your thing, you should go for it. I'm happy with whatever. But be warned: Brian's determined to bring a science-fiction renaissance to MadLibs. He and a few other people are promoting faves. *Star Wars* might take it." She bumped him with her shoulder as they walked. "You should promote, too."

Laurent smiled down at her. "Maybe I will."

She nodded. "Good."

Ava had been right. The Metrograph was packed. Row after row of refurbished seats was filled with a sea of strangers, their eyes following Laurent, Chantal, and Madi as they waded into the tide. Madi touched Laurent's sleeve as her fears took hold. He glanced back.

"Are there any seats left?" she whispered, scanning the rows for an open section. "It doesn't look like there are."

"I'm sure there are some left. Ava texted me that she's up near the front." He glanced at his phone's screen. "She says she saved four seats for us."

Madi's eyes skittered to the crowd. "I don't know . . ."

His hand brushed hers, then moved away. "Trust me. All right?"

She nodded.

Whispers rose from the gallery as they came forward. Madi didn't want to hear the people talking, but with the limited walking room, she couldn't help it. Hissed phrases pushed at her from all sides. People leaned forward, staring.

"Is that her?"

"Not sure—"

"She doesn't post pictures online. . . . Don't know what she looks like."

"But that's Laurent, isn't it?"

The sounds rose from a hiss to the sound of a swarm of bees.

"—he said he'd bring MadLib along."

"It is her! I'm sure of it!"

"Madi!" a voice shouted. "MADLIB!"

Laurent took Madi's hand, his warm fingers drawing her attention. She looked up. "C'mon. We're over here."

The crowd's chatter had risen to fill the theater with the roar of a hundred voices. Madi could no longer make out individual words.

Laurent stepped into a row of seats near the front of the theater, but before Madi could follow, a middle-aged woman stood, blocking her way.

"You're MadLib, aren't you?" she exclaimed.

"I—I—"

Laurent leaned sideways, catching Madi's eyes. "Got to go," he said, cheerfully ignoring the human barrier that separated them. "Ava's halfway down." Laurent pulled her in front of him. Suddenly, his hands were on her shoulders, guiding her, and all Madi could focus on was the warmth.

"You looked worried."

"Thanks, I was. . . . I'm okay now." Her gaze lifted to the rows of the theater. People stood on chairs, pointing, and for once in her life Madi was glad she was barely five feet tall. "Where's Ava sitting?"

"Just a little farther."

"MadLib!" a voice nearby shrieked and Madi jumped.

Laurent leaned in, his mouth near her ear. "Sorry about all of this. You're a bit of a celebrity with the MadLibbers, you know."

"I'm starting to realize that." Madi tucked her chin and walked faster.

"It IS MadLib!" someone cried.

Madi ducked down as soon as they reached their seats. Laurent sat next to Ava, Madi next to him, Chantal on Madi's other side, buffering her from the crowd on each side. For a few seconds, Madi thought things might calm down, but then the woman sitting in the seat ahead of Madi turned around.

"Oh my God! It's you! You're really MadLib!" She stared over the back of her seat while Madi avoided eye contact. This was growing weirder by the second! "I heard you might be coming," she gasped. "I didn't believe it, but you're here—with us—like really, *really* here!"

Madi's gaze flicked up to discover the woman had leaned halfway over the seat. Ava snorted with laughter.

"Madi," Ava said drily, "this here is Steph, though you probably know her as @antebellumintro. Steph, this is MadLib—also called Madi."

"It's good to put a face to the name," Madi said, though she had no recollection of that MadLibber's name. There were simply too many fans.

"It's so great to meet you!" Steph cried. "I couldn't believe it when Ava said she needed seats, but not just for anyone. For MadLib herself!"

"Thanks." Madi sank lower in her chair, but Steph leaned closer.

"I'd heard Laurent was bringing you," she continued. "But I didn't think you'd actually come. I've followed your blog for almost two years. You've never met your fans before." She reached out her hand to shake. "It's seriously awesome to meet you!"

"Thanks."

Madi slid down until she was almost reclining.

Ava stood and gently took Steph's shoulders. "Honey, you're overcrowding the talent. Maybe some breathing room?"

"Of course! Let's talk later, all right?"

"Um . . . okay?"

Steph grinned and slid back into her seat.

For a second, Madi thought the worst was over. "Thanks, Ava," she said. "I appreciate you—"

But before Madi could finish, a new face appeared, leaning across the aisle in front of Laurent to get Madi's attention. "Hey, Madi!" he shouted. "I was wondering if you could sign the coffee mug I got from your store!" He shoved it toward her.

"Sorry, do what?"

"Sign my mug!" A Sharpie marker appeared in the man's grip. "If you could write: 'To Ben, from MadLib,' that'd be great!"

"I guess," Madi said, "but we've got to hurry. The movie will be starting in a minute, and I don't—"

"It'll only take a second. Besides, there's a bunch of people waiting to talk to you."

Madi looked up from writing. Her eyes widened. "Oh hell no. . . ."

In the last seconds of stilted conversation, a line of people had appeared in the row. The queue of fans stretched down the length of the chairs and wound up the aisle, as at least thirty people waited for a chance to talk to her.

"MadLib! Madi! MADIIII!"

For fifteen endless minutes, Madi signed and talked and shook hands with a blur of fans who'd made the incongruous jump from her online world to real life. Everyone had a story to tell. Each person a request. Every once in a while, Madi caught Laurent's gaze, but he seemed as helpless to stop the tide of MadLibbers as she was. The theater lights dimmed, but the MadLibbers kept coming.

"I'm sorry," Madi said, wobbling from exhaustion. "But the movie—"

Suddenly, Ava rose and pushed her way in front of Madi, directly into the line of fire. Her voice rang out through the theater. "Madi's only got time to say hello. No signings, no requests!" she bellowed. "If you want to talk after the show is over, she'll be available for fifteen minutes. No more!"

"Thank you for following my blog!" Madi shouted as they turned away. "I'd love to talk to you after the movie!"

With a few shouts of "MadLib!" the line dispersed into the growing darkness.

Grinning, Madi sat down. "Thanks for wrangling the crowd, Ava. I didn't think I'd ever get through that."

Ava smirked. "Not a problem. But you'd better be ready for more meet and greet after the movie ends. I gave you a breather, not an out. There'll be die-hards waiting the second the credits roll."

Madi peered over her shoulder. If the theater had been busy before, it was now full to capacity. Attendants walked the aisles, guiding the people huddled on the stairs to the nosebleed seats in the back.

"This is all so crazy." She laughed.

"What's that?" Laurent asked, sliding his coat from his shoulders. The koi flashed to life, swimming in the tan depths of his arm.

"There are so many people here tonight."

"They came out for you," Laurent said, smiling.

She blushed and looked away. It felt like he was saying something else, but she didn't dare ask if she was right. On-screen, the previews began. As if on cue, the entire group of them pulled out their phones. Even Laurent—ever attentive—checked through his messages. Unlike Madi's parents, who insisted on talking face-to-face if they were in the same room together, the MadLibbers seemed to have an intrinsic understanding of the digital interface. Ava chatted to the girl next to her, but her hands blurred over the screen at the same time. Even Laurent seemed caught up in his own list of notifications.

Madi sighed. With everyone drawn into their own devices, she could finally relax. Laughter rose from one end of the theater's aisle and was echoed at the other side. There was a quiet camaraderie. Voices balanced by the *ping* of text notifications and the warmth of laughter. Madi leaned back in her seat.

"You look a little more relaxed," Laurent said.

She smiled. "I just needed a few minutes to get used to this kind of . . ." She waved at the theater. "Notoriety."

"Of course. And for the rest of us to get used to you, too."

Madi nodded. She could feel it now, a different kind of excitement. These were MadLibbers, her people. They'd come because of her posts. *Because of HER.* The smile grew until it filled her expression.

"I'm glad you're here," Laurent said.

Madi nodded as her phone buzzed. She glanced down to discover both Ava and Chantal had tweeted at her to ask her what the new focus of the MadLibs blog would be. Undecided, Madi searched her dashboard for "MadLibs" to see if anyone besides Brian was on the campaign trail. She snickered as a post appeared. Somewhere, among her countless fans, a MadLibber had started yet another MadLibs meme.

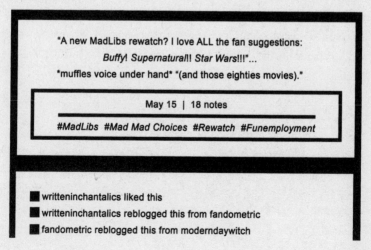

"A new MadLibs rewatch? I love ALL the fan suggestions:
Buffy! *Supernatural*!! *Star Wars*!!!"...
muffles voice under hand "(and those eighties movies)."

May 15 | 18 notes

#MadLibs #Mad Mad Choices #Rewatch #Funemployment

▆ writteninchantalics liked this
▆ writteninchantalics reblogged this from fandometric
▆ fandometric reblogged this from moderndaywitch

Laurent leaned closer. "What is it?"

Madi turned her phone's screen to him and he scrolled up to read the tags. He chuckled, the rumble moving from his arm to hers. The houselights faded into full darkness, but he was close enough she could still pick out details. Laurent's face, in profile, looked like a statue: jaw perfectly cut at a ninety-degree angle, the muscle visible under the skin. The smell of his cologne was distracting. He was too close. Too beautiful. Madi's heart pounded so loudly she could feel her chest vibrating with each *thud*.

"So you like old movies, huh?" she whispered.

"Mm-hmm," Laurent said with a wink. "I really do."

She grinned. "Me, too."

She was going to say more, but Ava said something to Laurent, and he turned away, ending their conversation. His head tipped to the side as Ava animatedly whispered, then Laurent laughed and whispered something in return. Madi's smile faded.

Laurent certainly liked Madi as a friend, but more than that, she couldn't say. Distracted from the movie, she could only think of how confident he seemed, how at ease. But that wasn't her . . . at least not in real life.

Hours later, Madi and Laurent headed out of the theater onto the nighttime street. The MadLibbers swelled around them, and Madi forced herself to face them. She smiled and nodded, talking to more people than she could remember interacting with in her entire life. Ava had promised the crowd fifteen minutes, but it was closer to half an hour before they started to disperse.

"Thank you!" Madi shouted to them as they finally headed their separate ways. "It was great meeting you all!"

The small knot of friends tightened around Madi to block the rest out: Laurent at one side, Ava at the other, Chantal on her heels, and a few MadLibbers whose names Madi couldn't recall making a human shield as they headed away from the Metrograph. Her mind buzzed with the excitement of finally meeting her fans firsthand.

"That was crazy," Madi said with a laugh.

"Crazy *awesome*!" Chantal said. "Tonight was incredible! I still can't believe you actually came."

"I can," Laurent said, smiling. "But I'm glad all the same."

"Thank you—all of you—for helping me out," Madi said. "It was a little overwhelming."

"Anytime," Ava said. "It's no problem."

"We're here for you," Laurent added.

Madi grinned. "I know you are."

As they headed back toward the subway station, Madi fell to storytelling. *This* was her element, her forte, and her hands danced through the air as Laurent and the rest of the group listened. She found herself describing her reactions to *Blade Runner* much as she would on her blog. It surprised her how easy it was.

Madi was amazed by how many details she had missed by watching *Blade Runner* on the small screen. There was a photograph she hadn't noticed in one scene, and later, a small flicker of gold in one character's eyes, which set her thinking of Laurent. She was almost certain of what the ending meant, whereas before she'd been a little confused as to whether or not the character had been human.

Doing an impromptu "live" version of her MadLibs blog gave Madi a rush of energy. She felt completely at ease, so different from when she'd arrived mere hours before. Walking down New York's nighttime streets felt more like home than home did, and she wondered why she'd never thought of reaching out to her online friends before. Barring the obvious challenge of coordination, it had been surprisingly easy.

The first person to leave was Chantal. They waved her off as she headed into a nearby apartment. Next was Ava. She texted her good-byes as she disappeared at the end of Ludlow Street. The last few MadLibbers drifted off in different directions, and then only Laurent and Madi remained. They took the subway back to Penn Station, where Laurent insisted on waiting until her train arrived.

"It's fine, Laurent. I don't want to waste your time."

"I don't have to be anywhere." He slid into the seat next to her, his knee brushing hers for a split second. "Unless you want me to go?"

"No. No, it's fine." Madi felt a bout of nervous laughter bubbling to get out of her chest, but she forced it down. *Play it cool,* her mind warned. Unfortunately, "cool" had never been one of Madi's skills. "Stay if you want."

"I've been thinking about that story you didn't want to tell me the other night," Laurent said.

She stared at him in confusion. She'd been talking almost nonstop since leaving the Metrograph. "What story?"

"When we were talking on Skype. You said that you sometimes get in trouble for saying whatever is on your mind."

Madi groaned. "Oh, right. I was kind of hoping you'd forgotten about that."

"Not a chance. I have a friends-fic in my mind for you."

"A fanfic?" Madi snorted. "What fandom?"

"No, no. A *friends*-fic about you."

"A *what*?"

"It's like . . ." Laurent tapped his chin. "It's like a story you make up about a friend when you don't know what the real answer is."

"Like me thinking you were a girl?"

He chuckled. "Something like that, I suppose. But friends-fic tends to be *much* more elaborate. It's a fantasy. *Un conte de fées.*" He winked. "And this one is about you."

Madi felt the color creep up her neck to her cheeks. Even her forehead prickled. She looked away, trying to force her voice to be steady. "About me?" she said.

"Uh-huh. Want to hear?"

She wiped her hands on her pant legs. "I guess."

"You guess?" He laughed.

"Well, yeah. But only if you want to."

Laurent grinned. "Oh-ho! But I'm only going to tell you my friends-fic under one condition."

"And that is . . . ?"

"That I get the *real* story about what got you in"—he did air quotes around the words—"'serious trouble' when I'm done."

"You haven't forgotten about that part, huh?"

"Not at all. It'll be our little *secret entre-nous.*"

A shiver ran the length of her spine. "Sounds fair."

Laurent dropped her gaze to look out at the waiting room. "Hmmm . . . Well, in my friends-fic, your name is Madeline Li—"

"BRZZZZZZZ!" Madi interrupted him with a buzzer sound. "First mistake!" She laughed as he gave her a horrified look. "My full name isn't Madeline, it's Madison."

"Really?"

"Yes, really. Though I'm not named for Madison Square Garden; I'm named for the street."

"The street?"

"When my mom was a kid, a movie called *Splash* came out," Madi explained.

"Never heard of it."

"Not surprised. It's way before our time. Anyhow, my mom really loved that movie. She got kind of obsessed over it, and the story's about this mermaid who—"

"Hold on," Laurent said, pulling out his phone and typing. "Mermaid. Ah! *Une sirène.*" He looked up. "Go on, please."

"So this movie takes a cute turn when the mermaid has to come up with a human name. She looks around and sees the sign for Madison—"

"Wait. The mermaid can read?"

"Yeah, I guess so," she said with a shrug. "Anyhow, she names herself after Madison Avenue. So when I was born, my mom decided it was a cute name, and that's why I'm Madison. Only a lot of other people got the same idea, and by the time I got to kindergarten, I was Madison N. Argh! To have that stupid little initial tacked onto my name every day for the next eleven years was the worst."

"But why? I like Madison."

"I guess I just wanted something unique. Different. Instead I got a leftover." She shook her head. "Back to your friends-fic. I want to hear the rest of it."

"You sure?"

"No more buzzers." She raised a hand. "Scout's honor."

"All right. Well, your name is . . ." He peeked over at her and smiled.

"*Madison*, named after the epic tale of the New York mermaid, and your last name starts with N. And you *hated* being called 'Madison N' in school."

"It's like you're psychic."

"Oh, I'm not done," he said. "You're the eldest child of three children. That's why you're so strong-willed. So honest. *Tu ne mâche pas tes mots.*"

"Two kids, actually. But close enough."

"You started your MadLibs blog because you needed a place to express your personal thoughts. I've read back to your older posts, you know. They don't all sound as happy as you seem now."

Madi's smile wobbled. "They weren't."

Laurent stared out at the rapidly emptying waiting area. "And once you started your blog, you found you *had* to keep going. It became your link to the world, a place to say it as it is. . . ." He frowned and lifted his phone from his pocket, typing as he searched for a word. "A-a—"

"Soapbox?" Madi suggested.

"No, no. The thing like a table, but tall, like—like a—*Ah! Quel mot? C'est ennuyant!*" Laurent sputtered for a few seconds in French, cheeks flushing.

From the speakers above, a voice announced the arrival of the train. Madi groaned. She and Laurent had been friends for almost two months, but having him face-to-face changed everything. She wanted so much more than texts and tweets.

"There's a word," Laurent grumbled. "It means this place where you make a speech. A table, but not a table, a—"

"A podium?"

"Yes! Exactly." He put the phone back in his pocket. "So the blog became your podium, and that gave you a chance to connect with the world, but when you did that, it caused trouble with your family." He winced. "I'm guessing your mother must have seen your blog at some point. She didn't like it at all."

Madi's smile dimmed until it was just a shape painted over her lips. Her heart began to pound. "It was my father who saw it, actually," she said. "He cares a *lot* about what people think about him . . . about all of us. Our family."

Laurent wasn't smiling anymore, and neither was she. "I'm sorry," he said quietly. "I didn't mean to upset you, Madi."

"Don't be. I'm the one who asked. And you're right, you know. I—I said things to them I couldn't take back."

"I could tell from your tweets and texts." His knee bumped hers. "We've been friends for months. It's not like you've never talked about it. I just wanted to know if I'd guessed right."

"Yeah, you did." Madi stared down at her lap, wondering why things felt weird all of a sudden. Laurent was someone she went to for support. Only she'd been thinking of Laurent as *Lauren*, at the time, and now there were other, more sticky emotions getting in the way. Crushing on someone made a cool façade a lot harder to manage.

"Are you all right?" he asked.

"I'm fine."

"You sure?"

"I'm just remembering."

At the far side of the room, travelers began moving through the doors to the waiting train. They had minutes left.

"Do you want to know what I said to them?" Madi asked, then looked away.

"Only if you want to tell me."

"I told them what had happened to Sarah was their fault. I told them if Mom hadn't taken off that summer, Sarah wouldn't have had such trouble changing schools and things wouldn't have fallen apart." She flinched. "But that's not entirely true. Sarah's *always* had challenges. They're just harder when schedules change." She looked up, throat aching. "I said it because I *knew* they'd been thinking it. And because I knew it would hurt them."

"How'd they take it?"

"My dad was fine. He laughed off my behavior as 'teen angst,' and that was the end of it."

"And your mom?"

Madi sighed and closed her eyes. "She told me if that was how I felt, I should do more to help out."

5

"I have had people walk out on me before,
but not . . . when I was being so charming."
(*Blade Runner*, 1982)

The door to the train sat open, though most of the other occupants had long since climbed inside. Only Madi and Laurent remained, half in and half out of the door, the occasional stranger stepping past them on their way inside.

Madi peeked over her shoulder into the busy interior. "I should probably go."

"You should." Laurent smiled sadly. "I'm happy you came out tonight, Madi. And I'm glad meeting the MadLibbers wasn't weird for you."

"Oh, I wouldn't go that far," she said with a chuckle.

"Well, I'm glad they weren't *too* weird for you."

Madi smiled. "Me, too."

"You think you'll come next time?"

Butterflies fluttered in her stomach. She flicked her hair in what she hoped was a look of nonchalance. "I think there's a good chance of that . . . if you'll be there, too."

"Of course. I can't wait!"

A giggle broke free of Madi's chest. He was too honest for his own good.

Behind Laurent's shoulder, a woman's flushed face appeared. She had her purse clutched to her chest and was trying to get past, but Laurent blocked the way. "Are you getting in or out?" she snapped.

"Ah! So sorry!"

Laurent stepped back and the woman pushed her way inside, grumbling. The moment to go had arrived, but Madi clung to the last seconds. She'd been so hesitant when she'd stepped off the train, but now she was desperate to stay. Everything had changed.

"Well," she said. "This was fun, but I really *should* go."

"I know."

Madi lifted her fingers, meaning to shake Laurent's hand, but he moved toward her at the same time, and suddenly they weren't shaking hands, they were hugging in the doorway to the train. Madi's face pressed against Laurent's chest, the top of her head bumping under his chin as his arms wrapped her in a warm embrace. *My God, he's tall!* Laurent smelled like aftershave, and cinnamon, and the hint of popcorn from the theater, the scents all mixing together into an intoxicating bouquet. This wasn't a quick hug, like when she'd first arrived. This one lingered, slow and warm.

She felt his stubbled cheek brush her forehead as he leaned down to whisper in her ear. "This was more than fun. It was *merveilleux*."

"I don't know what that means, but I'm glad I came."

This wasn't just friends saying good-bye, she realized—it was like a scene from a movie. *Oh my God! What do I do?* Moments like this didn't happen online, and she was completely unprepared to deal with the emotions. Her smile wobbled as he released her.

"*Merveilleux* means I liked it a lot." He reached out and tucked a stray hair behind her ear. "I liked meeting you, Madison. . . ." His smile grew softer. "*Minette*. I liked it so very much."

"M-me, too."

His fingers brushed her cheek, and for a heartbeat she was certain Laurent was going to kiss her. Madi couldn't breathe.

Suddenly, a voice interrupted from right beside them.

"We're on a schedule here!" the stranger announced. "You gonna kiss this guy or what? 'Cause I want to leave." Madi looked up to discover a middle-aged man glaring at her. Her gaze lifted to the train's interior. A wide-eyed boy near the door stared at them from the front seat, his finger half up his nose.

"Oh my God!" Madi jumped away from Laurent, face in flames. If there'd ever been a chance of an "accidental kiss," the man's prompting had effectively ended it. "Sorry," she said. "But I've gotta go, Laurent."

"Next time, then?"

She didn't know whether he meant the visit or the almost kiss, but she couldn't wait to find out. "Definitely next time."

Laurent waved as she stepped into the train and found her way to her seat. She expected he'd leave at that point, but he waited until the train pulled away, his hand upraised until she lost sight of him in the flicker of lights and darkness. Madi's lashes fluttered closed, and she let the wide grin she'd been holding back release, her cheeks aching as it spread ear to ear. This had been—bar none— the most exciting night in her entire life. It felt like a movie, and she wasn't ready for the credits to run.

A few minutes into the ride, her phone rang. She pulled it from her pocket with shaking hands, certain an unexpected phone call must mean she wasn't the only one who'd felt the growing connection between them. She slid the release without checking the caller ID and put the phone to her ear.

"Hello?" she said breathlessly.

"Madi?" her father's worried voice echoed in her ear. "Where are you?"

It felt like the train had gone off the rails. Her stomach dropped. "I-I'm on the train," she stammered. "I told you I was going to New York to see—"

"Yes, but *where*? Where are you right now?"

Madi looked out the windows at the fading lights of the city. Somewhere out there, Laurent was taking the subway home. "On the way to Millburn. The train left the station a couple minutes ago."

"And when will you be home?"

She blinked in shock. "In about an hour, I think." Her fingers tightened around the phone as her mother's face flashed to mind. She was on a plane right now, somewhere over the Atlantic. "Why? What's going on, Dad?"

"Your mother and I sat down to explain things to Sarah. She seemed fine, but when the cab arrived to take your mother to the airport, Sarah started asking for you. . . ." His words faded. Images from the year Sarah started high school filled Madi's mind. She could see her sister's face wracked with tears, the keening scream behind locked doors. Chaos had engulfed the household in the days after their mother had left. And though that event had been two years ago, the echoes of it carried through to today.

"What happened?!"

"Sarah ran away."

"She what?!"

"The police think she's probably fine, but they have patrol cars out, checking the roads. The whole neighborhood is out searching for her, but so far, no luck. I think she might be hiding, refusing to answer the searchers."

"Oh my God!"

"I need you to come home as soon as you can. We need your help to find her."

"Of course, Dad. I'm on my way."

"Thanks, Madi. Just call my cell when you get here."

"Right."

And with that, the line went dead. She stared down at the phone in her hand, barely able to keep the fear at bay. This, right here, was what she'd been waiting for. It had happened.

A post appeared on-screen, and her phone chimed happily. Distracted, Madi pulled it up. She cringed.

THE TEEN YEARS

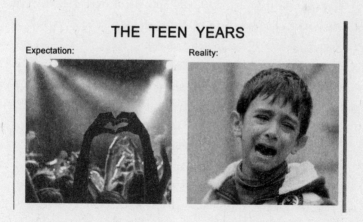

Expectation:

Reality:

"Isn't that the truth."

Madi closed her eyes and let her head fall back against the seat. Her life was coming to pieces, and she didn't know how to put it back together.

The Millburn subdivision where the Nakamas lived was a secluded enclave left over from the previous century. Retrofitted Victorian homes backed onto a small tract of treed land that made up the South Mountain Reservation. The streets were quiet, the pace slow. It *should* have been easy to locate Sarah, but if there was one thing Madi knew about her sister, it was that if she didn't want to be found, she wouldn't be. Her father wasn't answering his phone when the train arrived, so she walked the twelve blocks from the station. Finding the house deserted, she headed to the park beyond the last line of houses. Flashlights moved through the trees.

"We've already done a sweep of the area," the officer told her. "Your sister's not there."

The parkland that ran behind the residential neighborhood included a small lake. The body of water's official name was Diamond Mill Pond, though Madi and Sarah simply called it "the lake." When they'd been children, it had been a favorite spot to play.

"Has she shown up anywhere else?" Madi asked.

"No, but—"

"Then let me go. I need to check one more place."

He seemed poised to argue when Madi's father appeared, elbowing his way through a group of volunteers to reach her side.

"Madi, you're here." He pulled her into a hug. "Thank God." His hands were shaking, his face gray. "Sorry I missed your call."

"I came as soon as I could, Dad."

"Thank you. And again—sorry for wrecking your night."

"It's fine. I was coming home anyhow. This is more important."

Her father nodded and turned to the officer. "May we talk a moment? I had a few thoughts about the search."

"Of course, Mr. Nakama. What can I do for you?"

With the officer diverted, Madi darted around the cordoned-off section of trail and past the houses that overlooked Diamond Mill Pond. In minutes, she reached the paved path. The three-story, Federal-style Colonial Inn glittered behind her, lights dancing like fireflies behind mullioned windows. At the edge of the trees, ruins rose like spectral fingers, clawing their way from the ground where she and Sarah had played as children.

Madi tiptoed through the dark, her eyes in the shadows. "Sarah," she hissed. "Sarah, you there?"

As she neared the ruins, the shapes shifted into the remains of a long-destroyed building. The rough-hewn stone foundation predated most houses in Millburn, the roofless structure a ghostly reminder of another era. Though it was now a trendy spot for wedding photographs, the darkness made it malevolent.

"Sarah?"

The sound of the lake seemed to fade and Madi turned the other direction. She'd heard something, but what? *Maybe it was the other searchers.* She looked back. A shadow that hadn't been there moments earlier had appeared in the corner of the destroyed building. Madi waited, heart pounding.

"Sarah? Is that you?"

A sniffle answered her.

Madi released her breath and walked slowly forward. "What're you doing out here so late?"

The shadow took two steps sideways. Madi stopped. (Spook Sarah, and she'd never stop running.)

"You scared me tonight," Madi said.

Another sniffle.

"I'm glad I found you. Why're you out here, Sarah?"

The wind rose off the lake, almost obscuring her sister's words. "I thought you'd left, too."

Madi's chest tightened until she couldn't breathe. She took a single step. Sarah hadn't moved, but she could sense her wanting to.

"I didn't leave. I went to a movie with my friends. I told you that, remember?"

"No."

Madi took another tentative step. Now she could see Sarah's features. Her sister had been crying. Silver tracks lined her cheeks.

"Before I left, I told you I was going into New York. I went to see *Blade Runner* and—"

"Mom's leaving again!" Sarah shouted. The anger in the words bounced around the broken stone structure.

"I heard that." Madi waited, let the words sink in. "Do you want to talk about it?"

"I don't wanna talk! Mom's leaving, Madi. She's leaving!"

Madi inched closer. "Sarah, I think we should go home so we can talk."

"But she's leaving us; she's leaving! SHE'S LEAVING!" Her screams rose into a howl of fury.

Sarah turned to run, but Madi tackled her and the two of them tumbled onto the manicured lawn.

"Mom's LEAVING! She's going AWAY and she's not coming BACK!"

Madi's ears crackled, but she pulled her sister tight, holding Sarah's arms down and rocking her. Deep pressure was one of the ways Sarah coped with overstimulation, but the weighted blanket she used was at home.

"Shh . . ." Madi whispered. "It's okay. I'm here. You're going to be okay."

For a few seconds Sarah struggled against her. Madi could hear other people coming through the trees, could see a flashlight beam bobbing in the bushes up the shore. Somewhere, Madi could hear her father shouting Sarah's name.

"Shh . . . Breathe, Sarah. Everything's going to be all right."

"No! It's NOT!"

With a final lunge, Sarah's body went limp, the fight disappearing as quickly as it had arrived. Sarah pressed her face to Madi's neck. "Sh-she's leaving us," she choked. "She's leaving us b-behind just like she did last time."

Madi patted her back, wishing there was something she could say—some way she could deny it—but it was too late. Both of them knew the truth.

"Yeah, she is," Madi said. "But I'm still here."

6

"You want out of here so bad, you
probably memorize bus schedules."
(*Footloose*, 1984)

> Dear Madi, Just arrived at Oxford. Thought I'd check in with everyone. What a trip! The plane was packed so tight it felt like we were canned. I haven't heard from your dad yet. How are things on the home front? From: Mom

fine

> Fine, as in they're good at home? Or fine as in you don't want to talk about it with me? Mom

both—u should just talk to dad

> I will, but I want to hear from you, too. Is everything all right at home? As an aside: Have any papers arrived from my research assistant? She's not answering my texts and I need the next grant proposal in before the deadline. Mom

a: i'm not watching the mail for u
b: i've been a little OCCUPIED

Occupied with what? Mom

what do u think? u left. AGAIN.
god, mom. do u even care about us?

Madi, please stop being melodramatic. It's
exhausting. Of course I care. I'm your mother.
Mom

funny, u would expect a mother
to be at home with her kids

Honestly, Madi, it's not like you and Sarah are
little children. I think a bit of independence will
be good for both of you. Besides, I've put my
career plans on hold for years. I have to do this
while there's time. Mom

...

And I might not have said it in so many words, but
I am grateful you are helping out with Sarah. Mom

well I didn't really have a choice about it, did i?

You sound angry, Madi. Mom

it's been a long night. 🙁 also, you don't
have to sign "mom" to each text. i know it's
u. ur number shows up on the screen

Why? What happened?

sarah took off JUST LIKE LAST TIME. what did u expect would happen?!

Damnit! I didn't realize.

...

And sorry about writing "Mom" on everything. I'm not used to this technology yet. I prefer the phone, to be honest, but no one was answering when I called. I suppose everyone was out looking for Sarah.

...

Also, I know you're angry, but I do think you'll understand when you're older. Sometimes people have to make difficult choices. Sarah will cope. She did before.

...

Madi? Are you still around?

...

Good night, Madi. I'll try to arrange a video chat with you later so we can talk in person. Say good night to Sarah for me. I know it's hard, but things will settle down. They will.

I love you both. Mom

Madi closed her mother's texts and took a slow breath. Freaking out wasn't going to change anything. (Not with her mother on a different continent.) She thumbed her phone's apps sideways until she found her dashboard, popped it open, and scanned through the latest blogs, reblogs, and comments. The relief she felt as she scanned through the posts was tangible. If she was on the Internet, her mother's disappearance from their lives felt like a distant issue that didn't need to be dealt with. (At least not as long as she stayed online.) Everything she wanted to see and everyone she wanted to talk to was here. There was plenty to read, comment on, and do. It was easy.

She ran her thumb up the screen, skimming posts until one caught her eyes. She smirked. MadLibbers were always creating posts for whatever rewatch she was doing.

"If only it *did* have an opt-out button. I'd be the first one to sign up."

Real life didn't have that option, but it *did* have fandom, and that was as close as she was going to get. Hitting REBLOG, she closed her dashboard and popped open the last fanfic bookmark she'd saved: JoesWoes's long-fic "Shadow Soul." Tonight she found herself imagining Laurent in Spartan's role.

Content, Madi read until dawn.

By Saturday evening, the Nakama household had returned to its usual precarious balance. Madi and Sarah played video games. Their father sat in the kitchen, writing his newest "Down Home" for the *Herald.* Only one person was conspicuously absent. *Mom.* No one mentioned her, and she didn't call. By the time Sarah headed up to bed, Madi knew the worst was over. Her father caught her eyes as Madi came into the kitchen.

"Thank you," he said quietly. "For everything."

"It's fine."

"It's not fine, but it's appreciated. I don't . . . I don't think I could do this alone."

The sound of his voice was oddly empty. Madi nodded, unable to answer, and headed up to her room to work on a blog post. She wanted—*needed!*—something other than the drama going on at home to think about. Fandom was one outlet, writing another.

By the time the quotes for the MadLibs post had been selected and the rough draft written, she was smiling again. Madi plugged in her laptop and crawled into bed, hoping for a dreamless sleep. She dreamed of Laurent instead.

Sunday, everyone spent the morning following Sarah's schedule like clockwork, giving her the structure the psychologist insisted was key to her success. Charles made pancakes. Madi fried bacon. Sarah set the table. Most weekends their mother taught at Princeton, or went in to do grading, generally leaving before anyone else in the house woke, so it didn't feel like things had significantly changed. By the time Sarah and Madi finished eating, Sarah was humming to herself, a sure sign that she was feeling settled again. Madi felt her shoulders release. They'd gotten through the first two days relatively unscathed.

"Only six weeks to go," Madi muttered as she headed up to her room to edit her latest MadLib.

Blog Post 209, Sunday 1:02 p.m.:

The decision is MADE!

After a LONG process of elimination and an unexpected SURGE of popularity on the '80s movies choice (due to @laurentabelard's tireless campaigning this weekend ;), the new MadLib topic has been selected. For the next six weeks I'll be rewatching/liveblogging a variety of scintillating 1980s gems of the big screen. Our first MadLib of *Sixteen Candles* will go tonight at 7:00 p.m. EST. It will kick off with a group-focused liveblog—so please join in!—after which I'll be writing up a MadLib summary post. Check in for that tomorrow.

Thanks for the support, and as always, clickety-click on those links. (I need pizza money. ;)

exit stage left

MadLib

Comments enabled.

Tags: #MadLibs #80s Movies #Madi watches things and then blogs about them #Still a little sad I don't get to watch *Buffy* #Funemployment

With a smile, Madi hit POST. It was done, and now she could really let the excitement build. It was a new beginning, a new rewatch, a new—

"Madi . . . ? Madi?! MADI! Where are you?" Sarah's voice rose, panicked, from the main floor. "Dad! Where did she GO?! Where's Madi?!"

Madi cringed and pushed her laptop aside.

"Up here, Sarah. Just a sec."

By the time dinner had been cooked and served, and Madi found time to get back online, her blog post had nearly twenty-five thousand hits. An hour later, after dishes had been loaded into the washer, it had climbed to over forty thousand. She grinned as she scrolled through the discussion going on online. MadLibbers across the globe were excited for the newest MadLib to begin!

Her smile dimmed as she reached @StarveilBrian1981's tweets. In the last hours, Brian had taken it upon himself to champion the lost cause of science fiction. Irritation prickled under Madi's skin.

@StarveilBrian1981: I have to say I'm a little disappointed you didn't select *Star Wars*, @MadLib. IMO the election was rigged.

Madi bit her lip as she composed her reply. It had grown increasingly difficult to keep all her fans happy. A year and a half ago, she'd had a group of twenty thousand steady followers, but in the last year her fan base had exploded. Legions of MadLibbers—from all parts of the world—waited on her every post, their numbers increasing exponentially. They bought merchandise from her store. Money made its way from their pockets to hers. The site even had a "special features" section of exclusive content available for download after payment. Madi was no teen blogger hobbyist. She was a successful entrepreneur!

Madi was grateful for it . . . *most of the time.*

@MadLib: @StarveilBrian1981 It wasn't an election, Brian, it was a vote. But thanks for your concern. And there's always the next time for *Star Wars*. #UseTheForceLuke

Madi posted her reply. She groaned as another tweet from Brian appeared almost instantly. *How fast can he type?!*

@StarveilBrian1981: @MadLib Nonetheless, I think you should check the IP addresses for the people who voted in the last 24 hours. There's no way that should have changed that much.

@MadLib: @StarveilBrian1981 It was pretty close all the way through, but there was a lot of campaigning for the '80s movies in the last 24 hours. I watched the tally come in. #TrustMe

@StarveilBrian1981: @MadLib I wish I had your certainty.

@MadLib: @StarveilBrian1981 Yeah. Me, too. :>/ Moving on . . .

@MadLib: All right, #MadLibbers across the internet, are you ready to LIVEBLOG #SixteenCandles?

@laurentabelard: @MadLib Absolument! I mean—absolutely—YES! A thousand times, YES!

@ArtWithAttitude: @MadLib Signing in for blog duty! Woot! Let's get this party started!

@fandometric: @MadLib Netflix is open to #SixteenCandles and my computer's humming. Let's start! #MadLibbers #Rewatch #TheJourneyBegins

@MadLib: All right, #MadLibbers, hitting play NOW! *archaic Universal logo appears* *a hush falls over the room*

@laurentabelard: @MadLib EEEEEEeeeee!!! SO EXCITED SO EXCITED!

@MadLib: @laurentabelard You see? It's because of THAT kind of gratuitous use of all caps that I expected a Lauren (f) . . . rather than a Laurent (m). LOL

@laurentabelard: @MadLib I trust you aren't disappointed with me. ;)

@MadLib: @laurentabelard Not in the least. *flutters lashes* You are perfect, especially in person. :D

@ModernDayWitch: @MadLib @laurentabelard Hmmm . . . Sounds like I missed more than just *Blade Runner* last weekend. LOL Anyone feel like giving me details? ;)

@fandometric: @MadLib Are we watching this film or what?

For a split second, Madi considered tweeting a snarky reply to fandometric. What was his problem, anyhow?! She posted a neutral tweet instead.

@MadLib: All right—back to the liveblog.

@fandometric: @MadLib YES!

@MadLib: We start with a pristine snapshot of suburbia. Sprawling houses, lush lawns. Then BAM! An alarm goes off! Who wakes their kids like that?!?

@ArtWithAttitude: @MadLib My dad used to. (Mind you that was the only way I'd get up in high school.)

@ModernDayWitch: @ArtWithAttitude Sweetie, why does that NOT surprise me? ;P

@MadLib: First thoughts: WAY too much household stress. Kids fighting, parents yelling. I'd be hiding in my room like poor Samantha.

@laurentabelard: @MadLib Me too. :(

@MadLib: Samantha's getting lots of internal monologue/camera time which makes me think our main is . . . the indomitable MOLLY RINGWALD!

@fandometric: @MadLib Miss Molly is the QUEEN of '80s pop culture. #SixteenCandles

@ArtWithAttitude: @fandometric PREACH.

@MadLib: Poor Samantha's dealing with body issues (clearly a universal problem!) and a family that has . . . *gasp* forgotten her birthday.

@ArtWithAttitude: @MadLib I can't believe that's the premise of the film. Ha ha!

@MadLib: Side note: WHAT SCHOOL LOOKS LIKE THAT? It's like some Utopian version of 1980s America. O_o #MadLib #SixteenCandles

@laurentabelard: @MadLib See? THIS is why I wanted to come to America!

@MadLib: Whoa! Did they actually use TEENS to play the teenagers in this movie? That's surprising. Two points for realism!

@MadLib: Holy hairspray, Batman! Did you SEE that kid's hair?!? CRAZY!!! LOL Defying gravity FTW! #ByThePowerOfHairspray

@MadLib: Aaaawwww!! Look at all these ADORABLE 1980s styles. LOLOL I can't believe my mother probably wore those.

@ArtWithAttitude: @MadLib Yuck! Can you imagine? LOL

@MadLib: Two points for catchy music during boring credits. It's all synth and electric guitar. Does ANY sad music exist from the '80s?

@fandometric: @MadLib Nope. The '90s absorbed it all. #ItsFunnyBecauseItsTrue

@MadLib: @fandometric EXACTLY! :D Now back to #SixteenCandles. Her parents have missed her birthday. Woe is me! Let the #RomCom antics begin . . .

"I didn't like it," Sarah announced.

"You didn't?" Madi peeked up from her phone to discover her sister glaring at the Netflix "Top Picks for Madi" page. "Why not?"

"It wasn't real. The plot was all wrong."

Madi bit back a smile. For someone who had difficulty with social interactions, Sarah was unexpectedly astute at finding issues with logical progression. It was one of the many reasons Madi loved doing the rewatches with her.

"What was wrong with it?"

"There was too much left to chance. The dropped note, the people talking behind one another's backs, the friends showing up at the last second." Her gaze flicked over to Madi. "Life doesn't work that way."

"No. It sure doesn't."

Sarah glanced over at the clock on the fireplace mantel, then clambered from the couch and headed out of the room. She didn't pause to say good night. (She never did if she fell behind schedule.)

"G'night, Sarah!" Madi called after her.

Madi's phone vibrated, and she glanced down to see the MadLibs blog had received an anonymous message. Grinning, she popped it opened. Her breath caught.

NEW Message, *anonymous*: 11:05 p.m. EST
Subject: Sixteen Candles Liveblog

That was the worst liveblog you have EVER done. Stop fooling around with Long Duk Dong and RESPOND to the movie! People WAIT for your liveblogs, MadLib. THEY WATCH THEM. The least you could do is make it worth our time. I hope to hell the recap makes up for that piece of shit. SCREW. YOU. MADLIB.

Shocked, Madi jerked her hand back from the screen as if she'd been bitten. She popped open the REPLY button, then paused. Anons meant unless she wanted to air this in front of the entire MadLibs group, she couldn't answer. In her sophomore year of high school—when Madi had been involved in a completely different group of friends and fandom—she'd had a run-in that had involved months of online harassment. It had only ended when Madi had deleted her entire online profile. That was when she'd made the decision to start up MadLibs, where she could control who could post and which allowed her to remain anonymous.

She reread the post, temper rising. *Screw you, troll.* With a muttered swear, she hit DELETE. The best thing to do with trolls was to ignore them.

"Stay under your bridge," she muttered.

Madi did her best work long past midnight. Though she'd hated taking piano lessons as a child, it had given her an uncanny ability to touch-type. Lit only by the glow of the laptop, her fingers blurred over the keyboard, paragraph after paragraph flowing from her fingertips. Unfortunately, tonight she was deleting as much as she typed.

The troll had thrown off her writing game. She wished now that she'd never read his comment. It preyed on her mind and made her struggle with the flow of her writing. *Maybe he was right. Maybe I was being too flirty with Laurent. I was just excited to talk with him.* She shoved the thought aside, forcing herself to summarize the plot.

"C'mon," she muttered. "You can do this."

Madi was still up at two, when she was hit by the much-delayed urge to eat. Stomach growling, she tiptoed down the stairs. Reaching the kitchen, she discovered her father sitting at the table in the dark, his own laptop open before him, a hazy blue light cast over his face.

"Hey, Dad," Madi said. "What're you still doing up?"

Her words faded as a tinny voice—recorded on one side of the planet and relayed back home to New Jersey—echoed through the speakers. Madi's mother could have been anywhere at all, but all Madi cared about was that she wasn't here.

"And there's a great faculty support center. We're using Moodle, of course, but there's an entire tech wing devoted to providing access to online students. I'm learning so much, Charles. It's amazing!"

Madi's father absently smoothed his mustache. "Good to hear, good to hear."

"And I've been thinking about doing some extra research here, if time allows. They have a great microbiology program. Cutting-edge."

Charles's throat bobbed. "Extra research, you say?" (Madi wondered if her mother even noticed how much her prolonged absences affected *everyone* in the family.)

"If there's time before I come back."

"I thought you said you'd be back home by the end of June."

"Oh, I will. I'm just saying I'd do it if I could fit it in after my sessional work. It's so wonderful to have access to something like this. I really think it'd be a shame to pass it up. And if I can use the lab while I'm here, why not?"

"Sounds like something you should go for," Charles said. His smile dimmed. "Like you said, Oxford's a once-in-a-lifetime opportunity."

"I know, right? And now that the girls are settled with the change—"

"We're *hardly* settled," Madi interrupted. She stepped out of the shadows, moving behind her father so she could see the screen. The room behind her mother was a yellow splash of sunshine. Outside the window, golden stone buildings rose from a lush green landscape, a few early morning students moving like ants on the quad. It looked like Hogwarts.

Her mother's face rippled in shock as Madi came into view. "Madi. I didn't realize you were still up."

"I did another rewatch tonight. I'm working on the post now."

"That's nice. What movie?"

"*Sixteen Candles.* I'm on an '80s theme. You'd like these ones." Madi's tone sharpened. "Too bad you're not around to join in."

"I don't really have time for rewatches. I'm still setting up my course work."

"Of course you are."

Next to Madi, her father shifted uncomfortably in his chair. "Maybe we should . . ." Charles began.

"You're keeping up with your schoolwork?" Madi's mother asked.

"You've been gone less than a week, Mom. My grades are fine."

"Glad to hear it. So . . . things are good with you, Madi?"

Madi grimaced rather than answer.

There was a lengthy pause as her mother's expression grew wary. "Did . . ." Her voice faltered. "Did Sarah watch the movie with you tonight?"

"Yeah, she did." Madi's hands rose to her hips. "You could talk to Sarah about it if you wanted to. I'm sure she'd be happy to discuss it. Her light was on when I came downstairs," Madi lied. "She might even be awake."

Behind her, Madi's father made an uneasy sound like he'd tried to clear his throat but had choked in the process.

"It's a bit late for a call," her mother said. "Let her sleep."

"It's no problem. I don't mind waking her."

"I—I don't think that's a good idea. I wouldn't want to upset her unnecessarily."

"Of course you don't. Not like you've ever done *that* before."

"Well, then," Charles said. "I think we should probably finish up." He nodded to Madi. "If you could give me a few minutes alone with your mother, I'd like to say good night."

"Fine. Give me a second."

"Good night," her mother said.

Madi turned away from the screen without answering. She rifled through the cupboard for a granola bar and a juice box, and headed out of the kitchen. She wanted to rage at her mother, but there was no point. And Madi's father was *not* going to talk about it. Charles Nakama was everyone's friend, and it wasn't just because of his semicelebrity status writing "Down Home" for the *Tri-State Herald*. He simply hated conflict.

If there was one truth about the Nakama family, it was that they kept private family matters *private*. This rule had been drilled into Madi since childhood, and she knew talking to anyone about the latest upheaval would infuriate her parents like nothing else. Even the few friends she kept in contact with from her first two years of high school were off-limits for any sort of venting.

Temper bubbling, she locked herself in her room and returned to the Word document. She reread it once. She did a spell-check. She read it again. Seething with annoyance, Madi could not make the words come. After a moment, she pulled out her phone and tapped in a message. Laurent wouldn't get it until morning, but she needed to tell *someone*. She felt like her chest was about to explode.

> my whole family life is fake.
> it's all a LIE!

> what happened?

> OMG—did my text wake u?!
> I'M SORRY!!! 😮

> ha-ha! no, you didn't wake me up.
> i was already awake.

> why? do u have insomnia?

> no. i sleep. i was just online a minute ago.

> don't u have school tomorrow—i mean
> today?

> i do.

> but it's like two in the morning 😴

> aha! but it's 8:00 a.m. in france! i set my alarm
> so i can talk to my friends before they go to
> school. then I go back to bed again.

aw . . . that's sad 😴

why? think about it. i'm here in ny, but when I make a point of chatting each morning it's like i'm home, too. i get my own hours (when they're asleep), and their time, too.

i guess so

besides, who would i talk to if i got lonely here?

u could always talk to me

really?

yeah, laurent, u could

maybe i will. 😊 so tell me about this lie. is this related to the "family drama" from before?

the one and only 😕

what happened? (only tell me if you want to. i'm not prying.)

i'm the one who texted u at 2:00 a.m. ur off the hook. promise. 😜

so what was it this time?

my mom called home. we had a disagreement

oh no.

that wasn't the only thing, though. i was already in a pissy mood. i got some anon hate on the madlibs blog

you did? but why?!

i don't know. i guess the anon didn't think i was on my a-game for liveblogging. trolls bug me! 😡

so respond to him. air the matter.

not a chance

why not?

bc that feeds them

it does?

sadly, yes. i've dealt with trolls before. a few years ago i got targeted

targeted? (i don't understand.)

not everyone appreciates enthusiasm & there was a lot of anon hate going on. it was only 1 or 2 people (i think) but it got so bad i finally just left that's sad, madi. you love fandom.

i do. 😞 it made me kind of paranoid about trusting people. (it's part of the reason i prefer online school.) i like NOT having to deal with people. u know?

um, no. but I hear what you're saying.

it sounds weird, i know. i'm not JUST a shut-in. LOL i met you in RL, didn't I?

you did—thank you 😊 and i'm glad you came out, BTW. it's good to meet new people. get a sense of who they are.

strangers freak me out

did I freak you out?

at first maybe? *grins* i don't know. i was a little distracted by you when we first skyped

distracted, hmmm . . . ? and how about once you met me? did i pass your face-to-face test?

i'm warming up to u 😊

good. i'll keep warming myself up to you, too. 😆

that sounds . . . LOL worse
than i think you mean it, laurent

maybe. hard to tell if you're not face-to-face.
(i'd be happy to warm you up then.)

LOL stop! srsly

why? 😄 X 1000000

bc i keep laughing and my dad's going to
wonder what's going on up here

he wouldn't wonder if I was really there.

LOLOL—stop, seriously! he's going to think
i'm looking at porn or something

sorry. did I take the joke too far?

no—it's good. i just need to keep it down 😄

i'll save teasing you for another time, then.

another late-night chat?

definitely. and i hate to say this, but now i
should go. it's 8:30 a.m. france time, 2:30 a.m.
in nyc, and i have school in a few hours. ugh.
(i wish i didn't, but i do.)

yes, i know, but i'm glad u were awake

me, too.

good night

bonne nuit, madi. text me
tomorrow night if you're up.

i will. now go to sleep. it's
WAY past your bedtime 😜

ZZZZzzzzzzzzzzzzzzzzzzzzz . . . 😴

7

"Don't ever invite a vampire into your house,
you silly boy. It renders you powerless."
(*The Lost Boys*, 1987)

nline school was heaven. After more than a decade of stuffy classrooms and classmates whose highest cognitive skills seemed to be diverting their teachers off task, Madi had found her niche. Two years previous, she'd taken a single class at OMA—the online branch of Millburn Academy—to boost her freshman math grade. What she'd discovered was a completely unique way of learning.

Madi set her own schedule, and the teachers facilitated her learning. The students at OMA could finish a class as slowly (or quickly) as they were capable. The courses were broken into modules, with a focus on large projects. Madi loved it. By the end of her first OMA math class, her grade had jumped from an acceptable B- to an A+, but more important, she'd finally *understood* what she was being taught. There were no loudmouths to interrupt her learning. Madi had known that online schooling was for her.

The trick had been convincing her parents of the same thing.

In an unpleasant twist of fate, Sarah's first semester of high school and her mother's first out-of-state fellowship had coincided, resulting in chaos. Madi, who was struggling to balance her sophomore classes with family stress, pointed out that if she attended OMA rather than regular classes at Millburn Academy, she could drop her sister off in the morning and pick her up after school. (The fact that Madi was able to complete her schoolwork, without distraction, in half the time it'd taken while sitting in a classroom, was an added bonus.) Overwhelmed by competing work/research loads and Sarah's needs, Madi's parents agreed. So far, it was a balance that worked.

Today, Madi arrived at Millburn Academy mere minutes before the bell. With a relieved sigh, she slumped against the lockers. Online school gave her a stress-free high school schedule, but her MadLibs all-nighters were starting to catch up with her. She wobbled in place, half-asleep, until the sound of Mr. Wattley's door banging open jarred her awake.

Sarah rushed down the school hallway, leaving Madi staring after her.

"Sarah?" she called. "You're going the wrong way."

Her sister's steps barely slowed. "Got to study today."

"Why didn't you text me?"

"I'm telling you now."

Madi reached her sister's side, falling into step next to her.

"There's a physics test next Wednesday," Sarah continued. "I want to review, and Robbie's supervising a tutoring session tonight."

"Robbie?"

"Robbie Sullivan. Mr. Wattley's got him leading a study group for freshmen."

Madi stifled a yawn behind her hand just as the final bell rang. "So, where's this study group meeting?"

"The library." Torrents of students poured from open doors and Sarah hunched her shoulders, sidling to the edge of the hallway. "Come pick me up there."

Most days they were out of the building by this point—another part of Sarah's schedule—but today they were caught in the crowd. Madi's gaze darted as her sister pushed grimly onward.

"Wait!" Madi called. "The library at the school, or the one downtown?! Where am I supposed to get you?"

Her sister slowed as a red-haired boy walked out of the open door of a classroom. "Is the study group still on today?" Sarah asked.

"You bet." He waved. "Hey, Madi."

She gave him a weak smile. It was the boy from the hallway. Seeing him, a memory of Robbie borrowing her notes in tenth-grade AP History floated to mind, the name and face clicking into place. She'd barely given him a second thought in the years between.

"You coming to the study group, too?" he asked.

Two steps behind Robbie, a black-haired senior in a death-metal T-shirt slouched against the doorway, waiting to get through. He caught Madi's eyes and shot her a seething glare.

"You looking at something?!" he snarled.

She blinked in shock. *What did I ever do to him?*

"Madi?" Robbie prompted.

"Don't think so," she said, distracted. "I've already passed physics." She tapped her sister's shoulder. "What time do you need me to pick you up?"

"If we start studying right away, then we should be done by—"

"Move it, Sarah!" The nameless angry teen shoved between the two sisters, grunting: "Jeez! Get outta the way, cows!"

"Jerk!" Sarah glared at the receding figure of the black-haired boy as he disappeared into the crowd. *This is why I hated high school,* Madi thought. *This is why I left.*

"I could walk Sarah home after I'm done with tutoring," Robbie offered. "No problem."

"I don't know if—"

"No," Sarah snapped. "Madi always picks me up. The public library closes at five. I'll be waiting outside the doors for you at four thirty."

"The *public* library?" Madi's shoulder dropped. That was even farther than the school.

"Sure you don't want to hang out with us?" Robbie asked. "It's a small group, mostly one-on-one review. I wouldn't mind you being there."

"Thanks for the offer, but I'll pass. I hardly slept last night, and I want to post my next blog when I get home."

His eyebrows rose in surprise. "You have a blog?"

"Er . . . yeah."

"Cool! What's it about?"

"Stuff."

"What kind of stuff?"

"Just . . . stuff," Madi said lamely. She nodded to Sarah. "Four thirty, then. I'll be waiting for you."

"Got it."

"You have your phone if I'm late or something?"

Sarah's expression rippled into concern. "Are you going someplace? Are you leaving?"

"No, I'm just saying in case someth—"

"Where are you going, Madi?!"

"I'm not going anywhere, but just in case something happens, I want you to be able to text me."

Sarah's lip quivered. "Madi . . ."

"I'm not going anywhere." She sighed. "I'll be there."

Sarah clutched her arm. "Four thirty. Promise?"

"Promise."

And it wasn't until Madi was back on the street, lumbering home, that she thought about how exhausted that promise always made her.

Heavy-lidded, Madi sprawled across her bed, reading through the blog post, her mind struggling to make sense of it. The truth was, she wanted a nap, but she couldn't take one. Sarah was expecting her. Instead Madi focused on her upcoming post, braiding a long string of hair then tugging it apart as she reread the words. This was the first MadLib of the '80s movies theme, and she wasn't sure it did what she wanted. She could change it. *Lie.* But that had never been the point of the blog.

Escape. That was the beauty of the MadLibs blog and all the rereads and reblogs she created. MadLibs let those feelings she usually carried in silence out into the world. She could say what she needed, share what she thought. She could be herself.

Madi scanned the final paragraphs, retyping the ending.

In the end, *Sixteen Candles* didn't hold a candle for me. Now, before the backlash I know is coming—*dodges thrown comments*—stay

with me. Here are my reasons: It was the '80s, and given that, I can forgive a lot of the weird subtext, bad jokes, and, let's be honest, terrible hair! But it fell flat for a different reason.

I didn't escape.

I want a movie that lets me run away from my own life (if only for two hours!) I want love and romance, action and laughter . . . I want ALL the good, and none of the bad. Because if I can't escape through movies and fiction, what's the point? I read and view because I WANT to disappear from my life, if only for a little while. Hopefully the next rewatch will give me that escapist thrill I love so much!

Final stats below.

Movie Rating: 7/10 Mad!Cows, with a warm fuzzy of Mad!Love going out to the incomparable Molly and her sassy ways, and an extra bit of Mad!Love for director John Hughes for kicking off our '80s rewatch. He really is the KING of teen movies, and I can't fault his direction in the least. (There are many more Hughes movies in the queue.)

Would I rewatch it? No thank you. One birthday was enough for me.

Thanks for reading and watching, MadLibbers! It's been a blast. Pop by the comments and let me know what YOU thought of *Sixteen Candles*. Blogs are made for opinions, and I want YOURS.

Until next time . . .

chorus sings

MadLib

PS: Click on the side links if you have a minute. You don't have to buy, just visit the site for me to get my kickback. FUNEMPLOYMENT: It's not just a job, it's a way of life. M :)

Comments enabled.

Tags: #MadLibs #SixteenCandles #Madi watches things and then blogs about them #Funemployment

In the two years Madi had run MadLibs, she'd never avoided controversy, and she didn't intend to start now. Nevertheless, she fought a niggling sense of unease as she prepared to post. She still had time to change it, but she didn't want to. Blogging was her escape, and it only worked if she could write what she wanted: *Honest reactions.*

"Now or never," she said and hit POST.

The comments began within minutes, replies almost as fast. In stunned silence, Madi read through them, unable to absorb what was happening. The troll— whoever he was—had returned, angrier than ever.

Comments on Blog Post 210: Blowing out the Sixteen Candles
Comment 1.1, *anonymous*: You really think you should be commenting on something you DIDN'T ACTUALLY WATCH? Screw you, MadLib! This is bullshit. You're such a FAKE!

> **@laurentabelard:** Why don't you try saying that without the convenient mask of anonymity?

>> ***anonymous*:** Don't like me messing with the girlfriend, Long Dong? LOL Eat me!

>>> **@laurentabelard:** I don't like *you*, if that's what you're asking. As to your other asinine comment, I've no idea what it means.

>>>> ***anonymous*:** Ooooh . . . Someone's playing with their dictionary again. *slow clap* And I don't really give a shit whether you like me or not. I call it like I see it, and I CALL BULLSHIT. MadLib needs to be taken down a notch or two, and I'm happy to do it. Get out of the way! I'm taking this blog DOWN.

Furious, Madi hit the REPLY button. "This is *not* okay," she said through clenched teeth. "Not okay at all!" While Laurent's defense of Madi's post was endearing, she couldn't let him deal with the troll alone.

>>>>> **@MadLib:** Dear Anon—anon posting doesn't mean no IP address. Please refrain from spreading your hate on this blog.

anonymous: Or what?

@MadLib: Or I'll block you. :>/

anonymous: I'd like to see you try.

@laurentabelard: Why don't you go back to the kindergarten where you came from? Putain! C'est trop relou!

anonymous: Uh-oh! Long Dong's back to defend MadLib's honor, huh? Well, FUCK YOU, TOO. Why don't you go back to France, where you BELONG? You're not wanted here!

@MadLib: Aaaaaaaaand BLOCKED. Anonymous posting is a privilege, folks. Let's keep this classy. Comments are disabled while I deal with this mess. Later. MadLib. :(

Session closed.

Comments disabled.

Madi pushed the laptop off her lap with shaking hands. She'd never been so angry in her life. Not when her mother left the first time, or when she'd told her she was doing it again. Not even when she'd encountered a troll in her sophomore year of high school and left a beloved fandom because of it. Shattered by exhaustion, Madi felt tears well along her lower lashes. She needed to scream, lash out. She *needed* her blog! But she'd effectively closed it down to stop him.

"Bastard!"

Her eyes caught on her phone, and she grabbed it with trembling fingers. She dashed tears away with the back of her hand. Everything was off-kilter today. It had started with the jerk outside Sarah's classroom who'd snapped at Madi for no reason, but the troll was far worse. That wasn't just attitude—that was hate. She wasn't putting up with it!

The scream that had been building since the first comment arrived released in a blur of thumbs.

@MadLib: OMG—I'm going to KILL that freaking troll! *rage face* What is WRONG with people?!? It makes me want to BURN THE INTERNET TO THE GROUND! Gah! D:

@ModernDayWitch: @MadLib What say I hex him for you? #NoChargeOrAnything I can you know. Just give me the word. ;)

@MadLib: @ModernDayWitch OMG—please do! I just can't BELIEVE he's bugging me again. I thought I was DONE with him. #FlamesOnTheSideOfMyFace So furious!

@StarveilBrian1981: @MadLib He might be a she, you know.

@ModernDayWitch: @StarveilBrian1981 I get a definite male vibe from him, Brian. #Auras

@ArtWithAttitude: @MadLib I know the situation sucks, but I thought you handled the whole blowup pretty well. #TrollsBeTrolling

@WrittenInChantalics: @MadLib OMG—just saw that post. O_O Are you okay?! Skype me! I need to know what's happening.

@laurentabelard: @MadLib That idiot was AWFUL to you! I was so angry at that COMMENT!

@WrittenInChantalics: @laurentabelard What does putain mean, btw? LOL #LearningNewSwearsOnline

@laurentabelard: @WrittenInChantalics Er . . . don't repeat that. All right?

@fandometric: @MadLib Awful or not, it was kind of funny to watch. Just saying. LOL

@MadLib: @fandometric WELL, IT WASN'T FUNNY TO ME.

@fandometric: @MadLib :(

@MadLib: @ArtWithAttitude @WrittenInChantalics @laurentabelard @fandometric It's fine, guys. I just . . . I need a minute to decompress. AARGH!!! I HATE dealing with trolls. Fandom is supposed to be fun! But thank you for listening to me rage.

@ArtWithAttitude: @MadLib Is there anything we can do to help? #FandomWoes

@MadLib: @ArtWithAttitude Not really. >:>/ The IP address was to a public broadband site somewhere in NY state. Talk about NOT NARROWING IT DOWN.

@MadLib: @ArtWithAttitude I have a feeling I just made things worse by confronting him. ARGH! #WhyNow

@fandometric: @MadLib Feel free to vent. We're all here for you. #MadLibbersUnite

@ModernDayWitch: @MadLib Breathe, honey. You did just fine. Maybe have a cup of peppermint tea to soothe your nerves.

@laurentabelard: @MadLib I'm so sorry for commenting. I should have left him alone like you said. :(

@MadLib: @laurentabelard It's not you. It's trolls in general.

@laurentabelard: @MadLib I apologize, minette.

@MadLib: @laurentabelard It's fine. It is. I just need to deal with this one on my own.

@ModernDayWitch: @laurentabelard @MadLib Aw, you two. <3 *huggles you together*

@MadLib: Gotta go, peeps. I need a breather. *waves on the way out*

She closed the app at the same moment her phone buzzed with a private text. For one irrational moment she wondered if it was the troll, though she knew it couldn't be.

> i'm so sorry, madi. forgive me. 😔

She let out a teary laugh. *Laurent.* Of course he'd message her to make sure she was okay. She sniffled as she typed her reply.

> it's fine

> it's not. i shouldn't have interfered.

> it's okay

> he made me so MAD.

> that's what trolls do, but provoking them makes it worse 😫

> sorry, madi. i was wrong.

ur sweet, I. it's fine

i was hotheaded. (that's the term, yes?)
but i have a plan to win you back.

u never lost me

open your snapsed.

why????

just watch, please?

okaaaaaay . . . what am I looking for?

i'm taking you out on the town.

how? i'm in nj, ur in ny

keep watching.

#

"Roads...? Where we're going, we don't need roads."
(*Back to the Future*, 1985)

okay, i've got the app open. what now?

first, get ready to go.

all right . . . ?

grab your shoes. ny is a city to explore by foot.

Ready to go?

lol—okay, ready & waiting. (fyi: i'm not actually leaving my bedroom unless i have to. i'm wiped and i have to pick up my sister in an hour.)

trust me.

okay 😊

first we head down to the street. (the family i live with is on the third floor.) follow me, madi.

ugh. stairs are NOT my thing.
short legs = awful

short legs = perfect. 😝

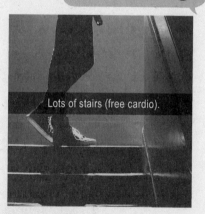

Lots of stairs (free cardio).

wait. if those are ur legs, who took the picture?

the one on the stairs? mrs. marcioni. (she lives on the first floor with her three cats and her grown son.)

u walked up & asked her?

well, yes. i knocked on the door first.
i didn't just walk into her apartment uninvited.
(that would be rude.)

u just ASKED?

mrs. marcioni is super nice. (i carry her
groceries sometimes.) i told her i needed
an action shot and she was game. i
always talk to people. (not always well,
but gestures go a long way.)

that's one of the things i like about u

only one? 😬

more than one, i promise. okay, shoes on.
stairs done. where r we now?

look around, breathe the air. it's a beautiful day.

Painted city.

that's gorgeous! it looks like another world!

i love street art. it's alive like nothing else. i have hundreds of photographs of it.

rly beautiful laurent.

come to ny some weekend, i'll show you all the things i love. there are so many galleries and hidden places—like this.

maybe 😃 😃 😃
grins this is fun.

yes. (but it'd be better in person.)
oh-ho! grab my hand.

why?

we're running across the road.

to where?

the . . . (hold on) . . . the bakery, the tea shop, the . . . COFFEE SHOP! aha! i knew there was a phrase for it.

still don't see it. but god, do I ever need some caffeine right now. soooooo tired today. 😵‍💫

Yikes! Watch out for the cabs!

that was closer than I wanted. sheesh!

OMG r u okay?

totally fine. are you?

that depends, r u still holding my hand? 🙂

of course i am. *whispers* why would i let go when we're almost there? we're walking along the street, and i've just opened the door for you.

show me 😃

Caffeine is a lifestyle choice.

AWESOME! i love coffee!

i'm french. coffee isn't just a beverage, it's a sacrament.

LOL

you think i'm joking, but i'm not! i have a serious coffee addiction. cappuccino is my kryptonite. i'd sell state secrets for a good french roast.

mmm . . . sounds delicious

you don't have to wait, madi. i'll stay in line. you go find us a table.

how exactly?

just step over there. see? that empty table.

One for me, one for you.

LOL—did you actually buy me a coffee?!? ur CRAZY! 😃

what? you're not going to drink it? i'm hurt. 😜

no, i will. 😊 yum!

Barista thinks I look "lonely".

srsly? 😄

to be fair, i am sitting at a table with 2 coffees and no one else. that's a little odd.

but we're having coffee together.

yes, and while i know you're here, minette, no one else does.

what's in mine?

what do you mean?

the foam. what did the barista put in mine???

Yours was by request :)

aw . . . 🖤

mmm . . . delicious!

🙁 i'm sad i'm not there—in person, i mean

next time. now, i'm going to drink my (two) cappuccinos, but that means it's your turn to keep the conversation going.

okay. about what?

whatever you want to talk about.

that's kind of a broad topic. 😕

then tell me about you. tell me what makes madi who she is.

um . . . i've got stage fright all of a sudden. *hides face* i don't know what u want me to say. it's embarrassing. 😨

but why? you talk to the world all the time with your madlibs blog.

exactly—the world—not u

why's it different?

it's different bc if it's the world, i'm anonymous and i can be who i want. say what i want.

and you can't in RL?

 not even close

but why?

bc in millburn, i'm madi nakama, the daughter of charles nakama. people know him . . . and so they know me (or think they do.) i have to BE that person all the time.

why does it matter whose daughter you are?

my dad writes the "down home" column. it's in newspapers across the states and online. i can't mess up, bc of that. everyone's watching our family, judging us by all the stupid "family values" my dad always writes about. (that's part of the reason i prefer online school.)

having to live up to those expectations doesn't seem fair.

it isn't, but it's just the way it is. our family has to look a certain way. sarah's behavior has to be "handled"

i'm sorry. that sounds stressful.

it's just the way it is 😕

and online you're not that person.

exactly 🙂

is that why you were so worried about meeting the madlibbers in RL?

um, yeah, i guess so

i'm glad you came out that night. very glad.

me, too. 😄

and thank you for telling me. i'm done with my coffee now, BTW. ready to keep going?

sure. where are we headed?

to one of my favorite places. it's where i go when i need to chill out. i'm going to sneak you in!

Almost there.

SNEAK me in? where are we going?

shh . . . it's a secret. 😜 i'm not even supposed to go there. But i was out one morning taking photos and discovered i could jump the fence. it's way up above the street.

Just a little bit farther . . .

UP?????????????

okay, i'm going to give you a boost, all right?

LOLOL—i am actually a little freaked out right now (from the comfort of my bedroom). I DO NOT LIKE HEIGHTS. where are we going?!?

close your eyes, madi.

okay. open them again.

do you feel the breeze coming from a thousand different corners? hear the hum of the city? sense the lives moving below us like ocean waves? THIS is where i go when i get down or upset (or when i miss home so much i can't breathe). you'll see when you really visit.

Imagining you here.

planning that out, are u? ;)

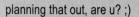

of course I am. aren't you?

The pounding on her door woke Madi from a deep sleep. Laurent had been in her dreams, the two of them laughing over coffee in New York. She sat up and rubbed a hand over gritty eyes.

"What time is it?"

The pounding started up, matched by her sister's voice. "Madi!" she shouted. "Where ARE you?!"

Madi yawned and rolled off the bed. Outside the window, sunset painted the sky a brilliant pinkish gold. Her eyes widened. *It's time for supper,* she realized. But she'd totally forgotten to start making it. The pounding redoubled.

"Oh shit!" she gasped. "And I forgot to pick up—"

"Madi!" Sarah shrieked. "MADI!"

"I'm in here, Sarah!" she shouted, half walking, half hopping to the door and pulling it open. "Why are you—"

Her sister barreled through the doorway, throwing her arms around her. Tears rolled down her cheeks. "I thought you were gone!"

Madi patted her sister's back. "I just lost track of time," she said. "Sorry."

Sarah's sobs grew in intensity. Her fingers dug into Madi's shoulders like claws. "I—I tried to find you, but you weren't there. Robbie walked me home, b-but when I came in, you weren't in the kitchen, either. I called, but you wouldn't answer. I thought you'd left!"

"Shh . . . It's okay. It's okay."

"Madi?" their father's voice echoed up the stairs. "What's going on up there?"

"Sarah's upset."

"About what?"

"She couldn't find me," Madi said (leaving out the fact she'd forgotten her sister at the library).

She heard her father take three steps up the stairs. "Can you calm her down a bit?"

Madi rolled her eyes. "I'm trying to, Dad."

The footsteps retreated.

If there was something she'd learned in the last few years, it was Sarah's reactions were never dealt with in regards to *Sarah*, but in regards to how efficiently she could be calmed. That was often Madi's job. Most days, she tolerated it. Tonight, it made her angry.

"Breathe, Sarah. You're fine. Robbie got you home."

Sarah's sobs continued.

"C'mon, Sarah. I'm right here." Madi stepped back, extricating herself from her sister's steely grip. "You need to calm down."

The weighted blanket was in Sarah's room. She needed it. Madi headed for the door, but Sarah grabbed hold of her shirt before she got through.

"B-but, Madi, I th-thought—"

"I never left. I was tired and fell asleep. I forgot you were at the library."

"But I waited!"

"And I was in my room the whole time. You could have just texted or called me like I told you!"

Madi's phone buzzed, but with her sister's fingers tight on her arm, she couldn't get it from her pocket.

"B-but you never came! And when I got home, you didn't answer." Her voice sharpened. "You're usually in the kitchen before dinner! I didn't know!"

"I don't *always* have to be in the kitchen. You should have called."

"But I thought you left me!"

"Sometimes I need time on my own." Madi's voice rose. "You always—"

"Girls?" their father called up the stairs. "Why all the commotion?"

The phone in her pocket buzzed again. *Laurent.* Madi jerked away from her sister. Sarah followed, hands outstretched, the way she'd done as a child.

"Don't go! Don't GO!"

"Just STOP IT, Sarah!" Madi ran her hands into her hair. "I'm not going anywhere!"

"Girls, please!" their father shouted. "The neighbors will hear."

With a roar of frustration, Madi dodged past her sister, pounding down the stairs as fast as her legs could go. Sarah's screams rose behind her as she rounded the corner. Intent on getting away, she barely avoided a head-on collision with her father, who was standing at the bottom.

"What's going on up there?" he asked.

"Sarah couldn't find me and she got upset."

"Madi!" her sister wailed. "MADIIII!"

Her father's gaze darted up and back. "You need to deal with her." Above them, Sarah's wails grew deafening. "Your sister's upset. You need to go back and calm her down."

"I don't *need* to do anything!"

"But you can't leave her like that. You *know* how Sarah gets when her schedule's thrown off."

"But I—"

"Your sister is sensitive to routine. You know what changes do to—"

"Then WHY did Mom take off in the first place?!"

Her father's mouth snapped shut midsentence. Upstairs, Sarah's voice expanded into a deafening siren.

"You and Mom always leave ME to deal with her!" Madi shouted in a broken voice. "Well, she's not my kid! She's not my responsibility! She's YOURS!"

Her father's mouth hung open, eyes glittering. For a moment, Madi thought he was going to cry.

"I'm sorry, but we all have to—"

"If Mom hadn't left, Sarah wouldn't be freaking out like this! I can't do this anymore! I just CAN'T!"

And in seconds, she was the one running out the door, leaving behind the house and her sister and all the things she couldn't fix.

Madi could feel her phone buzzing, but she didn't stop until the house was far behind. She stumbled to a halt on the sidewalk, then leaned over and put her hands on her knees. Dry heaves wracked her body.

"Oh my God," she gasped, the quiet houses of the subdivision blurring in her teary eyes. "I'm in so much trouble."

Her phone buzzed again, and Madi pulled it from her pocket, reading through the series of texts. Two were from her father. The others were from Laurent.

> coffee was really fun, madi. we should do that for real sometime.

> the madlibbers are meeting up in schenectady next weekend. (that's where @moderndaywitch—morag—is from.) she's offered her house for a movie rewatch. any chance you'll be able to make it? 🙂

> hey. um, i'm not sure what's up, but drop me a text when you get this. was the virtual coffee thing too weird? sorry. 🙁

> all right, then, later.

Madi tried to answer him, but her body was quaking with the downward spiral of adrenaline, and it took her two tries to get the message right before she hit SEND.

OMG laurent. i'm in so much shit.

His reply appeared a moment later.

why? (is this why you were offline?
i texted a couple times.)

i usually pick my sister up from school. when we
were out for coffee i forgot to go get her & my
sister had a MASSIVE freak-out bc she didn't
know where i was. (i forgot her at the library, but
a friend walked her home.) ugh. DNW!!! 😨

i thought you said you were at home.

i was! but I had my headphones on & door locked.
i dozed off. AAARGH! this is NOT what I need
right now. sarah was totally freaking out when
I left

oh no.

oh YES! 😫 my dad is so upset

but why?

bc I know how much routine affects sarah.
i should've been at the library to get her.
i should've been downstairs when she came
home. i should've calmed her down. 😫
WHY IS THIS HAPPENING RIGHT NOW?!?

110

are you okay?

no, i'm NOT okay. i'm anything BUT okay. damnit!

sorry. what can I do to help?

nothing. there's nothing TO do. i lost my temper & i shouldn't have.

can you go talk to your sister?

not yet (i'm not at home) i'm out walking

where?

just around the neighborhood. i need to NOT be at home for a bit. it's peaceful. calm

sounds nice. (if not for the drama.)

it is. :(but I can't stay here & I can't go to the next madlibbers event

no?

sorry, no. i just can't

i understand.

don't BE like that, laurent!

like what?

don't be so understanding all the time!

???

be mad at me! say how stupid I am! YELL!

Why would I do that? your sister's upset. i get that. why would that be YOUR fault? (and what kind of creep would yell at you over it?) madi, are you all right? seriously. you're worrying me.

no I'm not all right & i'm crying now.
u shouldn't be this nice to me 😒

i should and i will. i'm sorry, madi.
i wish i was there to fix it.

no one can fix this except me 😩

The porch light was on when Madi finally made her way home. She'd been expecting to hear sirens for the last three-quarters of an hour, but apparently the older of the two Nakama girls didn't warrant a call to the police.

Madi slid her key into the lock and paused, taking a breath. *Now or never.*

With one baleful look back to the empty street, she pushed open the door. The house was dark with the exception of the kitchen. Her father sat at the table behind his laptop, a cup of coffee on one side, his phone on the other. He looked up as Madi came inside.

"Madi, thank God you're back." Low and gravelly, his voice sounded like a poor recording of his robust self. "You didn't answer my calls or texts. What happened?"

"I took a walk."

"For three hours?"

Madi nodded. She toed off her shoes and set them on the mat next to Sarah's. When she saw her sister's sneakers—two sizes smaller than hers—sitting there waiting, her chest finally released. *Sarah's still here.* She hadn't considered it until this moment, but part of the reason she'd been waiting for the sirens had been because of Sarah. Thankfully, her sister hadn't run away again.

She took two steps up the stairs, but her father's voice called her back. "We should sort things out before you go up for the night."

Madi trudged to the kitchen with the enthusiasm of someone heading to the electric chair. "Can this wait until morning?"

"No, it can't." He pulled out the chair next to him and gave her a wan smile. "C'mon, Madi. It'll only take a minute."

She groaned and slumped down in her chair. "Fine. Let's get it over with."

"I'm not angry at you, but I think we need to talk."

Madi stared at her father. It felt like she'd walked into the wrong house. This wasn't how things went. "I . . . Okay," she said. "I guess talking's probably good."

"Yes, it is."

Her father cradled his coffee in his hands, smiling sadly at her. The house was quieter than usual, the sounds muffled and soft. It made her throat ache: the darkness, the kitchen, the single light. It felt like she was watching a movie of her life from an earlier era. *Before Mom left, before all the trouble.* Guilt twinged in Madi's stomach. *Before I took off and left Dad to deal with Sarah alone.*

"I'm glad you came home. You had me pretty worried."

Madi winced. "Sorry about that. I just needed a little time to think."

"That's to be expected. Sarah can be a bit much sometimes."

Madi chewed her lip. She'd expected anger, but her father's exhaustion-born patience was somehow worse.

"Your mom called while you were out," he said.

"She did?"

He nodded. "Yes. But I was dealing with Sarah and couldn't talk."

"Sorry."

"It's fine," he said. "I called her back." His mustache twitched. "I told her you were over at a friend's house. Didn't want to worry her unnecessarily."

"Thanks, Dad. And again, sorry, I just—"

"It's okay," he said, interrupting. "I get it, Madi. I do. We're all under a lot of stress with your mother away." He reached out and patted her hand. It made her want to cry. "I . . . I just think it's time we laid down some ground rules. We need everyone on the same page. You, me, Sarah . . ."

Madi waited for the last name, which didn't come. Her gaze flicked to her father. He looked old, and that worried her. "What kind of rules are you talking about?"

"You've had a lot of freedom the last year; doing your classes through OMA has been a great opportunity." His smile faded. "But that only works when you hold up your end of the bargain. What's done is done. But now we move forward. Agreed?"

Throat aching, Madi nodded.

"First, your grades have to be maintained. That was always part of the deal."

"My grades are fine," she said.

"There was a message from the school on the machine."

"About what?"

"I'm not sure. All the person said was that you were supposed to contact the office for some important information. Are you certain everything's okay?"

"It's probably to remind me about graduation. School's done in less than a month." Madi forced a smile. "You don't have to worry about me, you know."

"Fair enough. But the rest of your responsibilities haven't changed."

Madi frowned. "Meaning what?"

"You drop Sarah off in the morning, pick her up after school, and make dinner on your assigned nights."

"That's all stuff I already do."

He nodded. "I *know* that you do it. You help with Sarah more than anyone else. Thank you for that. But you're also my daughter, Madi, and I—" His voice broke. "I worry about *you*, too."

Madi blinked away unwanted tears. "Sorry," she whispered.

"Please just work with me when things get rough. Don't take off. Don't leave me out."

A tear ran down Madi's cheek, and she brushed it away.

"If we stick together, we can make this work."

"Okay," Madi croaked.

"We're a family, and everyone in a family is expected to pitch in. You and I had a deal about online school. You broke your end of the bargain."

Madi's mouth opened, but no words came out. Her father cleared his throat and steepled his fingers. Charles Nakama was a mediator by nature, but it was obvious that he'd had time to think about this in the hours Madi had been gone.

"Look, if you do your part," her father said, "then everything stays the same." He gave her a tired smile and patted her on the arm. "Keep it all on an even keel, you know? Until your mother gets home."

"And if I don't?"

Her father's expression cooled. "Then I'll have to limit your Internet access."

Madi blinked. "Wh-what? How?!"

"The code to the Wi-Fi is a privilege, not a right."

9

"I'm in the prime of my youth, and I'll only be young once!"
(*Stand by Me*, 1986)

laurent, you around?

just walked in the door. how are you?

missing u 🙁

missing you, too.
are things better today?

yes and no. dad was weirdly cool about me
taking off last night-at least for the most
part-but if I mess up now, it's over

over???

if I don't hold my end of the bargain,
he'll switch the wi-fi code

ugh. that sucks.

no worries. i'll figure it out. besides, everyone deserves a screwup once in a while

you're hardly a screwup.

thanks 😊

do you have any plans today?

just picked sarah up from school. why?

do you have time to hang out?
(for real?) 😃

i'd love to, but there's no time for me to head into ny. sorry! i'm doing a rewatch with sarah tonight. u want to join in?

can't tonight. dinner's at 8.

aren't you starving?!

ran into mrs. marcioni on the stairs. she took pity on me and gave me a cinnamon bun. 😊

mrs. marcioni???

the lady who took the shoe pic for me.

ha-ha! now i remember

so no time for ny???

sorry, no. ugh . . . schedules suck

do you want to go for coffee instead?

another snapsed date?

no, a real one this time.

Getting closer . . .

. . . and CLOSER!

Madi couldn't stop grinning.

"This isn't coffee," Laurent said as he carried his cup to the table. "It's pretending to be, but . . . I know coffee beans when I smell them."

"Yes, it is." Madi giggled. She settled on one side of the table, nudging the chair out for him with the toe of her shoe. "Millburn's finest."

Laurent took another whiff and coughed. "This is nobody's finest, but I like the ambience." He glanced around the Millburn station, catching sight of the announcement panels listing the times for the New Jersey transit to New York. He had exactly thirty-seven minutes before he needed to be back on the train again.

"So you're some expert on coffee now?" Madi teased. "Are these more skills I don't know about?"

"Perhaps not an expert, but a discerning drinker." He swirled the dark-colored liquid, staring in horror as it stained the sides of the paper cup. "It's the right color, but . . ." He lifted the cup to his nose and took a deep breath, gagging. "This is not meant for human consumption. It's almost as bad as vending-machine cappuccino."

Madi snorted with laughter. "You're insulting the delights of the Millburn train station, you know. This is the finest brew you'll find here."

"*Finest* is *not* what this is."

"I don't know, Laurent. I happen to like it." She took a sip and made an (almost believable) sound of contentment, then gestured to the people milling past them on their way to the trains. "Bet they'd agree."

"Doubtful."

She took another sip and cringed. "Mmmm . . . yummy."

Laurent couldn't stop the laughter that bubbled up from his throat. "You are a good actor, Madi. Worthy of so much better than this."

She grinned and set her coffee aside. "If the wrong person hears you complaining, you could cause an international incident." She held out her hands as if framing a television shot. "French exchange student insults local coffee. Caffeine-deprived patrons demand an apology!"

"International politics aside, the barista definitely got my order wrong. This isn't a latte."

"Pretty sure the lady at the counter isn't a barista, either."

Laurent followed her gaze to the hairnet-wearing woman handing out sloppily poured beverages. "I wouldn't want to cross her," he said. "She might force another coffee on me."

Madi laughed, her cheeks growing pink as she tried to muffle the sound. The woman at the counter turned and glared at them.

"Oh my God." Madi gasped. "She heard us."

Laurent leaned in, his voice a stage whisper. "She is not amused at our discussion of her coffee-making skills."

His words set off another bout of laughter. Madi wiped tears from the sides of her eyes. Seeing the coffee matron watching, Laurent lifted the cup tentatively to his mouth. He nodded to her. "Wish me luck." Then brought it to his lips.

He took one swallow and his throat closed. The scalding liquid did little to hide the muddy taste of overroasted beans laced with sugary sweetener. He tried to swallow, but his throat refused. His eyes watered. His hands shook.

"Laurent?" Madi said. "Are you okay? You're turning purple!"

He grabbed a wad of napkins off the table, spitting into it while Madi cackled with laughter. Passersby on their way to the trains stared at the sight. When he could breathe again, Laurent set the cup aside.

"This," he said in mock-seriousness, "was not what I had in mind when I suggested a coffee date."

Madi grinned and leaned closer. She pushed his cup aside. "Then next time you'll have to buy."

"If it can be our coffee shop, you've got a deal."

"Our coffee shop?"

"The one in New York."

Madi's smile grew until her whole face seemed to glow with joy. Laurent reached out and touched the tip of her nose.

"Yes. Because next time I want *you* to visit *me*."

She blushed and looked away. "I'd like that."

"Me, too."

Madi's elation at Laurent's impromptu visit quickly spiraled into depression. She dawdled for twenty minutes after she got home, but when Sarah still hadn't finished her homework, Madi finally gave in and started the movie. The repetitive ticking had already ended and the "Power of Love" theme song begun when her sister's footsteps pounded down the stairs.

"You started without me!" Sarah cried. "I'm not ready!"

"Sorry," Madi said, not looking up from the screen. "The other MadLibbers were waiting." Her mind was still on Laurent and the terrible coffee they'd shared at the Millburn station. He'd be home by now, probably finishing dinner. She wished she were there, too. Her disappointment was a tangible thing.

"I told you I wanted to see this one," Sarah grumbled, taking her place on the couch. "I love *Back to the Future*."

"Then why does it matter if you miss the credits?" Madi asked. "You already know what happens."

"Yeah, but I want to *see* it."

Sarah leaned closer, but Madi nudged her away. She hadn't forgotten her sister's meltdown the other night. "I need room," Madi said.

"All right. I'll move." Sarah slid half a couch cushion sideways, her frown deepening. "You don't have to take it out on me, you know. I'm not the reason you're in trouble."

Madi made a choking noise. "I'm *not* in trouble. Dad and I talked things out." She had just opened her mouth to explain that the problem was she *wanted* to be in New York with Laurent, not stuck at home, when Sarah spoke again.

"The school left a message on the answering machine. Dad's worried about you, Madi. He asked me about it twice while you were out."

Madi rolled her eyes. "That'll be about grad."

"Oh?"

"Don't worry. I have no intention of going."

She expected her sister to argue with her. (Sarah never seemed able to let things go.) But tonight the movie already had her in its thrall. For nearly half an hour, they watched in silence. Madi glared at the screen as Einstein the dog was strapped into Doc Brown's vehicle for its first test run.

"I like this part," Sarah said under her breath. "This is where he goes back into the past."

"I know. It's, like, the whole point of the movie." Madi crossed her arms, annoyed at how petulant she sounded.

"Marty's gonna take the DeLorean. He's gonna go back."

Madi's phone buzzed with a text and she jumped to answer it. When she checked the screen, it was only her father telling her that his interview in the city had run late, but that he'd be home as soon as he could. She slumped lower on the couch. She hated being trapped in Millburn. Hated her mother for being gone. Hated her father for being so busy. Her gaze flitted over to her sister, and her chest was filled with remorse. She didn't actually hate Sarah, because Sarah had no idea she was part of this mess. She was caught up as much as Madi was.

"Sorry for being a bitch before," Madi said.

"Shh . . . Marty's got to save the doctor. I don't want to miss this."

"Me, neither."

Madi slid until she was next to her sister, and, like always, Sarah leaned in, her head resting on her shoulder. Sarah's expression was rapt, a line of concentration between her brows. Madi wished she could lose herself in movies as easily as Sarah could. Because if life owed anyone a do-over, it was her.

A do-over where Laurent and I live in the same city.

"Sarah," Madi said after a time. "Do you think it's possible to fall for someone you hang out with online?"

Sarah's eyes flickered, almost too fast to see. "Like someone you've never actually met?"

"No. Someone you've met, just someone you don't hang out with very much. Someone who lives in another town."

Sarah shrugged. "Sure. Why not?"

"I don't know. I mean, you wouldn't get to—you couldn't—" She cleared her throat. "Do a lot of stuff together."

"Stuff like what?"

"Like . . . touch or things. You'd only be able to talk and text and stuff." Madi's cheeks began to burn. "I mean—except for once in a while, when you could find a way to be together."

"So nothing lovey-dovey most of the time?"

Madi's expression faltered. "Yeah."

"Sounds like the perfect kind of relationship, if you ask me."

Madi smirked. "Thanks, Sarah."

By midway through the movie, Madi had taken to multitasking. *Back to the Future* was one of the films she'd seen several times, and she knew what to expect. She flicked through her dashboard posts, smiling to herself as she discovered a new meme. The MadLibbers had embraced the '80s theme.

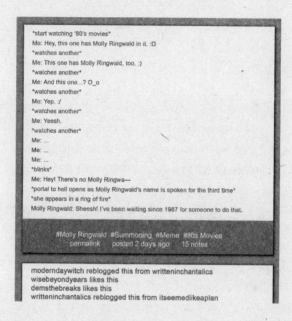

start watching '80's movies
Me: Hey, this one has Molly Ringwald in it. :D
watches another
Me: This one has Molly Ringwald, too. :)
watches another
Me: And this one...? O_o
watches another
Me: Yep. :/
watches another
Me: Yeesh.
watches another
Me: ...
Me: ...
Me: ...
blinks
Me: Hey! There's no Molly Ringwa—
portal to hell opens as Molly Ringwald's name is spoken for the third time
she appears in a ring of fire
Molly Ringwald: Sheesh! I've been waiting since 1987 for someone to do that.

#Molly Ringwald #Summoning #Meme #80s Movies
permalink   posted 2 days ago   15 notes

moderndaywitch reblogged this from writteninchantalics
wisebeyondyears likes this
demsthebreaks likes this
writteninchantalics reblogged this from itseemedlikeaplan

Madi grinned and clicked REBLOG at the same time her phone buzzed.

Madi, are you around? (It's your mom.)

For a minute, Madi considered not answering her, but knowing her mother it would only make the situation worse. Her father was out at an interview. Madi knew not to interrupt him, but she also knew he'd answer his cell phone if his wife called. Madi's mother *would*, if she got no answer from home . . . and then her father would be worried. They could have a complete rehash of the previous night if she wasn't careful.

Annoyed, Madi tapped in a speedy reply.

yes, i'm here. (u know ur name pops up, right?)

Oh, right. Of course. (I'm just not used to it yet.)
Do you have time to talk?

i'm watching a movie with sarah right now

How are things going at home?

what things?

Please don't play games with me, Madison. How
are things going? How are Sarah and your father?
How are you? As a separate note, I checked in with
the CUNY admissions office, and the receptionist
told me they hadn't received your finished course
registration information yet.

i'd appreciate you NOT checking
up on me. things are fine

Fine meaning what, exactly?

. . .

Madi? Did my last text make it through?
My phone shows it on-screen, but I don't know. Why
does it have a different color? Does that mean it arrived?
Oh, I wish this formatted things like e-mail does.

. . .

Madi? Are you still there?

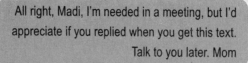

> All right, Madi, I'm needed in a meeting, but I'd appreciate if you replied when you get this text.
> Talk to you later. Mom

Madi set her phone down on the coffee table rather than answer. (If her mother called, she'd claim she hadn't seen the last texts.)

Sarah glanced over at her phone and then at Madi. "You okay?"

"Aren't I always?"

"I guess . . ."

There was the sound of gunfire on-screen and Sarah turned back to the TV. Marty McFly threw himself into the DeLorean, ready to go back into the past and change the present. Madi shook her head.

If only life was that simple.

Madi reread her synopsis for *Back to the Future*, her finger hovering over the POST button. The movie had underscored what she already knew: She needed a change in her life. Problem was, Madi had no idea how to make it happen.

And by the end of *Back to the Future*, I was shouting at the screen for Marty to reach the top speed and make it back to his present in time to save the Doc.

I laughed. I (almost) cried. I hooted and cheered aloud when the lightning struck the clock. Bravo to ALL those MadLibbers who suggested this film. I've seen it at least five times before now, but it was SO worth a rewatch. It's definitely one that stands the test of time.

Here's the final stats for my love-fest.

Movie Rating: 10/10 Mad!Cows—a rarity on this blog! If you love underdog stories, then *Back to the Future* is for you.

Would I rewatch it? Heck YES. Who wouldn't want to go back and change their past? THAT is why this movie works. We all would. And if you haven't watched this yet, then you need to.

Go.

shushes you off

Go now.

taps fingers on laptop

Seriously, I'll wait until you watch it.

Done? Good. :D See? Wasn't that awesome? EXACTLY.

And with that, your latest installment of MadLibs comes to an end. Thanks to ALL the MadLibbers who came along this time. (Watch your posts for details on when the next movie will play.) And as always, clickety-click on those sparkly side links and give the comments a whirl to tell me what you think.

lightning flashes ominously on a clock tower

MadLib

PS: Please note, anonymous comments are disabled for today's post.

Comments enabled.

Tags: #MadLibs #Back to the Future #Madi watches things and then blogs about them #Funemployment

Madi chewed her thumbnail as she reached the final line of tags. She *wanted* to add in something else—about real life and the challenges of growing up—but she didn't dare. She tried to keep her online and real lives separate if at all possible. And this post wasn't the one where she'd break her own rule. Besides, she *had* enjoyed the movie. She and Sarah had talked about it long after it finished.

Sarah. She was one reason things in Madi's life couldn't change. Her schedule linked her to Madi as much as any grade, school, or group of friends. Her sister was a hashtag that couldn't be altered. Madi couldn't even be upset with her for it.

#Nothing to do but keep going.

With a resigned sigh, she hit POST.

10

"Nobody puts Baby in a corner."
(*Dirty Dancing*, 1987)

Madi was working on an English assignment when a text from Laurent appeared.

> did you just send me a friend request?

She frowned as she answered.

> no

> oh. okay. that was weird.

> a friend request on what?

> on FB.

> u still use that?!? LOL even my mom's on that (and she's completely LOST when it comes to technology)

> my parents and grandparents are on FB (which is why I pop in every now and then).

so the madi nakama who tried to friend me isn't you?

nope. not me.

weird. looks like you, just younger.

rly?

yeah. she's wearing a blue sweater and her hair is over one shoulder.

WTF??? hold on a sec, i'm going to check something

okay.

...

you back yet?

...

madi?

AAAAAAARGH!

oh dear. 😫 what's wrong?

my account's been hacked. damnit! I KNEW I should have deleted my FB account.

(haven't used it in years)

yikes! what now? should I tell someone?
(report it?)

it's fine. i just need to contact support &
change the account back to my control.
thanks for letting me know. got to go

talk to you later?

definitely! (go check out my blog
if you have a second. just posted
my newest.)

EEEEEEeeeee!!!!!! AWESOME!

LOLOL u r the BEST, laurent! even when
i'm crabby you make me feel better. Now
go read the blog 😆

as you wish.

love that movie!

Madi smiled to herself as she set her phone aside and opened her laptop.
The MadLibs blog was her home page, and she immediately scrolled down to
the comments, wondering what kind of reaction her rewatch post was getting.
She hoped her excitement for the film had spread to her readers, too.

Comments on Blog Post 211: *Back to the Future*!
Comment 1.1, @laurentabelard: What a fantastic movie and a great

post. It made me wonder whether or not you'd go back in time if you had a chance. (Anything you'd change?)

Madi giggled as she read Laurent's comment. For some reason it mattered how he felt more than it did with her other readers. She considered her reply—should she play it cool?—then went from the gut.

> **@MadLib:** At the risk of screwing my life up now? No. Probably not. (Knowing me, I'd end up blurting out some terribly important fact and the universe would implode.)
>> **@laurentabelard:** Wouldn't want to meet me earlier? (I'd want to meet you.)
>>> **@MadLib:** And mess up the perfect balance of flirting and angst we've got going on now? ;) I'd have to think about that one.
>>>> **@laurentabelard:** :D Aha! I like that combination. But if someone shows up in a TARDIS, you should know it might be me.
>>>>> **@MadLib:** I'll definitely watch for you. :D

Comment 2.1, @fandometric: Love this movie so much!
> **@MadLib:** I did, too. Thanks so much for the comment!

Comment 3.1, @ArtWithAttitude: This wasn't so much a hit for me, but your writing always makes me grin. I'm REALLY hoping *Some Kind of Wonderful* is the next MadLib. That movie is ah-MAZE-ing!
> **@MadLib:** Haven't chosen the next one yet, but SKOW is certainly a contender! Thanks for reading!

Comment 4.1, @ModernDayWitch: Aw . . . so much love for this post. You GO, @MadLib
> **@MadLib:** :D X 10000 You are the BEST!

Comment 5.1, @Malwarning: Awwwwww . . . sweet little @MadLib going back to her so-sweet-my-teeth-hurt blogging style. How 1980s RETRO. Weren't YOU the one who said you didn't like '80s movies because they weren't escapist enough? So which is the REAL @MadLib, huh? The *Starveil* fake geek girl? The social justice warrior? Or the too-sweet Mary Sue? Or do you just spout off your drivel according to whatever you think will get you the most hits? Either way, I CALL BULLSHIT.

Madi's chest grew tight as she read through the irate comment. *Malwarning*. She didn't recognize the name, but whoever it was, he wasn't happy. Heart pounding, she typed in a terse reply.

> **@MadLib:** First—you've never even READ my blog before. (I know, because I actually read and respond to comments.) But new or not, I really don't appreciate the trash talk. Don't like my blog? Don't read it. It's a free world. *shows you the door*

She posted her retort. Seconds later, a reply appeared.

> **@Malwarning:** Oh, I'm not new, @MadLib. I've been following you FOREVER. Couldn't hack the Redux fansite, little girl? Or just too scared to play with the BIG BOYS? You gonna cry now? GOOD.

Madi knew she should calm down and think about things, but she was too angry. "You asshole!" she growled, typing as fast as she could. "Who do you think you are?"

> **@MadLib:** Let me just say one thing before I block your sorry ass: You are on MY turf now. This is MY blog, MY friends, MY words. And I'm sick of your kindergarten name-calling! If you're the Redux jerk who made my life a living hell, then I hope you're living all the karma you earned. Because I'm DONE with putting up with trolls like you! BLOCKED. BLOCKED. AND BLOCKED. PS: Learn some tech skills along with your manners. Your IP address is now sitting on my desktop. #pwned

Session closed.
Comments disabled.

Madi grabbed her phone, ready to tweet her frustration to the world. This newest MadLibber was a jerk! A post appeared on her dashboard before she did. Her fingers paused over the CLOSE button as she read it.

Fact A: The Internet is filled with people.
Fact B: A percentage of those people are trolls.
...
Fact C: By that logic, if you meet enough people online, you WILL eventually meet a troll.

#TROLLS #STATISTICS #THERE'S TRUTH TO THIS

PERMALINK   POSTED 1 YEAR AGO   3,109 NOTES

trappedinfiction reblogged this from voldemortician
snickerdoodle likes this
rollerboogie likes this

A shiver ran through her. "Malwarning was the troll," she said quietly. She set the phone down and stared at it. "He used a name this time, but it's the same guy. He's the troll from before."

Now that the thought had arrived, she couldn't shake her conviction. She glanced at her laptop. It sat open at the comments screen. With a rising sense of dread, she clicked on her e-mail tab. A message awaited.

NEW Message, @Malwarning2: 7:04 p.m. EST
Subject: Did you just BLOCK me?
I don't think you get this, Madi. I'm not going anywhere. So stop being a baby and DEAL.

Panic turning to anger, Madi hit REPLY.

Reply to Message from @Malwarning2: 7:06 p.m. EST
Subject: RE: Did you just BLOCK me?

Yes, I totally get this, jerk. And now you're blocked here, too.
I wasn't kidding. This blog is mine and trolls like you aren't
welcome. GO BACK TO REDUX.

In seconds, she had blocked the adjusted username. "There. That should—"
A new message appeared.

NEW Message, @Malwarning3: 7:08 p.m. EST
Subject: Oh, I can do this all day
Nope. I'm not going anywhere. Don't like it? RUN. That's what
you did before, didn't you? SJWs like you like to talk big, but you
can't hack it face-to-face.

"SJW," Madi muttered. "What the hell's that supposed to mean?!" She
started to type in a reply, then stopped and popped open Malwarning's full
header. Once she'd selected VIEW MESSAGE SOURCE, the IP address appeared. She
smirked. "Take that, asshole."
She finished typing her return e-mail and hit SEND.

Reply to Message from @Malwarning3: 7:09 p.m. EST
Subject: RE: Oh, I can do this all day
You realize, name change or not, I snagged your IP address.
Right? Harassment is ILLEGAL. And you are WAY past the line.
(BLOCKED again.)

A response e-mail—from yet another alias—appeared almost immediately.

NEW Message, @Malwarning4: 7:11 p.m. EST
Subject: Fuck. You.
Nah, bitch. If you had any way of finding me, it would have
happened already. And all this BS you're shoveling at me is
going to make it worse. You think this is all I can do to you?
You ain't seen NOTHING yet.

"You bastard!" Madi shouted.

From the living room downstairs, Madi heard her father bellow: *"Watch your language, please, Madi!"* She didn't answer. If this troll was hiding his whereabouts, she'd have more difficulty keeping him away. She typed in an angry reply.

> **Reply to Message from @Malwarning4:** 7:15 p.m. EST
> **Subject:** RE: Fuck. You.
> I've seen enough to know your IQ is even lower than your language
> skills. And I'm DONE talking with you. Get back under your bridge.
> You're not welcome here. Blocked, and blocked, and BLOCKED.

With her message sent, Madi opened an IP address search engine and pasted each of the different IP addresses from the incoming e-mails into it.

"Oh, please, please be there," she muttered.

While the search engine chugged, Madi turned off all incoming e-mail and set an automated message. As she watched, a series of incoming e-mails appeared and were bounced back just as quickly. Whoever the troll was, he was persistent.

> *Automated response* to @Malwarning5: 7:16 p.m. EST
> Private messaging for all e-mail clients on the MadLibs blog is
> currently closed. Please check back again later.
> *Automated response* to @Malwarning6: 7:17 p.m. EST
> Private messaging for all e-mail clients on the MadLibs blog is
> currently closed. Please check back again later.
> *Automated response* to @FUCKYOUMADLIB: 7:18 p.m. EST
> Private messaging for all e-mail clients on the MadLibs blog is
> currently closed. Please check back again later.

After a moment, the barrage stopped.

"And stay away," Madi said in a shaky voice.

She clicked on the ongoing search tab. The IP addresses she'd searched came from all points of the globe. Madi closed her eyes, breathing hard.

"He's hiding."

This situation had gone from bad to worse.

With the MadLibs blog closed down to keep the troll in the dungeon, and no one to talk to, Madi tweeted her exasperation. The anger and anxiety she'd been holding at bay for days spiked. She'd *dealt* with trolls before! She should be able to handle this.

@MadLib: So angry I'm literally shaking! #WhatDoWeSayToInternetTrolls #NotToday

In seconds, fandom friends were replying.

@ModernDayWitch: @MadLib Oh my goodness, hon! Are you okay?

@MadLib: @ModernDayWitch Not okay. I'm absolutely FURIOUS! The troll is BACK AGAIN!

@ModernDayWitch: @MadLib Oh no! I'm so sorry you're dealing with this! D: He sounds absolutely AWFUL. I'll do a cleansing spell for you, Madi. You need it. :(

@MadLib: @ModernDayWitch I need more than a cleansing. I need some kind of CURSE for this guy. GAH! Why are people so AWFUL?!?

@laurentabelard: @MadLib What an idiot! I can't believe it. You got the IP address, though, right? You can track him and block him.

@MadLib: @laurentabelard I did, but it's not that easy. He's using Tor, or something like it. #UseYourPowerForGoodNotEvil

@laurentabelard: @MadLib Sorry, I don't understand. What does Tor do?

@MadLib: @laurentabelard It bounces his signal from place to place. When I tracked it, the IP for @Malwarning showed up in both Nigeria AND in Toronto. He's not in either of those places. Guaranteed. THIS is why I hate trolls!

@ArtWithAttitude: @MadLib @laurentabelard Shit! That's not good.

@MadLib: @ArtWithAttitude @laurentabelard Exactly. :(I've probably made things FAR worse bc I answered his PMs. D: He's smart—way smart—I shouldn't have taunted him.

@ModernDayWitch: @MadLib Let us know how we can help you. :(You aren't alone in this. #MadLibbersUnite

@MadLib: @ModernDayWitch Problem is, I don't think there's anything you CAN do to help. #FML For now everything is closed— ask box, comments, EVERYTHING. Sorry, guys. I need to contain the fallout from this mess. #GetAHazmatSuit

@laurentabelard: @MadLib How awful. :(

@MadLib: @laurentabelard I know.

Madi tossed her phone on her bed and flopped back on the coverlet. She rolled over, burying her face in the pillow, and let out a primal scream of fury.

Seconds later the door to her bedroom opened and Madi looked up to find her father waiting in the doorway.

"Sheesh, Madi. Everything okay up here?"

"Everything's just peachy," she said in a bitter voice.

For a moment it seemed like he was going to disagree, but he shook his head instead. "Well, good. But try and keep it down."

Friday afternoon, Madi waited outside Mr. Wattley's door, heavy-lidded eyes staring down at the tiled floor. She'd had three sleepless nights after the explosive argument with the troll. It felt like the events that had chased Madi out of her last fandom—two years earlier—were starting again. Even Laurent's two-in-the-morning texting pep talks hadn't been able to dispel her gloom. *I need to get out of here,* her mind shouted. But where? There was no "out" that didn't require completely renegotiating her responsibilities with Sarah. Besides, she had final exams in two weeks.

They were the last hurdle to finishing high school. Classes ended mid-June, and then, as everyone loved reminding her, real life would begin. She'd be starting at CUNY in the fall, taking the train into New York each morning and back home each evening. Everything in her life had been tied up so neatly. Madi felt trapped.

She didn't even know if she *wanted* to go to college, but it had happened all the same.

You couldn't *force* someone to grow up, could you? Madi's lips twitched as she imagined the nuclear-devastation-level blowup that would occur should she try to explain *that* concept to her parents. Nope. Their understanding of funemployment was as narrow-minded as their fixation on academics. It left Madi coasting, refusing to decide. And so those decisions were made without her.

Her thumb flicked over the phone's screen, pulling up the series of late-night texts. She smiled to herself as the conversation with Laurent returned:

> i know i should ignore it. EVERYONE tells u that about trolls, but how can u put that kind of nonsense aside? And why should u? i'm doing the blog for me—not them—and trolls can get back under the bridge where they belong! 😡

> Can't you report him or something?

if it were a regular site, yes. (and in theory someone would do something about it) but i'm the site administrator in this case. it's ME who needs to deal 😩

that's awful. shouldn't you go to the police or something?

he hasn't really done anything, but I'm worried he might

???? OMG—now i'm worried. 😨

don't be. i'm not, like, afraid for my life or anything. (i'd go to the police if i were.) i'm just worried he'll out me in some way

out you?

post my name publicly.

i'm sorry if this sounds naive, but would that be bad? madlibs is a good site. there's no NSFW content. and it's not like you're doing anything you should be ashamed of

not me, no. but my family would FREAK 🙄

why?

it might mess up my dad's career

i don't understand.

"down home" is pretty conservative. dad's followers are, too. bc of this, dad's always been VERY nervous of things i post. he wouldn't even let me get a FB account until i was in high school. i'm only allowed to run madlibs because i DON'T use my actual name

can i help with the troll?

i appreciate the offer, but no. just leave him be. he's awful, and he seems to be good at tech stuff, too. that's a BAD combination. (the IP addresses are always hidden or fake.) just let it go. confronting him will make it worse

are you sure?

100% sure. i don't need u to ride in on a white horse & save me

but i'm totally up for it, you know. i mean, i've rented a horse and everything.

LOL—that WOULD be a sight. u on a horse? Hee!

just you wait and see.

oh, i will 😜

Madi's smile disappeared as the telltale sound of heels approached. She slipped her phone into her pocket, eyeing the hallway. The shiplike figure of Mrs. Preet was halfway to her, her bosom heaving as she strode forward, waving.

"Oh, for the love of—"

"You there," Mrs. Preet called in a singsong voice. "Could I see your hall pass, please?"

Madi stifled a groan. *Where is Doc Brown's DeLorean when you need it?*

She gave a halfhearted smile. "It's just me," Madi said. "Sarah's sister, remember? I don't go here."

Mrs. Preet's shortsighted eyes widened behind her thick glasses. Instead of turning away, she jogged to Madi's side.

"Miss Nakama," she panted. "What good luck! I was hoping to run into you today."

"You were?"

"You didn't return my phone call. I asked you to contact the office at the school for some very important information."

"I, um, I didn't really have a chance. Things have been a little crazy the last few days."

"Oh dear. Well, that makes this more difficult."

The hair on Madi's arms rose. "I—I don't understand."

"Are you sure you don't want to discuss this in my office?" Mrs. Preet asked. "It's just down the hall."

"No, the bell's going to ring in a minute. Sarah's coming." Madi swallowed hard. "What's going on, Mrs. Preet?"

"I had a concerning phone call the other day. One that my message requested you explain."

The door behind them opened and Mr. Wattley appeared.

"Explain what?"

"What you're planning to do for your final English Language Arts project? I mean, since your blog is no longer acceptable for submission."

The floor below Madi's feet disappeared. She was falling—*fast*—with no sense of when she'd stop. The MadLibs blog was her final major assignment for the class. Barring that, she only had finals. She was so close to graduation she could see the finish line, but if this fell through . . .

Mom and Dad are going to kill me.

"I—I don't know what you mean," Madi stammered. "I already talked to my online teacher. Ms. Rodriguez said I could—"

"Use it as long as it adhered to the school's code of conduct," Mrs. Preet said with a tight smile. "Yes, yes. I assume you read the agreement. OMA is very stringent about meeting state standards."

"I don't know what you mean."

Mrs. Preet spoke slowly, her words enunciated as if reading from a book. "The code specifically prohibits any work that has been submitted elsewhere for monetary gain."

"But I haven't been paid for any of my writing," Madi said. "I've never—"

"But you *do* make money from your website, yes? You have ads? Pop-ups that provide you with . . ." She tapped her lip. "What was the word you used on your blog? 'Funemployment,' isn't it?"

She waited for an answer, but Madi's words were gone.

Sarah came out of the classroom, pushing past Mrs. Preet and heading down the hallway without waiting.

"You'd better start a rewrite," Mrs. Preet said seriously. "The end of the year is only three weeks away and you have a semester-long assignment to redo."

"But I have final exams! I can't just drop everything and redo my whole blog. Can't you make an exception?"

Mrs. Preet crossed her arms. "I can't and I won't. Doing that would make it unfair for every other student in this school."

"But—"

"I don't have a choice on this, Miss Nakama. Rules are rules." Her expression was unwavering. "You will follow them the same as everyone else."

"There's no way I'll get it done in time!"

"I'm sorry, but if that's the case, perhaps you should consider returning to Millburn Academy for an extra semester, next fall."

11

"How do you explain school to higher intelligence?"
(*E.T. the Extra-Terrestrial*, 1982)

u still have that white horse
u told me about?

at the ready. ☺

bc I could REALLY use someone
to save me right about now 😩

oh no! what happened?

EVERYTHING! FML!
this month is cursed!

details?

i'm in so much serious TROUBLE

okay. breathe. is this drugs? alcohol? the law?
do you need bail money? (that'll take a bit.)
HOW CAN I HELP???

none of those. (jeez, laurent. what kind of person do you think I am?)

then what? because those are the big ones, IMO. everything else is manageable.

not this

???

i may not graduate. 😵

but I thought you were an A student.

i am.

and . . . ?

and the school got an anonymous tip I had been making money off my madlibs site. my english project is totally screwed

i don't understand.

THE TROLL MESSED UP MY REAL LIFE

oh no! merde! that's terrible!

it is. i'm so angry i could scream 👶

do it.

what?

go outside. scream it out! terrify the neighbors!

LOL—i can't, laurent. my dad will freak 😕

so what? you need to let it out. go!

don't make me laugh. all right? not yet. i'm just too mad right now

then how can i help? please. tell me.

aw . . . laurent. ur a beautiful cinnamon roll, too good for this world

i'm a WHAT? 😜

nothing. LOL ur perfect 😘 and thank u for being here for me. i appreciate that more than i can say

i'm never more than a text away.

i know & i'm glad. i just wish u were across the street

me, too, minette. me, too. here. i saw a post you might enjoy. it's a little less back to the future and a bit more fast-forward to the future. 😎

A link appeared and Madi clicked on it. She began to laugh.

ha-ha! i think being stuck in the '50s might be a better choice than panem

not up for the hunger games?

i'm not much of an athlete 😕

but you could use your computer skills to hack the arena. the rest of us would be at your whim!

would u be a competitor?

not a competitor. an ally.

the future is looking better and better

Laurent and Madi spent the next ten minutes texting. He wanted to know about Millburn. How small was it? And how close to the lake were the houses? Was the Nakama house actually in the forest, or was it on a street? Smiling, Madi sent him a pin on Google Maps as she described the town where she'd spent her entire life. And then, without explanation, he disappeared. She waited a few minutes for a reply that never came, then slid her phone into her pocket.

It was time to deal with the mess she'd created.

Half an hour later, Madi was still typing. She'd completed all the minor assignments for the week and was now ready to tackle the big issue: her contested major assignment. She was writing an e-mail to her English teacher when Sarah knocked at her bedroom door.

"Just a minute," Madi said, stretching her back. "I'm busy right now."

She scanned it one last time. The wording needed to be exactly right.

UNSENT Message, MNakama@MadLibs.com: 6:33 p.m. EST
Priority: HIGH
Subject: Possible Alternate Projects for English

Dear Ms. Rodriguez,

Mrs. Preet contacted me at school today to let me know my MadLibs blog was no longer an acceptable final project for your course. I apologize for misunderstanding the school's code of conduct, and for not contacting you as soon as Mrs. Preet left a message on my home phone.

Mrs. Preet suggested the two of us talk about options for an alternate project. Given the time frame and the upcoming finals, I'd appreciate if you could be flexible. Please let me know what assignment would be acceptable.

Sincerely,

Madison Nakama

Madi chewed her lip, considering what she'd written. She needed to walk the line between supplicant and assertive. She would *not* be returning for another semester of high school, and flunking out in her last semester was not an option. (If she didn't die of embarrassment, her parents would kill her for letting them down.) She winced. The only choice was to suck it up and fix it. That meant a new project. She closed her eyes, sending a quick prayer to the academic gods, hoping they were listening.

"Please let her go easy on—"

Another bout of knocking interrupted her celestial plea, and Madi squeaked in surprise.

"Madi!" Sarah shouted. "Can I come in now?"

With a sigh, Madi hit SEND. "Just doing homework, Sarah. What's up?"

Her sister opened the door a crack. "There's someone downstairs for you."

Madi spun in her rolling chair, staring at her sister in confusion. "Who?"

"A boy; I don't know his name. He's downstairs talking with Dad."

"Who in the world . . . ?"

Madi stood from the chair, walking toward the door and peering over Sarah's shoulder. She could hear her father talking to someone, but the voices were too low to discern. She touched her sister's arm.

"What does he look like?" she whispered.

Sarah pursed her lips. "He has a straight nose, kind of highlighted dark hair, clear skin—*really* clear—like almost perfect. He has a backpack, and he's got a camera, too. The kind with the lenses and everything. It's around his neck. A Canon, I think. Maybe DSLR."

"Yes, but what does he *look* like?"

"Do you know Jack Shriveton?"

"No."

"Well, he's this boy in my chemistry class who sits two rows ahead of me. Tanned. Athletic. He was state champion for high jump. This guy kind of looks like him."

"So he's in high school, then?"

"Not sure," Sarah said with a shrug. "Seems more like a college guy to me. His clothes are different."

"*Different*, meaning what?"

"Like they're not from the mall. They look . . . nice. Fancier, I guess. Oh, and he has a tattoo of some fish on one arm. I thought Dad would freak when he saw it, but he didn't say a thing."

Madi was out the door and running down the stairs before her sister had finished, panting by the time she reached the foyer. She skidded to a stop. Her father and Laurent stood chatting like old friends.

"Madi," her father said, giving her a beaming smile. "Your friend Laurent, here, popped by to say hi."

Laurent waved. *"Salut."*

"H-hey, Laurent. I didn't expect you." She peeked out the window, half expecting a white horse on the lawn. There was only the next-door neighbor creating a grid with his mower.

"I figured you were probably studying, so I walked from the station rather than texting," Laurent said, answering the unspoken question. "I thought you might want to grab a coffee." He grinned. "Pretty sure I owe you one."

"Yeah, you do," Madi said with a nervous laugh.

Laurent turned to her father. "If that's okay with you, sir."

"Of course it is."

"It is?" Madi stared at her father.

He was in superfriendly mode, and she was relieved she hadn't admitted the massive storm about to descend on her academic life. He would never let her out of the house if he knew how she'd screwed up her English project.

Laurent stuck out his hand. "It was very good to meet you, Mr. Nakama. I'd like to hear more about 'Down Home' and your career at the *Tri-State Herald*." He glanced at Madi, winking, and she rolled her eyes. Laurent was laying it on a little thick. "I'd love to hear how you decided on a career in journalism."

Charles's face brightened into a beatific grin. "Well, then," he said, chest swelling. "Next time you visit, Laurent, we'll continue our little chat." He nodded to Madi. "You two kids go on and have a good time. Just keep your phone on, Madi, and give me a shout if you need me to pick you up somewhere. I'll let Sarah know you've gone out."

She stared at him, expecting at any moment for some type of prankster film crew to come exploding out of the kitchen, and for her to be dragged back to her room. This was *not* her life.

"You sure?"

He nodded.

"That's only if you *want* to go," Laurent said. "I never actually asked. Are you busy, Madi?"

She turned back to find him staring at her with pleading eyes. Like this, he seemed young and uncertain, a high school student once more. The moment in New York—when she'd been almost certain Laurent was going to kiss her—returned in a wave of yearning. She had no idea why life had just done a one-eighty, but she wasn't about to question the bright turn of fortune.

Rewrites could wait.

"Of course I want to go." She couldn't keep the grin off her face. "Ready to explore the booming metropolis of Millburn and mingle with a few of its cosmopolitan residents?"

Laurent tapped the camera hanging around his neck. "If you don't mind being the guide, I'll play photographer."

Madi grabbed her coat and swung open the door. "Let's check out the sights."

"Sights?"

"First stop: a taste of Millburn's best coffee."

Laurent's face took a decidedly greenish tint. "Oh no. Please tell me we are *not* going back to the train station."

She laughed. "Definitely not."

They were halfway down the block when Sarah's first text message appeared.

> When are you getting back?

Madi groaned, and Laurent looked over at her in concern.

"Everything okay?" he asked.

"Just fine," Madi muttered as she typed in a reply.

i don't know. (i just left, sarah!)
is something wrong?

No. But I thought we were gaming tonight.

we can do that later

When?

SARAH i'm busy right now

But when can we hang out? We are supposed
to be gaming right now. The rest of the team is
ready to go. @StarveilBrian1981's freaking out!

go ahead and play without me.
tell brian to lead the team

I don't want to.

then don't! srsly, sarah. i need some
space—all right?! (i'm with a BOY!) can
you talk to dad about this or something?

He said I should text you.

i'll be home later. chill please

Promise you'll come back?

YES. please relax. i'm allowed to be out.

Promise me. You never promised.

PROMISE ME, MADI.

"Are you sure everything's okay?" Laurent asked. "You look . . . tense."

"It's nothing. I mean, it's something. It's my sister. But I'm fine." She gave him a tight smile. "I'm okay. Just let me send one more text."

"Of course."

Madi sent one last text, but she flicked off the phone's ringer before she sent it.

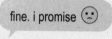

They walked down the shadowy street, warm patches of sunshine heavy on their shoulders, spring's chill waiting in the shadows. With Laurent at her side, Madi hardly noticed. He paused at random moments, snapping pictures: a silhouette of a house, a single flower, an unfurled leaf.

They were halfway to the coffee shop when he stopped dead in his tracks.

"What?"

"The light through those branches," he said breathlessly. "See there?"

It fell in bright bands. Any other moment and Madi would have walked past without noticing, but Laurent seemed attuned to beauty. She waited as he took a series of photographs.

He turned the camera on her. "And now my *real* reason for the camera . . ."

"Oh God, no." She laughed, turning away. "Please don't."

She thought he'd do it anyhow. (She would have.) But Laurent dropped the camera back to his chest as soon as she said the words.

"I . . . I just don't like how I look," she explained.

"You don't?"

"I—Yeah, no." She laughed. "And pictures make me look weird."

"All right. No pictures of you." The corner of his mouth curled. "Unless you change your mind and ask."

"I won't. Promise."

He smiled and they walked on.

"So why'd you decide to come out?" Madi asked. "Surely you couldn't be craving Millburn coffee."

"Ah, no! But I had other reasons."

Madi smirked. "Those reasons being . . . ?"

"You sounded upset when you texted, so I decided to visit." He ducked his chin so his hair fell over his eyes. "And not just for half an hour of drinking terrible coffee." He lifted his eyes and grinned. "Besides, I wanted to share my news with you."

"Your news?"

"I've been accepted to the College d'Arts in Paris. I've been waiting and waiting. And today I got my answer." Laurent grinned. "Next year I'll be learning professional photography. I'm in!"

"Oh my God, that's—that's—that's freaking AMAZING!"

"I've been dying to tell someone! And then when we talked, I wanted to tell you, but you were upset, so—"

"You came out!" Madi laughed. "I'm so happy for you, Laurent. That's fantastic! You'll be a famous photographer someday."

He reached out, tucking a stray piece of hair behind her ear. "Maybe you'll let me photograph you then?"

She looked away, smiling. "Maybe."

"*Maybe* works for me. Just means I'll have to convince you."

He seemed to be waiting for her to say something, but Madi couldn't reply. Her eyes skimmed the street. They were far from the Nakama house, but she could sense people watching behind half-parted curtains. The sense of being on display pushed away her excitement, and she walked faster, Laurent easily matching her pace.

After a moment Laurent spoke again. "I'm relieved about the College d'Arts. I wasn't sure if I'd get in or not. My grades aren't what yours are." He chuckled. "I applied for a couple here in the States, too. The Rhode Island School of Design and the School of Visual Arts in New York both have great photography programs."

Madi's breath caught. *Please let Laurent stay here!*

"And . . . ?"

His smile dimmed. "And nothing. It's all right, though. The College d'Arts is a fantastic choice. I honestly didn't expect to get accepted. The admittance interviews are much harder to do when you live on another continent."

"I'd think so."

"Thankfully, videoconferencing seemed to work."

"That's fantastic!"

"It's an amazing program. And the college is close to my family's apartment in Paris, so I'll be able to save money."

"That's so cool. God! Living in Paris? What an awesome life! I'd kill to have a chance to do that."

"I'm hoping to complete the photography courses in three years, rather than four. Maybe get out and do a work term in my last semester. I've been looking forward to learning more about photography. But the College d'Arts is beyond my expectations! During my interview I showed them a bunch of pictures I took in New York this year. The portfolio was a big factor in my favor."

Madi reached out and squeezed his hand. "That's really awesome, Laurent!" Nervous, she giggled and let go again. "I'm kind of starstruck here. That sounds like my dream life!"

He grinned. "I think so."

"Paris . . . wow. What I wouldn't do to live there!"

Laurent tugged her gently to a stop. They stood on the sidewalk, the sounds of the city echoing around them. He stepped forward, so close she had to crane her neck to see him. His hands slowly slid down her shoulders until he caught her fingers in his. He didn't let go.

"I'm glad I came to tell you," he murmured.

Heart pounding, Madi smiled. "Me, too."

And they walked, hand in hand, the rest of the way to the coffee shop.

12

"Verdict?" Madi asked as the lingering taste of perfectly roasted coffee and steamed milk faded on her tongue.

"Mmmm . . ." Laurent took the last swallow of his coffee and closed his eyes, breathing slowly.

"It's good, right?"

"Well . . ."

"Well, what?"

He opened one eye. "I haven't decided yet."

"You're stalling, Laurent," she said drily. "I can tell, you know."

"Not stalling. Deciding."

"If you can't decide, it's got to be good."

He grinned and pushed the empty cup aside. "You think so?"

"Oh, come on! You *know* it's good. Better than good . . . great, even!"

"Fine. The coffee was very good," he said with a wink. "But . . ." He paused dramatically. "I've had better."

A swell of laughter broke from Madi's throat. "I don't believe it!"

"It's true."

"This here," Madi said, "is the best coffee in the world!"

Laurent covered his mouth with his hand. "In Millburn, maybe," he whispered.

"What did you say to me?"

He stood, dropping money onto the table. "Nothing at all."

"You did!"

"Nope. You're imagining things."

Madi tried to block him, but he dodged past and headed out the door to the owner's shout of *"See you again soon!"*

"I'm not imagining anything," Madi said, laughing. "You said something there. Is this a comparison to Parisian coffee or something?"

Laurent turned, putting his hands on her shoulders. "It was very good coffee, Madi," he said. "Wonderfully so."

She stuck out her tongue. "Told you so."

"You did, and it *was*. Almost perfect."

"So you admit it!"

"Of course I do. Why wouldn't I?"

"I don't know. To be stubborn?"

"Ah, but stubborn is your thing, not mine."

She laughed, and Laurent slid his arm over her shoulder, resting it there. "I like that about you," he said.

"Good thing."

They were coming up with excuses to touch now. Little moments—passing the cream and sugar, or sliding into the booth—became tiny excuses for exploration. Ever so slowly, Laurent's hands slid down her arms, catching hold of her fingers. Madi's gaze flitted around the empty street, and then she relaxed. There was no one here who she knew.

"This was really fun today," she said.

"It was." Laurent checked his watch, and her expression saddened.

"Is it time for you to leave already?"

"Oh no. I've still got a couple hours before my train leaves. There's time for more."

Madi turned around, still holding his hand. "Doing what?"

"It's almost sunset. Let's go someplace different."

Madi raised an eyebrow. "*Different*, meaning what?"

"I don't know. A park or downtown or something. Train yard, maybe?

Someplace I can take pictures. What was the place you were telling me about? The place you and your sister used to play."

"The ruins!"

A short fifteen-minute walk took them to the Colonial Inn. As they followed the path into the park that surrounded it, the heat of the day leeched away. Birdsong filled the trees. Careful to avoid the guests and owners, Madi and Laurent tiptoed across the manicured lawn.

"We used to play here all summer," Madi said, leaning against the rock foundation. "Just Sarah and me, for hours and hours. I love it here at the ruins."

The sun dropped in the sky, brightening the surrounding houses, blue shadows contrasting with warm, sun-drenched colors.

"It's beautiful." Laurent lifted his camera, focusing on the lake, visible beyond the ruins. "Do you mind if you're in this one?"

Madi grinned and turned away. "Not really. But are you sure you want me in the picture? Won't I wreck it?"

"You're just a silhouette," he said, taking several shots. "It's better this way. A little contrast with the landscape. Hold on, I'll show you what I mean."

Laurent set to work, moving from one side to the other. The light faded until the clouds were only painted crimson. A bright canvas against the black.

"Perfect," he murmured. "Just perfect . . ."

An endless time later, he finished to find Madi watching him, a pensive smile on her face. He dropped his chin in embarrassment.

"Sorry. That took longer than I thought."

"I liked watching you work," she said. "You're very intense when you're behind the camera. Very focused."

Laurent grinned. "It's where I feel the most 'real,' you know? Everything else fades until it's nothing but me and the lens."

"Writing's like that for me."

"That's your art."

A flurry of movement from the side caught his eye and he lifted the camera, taking a series of snapshots as two birds took off from the underbrush and flew across the lake.

"Can I see?"

"Of course." Laurent brought the camera to Madi, flipping through the digital images on the screen.

"Oh, wow! That's really beautiful, Laurent." Her fingers brushed his as she pulled the camera closer and squinted at the screen. "The lake looks like it goes on forever. And the ruins are gorgeous."

"Here," he said, zooming in the frame. "You can see them better this way."

Madi moved through, one by one, inspecting the photos. After a long while, she turned to him and smiled. "This one with the birds is my favorite."

"I'll send it to you," Laurent said. He turned his gaze back to the lake. The clouds parted and a line of light appeared above the horizon, sunset's final blaze.

"Ah! Look there!"

The top of the highest stone on the ruins was bathed in gold, but the light would only last a minute.

"I'm going up!" Laurent clambered to the edge of a broken stone wall, finding footholds, and climbed to the top. He stood slowly, hands outstretched. From here, the perspective changed: the small lake and the paved path around it, the rooftops and the lights of the Colonial Inn twinkling in the distance.

"Come up," he said, offering his hand. "You can see forever from up here."

"I'm scared of heights, Laurent."

"Pfft! It's hardly more than ten feet off the ground," he said, waggling his fingers. "I won't let you fall. Promise!"

"You go," she said, giving him a lingering once-over. "The view from down here is just fine. Thanks!"

He laughed aloud, then jumped from the top straight down to the ground.

Madi squeaked in surprise. "You're crazy!" she laughed.

He put his hands on her shoulders. "You're right. The view from down here *is* pretty amazing."

He caught hold of her hand and pulled her toward the paved path that circled Diamond Mill Pond, around the inn, and behind the line of houses.

"*Quel bel endroit!*"

"What?"

"It's so beautiful. No wonder you played here as a girl." He took another photograph and another.

Madi reached out to touch his hand. "Hold on a second," she said. "It's going to be dark soon. I wouldn't want to trip."

"Of course not."

They strolled hand in hand, watching the disk of light travel the last few degrees, sky and water blending together. The circuit was an easy walk and barely ten minutes later they were back around the other side, the Colonial Inn shining like a lantern behind them. The voices of guests on the veranda wafted forward, music coming from the dining room.

Madi knew that someone there might see them together, but at this moment, she didn't care. Her fingers tightened in Laurent's. Tonight everything felt exactly *right*.

Madi was almost out of breath when they made it back around the path to the ruins, but she had no intention of telling Laurent that his long legs were an issue to keep up with. She'd gladly do cardio if it meant another moment holding his hand. When he stopped to photograph a swirl of night-flying insects around a lamp, she perched on a stone slab, watching. He was in his element here, taking pictures. She liked seeing it.

After he finished, Laurent sat down beside her and set his camera aside. It wasn't until his hand brushed her back that Madi realized he'd moved closer. His leg was pressed alongside hers, the warmth spreading from one to the other.

Madi looked up. "What are you . . . ?"

Her words faded as she realized he was staring down at her, so close she could see how his eyes held flecks of gold in the depths of mossy green, the same shade as the glitter on the lake. Laurent reached out, his fingers tracing the shape of one black brow, then moving to her lips, before sliding along her jaw, to bury themselves in her hair.

"I wanted to kiss you at Penn Station that day."

Madi tried to answer, but couldn't. She was trapped by his eyes.

"May I?" he asked, moving closer.

She wanted something funny or smart to say—like some kind of moment from the movies when the sassy heroine tells it like it is—but she was no Molly

Ringwald, and her words and brain had parted ways. When Laurent moved no farther, she realized that he was still waiting for her agreement, and since she was mute, this moment was going to end before it began.

He pulled back. "Sorry, Madi. I shouldn't have——"

His apology jarred the words from her chest. "Y-yes. I . . . You can. Yes, you can kiss me!" Her embarrassment was matched only by her panic. (Molly Ringwald would be eye-rolling at the lame response.)

Laurent smiled, a crinkle of lines reaching all the way from the edge of his eyes to his hairline. *"Merci, minette."*

Their lips met.

Madi had kissed a few boys before: one at a middle school dance, two in high school, but they were nothing like this. It was like comparing deep-sea diving to wading in a paddling pool. Laurent's lips were persuasive as he moved them against hers. His hand in her hair guided her forward ever so slightly, and Madi's hands slid up his shirt, moving almost without her realizing it. He tasted like the cinnamon gum he'd offered her during their walk. She breathed him in—the scent of water, and green growing things, and under that the scent of Laurent's cologne, flooding her senses.

The kiss deepened. Where she'd been cold minutes before, she now burned. Laurent seemed to have an innate warmth. It spread from his mouth—tenderly moving over hers—to her cheeks—flaming with heat—to his hands—behind her shoulder and around her waist—all the way down to her toes. The kiss went on and on, until Madi couldn't think. She moaned as he released her mouth. But instead of ending it, Laurent's tongue traced its way back to the shell of her ear, his hands moving restlessly under her jacket.

"Si belle . . . si gentil . . ." he murmured.

The French endearments were so perfect—*too perfect!*—and that struck Madi as utterly absurd. She began to giggle.

"Oh God," she gasped. "I'm sorry. I didn't——"

Laurent froze. "Madi?"

Sudden laughter broke free again. "It just sounded so funny, so weirdly perfect and surreal—I mean, this doesn't happen in real life—It's not you, it's——"

Laurent took her laughter as a sign to return the kiss to her mouth. He pulled her closer with one arm while, under the cover of her jacket, his free hand explored. She gasped as his fingers traced over her shirt and bra. Everything disappeared except the taste and feel of him. There was no fumbling, no bumped noses. It was a lingering, endless moment, and Madi was certain Laurent must be able to feel her pounding heart through the layers of clothing. She gasped as he broke away, both of them panting.

"Je pourrais rester heureux toute ma vie, tant que tu seras a mes cotes," he murmured.

She fought down more laughter. "What does that mean?"

Laurent smiled, but it wasn't his usual lopsided grin. This one shone from the center of his face, spreading into the corners of his eyes and over his cheeks. Madi had never seen anyone so beautiful, so earnest.

"It means I'm happy to be here." He patted the rock. "Because you are here, too."

And then he kissed her again.

It was twilight when they walked down the paved path that led from the ruins to the residential neighborhood. Streetlights buzzed at intervals, but it was near dark, the sidewalk wrapped in shadows. Twice, Madi tripped. The first time, Laurent caught her before she fell, but the second he wasn't fast enough, and she ended up flat on her back on the grass on the side of the pavement. After the perfect evening in an otherwise dismal week, the universe's sense of humor had returned.

Nice, she thought sourly. *A real class act.*

"Madi? What happened? Are you all right?"

"I'm fine," she said as Laurent's worried face appeared upside down above her.

"Are you sure? You tripped on—"

"Totally sure. Just a klutz."

Laurent reached down a hand, hoisting her upright. Madi stretched cautiously. Other than her ego, nothing seemed damaged. "Now that you've seen my classy moves," she said, "you might want to—"

"Wait!"

"What is it?"

"There," he whispered. "I saw something move!"

"Where?"

"Over there. See? By that tree with the V branches." He leaned forward, eyes wide. "There it is again!" he gasped.

Madi peered into the trees. The first streetlights were a good two hundred feet away, the street that led to home glowing like a beacon, but there was nothing—as far as she could see—that barred their way.

"I dunno, Laurent. That just looks like a tree to me."

Laurent nervously shifted from foot to foot. "I've seen a lot of horror movies," he said in an anxious voice. "This is *not* a good place for us to be alone. The woods are the worst place to be."

Madi burst into raucous laughter. "Are you kidding me?"

"No, I just . . ." He stepped behind her. "I saw something move. I really did."

Madi tried to squelch the sound, but another wave of giggling rose in her throat. "This is Millburn, Laurent. You're totally fine. And this is hardly the woods."

"But the trees—"

"We're in the suburbs," she said, still laughing. "The trees were planted here."

"But there could be animals . . ."

"A raccoon, maybe."

Laurent grabbed her hand. "Are raccoons dangerous?!"

"Not really. I mean, they can be a nuisance, but they won't, like, sneak up on you and attack." She giggled again.

A branch broke in the bushes and Laurent let out a high-pitched yelp.

"Relax," Madi said, biting the inside of her cheeks to stop the laughter. Laurent really *did* look terrified. "It's going to be fine. Sarah and I always walk this way. Seriously! The night we went to the Metrograph, she was hiding out here by herself."

A dog barked, somewhere nearby, and Laurent jumped. "But what if it's something else? Someone dangerous. Like a—a—"

"Horror movie?" Madi said, fighting for composure.

"Exactly!"

Madi stepped forward. "Hey!" she shouted to the woods. "If there's a guy in a hockey mask out there, I'm gonna kick some ass."

"Don't!"

She lifted her voice. "Hear that, mask face?! You better move or I'm gonna attack!"

"Shh!" Laurent said with a nervous laugh. "I don't think you're supposed to goad strangers into attacking you."

Giggling, Madi grabbed his hand and tugged him down the path. "I really doubt it's a serial killer. It could, however, be someone trying to sell us life insurance."

"Are you sure?" Laurent's feet dragged the deeper they got into the treed section between shore and street. "In New York, I tend to follow my gut, and right now it's saying this is *not* the smartest thing I've done." His fingers tightened around hers. "I don't like this. Would it be okay if we went back the other way?"

"To the Inn?" She scoffed. "Not a chance. I'd rather face a serial killer."

The nosy owner would ask Madi a million questions about her and Sarah, why Madi had left the regular high school (as had happened the last two times they'd met), and—inevitably—about Laurent and who he was. Madi's burgeoning love life would be on the front page of the *Tri-State Herald* before they'd even made it to the street.

"Come on," she said with a grin, putting her arm around his back and leading him away. "There's nothing here. It must've been wind in the trees or something."

"Er . . . all right."

They were perhaps ten yards from the street when Madi felt Laurent start to relax.

"Thank you," he said with a sheepish smile. "I'm not used to being out in . . ." He waved at the trees around them. "Nature."

"I'd hate to see you camping." She laughed.

Laurent shuddered. "Not a chance."

"You sure? It might be fun."

"Not my kind of fun."

Madi grinned. "Don't worry, I'd protect you."

"You would?"

"Of course I would. Besides, I told you. There was nothing to worry about. The shadow you saw was probably just—"

"What's THAT?!" Laurent screeched as the bushes directly next to them began to move.

A hundred things ran through Madi's mind: that serial killers really *should* choose more productive ways to spend their time, that her sister Sarah was going to be out of control when their parents broke the news Madi had been murdered, that it was a really stupid twist of fate that Madi had found the man of her dreams only to lose him, and last—

That really looks like a squirrel.

"RUN!" Laurent bellowed as the little creature took two bouncing steps toward them and stopped, staring at them with interest.

"Wait, Laurent. It's just a squirrel!"

Between gales of laughter, she chased Laurent up the street. When she caught up to him, he was under a street lamp, gasping for breath.

"It was a squirrel." Madi giggled. "Just a tiny little squirrel."

"I didn't think it was. The shadow seemed a lot bigger. Perhaps a bear."

She wiped happy tears from her eyes. "That squirrel," she gasped, sides aching, "was *not* the size of a bear!"

He slid his arms around her and pulled her against his chest. "In either case, thank you for saving me. You're my hero."

Madi leaned in for a kiss. "Anytime . . ."

Madi sat in the front seat of her father's car, phone in hand, the trees blurring as they spun past. She replayed the last hours, a knowing smile on her lips. Laurent would text as soon as the train left the station, but there'd been no word yet, so she scrolled through the posts on her dashboard, waiting.

I just want someone who'll stay up late laughing over stupid television reruns, who'll sit on the counter and eat cereal straight out of the box while arguing fanon vs. canon, and who'll text me at two in the morning 'cause they just can't sleep.

2 weeks ago | 255 notes

#Love #Photography #Pixabay #I want this so badly

madlib likes this

johnlocker29 reblogged this from animaniac

animaniac reblogged this from nosferatoad

Yes, Madi thought. *That's exactly what I want.* Her smile faded. *But I can't see how it'll be with Laurent if he's returning to France when his student visa ends in a month.*

In the backseat, Sarah hummed tunelessly. In the front, Charles Nakama drove, looking inexplicably chipper. He whistled along to the radio. Madi flicked back to the messages on her phone. *C'mon, Laurent.* The impromptu date had been amazing, but as the night spread its dark wings over the town, she found herself caught between hope and fear. Things with Laurent were clearly heating up. Madi had no issue with that at all! It was that she couldn't see a way for it to work. He was leaving in mere weeks. As if drawn from her thoughts, a message from Laurent appeared.

the train is on its way. an obnoxious man is trying to talk to me, so i'm texting you instead. missing you terribly. 😕

me, too. thank u for coming today. i needed it 🙂

you're welcome. are you sure you can't come to schenectady next weekend? please, please, please, please, please, please!

sadly, no. i wasn't kidding about my english assignment or studying for finals. madlibs is going on hiatus until i get my rl figured out & that SUCKS 😩

would it help if someone guest-posted on your blog?

but who'd do that?

i don't know. maybe me or one of the other madlibbers? hey! we could do it from morag's house. (she's the one hosting the rewatch.) we could TOTALLY do that for you.

OMG—would u & morag do that for me??? not forever, just while i'm catching up on my new assignment. i could send a schedule, if that helps

for you, madi? anything. send details and i'll make it happen

u r the best. srsly 😍

merci. and now, sadly, I must go.

my phone is dying, and the man in the next seat
just pulled out a brochure to show me. (gah! I
may have to purchase insurance just to escape.)
talk to you soon. bye!

Madi glanced up as the sign for Millburn appeared, the transition occurring between one house and the other. The city was one part of a larger whole, more an appendage than its own entity, something Madi couldn't help but understand. She was here, but she wasn't anyone important. She had a role, but there was little more to it.

"You seem pretty quiet tonight," her father said.

"I just have a few things I have to do when I get home."

He cleared his throat. "Look, Madi. I . . . I know how difficult things have been for you since your mother left." His gaze darted over uneasily. "And I was thinking about it. You've always been so good with helping out with Sarah, and while that's great, the downside is that your mother and I have started *expecting* it." He stared forward, hands tight on the wheel.

"It's fine, Dad."

"Look—all I'm saying is it's really good to see you happy. You're smiling again these days."

"I am?"

"Yeah. You are. And it made me think about my own teen years. God! I didn't do half the things you do. Only had myself to worry about."

Madi had no idea how to respond. She'd always imagined her father born middle-aged.

"And I'm . . . I'm sorry about the pressure you've been feeling the last few weeks. It's just hard when your mother's away."

"I know, Dad."

"For what it's worth, I want you to know I'm going to try harder. Call me on it, if I don't."

"Um . . . okay?"

"So did things go all right with Laurent tonight?" Her father smiled to himself, and that left Madi uneasy. He was a worrier by nature.

166

"Yes. Why?"

"Well, I figured with school ending in June, you two might be making plans."

Madi felt her face begin to burn. "Plans for what?" she croaked. *Oh God, please don't answer that. PLEASE don't answer that!*

"I don't know. Something . . . together. Like taking a little day trip into the city or—"

"Dad, stop."

"Stop what?"

"Stop *this*."

"But—"

"I don't want to talk about Laurent, okay?" Madi's face was definitely on fire. She could feel the heat spreading down her neck, onto her chest. In a moment, she was certain she'd spontaneously combust.

"Why not talk about Laurent?" he asked. "I mean, you two seem good together."

"Dad, please!"

"Come on now, Madi. I've been in love before—"

"Dad! Seriously, though, STOP!"

Her father smothered laughter under his hand, hiding it by clearing his throat. She saw him look in the rearview mirror and she knew—without seeing—that he'd caught Sarah's eyes. It bugged her. She didn't want them talking about her.

"Look," her father said. "All I'm saying is that it's nice to see you happy and out again. Out with people." He glanced over at Madi. "Real people, as in *off* the Internet for once."

"Dad, Laurent is great, but he lives in New York."

Her father shrugged. "Didn't stop him from coming out to see you tonight."

"It's not only that. I just don't think the whole 'dating scene' is really my thing."

"But that's how you make memories, Madi. High school's a special time in your life. I like that you're getting out of the house a bit."

Madi didn't answer.

After a minute, her father spoke up. "I like your friend Laurent. He's very polite. Very personable."

Sarah's voice echoed from the backseat, "I'm pretty sure Madi likes Laurent, too."

Madi spun around, glaring at her sister. "I don't!"

"Do, too."

Her father smothered a chuckle.

And after that, all Madi could do was slouch in her seat and stare out the window, desperate for home. If her *sister* could see how bad she was crushing on Laurent Abelard, it must be obvious to the entire world. She hated the feeling. Online, she had the buffer of text. Here in the car, her blushing face was visible for all to see.

"Laurent's all right," she muttered. "For a friend."

"A friend, hmmm?" her father said with a wink. "Didn't look like that to me."

"Me, either," Sarah added.

The next time her phone buzzed again, Madi ignored it. What was the point? Laurent would be back in France by the time summer began.

Madi was stretched out on her bed, a pillow under her chin, when the phone in her hand buzzed. She flicked aside the dashboard posts to discover that a text from Laurent had appeared.

> you awake, madi?

"Laurent." The frown that had worn a groove between her brows since the car ride softened as she said his name. "What'm I supposed to do with you, hmmm . . . ?"

Although she appreciated her father's not-so-subtle efforts to nudge her toward social normalcy, she wasn't entirely sure she *could* be more than friends. Not when the deck was stacked so decidedly against them. Did she want to set herself up for relationship failure?

Unsettled, Madi rolled to her side and composed a quick reply.

> haven't gone to sleep yet. r u home now?

> just walked in the door. marco and jeannine—
> my host parents—were very snoopy about you.
> 😫 they worry about me, I think.

Madi smiled at his words. Her father—after years of watching Madi grow less and less involved with her peers—was pushing her straight into Laurent's arms. She wondered what Laurent's host family would think about that behavior. Shoving the pillow under her chest to give herself leverage, she typed in a reply one-handed.

> mmm . . . are they concerned i'm
> corrupting u or something?

> they're just protective. i think they're worried because
> i met you online. *gasp* not in the real world.

Madi smothered a bout of laughter into her pillow. She could only imagine their distress as Laurent tried to explain why he was running off to Millburn to meet up with a girl he'd connected with on the Internet. They must have thought the worst. She smiled as she sent another reply.

> hee! maybe they're worried i'm stalking you

> i'd invite you in if i found you
> lurking around under my window.

> u would, would you? (aside: that's actually a
> terrible idea, l. promise me u will never actually
> invite in a stranger waiting outside ur window.)

i'm KIDDING, madi. yes, i'll be terribly careful with strange women hanging out under the fire escape. 😄 but if it was YOU under my window, i'd invite you up.

this sounds like the beginning of a rom-com

would you come up?

u might convince me to climb up. But I'd probably be laughing. (i can't help it. i'm loud. ur host family would know i was there 2 seconds after we came inside.)

then i'd kiss you to muffle the sound.

and when you stopped giggling, i'd kiss my way down your neck.

Madi stared at the screen, heart pounding. The joking tone was gone. Laurent was dead serious, his words burning across her phone's screen. *I'm about to lose my phone-sex virginity,* she realized. She had no idea what she was doing! *Holy crap! This CAN'T be happening! What do I say? How do I sext?!?*

Madi's phone buzzed, jerking her away from Laurent's text. A message from her mother had appeared on the top of her screen. Scowling, she scanned through it.

Madi. It's your mom again. Are you around? I know it's late, but your father tells me you've been working on some school projects.

170

> How are things going? Have you checked out any study groups for your finals? Mom

Madi rolled her eyes. Leave it to her mother to walk in on her and Laurent at exactly the wrong moment. *Definitely a buzzkill.* Irritated, she ignored her mother's texts and returned to Laurent's message. She tapped in a quick reply.

> what else would u do, hmmm?

> i'd try to warm you up. 💕

> warm me up? (why am i cold?)

> because it's raining in ny tonight. you'd be chilled from standing out in the alley.

> brrr . . . 😄

> i'd pull you against me, and kiss you. my hands would touch you all the places i've imagined—

Madi's phone buzzed, but she ignored it, flicking the text aside. "Go *away*, Mom!" she growled, returning to the screen where a new text had arrived.

> Madi? You there?

> mmm . . . definitely. just imagining all the things u r doing to me

> What does that mean?

i'm still cold. waiting for u to warm me up

For a long moment, the pulsing dots told Madi that Laurent was replying. She grinned, imagining all the things he might say. Maybe they *could* figure out a long-distance romance. She held her breath. This was it. *The moment!* Her phone-sex virginity was about to be lost.

The text appeared.

Madison, are you on drugs? Please tell me the truth. I do NOT have time for this right now! I am very worried about your behavior. Mom

"Shit!" Madi dropped her phone, recoiling like it had stung her. In her rush to close her mother's text, she'd opened the wrong one to reply to. "Oh, no, no, no!" she chanted.

The phone buzzed again.

Madi? Answer me! I'm calling the house if you don't! Mom

Madi picked up the phone, fingers shaking as she typed in a reply. Her phone buzzed—Laurent was trying to message her, too—but she focused her reply on diverting her panicked mother.

sorry, mom. just woke up & my fingers are a little clumsy. my autocorrect did something weird there 😕

Are you sure, Madi? That sounded strange. What's going on with you? Have you been drinking tonight? You know that's not permitted. Mom

no, i haven't & nothing's wrong.

i'm just TIRED, mom. i need to go. i've been spending all my spare time studying

Please promise me you'll make good choices. Say no to drugs. Please!

first, calm down. I AM NOT ON DRUGS. god, mom. i need you to trust me, all right?

I'll talk to you tomorrow, I love you.

love you, too.

Madi flicked the text messages from her mother closed and reread the last text from Laurent, double-checking the name.

are you still around, madi?

just getting back. sorry, laurent. i kind of got intercepted by my mom. LOL (the mood's gone.)

c'est dommage! another time.

definitely

perhaps in person would work better. 😃

Heat rushed back to Madi's face and neck. His saying things like *this* was going to make it oh so much harder to say good-bye in the end. But right now, she refused to consider it. Falling in love wasn't something you decided on. *It just happened.* Her smile softened as she typed another text.

oh, laurent, now THAT is exactly what i needed to hear

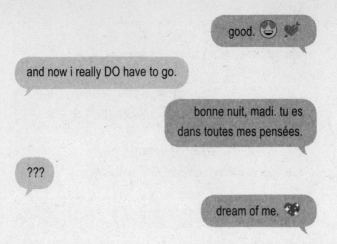

good. 😆 🥀

and now i really DO have to go.

bonne nuit, madi. tu es dans toutes mes pensées.

???

dream of me. 💘

Madi smiled and closed her messages. *Oh, Laurent. How's this ever going to work?* She scrolled through her dashboard one last time before bed. The first four posts were fandom-related, but the fifth seemed like it had been posted for her alone. She giggled and hit REBLOG.

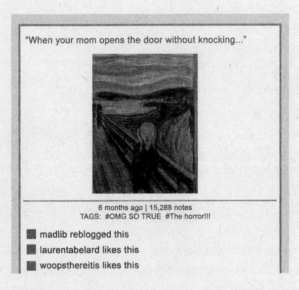

"When your mom opens the door without knocking..."

6 months ago | 15,288 notes
TAGS: #OMG SO TRUE #The horror!!!

◼ madlib reblogged this
◼ laurentabelard likes this
◼ woopsthereitis likes this

There were times she swore the Internet was sentient.

13

"This city is headed for a
disaster of biblical proportions."
(*Ghostbusters*, 1984)

An e-mail message was waiting for Madi when she flicked on her laptop. She read through it, her stomach twisting into a painful knot.

NEW Message,
AnnaRodriguez@MillburnAcademy.com: 7:51 p.m. EST
Priority: HIGH
Subject: RE: Possible Alternate Projects for English

Hello Madi,

Thanks for contacting me. I wish I'd been made aware of this issue earlier (so we could have arranged for some accommodation), but given Mrs. Preet's concerns, you are correct. The MadLibs blog is no longer an option.

I have listed four choices below. All are due on the same date as the previous assignment. I checked with Mrs. Preet, but given school rules, there is no chance of an extension.

Assignment Choice 1: An online blog of another topic. This will require the same number of discussion posts as the previous, so I'm not sure this is really an option, given the compressed time frame. If you do choose this one, be very careful regarding the school code. (Mrs. Preet has asked that I forward you the list of OMA's assignment requirements.)

Assignment Choice 2: A short story of between 15K and 25K words on a topic of your choice. See the attached grading rubric.

Assignment Choice 3: A series of five to ten nonfiction articles (with a total word count of between 15K and 25K) on a topic of your choice. As with the blog, this will need to have a thematic connection between posts. Rubric attached.

Assignment Choice 4: A digital video diary with accompanying written texts. These texts should be between 8K and 10K in total. The video diary must be at least four minutes long, with appropriate titling, edits, etc. (You may wish to contact the school's media instructor for assistance on the digital editing portion of this project.) Rubric attached.

Please let me know as soon as you've made your choice. And as finals are nearing, please note Millburn Academy has study groups on Tuesdays and Thursdays, directly after final bell. They're held in the library and are very helpful.

—Ms. Rodriguez

"Kill me now," Madi groaned, pushing the chair back from her desk.

No way was she getting out of this new project. She leaned back until she was almost reclined, staring at the ceiling. All the choices felt equally impossible, but if she didn't choose, she wouldn't graduate.

"It's not fair!" she snarled at the empty room.

With a weary sigh, Madi sat up and slid the chair back to her desk, scrolling through the options. She had no time to make a new website. No idea for a short story. And nonfiction articles were her father's passion, not hers. Her eyes caught on the final choice.

She hated all of them, but video making sounded the least like work. It just left her with one question: *What would her vlog topic be?*

Before she could decide, her phone buzzed and she fished it from her pocket. On-screen, a number of tweets jostled for position, Brian's irritated ranting taking up the most room. Rather than dealing with him, she closed the app and opened a Snapsed that had arrived seconds earlier. A smile ghosted over her lips as she saw it was from Laurent.

Wish you were here.

She started to type in a reply, then stopped. Her fingers hovered above the phone's screen. She needed to confirm that Laurent and Morag were willing to do a guest post. If she could arrange a week or two off, she'd have time to work on her English project *and* she wouldn't have to worry about losing traction with blogging. As much as she hated handing over the reins—even for a short amount of time—MadLibs could carry on without her . . . at least until she got her life in order.

"What could it hurt?"

Her phone vibrated in her hand before she could type anything. She looked down. Another tweet from @StarveilBrian1981 waited on-screen.

"God, Brian," Madi grumbled. "You need to chill, dude."

@StarveilBrian1981: @MadLib Why did you close the e-mails for the site? I wanted to send you a PM. #Disappoint

@MadLib: @StarveilBrian1981 Can't you just ask here, Brian?

@StarveilBrian1981: @MadLib I could, but character limits are pretty frustrating. It's a bit of a long one. :>/

@MadLib: @StarveilBrian1981 Fine. It's open again.
#CrossesFingers #TrollFreeZone

@ArtWithAttitude: @MadLib What's this I hear about you letting the
MadLibbers do a LIVEBLOG?!? #BestNews #AllTheThings

Madi stared at the screen in confusion. She reread Ava's tweet a second
time. "What the hell . . . ?"

@MadLib: @ArtWithAttitude How'd you hear about that?

@ArtWithAttitude: @MadLib @laurentabelard told me that he and
@ModernDayWitch are doing one. I'm so excited!!! CAN I DO THE
NEXT POST???

Madi frowned. It irked her that Laurent had already told someone about the
possible guest-posting. And *why* was Ava so happy about Madi going on hiatus?

@MadLib: @ArtWithAttitude Thanks, I think. Haven't decided on
official guest bloggers or schedule yet.

@ArtWithAttitude: @MadLib Really? That's not what I heard.

@StarveilBrian1981: @MadLib WAIT. Why are MadLibbers doing
the blog, not you? That isn't right. #QualityControl

@MadLib: @StarveilBrian1981 Long story, but things are a bit busy
right now. (End of the year.) I'll be back as soon as I can.

@StarveilBrian1981: @MadLib So no liveblog at ALL?!?

@MadLib: @StarveilBrian1981 Yes, a liveblog (online, like this), but
I won't be writing up the actual summary post.

Madi's frowned deepened. There was no use denying it. Ava had already made it public, so Madi might as well go for it. She added a quick second reply.

@MadLib: @StarveilBrian1981 Looks like @laurentabelard and @ModernDayWitch are working on the first one.

@ModernDayWitch: OMG I LOVE YOU @MadLib!! #GuestMadLibbing

@StarveilBrian1981: @MadLib I didn't agree to this.

@fandometric: @MadLib So where's everyone meeting up for this liveblog? #Awesomesauce

@ModernDayWitch: @fandometric Send me a PM, I'll get you details.

@MadLib: All right, guys. I gotta go. Schoolwork awaits.

@WrittenInChantalics: @MadLib Noooooo! You've got to STAY! I don't want a rewatch without you!!! :(

@ArtWithAttitude: WOOHOO!!! REWATCH TIME!

@MadLib: Sorry, @WrittenInChantalics. Got to go. *disappears*

Madi scowled at the phone's screen. She'd dealt with Brian's temper tantrum and had someone to cover her next MadLib post, but it left her feeling more exhausted than relieved. She rolled her thumb up the screen, rereading the conversation.

"What is your problem, Ava?" she grumbled.

Blogging was Madi's life. Handing it over to someone else took her freedom away. Having someone *try* to take it away from her was outright infuriating.

Irked, Madi opened up her e-mail from Ms. Rodriguez and scrolled through the choices for her final project.

Assignment Choice 1: An online blog of another topic.
Assignment Choice 2: A short story of between 15K and 25K words.
Assignment Choice 3: A series of five to ten nonfiction articles.
Assignment Choice 4: A digital video diary with accompanying written texts.

"Why can't it ever be easy?" she grumbled.

Madi was taking a break online when the guest blog, written by Morag and Laurent, popped up on her feed. She read through it with a growing sense of unease. It felt like someone had taken her favorite piece of clothing—her canvas shoes with the comic strip design on them—and worn them without permission.

Only, Madi had *allowed* them to borrow her blog.

Blog Post 214, Sunday 2:01 p.m.:
The Breakfast Club!

Welcome MadLibbers far and wide to MadLib's FIRST GUEST-BLOGGING EXPERIENCE. For those of you who haven't heard, our own @MadLib is in the throes of end-of-the-year drama, and to assist her, the two of us—@laurentabelard and @ModernDayWitch—will be serving as guest bloggers. We promise that @MadLib will soon be back and AT THE HELM! Until then, please be patient; we've no idea what we're doing. LOL

@ModernDayWitch: To begin, I absolutely LOVED *The Breakfast Club*. It starts off with a snapshot of high school society and the various cliques that make it up. For me (a little closer to the age of this film than the rest of you), it felt like a high school reunion. A little bit uncomfortable, but endearing all the same. How about you, L?

@laurentabelard: Er . . . This one wasn't my favorite. I *wanted* to fall in love with these characters, but I found myself losing track of who did what to end up in detention. They didn't speak to me in the same way individual couples in films usually do.

@ModernDayWitch: Aw . . . I love that you're a rom-com viewer at heart! <3 Beyond the main plot—which is pretty loosely stitched together, I'll admit—what I really loved was how the characters bring you into their experiences. I really *felt* them. They seemed like real people.

Madi's fingers drummed on the armrest as she read through the post. She wanted to like the post, but the fact it wasn't *hers* bothered her more than she wanted to admit. The comment box was open, but no one had left any replies, a rarity with a blog as massively popular as hers. She smirked. Was it wrong to be glad for that?

Her phone buzzed and Madi looked down to discover a text from Laurent had arrived.

so did you see it?

just reading it now

and????

still reading 😊

do you hate it? 😨 oh god. you hate it, don't you? (i knew you'd hate it.) c'est dommage. 😥

LOL relax. i like it, laurent

really? you actually like it?

yes, i really do. u & morag r a good mix 😊

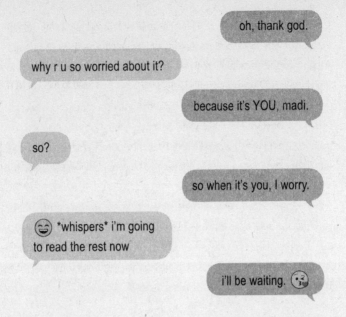

oh, thank god.

why r u so worried about it?

because it's YOU, madi.

so?

so when it's you, I worry.

😄 *whispers* i'm going to read the rest now

i'll be waiting. 😘

Madi smiled and set her phone next to the laptop. Knowing Laurent was waiting for her and worried about her reaction made her annoyance seem unjustified. The blog was actually pretty good. And it had been written specifically to give her time to work on her own project. They'd announced it was just a brief stint. It was ungrateful of her to dislike it on principle.

"And it's only for a little while," Madi said quietly. In a week or two, she'd be back. The thought excited her more than anything else.

She clicked REPLY and began to type.

Comments on Blog Post 214: The Breakfast Club!
Comment 1.1, @MadLib: Aw . . . thank you guys for doing this. It's great! (And I'm so grateful.) *goes back to studying*
 | @laurentabelard: For you, *minette*? Anything. :D
Comment 2.1, @TrollingLikeWhoa: I can't believe you guys pulled this kind of shit. WHO DO YOU THINK YOU ARE? I didn't think it was possible, but this is even WORSE than MadLib's garbage.
 | @laurentabelard: Casse-toi! You aren't wanted here.
 | @ModernDayWitch: I think you need to back off, @TrollingLikeWhoa.

> This blog has always been a welcoming place, and this type of flaming isn't tolerated. Consider yourself warned.
>
>> **@TrollingLikeWhoa:** Ooooooh! Whatcha gonna do about it? Burn some incense until I disappear? LOL Get used to me. I'M NOT GOING ANYWHERE.
>>
>>> **@MadLib:** Morag, text me—PLEASE.
>>>
>>>> **@TrollingLikeWhoa:** Well, well, well. If it isn't MADLIB HERSELF. How surprising to discover our MIA blogger isn't actually studying, but is sitting here in the shadows, reading her own blog. How's that feel, people? To know she LIED to you, huh? That she's the biggest FAKE out there?! You think she's your friend? MadLib is NOBODY'S friend but her own. She's just playing a game with you, and I'm going to STOP HER.

Session closed.
Comments disabled.

Madi stared at the screen in shock. The troll wasn't just back, he'd been waiting for her to appear. *And if he's watching the comments, then he's probably back at the private messaging, too.*

Stomach in knots, Madi opened the MadLibs e-mail service.

NEW Message, @TrollingLikeWhoa: 10:14 p.m. EST
Subject: Hi!
Helllloooooooo, Madi. You don't think I can see you there, but
I CAN.

Madi gasped, recoiling from the screen. She knew he couldn't actually see her, but she felt exposed. Another message appeared.

NEW Message, @TrollsCanPlayTheseGamesToo: 10:19 p.m. EST
Subject: No reply? :(

You disappoint me, Madi. I thought for sure you'd come out and play. (You played on Redux.)

Madi scrambled to open the e-mail settings for MadLibs, but another e-mail appeared before she'd finished resetting them.

NEW Message, @TrollYouOnce: 10:22 p.m. EST
Subject: Your Move
COME OUT COME OUT WHEREVER YOU
ARE!!!!!!!!!!!!!!!!!!!!!!!!!!!

She clicked INCOMING E-MAILS OFF, and the program began rerouting all incoming e-mails, bouncing them back one after the other.

Automated response to @TrollYouTwice: 10:23 p.m. EST
Private messaging for all e-mail clients on the MadLibs blog is currently closed. Please check back again later.
Automated response to @GetOutAndTROLL: 10:25 p.m. EST
Private messaging for all e-mail clients on the MadLibs blog is currently closed. Please check back again later.
Automated response to @EveryDayImTrollingYou: 10:27 p.m. EST
Private messaging for all e-mail clients on the MadLibs blog is currently closed. Please check back again later.

"Just leave me alone," Madi hissed. "I just want you to go away."

She didn't know what she'd done to cause this, but it was getting worse, not better. She wanted to scream. Sob. Disappear. With trembling fingers, she sent a text to Laurent.

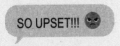

SO UPSET!!! 😡

let it go.
the troll's not worth it.

obv not, but I can hardly focus. ARGH!

will venting help? i'm here to listen.

it won't. (i mean u do help,
but i don't have time to vent.)

do you need me to come out?

u can't keep doing that, laurent! 🙁

i will if you need.

no. don't. (i need to study & i will
NOT be doing that if u r here. 😜)

i'm here, then. i'm around.

i know u r. thank you *HUGS* 😊

things will get better.

well, they can't get much worse

get some sleep, madi. you'll feel
better in the morning. 💕

But hours later, Madi was still wide-awake. Somewhere, she was certain the troll was laughing.

Madi yawned as she set the bowl and spoon in the dishwasher. "What do you mean, we're having a meeting at the school?" she asked.

Her father smoothed the edges of his carefully trimmed mustache. "The school called me while I was at the office, and said they needed to book a meeting with the two of us. I figured since you're home, we should just do it now."

"But *why* are we meeting?"

He stared at her over the top of his glasses. "I was hoping you could answer that."

"I . . . I honestly don't know."

"You sure?"

"Yes, I'm sure." Madi rubbed her palms on her sweater then tucked her hands under her arms. *Not good. This is so freaking not good!* "Did they say who called the meeting?"

"Mmph. Let me check." Her father reached into his pocket and pulled out his phone, scrolling through various appointments. "Looks like it was someone named Mrs. Preet. The message says she wants to clarify some kind of project requirements."

"Oh God."

Her father looked up from his phone. "Madi, what's going on? Is there something you're not telling me?"

"I—it's nothing, Dad. I just thought . . ." She darted from the room, pounding up the stairs. If Mrs. Preet wanted to out her, there was no way she could stop it from happening, but she wasn't going into the meeting without Ms. Rodriguez's emailed replies. "Hold on!" she shouted from her bedroom. "I've got to print off a few things before we go."

"All right. Meet me in the car."

Thirty minutes later they sat in Mrs. Preet's office. In the style of a modernist penitentiary, it had been painted a pale grayish green. Three framed pictures of poodles in tiny pink sweaters sat in a line behind her desk. Each one of them had hair with frizzy curls that matched their owner's.

"I'm certain you're both wondering why I called you here today," Mrs. Preet said gravely. "I'd hoped it wouldn't come to this. But I want to make sure we don't have any further confusion as the school year comes to an end."

Madi's father glanced over at her, raising his eyebrows in question. She couldn't even force a smile. *Oh my God, let me die now!* (God ignored her request.)

"As I'm sure you know," Mrs. Preet continued, "I'm in charge of Millburn Academy's online program, as well as vice principal of the regular high school."

"I'd heard that, yes," Mr. Nakama said.

"And have you heard about the issue with Madi's English project?"

There was an uneasy silence only broken when Mrs. Preet let out a weary sigh. "Oh dear, that's what I'd been afraid of." She straightened the pen and ink blotter on her desk before looking up again. "Madi made an error in her project requirements."

"Error?" Charles repeated.

"There are project requirements, Mr. Nakama. Rules *all* students must follow. Madi's blog broke one of the rules, preventing it from being submitted as a final project. It's put her in a bit of hot water."

Her father's eyebrows contracted together into a single, angry caterpillar. "Hot water?"

"Madi broke the school's code of conduct, Mr. Nakama. Her project was rejected."

Her father's gaze shifted onto her. "Madi . . ." He drew her name out in disappointment.

"I didn't know!" she cried. "No one told me I wasn't allowed ads on my site."

"And if that were the only issue," Mrs. Preet said quietly, "then I'd hardly be calling you in." She sat up straighter. "I called you because I've requested a formal reprimand be put on your daughter's record."

"A what?!" Madi surged to her feet. "You've *got* to be kidding me!"

"Madi, please," her father said.

"I can't believe this! Mrs. Preet is doing this on purpose. She's—"

"I'd like you to explain this reprimand, Mrs. Preet," Charles interrupted.

"She's broken the rules"—Mrs. Preet's mouth tightened—"a *second* time."

"Explain," Charles repeated.

"The school received an anonymous report," she said, shoving a pile of photocopied papers across the desk to Madi's father. He fiddled with his glasses, bringing them close to his face as he read. "A report the board has taken very seriously given the other issues with your daughter's classwork."

Madi nervously settled back into her chair. All the blood had drained from her extremities, and her hands were icy cold. "I—I don't understand."

"The informant claims you are plagiarizing the work of another student, who wrote the blog posts you submitted."

"But that's not true!"

"The informant says you used guest bloggers, who—"

"But it shouldn't matter!" Madi shook the e-mails she'd printed off from Ms. Rodriguez. "I'm not even using that post! It has nothing to do with—"

"At this point, our disciplinary committee is investigating the claim," Mrs. Preet said, ignoring Madi's outburst. "That's school policy whenever there is a complaint brought against a student. One of Millburn Academy's cardinal rules, and one that cannot be broken. But it's also important the parents of the accused be involved, since if Madi is found guilty, her final grades for English will be withheld." Mrs. Preet's expression was coldly unsympathetic. "Whether she finishes the alternate assignment Ms. Rodriguez has offered her *or not.*"

Charles's chin jerked up as if attached to a string. "Why *exactly* is my daughter doing an alternate assignment? She's been working on this blog all year. She's put hundreds of hours of work into it."

"I'm sorry to have to tell you this, but Madi's graduation is in jeopardy. She's broken the rules; she won't cross the stage unless she completes a new project."

"Why?!"

Kill me now, God. Please! Madi cringed, waiting for lightning to strike. (No luck.)

Mrs. Preet leaned forward. "She broke the code of conduct," she said calmly. "All her current blog postings have been rejected as inappropriate for submission."

Charles Nakama's face grew pale, his hands white-knuckled on the papers he held.

"I-I've got a new project started," Madi whispered. "I've started some preplanning. I'll get this done before the end of June, Dad. I promise!"

188

Mrs. Preet composed her hands in front of her. "I'm glad to hear that, Madi. And I hope that *this time* you've reviewed the rules."

Madi had the sudden, inappropriate urge to flip the desk over and attack. (That almost always worked in the movies.) Instead, she slouched lower.

"I read your stupid rules," she muttered.

"Good. And now that we've got all of this out in the open," Mrs. Preet said brusquely, "we should probably start talking about what this will mean for next year, since Madi—in all likelihood—will be returning for an extra semester of high school."

Her father was silent as they reached the car. Madi climbed inside, her heart pounding so hard she could hear it in her ears. Charles followed seconds later.

The door closed.

A minute passed. Then two. *Nothing.* Her father stared out through the window at the dancing leaves on the trees, the sun glinting on cars. His breath came in sharp pants, his face blotchy with color.

"Dad, please say something."

He glanced over. "Like what?" His lips were white, hands in fists where they gripped the wheel.

"I don't know. Something . . . anything. Please."

"I can't, Madi, I—" His voice broke.

"What?"

"I—I can't believe you lied to me." His voice was raw. "My own daughter. You . . ." He looked so broken that it rendered Madi momentarily speechless.

"I never lied."

Her father let go of the wheel, reaching up to pinch the bridge of his nose. "My God. What were you thinking?"

"But I didn't think . . ."

"No, you didn't. Madi, you aren't going to graduate unless you finish that class. You lied to me."

"I didn't lie. I just didn't tell you."

"But *why?*" For the first time, his voice rose. "Why didn't you come to me? You never said anything to me at all."

"Because I'm handling it."

"Handling it? You're about to flunk out of high school." He reached out for Madi's hand, squeezing her knuckles so tight it hurt. "I've been so worried about Sarah these last weeks, but I should've been thinking about you, too."

"It's fine, Dad."

He let go of her hand. "No, it's not. I just . . . I just can't keep up with everything these days."

"Sorry, Dad." Madi pulled her knees up and wrapped her arms around herself as her father started the car.

"Your mother is going to be furious when she hears about this."

"But I never lied. I just didn't tell you."

Her father ignored her explanation. He leaned his arm back over the seat to check that no vehicles were behind them before easing the car out of the parking spot. "I've never been so utterly embarrassed as I was today. Sitting there, finding out what had happened secondhand." Their eyes caught. "Oh, Madi, I wish you'd told me from the start. It's so much worse this way."

"I'm sorry, Dad. I should've said something, but—"

"You need to get this under control."

"What d'you mean?"

"We had a deal to keep things on an even keel at home. A deal where you did your part."

"But I have—"

"The Wi-Fi code is changing the minute we get back to the house. You can use your computer for submitting homework—I'll type the code in when you need to send in your projects—but no other fooling around online until Mrs. Preet tells me you've passed that course."

"But you can't just take away the Wi-Fi! That's not fair!"

He popped the car into drive and headed onto the quiet street. "I'm sorry. But I can and I have."

14

"Do . . . or do not. There is no try."
(*Star Wars: Episode V, The Empire Strikes Back*, 1980)

Madi's hands shook as she picked up her phone. She wanted to text, but with all the trembling, she couldn't get the letters to come out right.

> Omaha, I'm in so much troubadour!!!!1!

(Autocorrect was making it worse.)

"Damnit!"

She deleted the text and threw down the phone. Her laptop sat on her bed, but the code for the house's Wi-Fi had been changed the minute they walked in the door. (Sarah had argued with her father when she'd come home from school, but even *she* hadn't changed his mind.) Texting was fine, and the Internet access at the coffee shop and mall worked, too, but her phone's small wireless package would run out if she used it for more than the occasional peek. Madi's online access had been seriously impacted!

Luckily for Madi, their neighbors had coded their Wi-Fi with the simplest password ever: "Pickles," after their cross-eyed Pomeranian. As long as Madi stayed in the far corner of her upstairs bedroom—crouched by the windowsill—she could get a faint signal on her phone.

Madi typed in the neighbor's code and waited. After a moment, the phone connected to the wavering Wi-Fi signal, and a post appeared on her dashboard. She let out an angry laugh.

Parents: you need to get out of the house.

Me: i'd rather be online.

Parents: you have no idea what the real world is like.

Me: i have friends around the world.

Parents: PROBABLY ALL PREDATORS.

10 minutes later...

Parents: can you fix my e-mail?

Me: why? it's probably a predator.

Parents:

Me:

Parents:

Me:

Parents: this attitude comes from spending too much time online.

#parents #RL #frustrations

192 notes | 8 months ago

◼ roombazaboomba likes this
◼ kazieka-super-gurl likes this

Isn't that the truth?

Fighting another wave of tears, Madi closed the post and selected DIAL rather than TEXT, then waited as the phone clicked through the connections. The phone rang three times. She half expected it to go to voice mail—*does anyone answer telephones anymore?*—when Laurent's voice echoed through.

"Allo?" Laurent's voice through the phone was sleepy, and Madi had the sudden worry she'd woken him.

"Hey, Laurent," she croaked. "You have a minute to talk?"

"Madi? Is that you?"

She swallowed against the lump in her throat. "Yeah. It's me."

"You . . . phoned." He sounded like he'd just found the sky had turned pink without him noticing.

"Is that okay?"

"Totally fine. I just—I didn't expect a call. You sound sick."

Madi closed her eyes, leaning her head against her knees and focusing on the sound of his voice. "Not sick." She sniffled. "Crying."

"Oh, *minette*, but why?"

She tried to answer, but a sob came out instead. Madi fumbled around her dresser, searching for tissues. "I'm in so much trouble."

"Is this the English project? You know I'll help in any way I can."

"Yes, it's to do with English, but it's more than that, too." Another loud sob broke free of her chest. "Someone told the school I plagiarized. My projects are being reviewed."

"Plagiar . . ." She heard the phone being moved around, things shifted. "Let me check—"

"It means the school thinks I cheated!" she cried. She swiped angrily at her tears. "I need to graduate. Oh my God. I don't know what to do!"

"What are the options for the assignment again?"

Madi's hand reached out for her now-missing laptop before falling back to her side. "One was a short story."

"Sounds all right?"

"It would be if I had a single creative bone in my body."

"I think you're very creative."

"Not like that," Madi said. "Besides, it's a *long* short story. And I don't have any ideas right now."

"Fair enough. What're the other choices?"

"A new online blog."

"You're great at blogging! Do that one."

"Can't," Madi said. "The anon who turned me in for plagiarizing is definitely targeting my MadLibs site."

"You could make a new website."

"I could, but my dad's guarding our Wi-Fi code until I finish my stupid project. I'd need the Internet for website building. And I have to help with Sarah every day, so I can't very well spend all my time mooching Wi-Fi at the coffee shop. God, I feel like I'm trapped in a John Hughes film! I just need Molly Ringwald to show up and start complaining about her parents ignoring her." She made an angry sound of frustration. "I *wish* my parents would ignore me!"

Laurent began to laugh. "Oh, Madi. No one could ignore you. You're too loud." And for the first time since her father's angry explosion in the car, Madi smiled.

"Thanks."

"So, what's choice number three?"

"A series of nonfiction articles. But I can't think of a topic."

"Number four?"

"A bunch of video diary entries."

"That's the one," Laurent said.

"What? But why?"

"Just do what you did outside the Metrograph that night."

There was a long pause as Madi searched her memory. Had she done anything that night other than moon over Laurent and feel awkward? "I don't remember . . ."

"You did a running commentary on *Blade Runner*," he said. "You talked about the film, and then later, your family and school. You're a natural in front of people. You're funny and smart. A vlog would be great!"

Madi chewed her lower lip. Perhaps it *wasn't* such a crazy idea. "I don't know. It's different with a camera."

Laurent chuckled. "So pretend the camera's not there."

"But—"

"I'll help you."

Madi groaned. "I hate being on film. I don't even like having my picture taken."

"But you're *already* Internet famous. What's the difference if people see you?"

"It's different to me."

"Ah . . ."

She pressed her eyes closed, wishing she could rewind back to the moment they'd been walking on the path by the ruins. A memory of Laurent, crouched by a slab of stone, camera in hand, flashed to mind.

"Are you serious about helping me? 'Cause I'd need someone to film it."

"Of course I will." The phone shifted. "Hold on a sec. All right?"

There was the distant sound of a television, followed by the sound of a door closing. It grew quiet in the seconds before Laurent's voice returned.

"You still there?"

"Mm-hmm."

"All right, so what are you going to vlog about?"

Another roadblock.

"I, um . . . I . . ." Suddenly, the answer appeared. "How about I come into the city some weekend and liveblog the experience?"

"Awesome! And I could take all the footage."

"Thank you. I really appreciate this, Laurent."

"It's no problem. Besides, there are so many places we need to go."

Madi's eyes popped open. "Oh?"

"I mean, photos are fine, but I'd rather show you places, you know?"

Madi nodded to herself. "Yeah, I know."

"So plan a day you can visit," Laurent said. "You talk, I'll film. It'll be good, Madi. *Really* good."

She grinned. "You think so?"

"You and me teaming up?" Laurent chuckled. "I *know* so."

"Yeah. Maybe it will."

And for the first time, she actually felt excited about where this mess might lead.

Madi was on her unmade bed, typing out a rough plan for the vlog, when Sarah knocked on the door.

"Busy right now," Madi said.

"Dad says it's time for dinner."

"Tell him I'm not hungry."

Madi waited for Sarah to retreat downstairs. She didn't. The knocking started up again.

"What?!" Madi snapped, hitting SAVE.

"I want you to come down."

Madi closed her laptop and flopped face-first on the bed. "Why?" Her voice was muffled by the comforter.

"'Cause we *always* eat together."

Madi groaned and rolled onto her back, staring up at the ceiling. She had too much to do right now, and Sarah's schedule was *not* helping.

"I'm sure you can handle eating alone. I've got a lot of homework to catch up on." She closed her eyes. "And I don't feel like dealing with Dad right now."

She heard the door open and Sarah step into the room. Footsteps crossed the floor. Madi opened one eye to see Sarah frowning down at her in concentration.

"What?" Madi grumbled.

"Why're you so mad at me?"

Madi shoved herself up on her elbows. "I'm not mad at *you*, Sarah. I'm mad at all the other crap going on in my life."

"Is this about the phone call about your graduation?"

"Wasn't about graduating," Madi said. "It was a stupid issue at school."

"What kind of issue?"

"I have to redo an English project."

"Why?"

"Because the last one wasn't acceptable." Her sister opened her mouth to ask another question, so Madi rushed to explain. "There was an issue with my MadLibs site. It didn't fit the parameters of the project. I broke the rules, and Mrs. Preet *loves* her stupid rules. And that's why I'm stuck redoing it."

"Oh." Sarah's scowl deepened. "But didn't you read the project guidelines before you started the blog? You should always read the rules before you—"

"Yes, I read them! No, I didn't know about the rule."

"Oh." After a moment, Sarah spoke. "Sorry for bothering you."

Guilt twinged under Madi's annoyance. "Wait, Sarah. I'm coming, I'm coming." She climbed from the bed. "So that was my awful day," she said. "How'd yours go?"

Her sister paused in the doorway. "It was fine," she said. "Robbie asked if I wanted to go to a movie."

Madi's eyes widened. "He did?"

"Yeah, he and his friend Gavin are going."

"Gavin?"

"Black hair. Moody," Sarah said as she headed toward the stairs. "Anyhow, supposedly Gavin wanted *you* to come along, too."

"Huh. That's . . . weird. And?"

"And what?"

"And are you going with them?"

Sarah glanced back at her, pausing midstep. "No. Robbie only asked me to go to the movie because he likes you. I don't know what Gavin wants. I thought he hated everyone."

"Me, too."

Her sister shrugged, heading into the kitchen. "Doesn't matter either way. I don't feel like going to a movie with them."

"Why?"

"I prefer our rewatches."

If there was something Madi appreciated about her father, it was that he didn't hold grudges. Throughout supper, he made cheerful small talk while Madi answered him in grumbles.

"It's not the end of the world," he said.

"Feels like it."

"I promise it's not."

"Hmmph."

"Believe me." Her father chuckled. "When you get your first tax audit? *That's* a reason to panic."

"Thanks, Dad, but that doesn't help."

Planning out her new English project made time drag on forever. Near midnight, Madi came down to get a snack. Partway down the stairs she heard voices. Her father was online, Skyping with Madi's mother, their voices rising and falling in the darkness. She sat down on the step, listening.

"She didn't tell us because she thought she was handling it," her father said. "That speaks more to Madi's strengths than any perceived weakness."

"But she isn't going to graduate! My God, Charles! What will people think?"

"They'll think whatever they want. And an extra semester is only one option. Madi's redoing the project she missed. It's a large one, I'll give you that. But it's just one. I believe she'll get it in."

"She'd better."

"She will. We need to trust her on that, Julia. She needs our support, not our condemnation."

Madi tiptoed back up the stairs, throat aching.

By the following morning, Madi and her father had settled into a truce. Over the next week, she plugged away at the scripts for her New York vlog. The more she wrote, however, the more difficult it became. She needed to *be* in the city to channel its energy. She needed to react. *Feel.* Frustrated, she walked down to the train station and booked her ticket for the upcoming weekend. It was time to face her fears, stop planning, and start filming.

She looked down at the ticket and smiled. *A weekend with Laurent in New York . . .* If there was a silver lining to the situation, that was it.

After leaving a voice message with her aunt Lisa on Friday—confirming her arrival and departure times—she headed back to the school to pick up her sister. The hallways of Millburn Academy were blessedly empty, and Madi was grateful. (She wasn't sure she could control herself around the rule-fixated Mrs. Preet for one minute longer.) Twice on the return home, Madi pulled out her phone, but there were no new messages from Laurent. The separation from her online life with MadLibs had left her more anxious than usual, and after setting a frozen lasagna in the oven, Madi headed up to her room, taking her new favorite spot under her windowsill.

She was checking her e-mail with the faint Wi-Fi signal pirated from her neighbor when the message arrived.

NEW Message, Trollify@hackster.com: 3:49 p.m. EST
Priority: Normal
Subject: Knock, knock
Didn't think you'd get rid of me so fast, did you? LOL

"Oh, you little shit." Temper flickering to life, Madi typed in a terse reply.

Reply to Message from Trollify@hackster.com: 4:01 p.m. EST
Subject: RE: Knock, knock
Why are you emailing me?!? Actually, don't answer. I am DONE
and you are BLOCKED. Go away!
E-mail address blocked

She'd just finished checking the other messages in her e-mail folder when a *new* message appeared. Furious, Madi scanned it, her hands tightening around her phone.

NEW Message, TooTrueForYou@hackster.com: 4:04 p.m. EST
Priority: Normal
Subject: Little pig, Little pig, LET ME IN
You SJWs always underestimate me. And THAT pisses me off.
I'm not playing games here, MadLibs. I know where you live.

"I'm so sick of you," Madi muttered as she tapped in a reply. "GO. AWAY."

Reply to Message from TooTrueForYou@hackster.com:
4:06 p.m. EST
Subject: RE: Little pig, Little pig, LET ME IN
You think that gaslighting's gonna work with me? Not likely. I'm
going to keep blocking you. (The admin is already working on

blocking your server.) Go home and play with yourself. I'm not interested. >:>/ Good-bye. Troll.

E-mail address blocked

She was in the middle of reading a slowly loading information page on blocking all e-mails from a particular server when the next e-mail arrived. She swore under her breath as it popped open.

"Stupid trolls trying to flame my blog." Her words faded into shocked silence.

NEW Message, TestyTrolling@hackster.com: 4:08 p.m. EST
Priority: HIGH
Subject: I'll huff and I'll puff
You live on Farley Road. Your house has two levels. It's white with green shutters. Believe me yet? LOLOLOL

"Oh my God," Madi whimpered. This wasn't flaming, this was *doxing*. The troll had somehow uncovered her personal information. If he exposed her, he exposed her family. But beyond Madi's concerns for her father's journalistic career, she had a sudden, biting moment of real fear. *What if he comes after me?* The thought was too terrifying to consider.

Heart in throat, she composed a short answer, sending it off before she could think better of it.

Reply to Message from TestyTrolling@hackster.com:
4:10 p.m. EST
Subject: RE: I'll huff and I'll puff and
This isn't funny anymore. :(
E-mail address blocked

She flicked back to the help site, searching for details on blocking a server. "Come on . . . come on!" A new message appeared just as she finished resetting the permissions to her e-mail.

NEW Message, DevilsInTheDetails@hackster.com: 4:11 p.m. EST
Priority: HIGH
Subject: I'll BLOW YOUR HOUSE DOWN
LOL I disagree. This is HILARIOUS. I'm having a GREAT time
playing with you.

Rattled, Madi deleted the e-mail, then followed the directions for blocking a server. In seconds, she had the settings altered. On-screen, the automated reply appeared—following the newly arriving messages and bouncing them back before they could make it to her inbox.

Automated response to *all users*@hackster.com: 4:12 p.m. EST
Messages from this server have been rejected by the e-mail
client. Please contact the system administrator.
Automated response to *all users*@hackster.com: 4:13 p.m. EST
Messages from this server have been rejected by the e-mail
client. Please contact the system administrator.
Automated response to *all users*@hackster.com: 4:15 p.m. EST
Messages from this server have been rejected by the e-mail
client. Please contact the system administrator.
Automated response to *all users*@hackster.com: 4:17 p.m. EST
Messages from this server have been rejected by the e-mail
client. Please contact the system administrator.

Madi waited, phone in hand, until the direct message stopped appearing. Whoever the troll was, he'd given up.

"I-it's over," she said in a shaky voice. But somehow, she knew that wasn't the truth.

Sarah stood in the doorway, watching as Madi packed.

"I can't believe you're leaving," she said glumly.

Madi paused with a pair of half-folded jeans in hand. "I'm going to New

York, Sarah, not Mars." She set the pants on the growing pile. "I'll be home on Sunday."

"You always said you wouldn't go."

Madi groaned. "It's a weekend, not forever."

"I hate it."

Madi left the half-packed bag and walked to her sister's side. "I have a project to finish. New York is the topic. There's no choice about it. Okay?"

"You sure this isn't about that boy? The one who lives in New York."

Madi sighed. "Laurent's helping me film, but the trip's not *about* him."

"What if I want to talk to you while you're gone?"

"Then text or call," Madi said. "I'll answer."

Her sister scowled. "It's not the same."

"It's not the same, but it's close." Madi nodded to the hallway. "Step outside."

"Where?"

"Go into the hall." She nudged her sister out of her room. "I'm right here, okay?"

"Okay."

Madi closed the door and slowly turned the lock. "You can hear me, right?"

"Of course I can," Sarah said irritably.

"All right. You've got your phone?"

"Uh-huh."

"Now imagine I'm in New York."

The door handle jiggled.

"Madi?"

(She didn't answer.)

"Madi?!"

Sarah jiggled the door handle harder.

"MADI! Open up! I don't like this!"

Madi pulled out her phone and tapped in a quick text.

> stop yelling! dad's going to freak

"Then let me in!" Sarah's voice rose anxiously. "Why'd you lock the door?"

Madi tapped in another answer, hoping it'd arrive before their father did.

> srsly—stop YELLING, sarah! 😫
> text me

"Why can't I just talk to you?" Her sister's voice wavered, close to tears.

> bc I'm not in millburn, remember?

"But you're in your room and . . ."

Her sister's voice disappeared midsentence. A few seconds later, Madi's phone buzzed.

> I don't like texting.

> ur just not used to it

> It's weird.

> it's a different way of talking

> What do you mean?

> u know how sometimes u wish you could know what people r thinking instead of guessing?

> Yeah.

> this way you can, bc u get my thoughts directly. there's no guessing. i write it, u read it

I don't know about that.

ask me something 😜

Why are you leaving?

bc i have to finish my project

I hate when you're far away.

i know 🙁 but i'm still here for u, just not right beside u. make sense?

Sort of.

u can text whenever you want. i'll answer. u can phone me if you need to hear my voice 😃

I guess that's okay.

i love you, sarah. that's not changing. the space between us is just stretching a bit

Love you, too, Madi.

HUGS

I don't like hugging.

LOL i know

But I guess that one wasn't so bad. 🤗

Madi's father stood in the waiting area, his hand tight on her shoulder, Sarah two steps away.

"And if you need anything," her father said, "you call your aunt Lisa and she'll deal with it."

"I know that, Dad."

"Keep the extra twenty in your pocket at all times. Not your wallet; *your pocket*. That way if you lose one you've got the other as a backup."

"I know, Dad."

"And you make sure you don't go anywhere alone. Even during the day. New York is a much safer city than it used to be, but you're still young. It's a big place. Things happen."

Madi groaned. "Dad, I'm eighteen. I know how to take care of myself. I've been there like ten times before."

"You've never stayed overnight alone."

"I'm not going to be alone. I'll either be with Laurent or Lisa: overprotective escorts on both sides."

"Just promise me you'll be careful."

"I *will* be careful." Madi sighed.

"And you'll call me when you arrive—"

"And tell you where I go, and who I'm with, and when I'm leaving." Madi reached out and hugged her father. "I know all of this, Dad. You need to calm down about it."

She stepped back to find him frowning.

"I'm only agreeing to this because of Ms. Rodriguez's call," he said. "I'm still worried about you."

"I know you are."

"This is a test as much as anything," he said. "You go, you do your filming, you stay overnight with Lisa, and you come home Sunday morning."

"I know, Dad."

Her father's expression shimmered with something Madi couldn't decipher, and then he cleared his throat. "Well, then. You should say good-bye to Sarah and go."

Madi looked over to find her sister watching. Sarah's forehead crumpled as their eyes met.

"I'm coming back on Sunday," Madi said, answering the question before her sister asked it. "You can phone or text me any time you want. I'll let you know what I'm doing." She grinned. "I can even send you pictures if you want."

Sarah nodded.

"I'm coming back," Madi repeated.

Her sister didn't answer.

"I am. I promise."

Sarah sighed. "Okay."

Madi pulled her into a tight hug. As always, she got to the count of three before Sarah began to squirm. She didn't let go, just pressed her face into her sister's hair and breathed. There were some times her little sister felt like a lead weight tied to her foot, but other times she felt so protective of her it hurt to step away. This was one of those times.

"Madi," Sarah grumbled, her arms coming up to wriggle free.

"I know, I know." She laughed as she released her.

"You should board the train." Her father lifted her backpack. "And don't forget about keeping a twenty in your pocket, even—"

"I *know*, Dad. Stop worrying."

"Mmph."

"I'll miss you, too," Madi said, shouldering her pack and heading to the train. She took a seat by the window, watching as her sister and her father grew smaller and smaller, before fading from view. Madi's smile disappeared as she imagined her mother, thousands of miles away—a pinprick in the distance.

Was this how Mom felt when she left them behind?

Madi caught sight of Laurent the second she walked into Penn Station. (At his height, he was hard to miss.) He peered over the heads of the crowd, and Madi grinned as she watched him unawares. His lean, muscled build hinted that he might be a track star, but the longish hair and intricate tattoo on his arm threw the athlete look completely off. Laurent was hot.

"Hot damn," Madi murmured as she pulled her backpack onto her shoulders.

Laurent craned one direction, searching, before swinging back the other way. He seemed oblivious to the effect he had on people, but as he worked his way through the crowd, Madi noticed the appraising gaze he received from women of all ages. He shoved a hand through his hair, tucking it back behind his ear. His face broke into a wide smile as he caught sight of her.

"Madi!" He waved enthusiastically. "I thought I'd missed you!"

Madi waded into the milling crowd, Laurent immediately disappearing as she was caught in an ocean of strangers. *This* was what Madi hated about her height. She stood on tiptoe to peek over the sea of shoulders until she caught sight of Laurent again. He was grinning as he headed straight toward her. Madi pushed her way through the final knot, catching herself against Laurent's chest.

"You're here," he said, and leaned down to pull her into a hug.

"The train was late, and I—wait! Whoa! Oh my God, what're you *doing*?!"

Madi cackled with high-pitched laughter as Laurent lifted her into his arms. He held her up against his chest in a way that reminded her of the water-jumping pose from *Dirty Dancing*. It was awesome and silly, and she couldn't quite believe it. Her giggles faded as he let her slide from chest height, to face-to-face. *Like some scene from a movie,* Madi thought. *Only thing he missed was—*

Laurent leaned in and kissed her.

The crowd disappeared. Sounds faded. Time stopped. Madi wrapped her arms around his shoulders, feeling his mouth wander over hers, his hands holding her up as if she were a feather. Finally, he broke the kiss and set her down and brushed his hands over her shoulders. She beamed up at him.

"Hello to you, too."

"You need a hand with your bag?"

"I'm fine," she said, blushing. (Was everyone watching them? It felt like they were.) "It's only an overnight bag."

"Ready to go?"

"First I need to text my dad."

"You sure I can't hold that for you?" Laurent asked. "I want to help."

"I'm good," she said, shifting her bag to the other shoulder. "Just give me a sec." She fought her phone from her pocket and typed in a quick text one-handed.

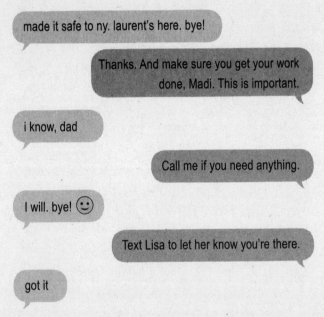

made it safe to ny. laurent's here. bye!

Thanks. And make sure you get your work done, Madi. This is important.

i know, dad

Call me if you need anything.

I will. bye! 😊

Text Lisa to let her know you're there.

got it

Her phone's screen pulsed with another reply, and Madi groaned. (Leave it to her father to become a mother hen at the worst possible second.)

And given your company, I'd prefer you did your homework first, and had fun with Laurent second.

A wave of heat rose up Madi's neck, and she tucked her phone away. She felt it buzz again but didn't answer it.

"Everything okay?" Laurent asked.

Madi reached out and took his hand. "Perfect."

"I thought we'd start with coffee." He glanced over in concern. "If that's all right with you."

"It'd be better than all right. It'd be awesome."

And with coffee on her mind, a pack on her shoulders, and Laurent at her side, Madi's New York adventure began.

Madi sat at the table in the coffee shop, her phone beside her, as she tried to connect to the MadLibs site with the free Wi-Fi. The café was smaller than she'd expected from Laurent's Snapsed pics, but cozy. Warm wood counters met exposed brick walls. Jazz played on the sound system.

On the other side of the shop, Laurent waited at the counter. When Madi's phone finally connected, she looked up and caught him watching her.

Just a second, he mouthed.

Madi nodded, her gaze drifting over him. If her entire life had turned into an '80s movie, Laurent was doing his best to play the part of the romantic lead. He towered half a head above the tallest guy in the coffee shop, and when he flicked his hair, he looked like a model from a shampoo ad. *Well, if he's going for the heartthrob role, he certainly looks the part.*

Madi grinned and looked back down at her phone. MadLibs was taking forever to load.

"My firstborn child for decent Wi-Fi," she groaned.

Before her eyes, the page's URL abruptly changed. Madi blinked in confusion, then hit BACK. The MadLibs site began loading, and then, a second time, the page launched to a secondary site. She glanced up at the html address bar, double-checking that she'd typed it in correctly. *MadLibs.* It bounced a third time. Confused, she watched as a series of lurid images appeared and a man's nude body flashed on-screen.

"What the hell?"

Behind her, someone snickered. She swiveled to see a young man sitting at a table by the door, his hand over his mouth as he laughed down at his phone's screen. With jet-black hair that hung in his eyes and an oversized hoodie, his face was nearly invisible. Madi's phone buzzed, and she glanced down as three more images—each more lewd than the next—appeared on the piggybacked site.

"Oh shit!"

This time the teen's chuckling was distinct. Her chin jerked up. *Who the hell is that?!* She slid her chair away from the table. *Could he be the troll?!* The thought was so bizarre—so completely out of the blue—that Madi couldn't breathe. She stared at the nameless boy, but his gaze was on his phone. He began to cackle.

"Who in the world . . . ?"

It was the troll, Madi realized. *It had to be!* And she needed to call the police. Heart thudding, she imagined what she'd say. There was a troll attacking her. He'd followed her to New York. He wanted to screw up her life—*her real life!* That'd mean hours of questions, her father involved. *No time to spend with Laurent.*

Forced to consider her options, doubt needled its way into Madi's certainty. What was her proof that this was the troll, other than a gut feeling that the kid in the hoodie was someone she knew? That he'd hijacked her site? It sounded crazy. Maybe it was. She squinted, trying to get a good look at the boy's face. There was something unnervingly *familiar* about him.

The hallway of Millburn Academy flashed to mind. *The day I picked Sarah up, I saw a black-haired kid who—*

"It's Gavin!" Madi rose shakily to her feet. She needed to find out for sure.

Before she'd taken two steps, the black-haired teen abruptly stood and stalked out the door, leaving her standing alone. Madi's hands trembled around her phone as she stared after him walking down the street. From the side, he looked far less like Gavin than he had before. Maybe it hadn't been him after all.

"Everything okay?" Laurent asked.

Madi squeaked and sat back down in her chair, flipping her phone—and the hacked site—facedown on the tabletop. Her face burned as she held the POWER button down, waiting for the phone to turn off. How much had Laurent seen? When she got to her aunt Lisa's, she needed to check the site's security settings and figure out who was hijacking her MadLibs URL. With a few tweaks, she should be able to block any outside attack.

"Madi . . . ?"

"Everything's fine," she said with a nervous laugh. "Just having some trouble with the MadLibs site. That's all."

"Anything I can help with?"

"Not really. It's fine. I'll fix it tonight." She glanced out the windows of the café. The teen was gone.

"Ah." Laurent set a cup in front of her. A waft of coffee rose to her nostrils, and she took a deep breath, the phone momentarily forgotten. "This is for you."

Madi forced away her anxiety over the black-haired stranger. *Think about that later.* She looked down at the complex image of a lotus, floating in the foam of her cappuccino, and smiled. "Oh, wow! Thank you."

"The barista says you're lovely," he added, sliding into the chair across from her. "She also thinks it's good I brought an actual *person* on a date, rather than just sitting here alone, looking pitiful."

Madi giggled and peeked over at the counter. A young man and a middle-aged woman with her chin propped in her hands were watching the two of them with obvious interest. Madi looked back to Laurent, dropping her voice.

"So, do you take all your dates here?"

"All?"

She smirked. "I'm assuming you're pretty popular, Laurent. I mean, those two"—she tipped her head toward the counter—"can hardly keep their eyes off you."

"Not so much." He laughed.

"What's that mean?"

"Let's just say dating's not my thing."

Madi grinned. "Now, *that's* something I need to hear about." He groaned, and Madi scooted her chair closer. "C'mon, Laurent. I want the rest of the story."

He crossed his arms on his chest. "There's nothing to tell."

"That's not true."

He ran his hand over the back of his neck, wincing. "No, I can't."

"C'mon, Laurent. I've told you lots of embarrassing things."

"Fine." He sighed. "Truth is, I'm terrible with women."

"Really?"

"Absolutely hopeless."

"That's not true. You're amazing."

As soon as the words were out of her mouth, she regretted it. Laurent's smile spread until his face was incandescent. "You think so?"

"Well, yeah," Madi said drily. "But it's not a matter of thinking. Everyone can see it."

"Not everyone. But I like that you noticed me."

"Um, yeah." On the street, a steady stream of people moved past. She wondered if anyone else was as terrible at blurting things out as she was. (If there were an Oscar for this sort of thing, she'd win it.) "Anyhow," she said, forcing her way through the awkwardness, "I remember you talking to me and the rest of the MadLibbers. That didn't seem too hard."

She looked up to find him smiling. It wasn't the wide grin from before; this was gentler. It felt like something meant for her alone, and she couldn't stop herself from returning it.

"That was only because I didn't care with them."

"What do you mean?"

He shook his head. "It's easy to talk to someone if you're not worried. If you don't care what they think. The MadLibbers were the same as I was." He sighed. "As soon as I start worrying about fitting in, I clam up."

"What's there to worry about?"

"I'm too much of a geek."

"Too much?" Madi said. "I don't think that's possible. Geekdom is a badge of honor online."

"Well, yes and no. That's how I got into your blog, you know. You were doing the whole retro comic reread at one point last year." He dropped his eyes. "I, er, have a bit of a comic book addiction."

"I didn't know that," Madi said, grinning.

"Not exactly the first thing I admit to dates."

"How many?"

"How many what?"

"How many comic books do you own?"

Laurent shifted uneasily in his seat. "I don't know if I should tell you."

"Please?"

"I don't think I should."

"Oh, come on!" Madi said, laughing. "You've got to tell me now."

"It'll make me seem crazy."

"Hardly! It's not like you're weaving sweaters from belly button lint or keeping toenail clippings in jars."

Laurent's face contorted in shock. "That's . . . horrible."

"See? Those are all things I've seen on the Internet. You're completely normal by comparison."

"All right," he sighed. "I have close to two thousand comic books. A hundred or so graphic novels, some signed. And most are ones I've read, but I, um, I have a few first editions, wrapped in plastic." He cringed. "That's really weird, isn't it?"

She smiled so wide her cheeks hurt. "No, Laurent. It's not."

He dropped his chin, studiously stirring sugar into his cappuccino.

"So you're a geek's geek, hmmm?" Madi lifted her cup, taking a sip. "I happen to like that about you. You're passionate about whatever we rewatch. I find you really easy to talk to."

"Ah, but I find it hard getting to know new people outside fandom. The few people I hang out with are connected to that culture. Friends I'd met at comic conventions."

"But you talked to me."

"Online first, then by Skype, and later at the MadLibbers get-together. Plus, I'd invited you, so when I went to pick you up, it kind of . . ." He fiddled nervously with his spoon, tapping it on the wooden tabletop. "Pushed me forward."

"Then fireworks, right?" Madi joked.

Laurent didn't laugh. His palm slid forward and he caught hold of her hand, pressing tight. "Yes, *minette*. For me, at least."

And to that, Madi had no answer at all.

15

"When you realize you want to spend the rest
of your life with somebody, you want the rest
of your life to start as soon as possible."

(*When Harry Met Sally*, 1989)

Saturday provided even more excitement. In a quiet side street, Laurent insisted Madi close her eyes and let him take the lead. Lids pressed tight, she stumbled blindly forward.

"Where are you taking me?"

She shivered as Laurent's mouth brushed the shell of her ear. "Just trust me. All right?" His fingers tightened around hers. "Almost there."

"Okay."

In the last minutes, Laurent had slipped on her backpack, taking one of her hands in his, the other hand sliding around her waist. She wasn't sure where they were, but she could smell damp cement, mildew, and decay. The sounds of the city had dimmed in the last seconds, the red glow of sun through her eyelids replaced by darkness.

"You know I don't like scary movies, right? No screamers on my dashboard. No trolls in the dungeon." She shuddered. "Definitely no trolls."

Laurent laughed. "This is good, Madi. I promise." His scruff brushed her cheek, voice low. "Just a little farther. Here. Take a step down. Don't let go of my hand. This is definitely something you'll want to include in your video of New York."

"If you're certain. I mean, I'm not even sure where . . ." Madi stumbled, but he caught her, the faint scent of cologne rising as he helped her regain her footing.

"And one more step," he said. "A little to your left. Aha, almost there now. Hold on."

He put a hand on either shoulder, turning her slightly. When he let go of her, Madi's arms rose in fear, but Laurent came back to her side.

"You ready?"

Madi nodded.

"Open your eyes."

Her lashes fluttered open to discover they were standing in the damaged interior of a building. She guessed it had been a brick apartment building, but a fire, sometime in the last years, had gutted the interior. Now it was a roughly rectangular box forming a massive chimney, three or four stories high, with charred beams and the wilting remains of fire-bent stairs clinging to one side. Below their feet, the floor was warped and uneven, but apparently sound. Above them, the wide-open sky.

Madi gasped as her eyes adjusted to the light.

Light poured in from many glassless windows, highlighting an explosion of imagery. Faces rose from floorboards. Intricate words twisted into strangely foreign shapes. Round and round, the interior walls had been painted into a massive mosaic of light and color.

"Oh my God. Did you paint this stuff?"

"Oh no, not me," Laurent said. "Though I've met the artists who did." His arm slid over her shoulders. "One of them is a MadLibber, actually."

"Who?"

He winked. "I'm pretty sure you can figure out which artist would have the attitude to do something like this."

Madi's eyes widened. "ArtWithAttitude? This was painted by Ava?!"

"Among others," Laurent said. "But don't tell her I took you here."

"Why?"

"She's, er . . . a little protective of this spot."

A line creased Madi's brow. "But this isn't *her* place. I mean, it's just a building. Right? Anyone could go here."

Laurent laughed. "You try telling that to Ava sometime. I'll go hide in the fallout shelter while she explodes."

Madi frowned, remembering the unexplained conflicts with Ava/ArtWith-Attitude that had started with their meeting at the Metrograph. "Fine," she said. "I won't say anything to her."

"Thanks for understanding." Laurent stared at the broken-down walls and vibrant graffiti with the reverence some people saved for church. "I love this place. I've photographed almost all of it." He looked down at her and grinned. "The murals are always changing. Come back in a week, and this'll be new again."

Madi smiled. "This is the inspiration for your photographs."

Laurent nodded as Madi turned in a circle, imagining how Laurent would frame her within this backdrop. She'd only seen the raw footage of her videos, but she could already tell the vlog would be far better than she'd expected.

"And the . . . the *feeling* of it is what you want to capture?"

Laurent's eyes widened, gold dancing in the green. "*Exactement!* I want to photograph the life and spirit of a place. Not just the structure, but what a building is because people have put their lives into it." His hand rose to cup Madi's cheek. "Because they've loved it. Their vision is imprinted on it for—for—always."

"Forever?"

"Yes. Forever . . . *Inaliénable. Indélébile.*"

His thumb brushed the edge of her cheek. It seemed for a moment like they might kiss, but then he looked away. His eyes moved over the graffitied walls, inspecting it like a Rembrandt.

"Is that why you started taking pictures?"

Laurent's face grew wary. "That was part of the reason."

"Why else?"

When he didn't answer, Madi moved closer. "Did I say something wrong?"

Laurent let out a long breath and smiled. "It's nothing. I just . . ." He shook his head. "There are lots of reasons, of course. Art and creativity and—like you said—capturing things like this. But . . ." His face grew intensely sad for a moment. "It's also because I wanted to be more than just an objet d'art myself."

"I don't understand."

Laurent turned back and wrapped her in a gentle hug. "Do you remember that day by the ruins, when you told me why it was easier to live online?"

She nodded.

"Well, it's kind of like that. When people see me—even you, Madi—they all assume certain things. The good-looking guy. Nice but dumb," he sneered. "Obsessed with appearance. But that's not me at all! I want people to know who I am, and I don't know how to do that sometimes."

"I like you for who you are," she said. "I liked you even before I knew who you really were."

Laurent leaned down, halving the distance between them. "I know."

Madi rose on tiptoes. The kiss started out hesitantly, a mere brush of lips, but soon grew into more. She clung to him, thoughts and emotions burning the fuel of his kisses. An unexpected thought popped into her mind: *This isn't just a crush anymore.*

The thought was so terrifying Madi couldn't breathe. Her heart thrummed in her ears. But Laurent's kiss broke through her fear. Her fingers tightened in the soft cotton of his shirt as his mouth slanted over hers. With him tasting her, only one thought remained: *More.* His mouth moved to her cheek, and then her neck, nibbling her earlobe as he caught her against his chest. Panting, Madi fluttered her lashes open, her gaze rising to the destroyed building and the illustrations that filled it. If Laurent could find beauty in *this*, then perhaps there really was a chance for them.

"*Ah, minette,*" Laurent whispered against the skin of her neck. "*Je t'adore.*" He moved back to her mouth, his hands sliding into her hair.

As happened before, he was so adorably earnest Madi couldn't help the laughter that bubbled up from her chest.

He looked up. "What?"

Madi tried to answer, but she was giddy with the sound of Laurent's voice. "N-nothing." She giggled. "It's great."

"No, really," Laurent said, frowning. "You keep doing that."

"It's nothing—I just . . ." Another gale of laughter overtook her.

"But why are you laughing?"

"It's—it's . . ." How could she explain what his French accent did to her, never mind the kissing, and the foolishly appropriate building with its graffitied murals? It was too perfect. He was too perfect! She doubled over, laughing harder, as the tears dripped down her cheeks.

"It's not you," she gasped. "It's me." Laurent sighed and she rushed to explain. "No, really, it is! I can't be serious and romantic. I really *can't*! And you're adorable, Laurent. You're perfect, but I'm just a huge nerd—"

"Not as big as I am."

"You sure?" Madi grinned, fighting for composure. "'Cause I'm the one with the blog, and all the followers, and the massive video project I'm not even sure how to put together."

Laurent pulled her forward. "Comics trump all."

"But MadLibs is way more popular."

He chuckled. "Mainstream counts against you."

"You think so?"

"I *know* so."

"And how do you figure—"

But before she could finish the question, he kissed her.

The rest of the day passed in a blur of video footage, coffee dates, and subway rides. Madi jotted notes and used them for the footage bites Laurent recorded of her in front of various NYC landmarks—both touristy and off the map. While they worked, they talked. Madi now knew he was the second youngest of four children, his parents had divorced when he was eight, and he spoke Spanish as well as English and French.

"The Romance languages aren't that different," he said with a self-deprecating wave of his hand. "English, though, that's a hard one to master."

"I think you speak English beautifully."

"When I'm not flustered." He reached out with his forefinger, drawing a line down the side of her face and winking. "And if I have the right inspiration to talk."

Madi giggled and looked away. "Well, I'm glad you did."

"Me, too."

Dinner was a smorgasbord of street-vendor cuisine. Aromas mingled like incense: the sharp edge of cinnamon on top of bacon's heady palate, citrus scents interspersing the homey warmth of bread dough and tang of sauerkraut. Faint hints of car exhaust added to the sensory overload. Laurent seemed to know every vendor by name, and several appeared to know about Madi, too.

"You're the girl who blogs about movies and stuff," said the man at the bagel cart. "I heard about you."

Madi reached out to take the bagel from his waiting tongs. "Books, too, sometimes."

"Laurent tells me you're gonna be a writer someday."

"Something like that."

"You gonna sign a book for me when you do?"

"If it happens."

The man slapped his side. "There ain't no *if* about it. You've got to go after what you want." He nodded to the bagel in Madi's hands. "Now eat that up, miss, before it gets cold."

Madi took a bite, letting out a moan of pleasure. "Mmph," she said through the mouthful. "Delicious!" And Laurent and Madi continued on their way.

Sunset was spent at the train yard. (Though Madi missed the actual shift of colors as day turned into twilight, too focused on Laurent's kisses.) She didn't think anything could surpass the burned-out building, but the backdrop of the trains was one of her favorite shots Laurent had taken. He had an eye for composition. Even Madi had to admit that she looked good on film when he was behind the camera.

When it grew too dark to film, she thought they'd leave, but Laurent had brought sparklers with him, and he took photos as they made wishes in the dark.

Then there was a brief moment of panic when Madi discovered how much easier it was to get *in* than *out*. (In the end, Laurent climbed back over the fence to her side, and Madi clambered clumsily up his back, then crawled over the other side.)

"You get to play the hero this time," she said as he jumped down beside her.

"Only fair after you saved me from the attack of the wild squirrel."

"True." Madi giggled. "And thanks for getting me out of there. I don't know how I'd explain *that* to my dad."

"For you, Madi? I'd break you out of worse," he said as he pressed a kiss to her knuckles. "Where next?"

She pulled up the list of notes on her phone, chewing her lower lip as she read through them. "I think I've got most of the scenes I need for the vlog. You ready to head back?" She smiled. "We can hang out at my aunt's place for a while, if you'd like?"

"Yeah. That sounds good."

As they walked, they fell to talking again. Madi had a million questions for Laurent.

"So what's on your bucket list?" she asked.

"Bucket list?" Laurent reached for his phone, but Madi stopped him.

"Like a list of things you want to do someday." She laughed.

"I've got a few things in the works."

"You do?"

He lifted an eyebrow. "I've been putting money away. Saving so I could come back to New York."

"But I thought you were planning on college in Paris."

"I am, but maybe someday down the road I might come back for a visit."

"That'd be really cool," Madi said, smiling even though it hurt the center of her chest. She wouldn't allow herself to think of that could-have-been future. It hurt too much.

"So, what else? What crazy bucket-list items are you working on?"

"I don't know. Real life, I guess. Planning my future adventures."

For a second, it was on the tip of Madi's tongue to ask, *Am I in them?* but she grinned and looked away. As much as it might feel like it, her life wasn't a romantic comedy, and she had no doubt Laurent's plans included some marquee poster–type adventure with a Parisian coed, while hers included attending the BMCC campus of CUNY so she could still take the train back in time to pick Sarah up after school.

After a day of traveling to all parts of New York City—taking the subway to each of the five boroughs—they took the subway back to Brooklyn, where Madi's aunt Lisa lived with her girlfriend, Rita. They hung out in the too-small kitchen until Laurent finally decided it was time to go.

"Let us know if you need privacy," Lisa called from the other room. "We can go out, you know. We were young once, too."

But Madi was too embarrassed to take them up on the offer, so she escorted Laurent out to the hallway.

He brushed her hair back from her face, tucking it behind her ear. "Lisa and Rita are nice."

"They are. Mind you, I kind of have to say that since I'm crashing here."

Laurent smiled but didn't laugh. "When do you have to be at the station tomorrow?"

"Early. Train leaves at eight."

"I'll be there."

"You don't have to do that, Laurent. It'll be a waste of time."

He slid his hands up her arms to her shoulders as his gaze drifted longingly over her face. Madi shivered.

"When are you going to start believing me?" he asked.

"A-about what?"

He leaned closer. "That you are *worth* my time," he murmured against her mouth.

"I don't know what you mean."

He kissed her rather than answering, his hands moving down her back to the pockets of her jeans, and then lower still. Madi squeaked as he lifted her up, pinning her between him and the wall. Suddenly, they were eye to eye. Laurent looked up, panting.

"This okay with you?" he asked. "My back was starting to ache from leaning over so much."

Madi glanced behind him. The hallway was empty, and if she held his shoulders, she was more than comfortable.

"Yeah, it's good." She pulled him closer. "Kiss me again."

He let out a quiet groan the second before he caught her lips in his. There were no other thoughts, no worries about leaving, just this perfect moment spinning out between them. Laurent's mouth warm against hers. The city around them. The future—*their* future—a page waiting to be written.

When the kiss ended, he let her slide slowly down to her feet. Madi wobbled, breathless as he brushed his fingers along her cheek.

"Madi, mon ange, je t'aime . . . je t'aime . . . je t'aime à la folie."

Madi began to giggle. "Oh God, I can't . . ." Her laughter grew louder. "Sorry! I just . . . I can't be serious."

Laurent grinned and stepped back. *"A demain."*

"What did you just say?"

Laurent winked. "Until tomorrow." And then he sprinted down the stairs before she could ask what else.

It felt like only minutes later Madi was back at Penn Station, waiting to board the train back to Millburn. She threw her arms around Laurent one last time, breathing in the mulled scents of clothes detergent and shampoo, his faint cologne—as familiar as his accent—and under all those other layers, the faint odor of young, unwashed male.

She sighed happily. "Yesterday was a really good day."

"It was."

With a final kiss—and a few more French endearments on Laurent's part, which left her grinning—she let go, heading to the train. As before, Laurent waited until she was out of sight before he walked away. When Madi's phone buzzed, she knew it would be him.

i miss you, madi.

Madi's forehead crumpled as the weight of her departure sank in.

> me too 😞

Laurent's answer appeared seconds later.

> i want to relive yesterday. i want to go back again and again and again. every kiss. every moment. je t'adore

Madi had held it together all the way to the station. She'd reveled in their last moments together. *The last perfect kiss.* Suddenly, the floodgate opened.

> great. now i'm ugly crying

> you could never be ugly. your heart is too perfect. you shine.

> i miss you 💔

> miss you, too, madi

By the time the train reached the outskirts of Millburn, Madi's tears had dried, but the ache had grown into a solid weight in her chest. She stared out the window, wondering at the feeling of leaving Laurent behind. They were too far away to have a real relationship. Even if they met every other weekend, and spent all their time on trains back and forth to New York, he'd be returning to France in less than a month. Long-distance friendships worked, but the pain of leaving Laurent behind would make a relationship torturous.

She was in love with someone she could never be with.

Madi's phone buzzed one more time as the train reached the Millburn station. She looked down at the screen, her breath hitching.

"Oh, Laurent," she whispered as the tears started anew.

None of them are you.

School had always been relatively easy for Madi—she loved to read, and that translated well in academia—but as June ticked by with the persistence of a time bomb, she found herself scrambling. There simply weren't enough hours in the day to study, never mind eat, sleep, pick up Sarah from school, and edit video. She was near the breaking point as she took her last final.

Shell-shocked, she stumbled out of the gymnasium at the end of the day.

The exit door swung open in her hand, the sun momentarily blinded her, and she slammed bodily into another student coming the other direction.

"Watch it!" an angry voice snapped.

"Sorry, I—"

"Fuck! It's *you* again."

Madi squinted at the person who stood before her, blocking her way. He was a black paper cutout, devoid of features.

"Why don't you watch where you're going?" he yelled.

"Why don't *you*?!" Madi stepped sideways, shielding her eyes. The shadow grew features as her eyes adjusted to the light: shaggy black hair, narrow lips, and an angry mouth.

"Do you even go here?" he snarled. "Or do you just hang out trying to look cool?"

"I—I don't . . ." Her words faded as she suddenly realized why she knew him. It was the emo kid who'd glared at her the day Sarah had studied at the library. *Robbie's friend, Gavin.* She thought she'd seen him at the café in New York, too.

"You're Gavin."

"And you're in my way!" he grunted, pushing past her. "Move!"

The door slammed shut behind him.

Shaken, she turned back around. The sun was dazzling, and she squinted as she searched for Sarah, who'd been working in the library. She wobbled down the steps, so distracted she almost walked past her sister.

Sarah waited in the shadows, Robbie at her side.

"Hey, Madi," he said, beaming at her. "How've you been?"

"Busy," she said, wishing that Sarah was alone. She didn't feel like making small talk with her ex-classmates.

"Haven't seen you around in a while."

"Mmph."

"How did you do on the final?" Sarah asked with grim interest.

"Fine, I think," Madi said. "At least it's over. Done is done, right?"

"This your last exam?" Robbie asked.

"Yeah. You?"

"I've got one more test, but it's not until next week." He stepped too close, and Madi stepped back, almost falling off the curb. Robbie was attractive in a boy-next-door way, but compared to Laurent, he might as well have been invisible. "I can't wait to be out of here."

Madi smirked. "I've been waiting for this moment for years."

"But what if you have to come back next semester?" Sarah blurted. Madi fought the urge to shout at her sister. If Robbie had personal-space issues, her sister had problems with sharing private information.

"That's not my fault," Madi snapped. "Mrs. Preet is obsessed with rules. She hates anyone who doesn't fit into her neat little box."

"Preet?" Robbie snorted. "She has it in for me, too. She practically dragged me to the office by my ear last week."

Madi's brows rose. "She did?"

"Yeah. I got a text during my math exam."

Madi giggled.

"If you had your phone on during the exam," Sarah said grimly, "what did you expect her to do?"

"I didn't know I couldn't!"

"Better stay in her good books," Madi warned.

Robbie dropped his voice. "I heard she got transferred because she couldn't get along with students at her last school."

"Get along? I bet she had kids chained in the boiler room."

"Apparently, some parents threatened to go to the board if she wasn't transferred."

"God, I wish they had."

"Sure would make my life better." Robbie chuckled. "I think she's got a dartboard with my face on it."

"Then mine's there, too." Madi grinned. "I swear that woman lives for drama!"

"Actually . . ." Robbie's gaze skittered around the sun-drenched school yard. "My dad says her trouble with parents had to do with inflexibility. She refused to budge."

Madi rolled her eyes, remembering the dismissal of her entire project based on the MadLibs ads. "I can imagine! Mrs. Preet's so fixated on rules, I bet she gives other people parking tickets if their meter runs out."

Robbie laughed, but Sarah scowled.

"She's the kind of person who keeps the plastic on their couch so 'guests'"—Madi made air quotes—"don't mess it up."

"She totally would!"

"And I bet when Mrs. Preet walks those ugly little poodles of hers, she—"

"Madi," Sarah interrupted.

"—makes them wear booties so they don't bring dirt into her immaculately clean—"

"Madi!"

"—living room, or leave a pee stain on the—"

"MADI!"

"What?!" she snapped. But her sister wasn't looking at her, she was looking over her head.

"There's someone coming to see you."

Across from her, Robbie's face went so pale his freckles looked like they'd been drawn in pen. Madi slowly turned around.

"Miss Nakama," a cool voice said. "A word with you."

Robbie scuttled out of sight just as Mrs. Preet broke through the crowd. From the depths of her embarrassment, Madi wondered how the situation could get worse. (Life seemed to revel in demonstrating that.)

"Mrs. Preet," she choked. *How much did she hear?!* "I—I didn't know you were standing there."

"Obviously," she said with a shake of her head. "I heard you were writing your final exam today. I wanted to catch you before you went home."

"What about?"

"I hear from Ms. Rodriguez you're nearly done with your project. She told me you've worked very diligently on it."

"Sh-she did?"

Mrs. Preet nodded. "Yes, and I was glad to hear it. Graduation is just around the corner, after all."

Madi was surprised to discover she no longer felt excited about the prospect. In the two weeks since she visited New York, she'd grown so accustomed to exhaustion that she'd stopped thinking about it. There were too many things going on to worry. She still had no guarantee she'd be graduating. And Laurent would be back in France—*gone!*—in a few short weeks.

"Ms. Rodriguez also tells me she's thinking of writing you a reference letter for a journalism scholarship."

Madi blinked. "She is?"

"Which is why I thought I'd speak to you myself about it. So there aren't any . . . *impediments* to that."

"Impediments?"

"As you know, the board takes any accusations of plagiarism very seriously."

Madi felt like she'd been doused with cold water. The sweat across her forehead grew cold. "B-but they cleared my work," she said. "I talked to Ms. Rodriguez about it myself. She told me they'd reviewed all my previously submitted work, and as far as the group was concerned, they'd seen nothing to suggest—"

"This isn't about the *last* plagiarism accusation, Miss Nakama," Mrs. Preet interrupted. "This is a *new* one."

"What?!"

"I received a very concerning e-mail regarding your alternate assignment. The video project you went to New York to work on." She frowned. "I'm hoping you can explain it to me. I really don't want to discover that you've misled me in some way. Not after you assured me you'd followed the rules to a *T.*"

Madi staggered back, blood roaring in her ears. It felt like she'd stumbled into a horror movie, and though she didn't know why it was happening, the serial killer had found her once again.

"I was so pleased to hear Ms. Rodriguez praise your revised assignments," she said gravely. "But let me make it perfectly clear: Anything plagiarized is, of course, inadmissible."

"But I—I don't understand. This is wrong!" Madi's voice rose in anger. "I haven't plagiarized anything! I've been working on this new project for weeks!"

"Lower your voice, Miss Nakama. I want to believe you, but I need you to explain—"

"No! No, this isn't RIGHT!" All the panic, anger, and pain rose to the surface. Madi jabbed her finger at Mrs. Preet's chest. "You're doing this on purpose! You hate me!"

"I assure you my feelings for you have *nothing* to do with this," she said calmly. "It's just a matter of school rules. When the e-mail arrived yesterday, describing your behavior, I—"

"Behavior?!" Madi's voice boomed. A number of students on their way out of the exam looked up in surprise. "I've done everything by the book! I redid that whole goddamned assignment! And I followed *all* your stupid rules! You're a horrible person—"

"Miss Nakama! That sort of attitude is unnecessary."

"—who doesn't give a DAMN about her students! And telling me about this at the last second is just your way of getting even with me!"

Mrs. Preet's face had taken on a vivid eggplant hue. Her mouth opened and closed like a fish out of water. Sensing the eyes of everyone around them, Madi turned. Students watched the interaction with saucerlike eyes. A nameless girl, slouching against the brick wall nearby, fought a bout of silent laughter, hand over her mouth.

"You tell her!" a voice shouted, and an uneasy titter rippled through the gaping crowd. *Robbie!*

Mrs. Preet's voice was unsettled by the heckler. "That's enough!" she said shakily. "You come to the office right this minute, young lady. I'll not be spoken to like that!"

"No!" And with that, Madi bolted down the street, leaving an openmouthed Mrs. Preet and a mob of laughing students behind.

"Madi!" Sarah shouted. "Wait for me! WAIT!"

Madi ran faster.

16

"Bogus. Heinous. Most nontriumphant."
(*Bill and Ted's Excellent Adventure*, 1989)

Shoulders hunched, Madi tiptoed past the kitchen where her father sat, phone in hand.

"But I don't understand what you're claiming, Mrs. Preet," he said. "How *exactly* is that plagiarizing? I mean, you can't star in a video without having someone to film it, right?" There was a long pause. "I understand that the rules may use that particular wording, but that is *not* realistic, at least not for a project of this nature." Another long pause. "Actually," Charles growled, "I take the rules *very* seriously. . . ."

His eyes were pressed closed, fingers pinching the bridge of his nose, a pose that told Madi that no matter how calm and placating her father's words might be, he was furious. The fact he'd told Madi he'd "deal with it" gave her a modicum of relief, but the unpleasant personal knowledge of Mrs. Preet's temperament gave her an equal balance of terror.

This situation was going to get worse before better.

"Mm-hmm . . . and I understand that, too," her father said, "but it doesn't change the fact that *twice* my daughter's schoolwork has been investigated regarding plagiarism, and *twice* the instructor of the course has stood by her work." His tone sharpened. "Speaking as someone who has done plenty of writing for the *Tri-State Herald* and who knows firsthand its guidelines, perhaps this is the correct time to bring in an outside mediator to review the situation. . . ."

"Oh God," Madi groaned. She couldn't listen to any more.

She crept into the living room, where her sister sat, flicking through channels. Sarah glanced up as Madi came in.

"Hey."

"You busy?" Madi asked.

"Just about to start a movie."

"Oh, right." Madi wracked her brain, trying to remember what rewatch she'd planned for today. She'd been so busy, she could barely keep up with the schedule she'd set up. "This is *Some Kind of Wonderful*, isn't it?"

"Uh-huh. Do you have time to join us?" Sarah slid one cushion over so Madi could take her usual place. "I could message everyone. Let them know you're here."

"Don't tell them yet."

"Are you watching?"

"Um . . . not decided. Maybe for a bit."

Madi slid her phone from her pocket to discover an active discussion already in progress.

@ModernDayWitch: @ArtWithAttitude It was my all-time FAVORITE movie when I was an angsty preteen. #WearingMyFuture

@ArtWithAttitude: @ModernDayWitch I've never seen it before, though I think I saw the actor in something sci-fi. Not sure. #Yummy

@WrittenInChantalics: @ModernDayWitch EEEEeeee!!! I love him, too! But he looks so YOUNG in this one. O_o #HelloGrandpa #NotMyKindOfWonderful

@ArtWithAttitude: @WrittenInChantalics LOL—Everyone starts off young, Chantal. LOL Yes, even you. ;)

@laurentabelard: Hello all! Just got off work. What did I miss?

@fandometric: @laurentabelard Nothing yet. The MadLibbers are just cuing up. WOOHOO! #MadLibs

@ModernDayWitch: Ready to start this liveblog, everyone? (Anyone seen @StarveilBrian1981 around? He should be here.)

@fandometric: @ModernDayWitch Not lately.

@ArtWithAttitude: @ModernDayWitch @laurentabelard @WrittenInChantalics @fandometric Ready and waiting! Let's liveblog! Woot!

@ModernDayWitch: @ArtWithAttitude @laurentabelard @WrittenInChantalics @fandometric Take your places. On your mark . . . get set . . . GO!!!

With a sigh, Madi flicked her phone's screen off and shoved it in her pocket. She'd arranged for the guest posts. She'd handpicked the guest bloggers. But it still irked her to see it under someone else's control. *One last post. Then MadLibs is mine again. If only the video project were done, then I could—*

"You all right, Madi?"

She turned to discover Sarah watching her, her young face sharpened with concern.

"I'm fine."

Sarah tipped her head, giving her a piercing gaze. "I don't think you are. When we start movies, you're usually on your phone, but you just put it away and frowned." She leaned closer. "Did something happen?"

Madi considered telling her sister the truth, that there was a flaw to Mrs. Preet's claim—that someone *knew* she'd had Laurent's help in New York. But she didn't know how to put it into words without launching into a discussion she didn't want to have.

She shrugged. "I'm fine."

"Why are you lying?"

Why? Because the horrible truth was that whoever had turned her in had *known* she was in New York with him, and that left a very limited group of people: Sarah, her father, her aunt Lisa . . .

Laurent.

"Just start the stupid movie, Sarah, or I'm going back upstairs again."

Sarah scrambled for the remote. "You don't have to get so crabby about it."

A swell of music leading into the brass rumble of cymbals filled the room as her sister settled back against the cushions and leaned against her. The pose was much the way they'd sat weeks and months before: rewatching movies, surrounded by a bevy of online friends who wanted to laugh and joke. She couldn't wait to retake the reins!

The beat grew louder as a pounding drum riff joined the main theme. Madi watched through half-closed eyes, almost missing the buzz of her phone. She pulled it out to find a message from Laurent had arrived.

> i know you're working on your video and i don't want to be a pest, but watching movies makes me miss you. 😕

Her stomach clenched as a worrisome thought filled her mind. *What if Laurent told someone he was helping me film? He told Ava about the guest-posting long before it was public. He could have told her about the vlog, too.* Madi slid away from Sarah, giving herself room to type in a reply without her seeing.

> i'm actually around right now. (taking a break.) glad i caught this

> WOOHOO!!! that's AWESOME! i was hoping you might join us!

> awww . . . that's sweet of u

i'm going to tweet to everyone that you're here!

don't! i can't stay long and i don't want everyone to think i can stay for the whole movie.

too late, minette! 😜 now you have to come chat.

Madi frowned. Her fingers tapped irritably on the side of the phone. *Why does he keep doing that?* After a few seconds, she wrote another reply.

what if I'd rather just talk to u?

even better! (i'll tell the other madlibbers you just popped in to say hello 😃

...

"Are you even watching this?" Sarah complained.

Madi slid farther away. "I'm just checking e-mail," she lied. "You remember what's happening. Okay?"

"Fine," Sarah said with a long-suffering sigh.

so what have you been doing? how is school? life? family? tell me ALL THE THINGS!

er . . . that'll take a bit. there's been a LOT 😕

i'm here. (I wish you were here, too.) 💕

i wish i were, too 😕

> i've been trying very hard not to interrupt you the last few days. i know you're close to finishing up the year. (i'm counting days.)

i took my last exam today

> that's AWESOME! congratulations!

that's not all there is, though. i still have to finish editing the vlog and things r not good

> what? but why? I thought you told me you were nearly done?

Madi sighed. How much did Laurent actually know about the accusation? She couldn't think of how to lure the information out.

Madi typed in a reply, then deleted it all.

Seconds later, she typed it again.

i am, or i WAS, but someone complained that i'd collaborated with someone on the vlog. the school is doing ANOTHER review. my dad is ready to blow a gasket 😡

> blow a what?

he's FURIOUS. (but not at me, thankfully.) he says mrs. preet has taken the situation out of context, whether or not i got assistance & I DIDN'T.

wait. assistance from who???
that makes no sense.

according to whoever reported me—it was
assistance from u

but who'd even know we talked? or met? or did
anything at all? i didn't tell anyone.

Madi stared at the message on-screen. And there it was, that part that she just couldn't wrap her head around. *If he didn't tell someone, who did?* It had to be someone who knew she was rewriting her final project, and that left her a limited number of suspects. Madi's gaze jumped over to her sister. *Could Sarah have told someone?*

Sarah's arms were crossed on her chest, her lower lip jutting forward in irritation. "You done yet?" she grumbled. "'Cause there's a lot going on."

Sarah loved schedules—thrived on them—and everything about the last month had thrown her life into upheaval. The first issue had been their mother's fellowship, but Madi's own drama had done just as much. She'd been slowly pulling away from her sister for the last few weeks, hatching out her own independence. The trip overnight to New York had been a major step, but it had come at the cost of Sarah's security.

Guilt rising, Madi dropped her eyes from Sarah back to her phone, ignoring Laurent's text to flick back to the continuing liveblog. Messages popped up one after another. The group of MadLibbers—minus herself and Laurent—were in the middle of an energetic discussion.

@ModernDayWitch: SKOW is an old-time ship, like Leia and Han, Lee and Kara, River and Eleven, Spartan and Tekla. #IllGoDownWithThisShip

@ArtWithAttitude: @ModernDayWitch Sooooooo yummy! I love a girl with drumsticks. #AllTheFeels

@WrittenInChantalics: THIS is how you treat the woman you love! #TakeNotesBoys

@StarveilBrian1981: Just showed up. What did I miss? #MadLibs

@ModernDayWitch: @StarveilBrian1981 Woohoo! Brian's in the house!!!

Madi's breath caught. *It could be any of them!* Every last one of the MadLibbers knew what was going on in her personal life. She'd spammed them with increasingly frenzied messages over the last weeks, giving them a play-by-play of her personal life. Another message from Laurent buzzed her phone—appearing at the top of the screen—and Madi closed the liveblog to answer it.

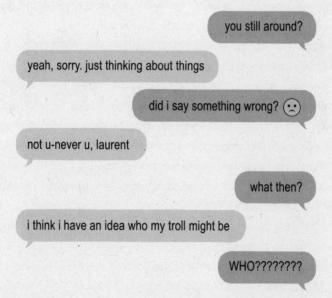

you still around?

yeah, sorry. just thinking about things

did i say something wrong? 🙁

not u-never u, laurent

what then?

i think i have an idea who my troll might be

WHO????????

Madi talked to her fandom friends all the time—some she'd even met—but how well did she *really* know them? Hands shaking, she wrote another text.

I think the troll is a MadLibber. 😲

"Hey, Madi?" her father called up the stairs. "Can you come down here for a minute?"

Madi tugged on her jacket and slid her phone into her pocket. The meeting at the school was in half an hour, but her father was determined to be early. She padded down the steps to find him standing in the kitchen, staring at his open laptop.

"Yeah, Dad?"

He looked up. "I need you to be honest with me about something."

"Okay . . . ?"

"Take a look."

Madi came around the other side of the table to find her father's laptop open to the Humans of New York website. A photograph of a young man standing against a graffitied wall graced the top half of the page, followed by the caption "The Art of Anarchy"—definitely not Charles Nakama's style.

More surprising yet was that Madi *recognized* the subject of the photo. "Hey, that's Laurent!" She laughed. "That's so awesome!"

Her father frowned. "You *knew* he was a graffiti artist?"

"Oh, he's not! I mean he takes pictures of graffiti, but he doesn't actually paint . . ." She leaned in as she scrolled down the page, reading: *"I've always been interested in the art that surrounds us, those perfect moments that photographs capture. Sunsets are fleeting moments of beauty, but no more than graffiti can be. A painting that took the artist hours to create might only last a day before it's painted out . . ."*

"I've seen this place," Madi said, grinning. "It's a burned-out building Laurent took me to. All of it covered in pictures. That's pretty cool."

"I'm not sure *cool* is the word I'd use."

Madi turned back to find him scowling at the screen. "Why not? What's wrong with it?"

"Besides the fact that graffiti defaces public property?" her father grumbled.

Madi groaned. "The building where that was taken is a burned-out shell, Dad. It's not like it's someone's house. Besides, Laurent's just documenting it. Capturing the"—she glanced back at the screen—"fleeting moment."

Her father sighed. "This worries me."

"Why?"

He cleared his throat. "Laurent seems nice enough, but dating someone who condones graffiti, Madi? I don't know how I feel about that."

"Dad. That's really weirdly conservative, even for you."

"Madi . . ."

"No, really. Why does it even bother you? Laurent's not doing the art, he's taking photos. Nothing wrong with that."

He reached out and closed the laptop. "I don't agree."

She rolled her eyes. "You realize how old-fashioned that sounds, right? Judging Laurent on what he does as a pastime?"

"I'm just a little uncomfortable with it. Graffiti is illegal and—"

"He's a *photographer.* All right? It's what he does."

Her father scratched his head. "I suppose . . ."

"Dad. I think you should relax. Laurent's a good guy." Madi touched his arm. "Just trust me on this, okay? I know him."

"Fine." Her father sighed and put the closed laptop into his bag. "Now, we should get going. The meeting's going to start in . . ." He checked his watch. "Twenty minutes."

Madi's expression grew wary. "Mom must be so mad at me."

"Don't you worry, your mother is on your side. Now we should probably go. I don't want to be late."

Madi plodded to the door with leaden feet. "Oh, yippee," she muttered. "As if this day couldn't get any worse."

Her father chuckled. "Relax, Madi." He squeezed her shoulder. "You're not going into this alone. I've got your back, you know."

"Thanks, Dad."

Her father smiled. "No problem."

Madi sat in Mrs. Preet's office, her father on one side, a laptop—projecting an image of her mother from Oxford—on the other. Across from them—directly below the trio of poodle pictures—sat the school's triumvirate: Principal McQuarrie, Vice Principal Preet, and a nameless representative of the school board. Mrs. Preet looked positively green, and Madi wondered how much trouble she'd be in if she flipped her the finger. Her father was in damage-control mode, smiling as he smoothed his mustache. Things couldn't get worse at this point. She just hoped—with her parents' support—it could get better.

"I appreciate you taking time to meet with us, Mrs. Preet," Charles said in his most persuasive voice. "I know you'll do everything in your power to assist us in this matter."

"Of course I will." Mrs. Preet nodded. "I'm just not sure why we need"— her eyes slid to Mr. Nakama's lawyer, Ms. Auryn—"outsiders involved."

The lawyer gave her a look of mildly bored interest. With her five-hundred-dollar shoes and Calvin Klein suit, she looked like she'd stepped out of the wrong television show. "Anything that may impact Mr. Nakama's personal interests are of interest to me," Ms. Auryn said drily. "And I'm sure you've followed the letter of the law."

Madi fought the urge to cheer as Mrs. Preet's face paled. "Well, of course, I believe so. But I'm . . . I'm no lawyer."

"Exactly," Madi's mother added, her voice echoing from the laptop's speakers. "Which is why we're going to get everything settled right now. This isn't something we're ready to slide on."

Madi turned to find her mother's gaze looking out at her from the laptop's screen. "This is far beyond a simple error. Our daughter, Madi, hasn't done anything wrong."

"Agreed," Charles echoed.

"We are determined to have this resolved," his wife added.

"Exactly," Charles agreed. "Madi's gone through enough."

In that moment, Madi knew both her parents were on her side, protecting her. She smiled, and her mother and father, on two different continents, smiled back.

The attorney slid a tiny recorder forward. "I'll be recording this, if you don't mind," she said. "It's easier than taking notes."

"Not a problem, Ms. Auryn," Principal McQuarrie said gravely. "Right, Mrs. Preet?"

"N-no. Not at all." Mrs. Preet stared at the recorder like it was something stuck to the bottom of her shoe. Madi bit the inside of her cheeks to keep from laughing. She might not be graduating. She might have an entire course to redo. But if she was stuck in a hole, Mrs. Preet had dug herself in a foot and a half deeper.

Madi stumbled out of Mrs. Preet's office, a grin plastered on her face. "You did it!" she said, throwing her arms around her father. "I can't believe you and Mom pulled it off!"

"I didn't do anything." The corners of his mouth tugged up into a smile. "Mind you, neither did you."

Beside them, the attorney cleared her throat, drawing his attention.

"Thank you for coming down, Maria," Charles said, offering his open palm and shaking her hand. "I appreciated your support."

"No problem at all, Mr. Nakama," she said. "Call me if you need anything else."

"I will."

With Ms. Auryn gone, father and daughter walked down the hallway to the exit. The meeting had resolved a number of items. According to the school board representative, the claim of plagiarism had been resolved based on Ms. Rodriguez's input. Any anonymous claims in the future would be treated with suspicion. Who exactly had accused Madi remained a mystery. She had completed all classwork except for the final video project.

"It still doesn't seem real," Madi said as they stepped out the doors into the June sunshine. "I was so worried about it all, and now it's fixed."

"You're home free," her father said. "How does it feel?"

"Good. Really good."

"Nothing but smooth sailing till college begins in the fall."

The day seemed to dim with his announcement. It was the one thing she hadn't dealt with. *College.* The issue she'd been avoiding for months. Was this the life she wanted to live? Madi frowned down at the sidewalk.

Now or never . . .

"Dad?"

"Yeah, sweetie?"

"I . . . need to talk to you about something." Buoyed by her parents' support in the meeting, she forced the words to come. "I want to talk about college."

"What about it?"

"I don't know if I want—if I can . . ." She took a deep breath, squeezing her eyes closed.

"It's okay, Madi. Just say it, all right? Whatever it is, we'll handle it."

"Dad, I don't want to go to college." She opened her eyes. "Not yet, at least."

She'd imagined this conversation any number of times since she'd gotten her acceptance letter, and in each one, it ended with yelling. Not today.

"All right, then," her father said. "What do you want to do?"

"I want to take MadLibs to the next level. I want to be funemployed full-time."

"Have you talked to your mother about this?"

Madi's smile faded. "You mean about Sarah?"

"No. Not about Sarah, about *you* and what you want to do with your life."

"I . . ." She winced. "No, I haven't."

"You should. I'm sure she'd love to talk to you. She loves you, you know."

Madi's voice dropped. "But what *do* we do with Sarah? I mean, she relies on me. I'm the one who picks her up and drops her off. I can't just leave you guys hanging."

"We'll figure something out."

"But I can't just leave her. I can't—" Madi's voice broke.

Charles put his hands on his daughter's shoulders, drawing her gaze. He smiled. "It makes sense to want to move on, to start your own life. And you *should*, Madi. This is when you've got to start living for yourself."

"But Sarah—"

"Will be just fine," he said. His hands tightened on Madi's shoulders. "Look at what happened when your mom took the position at Oxford."

"Sarah freaked."

"But once we got everything under control again, she was fine. Sarah just needs time to adapt to change. To get used to new schedules." He dropped his hands from Madi's shoulders. "We need Sarah to grow up just as much as we need you to. So don't put your plans on hold for her, or for us."

Madi stared at her father, unsettled by his words. Her little sister was the excuse she'd always used—for avoiding parties, for doing online classes rather than attending regular ones, for all the movies and dates she'd declined. If she didn't have Sarah, those choices were on her.

"A-are you sure?"

"I'm positive," he said with a grin that spread all the way from his mustache to the magnified wrinkles behind his glasses. "You're at the starting line for real life. You don't want to hold back. Your mother's career was a starting point, and I'm so proud we supported her in that. You deserve the same."

"I don't know what to say."

"You tell us how we can help. And that's what your mom and I will do."

"Thanks, Dad," she said thickly.

"You don't have to thank me. You just have to go for it. *Live, Madi.* You're only young once, you know."

Madi shook her head. "Once is one too many times, if you ask me."

Madi sat by the open window of her bedroom, waiting as the flagging Wi-Fi signal slowly processed the bits of information on the post she was trying to see. Outside, the sound of lawn mowers rose. A faint breeze rustled her hair, warm with the scent of flowers.

The post finished loading, and she glanced down at the screen.

Madi grinned and hit REBLOG. She might not be online today, or even tomorrow, but she'd be back, and MadLibs would be her escape once more. More than that, it was going to be her life. Her beginning.

Sighing happily, she let her head fall against the wall. It was a long ways from perfect, but things felt good. And that was a start.

17

"I gave her my heart, she gave me a pen."
(*Say Anything . . .* , 1989)

Eyes blurring, Madi watched the video for the tenth time, searching for errors. The titles were perfect. (Her father had proofread them all the night before.) So were the cuts. Even the few mishaps—when Madi flubbed a line or laughed midsentence—seemed to work. The vlog was polished and real, something Madi could be proud of!

She double-clicked on the final section, blinking gritty eyes as it launched. She'd entitled the piece "Real-Life Splash," and she liked it the best, despite it being the shortest.

She scrubbed through to the last scene: her sitting on top of the building near the train yards, night falling across the city.

"Perhaps that is what New York offers each of us: an ability to become the unknown, the faceless—to start afresh. That's what I want! New York is a blank page, waiting for my story, but unlike so many authors who've made the city their home, I don't intend to write mine in the words of a book. I want to share my thoughts, my ideas, my blog." On-screen, Madi grinned. *"I might be MadLibbing my way into adulthood, but it's as good a place as any to start."*

Madi nodded to herself, happy with the final montage. She was ready to make the leap. She attached the links to her e-mail, addressed it to Ms. Rodriguez's school account, and called her father to enter the Wi-Fi code. He squeezed her shoulder as he passed her chair.

"Good job, Madi."

"Thanks."

She waited until he left the room before turning back to the screen. *Time to jump.* Madi clicked SEND.

Yawning, she grabbed her phone, crawled back into bed, and pulled the covers over her head. Inside the cave of blankets, her phone became a warm campfire of connections. She thumbed through her online hangouts, exhausted but happy.

@ArtWithAttitude: Okay guys. The post on #SKOW is up. I'm a bit worried. Not sure @fandometric and I have the same style. O_o #BeGentlePlease

@laurentabelard: @ArtWithAttitude Just read through it. It was different—yes—but it sounded like you both. Great job! *applauds* #Madlibs

@ArtWithAttitude: @laurentabelard Not too angsty? :>S #MadLibbingIsHardYo

@laurentabelard: @ArtWithAttitude Not at all. To each his own. Besides—@MadLib didn't rave about every movie she watched. You both did great!

@ModernDayWitch: @ArtWithAttitude I thought you and @fandometric did a solid job.

@ModernDayWitch: @ArtWithAttitude @fandometric You balanced each other out, and I'm sure everyone will know emotions run high sometimes.

@WrittenInChantalics: @ArtWithAttitude @fandometric I'm sure it'll be good. (Unless the troll is around, that is.) *Checks under the bridge*

In her rush to complete her vlog, Madi had completely forgotten that @fandometric and @ArtWithAttitude had taken on writing the post for *Some Kind of Wonderful*, the final guest post before she returned to the helm. She flicked to the MadLibs page, anxiously scanning the comments.

No troll.

Relieved, she read through @ArtWithAttitude and @fandometric's *Some Kind of Wonderful* post. As with @laurentabelard and @ModernDayWitch, the article bounced back and forth between the two of them. The first few questions dealt mainly with plot, and Madi wondered why they were worried about backlash for too much angst.

She found her answer in the final discussion paragraphs.

@ArtWithAttitude: My favorite part of *Some Kind of Wonderful* was the romance that underscored the entire movie. I could identify with Watts more than ANY other movie lead I've seen. She had anger—yes!—but she also made her own future. This story doesn't have the stereotypical ending. #Spoilers: The guy doesn't really get the girl he thinks he wants, but he gets the person he needs. It was beyond perfect.

@fandometric: And that's where I have to call bullshit. Absolutely NO. Stories like this are half the problem with society. All lies! I wanted him to get the prize. Amanda Jones was supposed to be his! Why shift it partway through? It doesn't make sense.

@ArtWithAttitude: I thought it made sense. I mean, didn't you feel the vibes between the two leads all the way along? "Friends falling in love" is a much fresher story than "underdog guy gets a girl who'd never even give him the time of day." *gags* That's totally overdone.

@fandometric: Screw friends falling in love. Keith deserved better.

And as one of "those guys" hanging out and watching from the sidelines, I'm just saying this movie SUCKED. I'm glad I streamed it, because I'd never pay to watch this kind of crap.

"Yeesh! Calm down, dude," Madi muttered.

She reread @fandometric's comments, wondering how to address his angry tirade. She had a general policy not to provoke readers, but he'd given his opinion. It was undiluted. It was angry. But it was honest. For a few minutes, she mulled over the idea of commenting on the post, but in the end decided against it. With her final video assignment en route to Ms. Rodriguez, she was free to return to her spot at the helm of MadLibs.

She grinned as her eyes caught a final note on the bottom of the page:

ETA: @ArtWithAttitude: We're happy to announce that @MadLib will be returning to her regularly scheduled blogs starting next week. Welcome back! Your fans have MISSED YOU!

It felt like coming home.

Madi had just closed up the MadLibs post and opened her e-mail when she caught sight of a new message. It was from Anna Rodriguez, her English teacher. When Madi saw it waiting there, her breath caught.

"Oh hell no!" Her final assignment had been sent in less than an hour before. No way Ms. Rodriguez could have graded it in that amount of time! "This can't be happening again . . ."

Terrified, Madi opened the e-mail.

NEW Message, AnnaRodriguez@MillburnAcademy.com:
9:18 p.m. EST
Priority: Normal
Subject: RE: Final English Assignment

Hi Madi,

I saw you'd sent the video links to your final assignment this evening. Rather than forcing you to wait until the end of the semester to receive your grade, I went ahead and marked it. (See the attachment for the full grading breakdown and rubric highlights.)

Final Assignment: A+

Term Work: B+

Final Grade: A-

You have demonstrated a high level of skill and an ability to work under pressure that tells me what I already knew: blogging (in both written *and* video format) is your gift! I hope you will continue to pursue this.

Thank you for all your hard work and tenacity in the face of this semester's difficulties. Wishing you all the best in the future!

—Ms. Rodriguez

Elation rushed through Madi's limbs. "I did it!" she whooped. "I really DID IT!"

In the hallway, she heard Sarah's bedroom door open. "Madi?" she called tiredly. "You okay?"

"I'm better than okay—I'm awesome!"

Her sister appeared in the doorway, her hair sleep rumpled and eyes at half-mast. "I heard you yelling. What happened?"

Madi ran forward and threw her arms around her sister. "I did it, Sarah! I passed! I'm going to graduate!"

Her sister began to squirm and Madi let go, still grinning.

"So you're done? You passed everything for sure this time?"

"Yes!"

"You double-checked the rules?"

"Triple-checked 'em!"

Sarah nodded, her face caught in that intense expression that was a smile for anyone else. "Good job. I knew you would,"

Tonight, nothing could wreck Madi's good mood. With Sarah on the couch next to her watching reruns of an old television show, and her laptop on her lap linked into the Wi-Fi, she was free! The buzz of the reconnection to the web was a tangible thing.

u around, l?

madi! 😆 how are you?

SO HAPPY!

why? what happened?

i'm done with the course! I PASSED! thank u for all ur help with the project! what a RELIEF! *does a happy dance*

bravo! you deserve it!
(i didn't do anything at all.)

u did! u helped me film the vlog & u showed me around ny. (mrs. r said the locations were "spot-on" for the ny that new yorkers would know.)

okay, maybe i did those things, but it was all just part of my devious plan.

devious plan to what? LOL

to spend time with you.

well, devious or not, it worked

ah! but I'm not done yet.

should I be expecting u on my doorstep?

i wish i could. sorry! got to run.

let me know when u r back.
okay?

Madi sighed and put her phone aside, switching to her laptop. The MadLibs page, now free of the hijacked link, loaded in a heartbeat. "God, it feels good to be back."

Sarah glanced up. "What did you say?"

"Nothing. Just got to make a choice about the next rewatch."

Her sister's eyes widened. "Can I help you choose?"

"Um, sure, I guess."

"I want to watch *The Lost Boys*."

"But I thought you didn't like horror movies."

Sarah glared. "I don't like *slasher* movies. There's a difference. I think I'll like this one."

"You sure about that?" Madi teased. "These aren't the sparkly vampires, you know."

"I know that."

"All right, I'll tell the MadLibbers we're going to watch *The Lost—*"

Madi stopped in surprise as her sister threw her arms around her, hugging her tightly. Sarah rarely, if ever, initiated an embrace. Madi's hands wavered uncertainly in the air before she wrapped them around her sister's shoulders.

251

Sarah pulled away almost immediately. "This should be fun," she said.

And even though she wasn't grinning when she said it, Madi knew her sister was as happy as she was.

Madi twirled a strand of hair over her finger as she peeked at her dashboard post. She smirked, then hit REBLOG.

Monday Mashup: Some Kind of Wonderful Life

Keith gives up on his hopes of becoming an artist so he can stick around in the crummy little town and wait for Amanda to notice he exists. His best friend/real-life angel, Watts, shows him what life would be like if he actually followed his dreams.

2 WEEKS AGO | 3,791 notes
TAGGED: #SKOW #Some Kind of Wonderful #Wonderful Life

◼ antebellumintro likes this
◼ diabolicalmusings likes this
◼ miseenscene reblogged this from cesttropdelou

With Madi's plans for funemployment about to relaunch, the post felt like a good omen. *No more delaying my dreams.*

She reread her new MadLibs post one last time before she made the link live. She'd been offline for only a couple weeks, but it was a lifetime in Internet terms. Scrolling through the stats for the last few guest posts, she discovered there were thousands of new followers to the site. Her Internet fame might have been on hold for the last weeks of school, but she was set to return!

The thought gave her a rush of elation. She was back!

Blog Post 218, Tuesday 9:35 p.m.:

Back off, Twilight, *there's a new (old-school) vampire in town!*

When I started the rewatch for *The Lost Boys*, I knew it wasn't going to be the sparkly vampires that inspired my elementary school fangirling. *shudders* But could a new (old) vampire movie capture my attention the way the *Twilight* series once had? Before the MadLibbers live-blogging even took off, I was hooked. Angry teenagers? Check. Sexy death-metal vampires? Check. Kid on the outside, trying to figure it out before losing his already messed-up family? Check and CHECK.

I was down for the count ten minutes in.

When I usually write about a rewatch, I try to capture the highs and lows, but this movie swallowed me whole. I found I really cared about Sam. He's an outsider, struggling to figure things out while his life falls to pieces around him. (Too much truth there!) His love for his older brother, Michael, *fans self* was at once realistic and painful to watch. Difficult sibling dynamics are rarely explored in teen films, and this was one of many happy surprises from this rewatch . . .

Madi skimmed through the central paragraphs, her cheeks warming as she read the glowing descriptions of long-haired bad boy Michael. (She wondered if anyone else would know how much he reminded her of Laurent, or if she was the only one to see the connection.) She deleted one sentence, leaving her summary of his character more ambivalent, then jumped to the final summary.

Movie Rating: 9/10 Mad!Cows, with a HUGE dose of Mad!Love for a realistic portrayal of the ups and downs of a single-parent family with two siblings learning to get along, despite the challenges. Why not 10/10, you ask? Simply put—the GROSS factor. This film dripped with blood, guts, and gore, and while I appreciate it was a scary movie in its day, trying to calm my sister down in the middle of the Chinese-food scene was a bit of a downer. LOL

Would I rewatch it? Yes! This seems like a perfect date movie. *hint hint*

And that brings me to the end of my first MadLib since my hiatus. A HUGE thank-you goes out to the amazing MadLibbers who volunteered as temporary rewatchers. You are amazing!

And now it's time for you to let me know what YOU thought of *The Lost Boys*. Am I off on this? Were you swooning over Michael, too? I'm all ears.

invites you into my blog

eats garlic

MadLib

PS: I'm back on the FUNEMPLOYMENT bandwagon once more, so clickety-click on the links!

Comments enabled.

Tags: #MadLibs #TheLostBoys #ItsGoodToBeBack #Madi watches things and then blogs about them #Funemployment

Madi hit POST, then headed to the bathroom to get ready for bed. Sarah had her morning items—toothpaste, comb, toothbrush, and towel—all laid out in a neat line on the counter, and Madi was careful not to move them. Glancing in the mirror, she realized just how gross her hair looked. Usually falling in a shiny black sheet, in the last weeks it had grown dull from lack of care.

By the time Madi showered and blow-dried her hair, it was nearly eleven p.m. Returning to her bedroom, she found four texts from Laurent waiting on her phone. Her chest tightened as she read them.

> madi? you around? LOVED seeing you back at madlibs. admittedly a tiny bit jealous of your review of michael. 😆 seriously, though. so good to have you back. 😍

> really great post. don't let this commenting
> nonsense convince you otherwise.

> seems you're offline.
> text me before you look.

> madi, text me. PLEASE.

Hands shaking, she opened the MadLibs blog.

Madi felt like a truck had parked on her chest. Her breath wouldn't fill her lungs; her ribs ached. She scrolled through the comments, ears ringing. Comments blazed with anger. Replies seethed with disdain. The words *troll* and *fake geek girl* popped up again and again.

"My God . . ."

She'd walked in on an ongoing battle, her post in flames. While she'd showered, a troll war of monumental proportions had broken out between a number of MadLibbers and the anonymous commenter.

> **Comment 3.1, *anonymous*:** If I wanted to read about a teenage crush, I'd hang out on the *Twilight* page. This post made me PUKE. @MadLib needs to get out and get a REAL life. The more I read, the more I'm convinced she's a shut-in.
> **@laurentabelard:** You're not welcome. Stop posting. GO!
> ***anonymous*:** Or what? You'll yell at me in French? Thanks, Pepé Le Pew, but you're gonna have to woo your GF on your own time. I'm just telling it like it is. This. Post. SUCKS.
> **@StarveilBrian1981:** You need to read the posting guidelines, Anon. This is inappropriate content, and I'll be reporting this infraction.

anonymous: Ooooh . . . Baby Brian's going to REPORT ME. I'm dying of fear. LOLOLOL

@ModernDayWitch: Look. You've said your piece, now move on. You did this on @laurentabelard's and my post last week, and it wasn't appreciated then, and it isn't appreciated now. So go home. MadLibbers stick together. (*Madi, if you see this. Turn off anon postings—ASAP. Thanks.)

anonymous: Oh yeah—all the SJWs are coming out to play tonight. Mama Witch is ready to fight. LOL Careful you don't trip on your broom.

Eyes burning, Madi read through pages of angry comments. Five more replies appeared as she watched, the anonymous poster taking lower and lower shots as the argument raged. Almost all of her friends had come to her defense, but with anonymous posting open, there'd been no way to stop him. *Thought I turned that off,* Madi thought in dismay. Now it was too late to fix the damage.

She rubbed her temples as a stress headache began to pulse behind her eyes. She flicked open the settings page, only this time, she couldn't *access* her settings. The page was locked.

"What the hell?"

She refreshed again, but her password wouldn't work. Heart pounding, Madi tried a second time. PASSWORD INCORRECT appeared.

"No, no, no!"

Madi moved to her laptop and opened her e-mail with trembling fingers. There were a number of unopened e-mails, one linked site. She scanned through it, nausea churning her stomach:

NEW Message, MadLibs Site Manager: 9:48 p.m. EST
Priority: Normal
Subject: Password Change
This is an automated message to inform you that your password

for the MadLibs site has been updated. If you did not make the
changes, please click on the link below.

"GodDAMNIT!" Madi snarled, double-clicking the link. "I just got hacked!"

After ten minutes of double-checking security questions, she was back on-line where the battle raged.

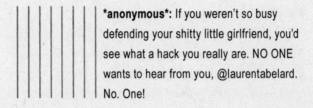

anonymous: If you weren't so busy defending your shitty little girlfriend, you'd see what a hack you really are. NO ONE wants to hear from you, @laurentabelard. No. One!

Madi took a sobbing breath. "Get the hell OUT!" she cried, taking the page offline with a single keystroke. Her phone buzzed, but she ignored it as she scrolled through the comments, trying to sift through the garbage. Failing, she deleted them all.

With that done, she opened the MadLibs e-mail server, knowing what she'd find.

NEW Message, *anonymous*: 9:36 p.m. EST
Subject: GO AWAY
Didn't think you'd be able to waltz back in here again, did you? I'm not giving up on this. You took off on your little NY fling to finish your stupid English course. YOU SHOULD HAVE STAYED AWAY.

"H-how would he know that?! I—I never posted about my class, or the trip!" Unable to breathe, she moved to the next e-mail.

NEW Message, *anonymous*: 9:41 p.m. EST
Subject: PUT UP OR SHUT UP
Too bad you're too much of a stuck-up bitch to stand up for

yourself. Or maybe that's how ALL you snobby girls are. Ignoring everyone else and expecting us guys to do your fighting for you.

NEW Message, *anonymous*: 9:49 p.m. EST
Subject: What—you SCARED NOW?
Aw . . . poor @MadLib's too scared to reply? Waaaaa! Stop being a baby. The silent treatment won't work! I'M NOT GOING ANYWHERE.

NEW Message, *anonymous*: 9:51 p.m. EST
Subject: I WON'T BE IGNORED
Don't like my e-mails? FINE. I'll give you something NEW to play with. Screw YOU! You're going to wish you'd taken me seriously when you had a chance, *minette*.

At that point, the e-mails stopped.

That's when he hacked in, Madi realized. She stared at the screen, blinking furiously. It was over for now, but how could she stop it from happening again? Her phone buzzed and this time she glanced down to see the two texts from Laurent.

> are you around yet? there's something up with your website. i just got blocked. did you do that?

> never mind. seems that everyone is blocked now. (did you do this or did the troll?) i really need to talk to you. answer, please, minette!

Madi started to type in a reply, then stopped. A cold sweat rose on her back. With shaking hands, she reopened the last e-mail.

"He called me *minette*," she gasped.

Her gaze flicked between the final e-mail and Laurent's text. The single word was burned into her retinas. That was Laurent's endearment. *His nick-name for her!* Seeing it echoed by the troll disturbed her more than even the doxing had. Her brow crinkled into deep grooves as a new thought intruded: *Why was Laurent so interested in me seeing what the troll posted? Why did he warn me when no one else did? Who else knows I went to New York to finish an English assignment?* The unsettling idea tightened its hold, and after a moment she deleted her unsent text.

As she became more unnerved, other instances of concern appeared: In the last few weeks, Laurent always seemed to be the first person to reply to the troll, but after that, Laurent would generally disappear from the comments. He was quick to get angry, but the first to console Madi and apologize for provoking the situation. It wasn't difficult to post from two different usernames—*heck, even a phone and a laptop would work!*—and if one of them used Tor to throw off the IP address, then it wouldn't even seem to come from the same place.

Other details popped to mind. Laurent was one of the newest MadLibbers; the trolling had only started after his arrival. Laurent was online at odd hours, then offline with no explanation. Laurent had shown up on Madi's doorstep, and weeks later, the troll had described her house. An easy task if he'd already been there! There suddenly seemed to be a hundred questions Madi couldn't answer. Her heart rattled against the walls of her chest as she looked back through the troll's messages to her.

"He knew I was in New York because he was there, too!" she cried.

Her phone buzzed in her sweaty palm, and she jumped.

> madi? you still there? i want to talk.

It was impossible! But was it . . . ?

"Oh my God," she whimpered. "This can't be happening."

She set her phone down as if it was a snake. She wasn't sure where the idea had come from, but now that it arrived, she couldn't shake it. As much as she didn't want to believe it, there were too many things that made sense.

Could the troll be Laurent?

18

"Les jeux sont faits. Translation: 'The game is up.'"
(*Ferris Bueller's Day Off*, 1986)

"Are you sick?"

Madi opened her eyes against the shimmer of sunlight to discover her sister standing just inside the door to her room.

"Hey, Sarah," she groaned. "Not sick, just tired." She rolled to the side, pulling back the covers to reveal yesterday's clothes. "Give me a minute to get ready, and I'll walk to school with you."

Her sister's frown deepened. "You really *are* sick."

"What? No, I'm not."

Her sister pointed to the clock radio/phone charger next to Madi's bed. She stared at it for several seconds, but the numbers were an equation that refused to add up. It was far too bright to be four in the morning, but that meant . . .

"Sarah, what time is it?"

"It's four-oh-nine," she answered. "You slept all day."

The grogginess disappeared under a rush of anxiety. She'd tossed and turned half the night as she dissected each moment she'd shared with Laurent. Sometime after midnight, she'd reread every one of his texts, but even that had left her uncertain. She didn't *want* to believe he was the troll, but the evidence was stacked against him. Madi had come to the uncomfortable realization that she just didn't *know* what to believe anymore. She was trapped.

Sarah waited in the doorway, her head tipped to the side.

"Wait," Madi said. "So if I overslept, who got you up?"

"Dad did."

"And who picked you up from school?"

"Dad. He went to the wrong classroom, though. I was certain you were coming, but when I started shouting for you, he came running down the hall." She rolled her eyes. "Totally embarrassing."

Madi let out a shaky laugh. "But you made it home okay?"

"Course I did. Dad said you were probably run-down from working on that assignment. So are you sick?"

Laurent popped to mind, and the possibility that he was the troll. It was impossible! (Unless it wasn't.)

Madi winced. "Maybe I am."

"Hope you feel better, then," Sarah said and walked away.

After dressing in clean clothes, Madi headed downstairs. It wasn't her turn to do dinner, but she pulled together a quick pot of spaghetti sauce, figuring she owed it to her father after foisting Sarah on him—planned or not. While she was measuring out the pasta, her phone buzzed.

> haven't seen you around at all today.
> is everything all right?

With a wave of guilt, she put the phone back into her pocket. It buzzed twice more while she was setting the table. Her feelings for Laurent aside, she needed to get his side of the story, but she really had no idea how to bring up the issue of the trolling. She didn't think it was him, but she wasn't entirely certain it *wasn't*, either.

Sarah came through the kitchen door at five thirty exactly, her father close on her heels.

"Smells delicious!" he said. "What's the occasion?"

"Nothing really. Just trying to say thank you for picking up my slack today. I don't know how I slept through my alarm." She filled her plate with pasta and headed to the table. Her phone buzzed, and Charles lifted his eyebrows, but Madi shoved it deeper in her pocket, ignoring it.

"I'd hardly say those grades are slacking," her father said, squeezing her shoulder as he passed on his way to his own spot. "Just a little worn-out from the effort, is my guess. Try getting more sleep."

"Madi slept all day," Sarah announced.

"Then she probably needed it."

The phone buzzed again. This time Madi pulled it out, ignoring Laurent's series of texts to open her settings. She flicked on the standard "User Offline" message. It was stupid, she knew. She was *never* offline. But that's what the troll had brought her to: hiding from the place she used to hide from real life. It hurt her that Laurent might be the cause.

"Everything okay?" her father asked.

"Things are fine," she said, dropping the phone back into her pocket.

"You sure? You seem—"

"Seriously, Dad. I'm fine."

"All right, then."

Dinner passed uneventfully. Her father chattered about his day. Sarah got into a deep conversation about the supervoid in the constellation Eridanus, and how it might actually be evidence of a parallel universe interfering with our own. Madi only halfway followed her sister's excited description—science was Sarah's passion, not hers—while their father made sounds of encouragement. *Perhaps,* Madi thought, *it's time to watch another sci-fi movie.* She squelched the thought almost immediately. She had no intention of going online until things calmed down. (The fact she was delaying was a niggling thought in the back of her mind.) She'd post for MadLibs again, but this time she'd be ready to block the troll the second he showed up.

As for dealing with Laurent—

Her thoughts were interrupted by the trill of a cell phone. For a second Madi thought it was hers. What would she say to Laurent if it was him?! But her father stood from the table, patting his lapel pocket as he fished his phone from its depths and put it to his ear.

"Charles Nakama speaking," he said. Across the table from him, Sarah stopped eating to watch. "Mm-hmm? Yes, that'd be my daughter, Madison."

Madi looked up in confusion. *What the hell?*

"It says what?!" Ashen-faced, her father stared at Madi before striding from the room. "No, I *don't* know anything about that! Do you know where it came from?" His footsteps disappeared down the hall to his office. "Just let me call my attorney and—"

The door slammed shut, cutting off his words. At the same time, an image flashed on Madi's screen, followed quickly by another. Her chest ached seeing them.

This felt like the beginning.

Maybe it was the end.

She looked back up to find Sarah staring at her, wide-eyed.

"What did you do this time?"

Madi shook her head, not knowing how to explain either her father's reaction or Laurent's. "I honestly don't know."

"Madi! We need to talk!"

Her father's bellow tore Madi from her trance. She still hadn't answered Laurent. Didn't know how.

Sarah caught Madi's eyes across the table. "I'll do dishes," she said. "You go deal with—"

"Madi—*now*!"

"Coming!" Madi shouted as she sprinted from the room. Down the hallway, a line of photographs showed the Nakamas through the years—Charles and his wife in various poses, the two girls in matching outfits in front of them—every photo projecting the perfect American family. Not in one of them, Madi realized, were her parents touching. Their hands were always on the shoulders of their daughters. The two of them separate. Disconnected.

"MADI!"

She slid to a stop at the entrance to her father's office. He sat at his desk, his laptop open, the phone balanced awkwardly between his ear and right shoulder. He looked up as she walked in.

"You need to explain this."

She walked toward his desk, anxiety rising with each step. What could it be? She caught sight of the screen and her breath hitched.

"Who took these?" her father growled as he clicked through the images.

They were pictures of Madi and Laurent, hand in hand: walking along the path to the ruins, laughing on a park bench, sitting in the coffee shop. They were grainy, but certainly visible. Madi stared at them, confusion mixing with fear.

"I—I don't know."

Her father flicked to the next photo, and Madi jerked. "Oh my God!"

It was a photograph of Madi and Laurent kissing at the ruins. Seeing it, Madi had her answer. The troll had followed them, photographed them; there was no way Laurent could be the troll! Her relief mixed with her terror.

"How do we prevent this from being printed?" her father snapped. He shifted the phone to the other ear. "My daughter's privacy—our entire family's privacy, for that matter!—is at stake here."

It took Madi a few seconds to realize her father wasn't talking to her, but to someone else on the phone—his attorney, Ms. Auryn, most likely.

Her father clicked the page and the last bit of blood drained from her face. A splashy tabloid image appeared from the popular Internet celebrity site, *HTR: Heard the Rumor?* Photos of Laurent and Madi—in various poses—splashed across the foreground while bright red letters crossed the center:

"Madison Nakama, the daughter of Tri-State Herald *journalist Charles Nakama, writer of the popular family values 'Down Home' column, in scandalous relationship with illegal immigrant!"*

Madi felt like she'd been kicked in the stomach. She tried to breathe but couldn't. "Th-that's my name," she gasped. "My *REAL* name!"

"It is, and mine, too."

"B-but they can't just publish that kind of stuff, can they? It's a lie! Laurent's here on a student visa."

"They can and they already have. HTR's site has the images up now. I was contacted by my editor at the *Tri-State Herald* about it."

"Why would they contact you? This is about me."

"My 'Down Home' column has a conservative readership. These claims are going to cause backlash with readers." He pinched the bridge of his nose. "Tabloids love exposing things like this. Doesn't matter if it's the truth or not."

Her gaze jerked up from the screen. "Tabloids?"

"HTR was the first to run the news, but a number of other tabloids, online and print, are following up on the story." Her father shifted the phone to the other ear. "As the writer of 'Down Home,' I've been asked to comment on it."

> i need to talk, laurent

> madi? i didn't expect to hear from you.

> it's a long story 😫 things have been CRAZY

> is that why you disappeared?

not exactly. there r other things going on, too. i need to talk. face-to-face

all right

the troll is back. it's a mess. he took a bunch of photos (of u and me). he's gone public with them. made up a bunch of lies. MY REAL NAME IS WITH THEM.

public?

yes! And now they're all over the INTERNET, laurent! that's it. i'm out! I CAN'T DEAL WITH PEOPLE KNOWING WHO I AM IN RL 😫

OMG

exactly

i'll come out to millburn. i can explain this to your father.

no—u can't! dad's at a meeting with his lawyer.

please let me help.

😥 ugh. i just don't know

PLEASE. I don't even know what's going on!

can we skype? i just need to talk

perfect. i'll turn on my laptop now.

okay hold on

In less than a minute she'd opened the video-chat program. The screen shimmered and Laurent's bedroom appeared. It wasn't tidy as it had been the last time they'd talked online. Clothes covered the floor and unmade bed, Laurent's backpack dangling, forgotten, off the closet door's handle. Laurent looked up and caught her eyes.

"Madi," he breathed.

Madi didn't move. *Couldn't.* In those few seconds before her voice returned, she had time to consider how unbelievably beautiful he was. His teeth were even, his disheveled hair shiny and full, his body athletic. Normal people—like those Madi interacted with on a day-to-day basis—simply didn't have that kind of symmetry and grace. *The perfection.*

"It's good to see you again," she said.

He took a shuddering breath. "God, I missed you."

"Missed you, too."

Tears filled Laurent's eyes, his face wracked with anguish as he neared the screen. "Why did you disappear on me? I thought I'd done something wrong. I thought—" His voice broke.

Madi opened her mouth, meaning to give him a half-truth about being busy with school, but the truth tumbled out instead.

"Because, for a little while at least, I thought it might have been *you.*"

Laurent frowned. "What might have been me?"

"The troll," she said, hands tightening into claws on the armrest. "I thought—I dunno—maybe you'd been doing it. Playing me along. Making it into some stupid game to hurt me. I wasn't *certain* it was you . . . but I wasn't sure it *wasn't.*"

He stared at her for several seconds as her words settled in. She remembered that afterward—how clearly she could see the moment when he understood what she'd said—when it cut him to the bone. They were miles away from each other, but she could feel the change in atmosphere. He leaned back in his chair.

"You—you thought I was the troll?"

"I thought you might be. I wasn't sure—"

"You thought I was attacking you."

"No . . . Yes. I mean—"

"Which is it?" he snapped. "Yes or no?"

Madi cringed. "I'd already figured it was one of the MadLibbers, and since I didn't really know you as well as some of the others, you seemed like an obvious choice. I-I'm sorry. I should have asked, but I didn't know how. I realized as soon as I saw the pictures it couldn't be you, but before then . . ."

On-screen, his brows tightened until a single line creased his forehead. "What did I ever do to make you doubt me?" His words were a cry of pain. "Why didn't you trust me?!"

"Because I didn't know why you'd spend time with me. I mean, look at us. We don't fit. You're gorgeous, Laurent, and I'm . . ." She let out a teary laugh. "Plain old Madi."

"I never treated you that way!" he cried. "Not once. Not ever!"

"I know, but you're perfect, and I'm just—"

She never got the chance to say the rest because Laurent reached toward the camera.

"I'm done." Her screen abruptly went black as he exited the chat.

Conversation ended.

Madi took a sobbing breath. "No!"

That was it. Her relationship with Laurent Abelard was officially over.

"Madi? You ready?" her father called. "We should go through this while we have time."

"Coming, Dad," Madi called, surprised by how normal her voice sounded. "I'll tell Sarah to get in the car." She felt like she was encased in ice. She stumbled to the kitchen on frozen limbs, barely able to breathe. Laurent had hung up on her. It was over. *Over!*

By nine o'clock Sarah was at school, and by ten Madi and her father at the Millburn police station. Charles waited at the counter, his attorney at his side.

While he filled out forms with Ms. Auryn, a police officer with a permanent scowl on his face took Madi into his office to interview her about the apparent stalker and who it might be.

"Do you remember anyone following you and Laurent when you walked to the Colonial Inn?" the officer asked grimly. "Someone who might have seen you there?"

"No. Not at all," Madi said. "Laurent thought he saw something in the trees, but it turned out to be nothing."

"Can you think of why someone targeted you? Anything you might've done that someone would be seeking retribution for? A schoolmate angry for some reason?" His gaze flicked to her and then back down again. "Cyberbullying is more common than you might think."

"Not really," Madi said. "I mean, I don't even go to a regular school."

"No?" The officer made another note in his file. "Which school do you attend?"

"OMA, their online program."

His pen scratched over the page for several seconds. "You said you run a blog online," he continued. "How many people follow you?"

"I can't even keep up with the stats," Madi admitted. "There're people around the world. MadLibs gets almost a million hits a month." She leaned forward. "So can you figure out who it is?"

The police officer set the pen down and looked up. His eyes had rings under them as if he hadn't slept in weeks, and a fan of wrinkles spread out from each side.

"We'll do everything we can to help you, Ms. Nakama. *We will.* But . . ." He nodded to a pile of folders on the corner of the desk. "Your case is one of many. Right now all we have are some photographs, a tabloid story, and some nasty e-mails and comments, plus your claims of online harassment."

"But it's all true!"

The officer nodded. "I'm sure it is. But it's still a hard thing to prove. And even if we had solid evidence—"

"But you do! The troll's been harassing me for weeks. You have to go after him!"

The officer leaned back in his seat and crossed his arms. "Look. This isn't like it is in the movies. We can't just click a couple keys to find him and send a SWAT team to his house. Without a name, I don't have a lot to go on."

"So you're just giving up on this?"

"Not at all. I'm passing your information on to our online crimes division. Cyber harassment is a criminal act in New Jersey—a felony, in fact—but it takes more than just finger-pointing to bring someone in. It's an even grayer area for juveniles."

"Meaning what?"

"This guy who's bullying you is probably a schoolmate, right? If he's under twenty-one, he'll only be charged with cyber-harassment in the fourth degree. If he's under sixteen, it'll be a special case, dealt with by the juvenile system." The officer tapped the file. "With the minimal evidence we have now, the guy will probably walk. At most he'll get a fine."

"A—a fine?" Madi choked.

"Truth is, there isn't a hell of a lot we can do without solid proof, and you just don't have it."

"But I showed you all the posts and e-mails!"

"All anonymous. The IPs are fake. And until our online division can locate him, my hands are tied." The officer closed the folders and added it to the pile on his desk.

Madi squeezed her eyes shut, breathing hard. "This can't be happening. . . . I can't believe it. . . . I—I—"

"Miss?"

Her lashes fluttered open to find the officer frowning down at her.

"I'm sorry," he said. "I really am. And we *will* go after him, but I need you to understand that it could take a while. Months, most likely."

"But—"

"The online crimes div will do their best to catch him in the act somehow so they can show, without question, what he's done to you. But . . ." He winced. "It's not going to happen right away. It's a matter of proof."

Madi's eyes narrowed. "Then I'll get the proof myself."

19

*"We're all pretty bizarre. Some of us are just better
at hiding it, that's all."*
(*The Breakfast Club*, 1985)

"Wow, you really screwed things up with Laurent."

Madi didn't stop walking, just glared at her little sister. "Gee, thanks, Sarah. I hadn't realized that until you pointed it out."

"So he just hung up on you after you talked to him?"

"Yup." Madi reshouldered her bag. Under June's heat, her back was sweaty from its weight. "That's pretty much it."

"And you haven't heard from him since?"

"No. He's not answering my texts, either."

"Can you e-mail him? Tweet, maybe?"

"I tried. He's offline. I even tried phoning, but it went to voice mail." Madi shook her head. "I think it's just . . . over."

Sarah plodded along until they reached the crosswalk. She paused—checking both directions, as she always did—but instead of walking, she put her hand on Madi's arm, stopping her.

"This is the troll's fault, not yours," Sarah said grimly.

"Tell me something I don't know."

"You need to find the troll. Get your proof."

"I've been trying, Sarah, but it's not that easy. The troll's smart. He knows how to hide. I can't just force him to show up on demand."

"This whole thing isn't going to stop until you do."

Sarah crossed the road, and Madi followed her to the other side. "The troll is doing this to hurt you," Sarah continued. "He's the one who messed up things with you and Laurent. And he brought Dad into it, too." She gave Madi a fierce look. "It's like Newton's first law of motion."

"I was with you until Newton, and then you totally lost me."

"Newton's first law says objects in motion tend to stay in motion. The troll's like that. He's got momentum. He *likes* what he's doing. You need to force him out because he's not going to stop on his own."

"You really think so?"

"I don't just think so, I *know* so," Sarah said. "It's physics."

Madi shivered despite the heat of the day. "Then I'd better get looking."

By the time she got home, Madi had compiled a mental list of the things she knew about the troll. He knew her from her previous fandom on Redux, which meant he'd been online for at least a few years, cutting out the youngest member of the MadLibbers: WrittenInChantalics. He had an obvious temper, which removed ModernDayWitch, who always took the role of the mama bear of the group, but leaving ArtWithAttitude, Ava, as a distinct possibility.

Ava and Madi had conflicted from their very first meeting at the Metrograph. Ava's competitiveness was a vague but irritating part of her interaction with Madi. There were the snide comments: *"Aren't you, like, a bona fide recluse? . . . Can't we, like, bribe you or something?"* And Ava's one-sided attraction to Laurent. The only thing that didn't fit was that Madi sensed the troll was male. He seemed to have connections to Redux—a sci-fi site—which made StarveilBrian1981 a front-runner. But Brian was as trustworthy as he was odd. In all the years she'd known him, he'd never wavered on that. His name was cut from the list, too.

As to the tens of thousands of other MadLibbers who followed her blog and participated to varying degrees, she couldn't even hazard a guess. There were simply too many to consider. But Madi's gut told her it was someone who knew her well. Someone who knew her weaknesses.

"Just need to figure out who."

She made a list of her most trusted online friends and wrote them each an e-mail. If her life had a soundtrack, Madi thought, this would be when the epic spy theme would play.

NEW Message, MNakama@MadLibs.com: 4:39 p.m. EST
Priority: HIGH
Subject: Need your HELP

Hi Brian,

I know this is a weird thing to ask, but I need your supersleuthing Internet skills. I've been having some issues with a troll the last couple weeks. (I'm sure you've noticed.) I figure if anyone can help track this guy down, it's you. My goal is some hard evidence so I can stop him. IP Addresses, information, etc.

Thanks. You ROCK!

—Madi

PS: Please don't do anything illegal, okay? I have to take this information to the police afterward, and I wouldn't want you to get in trouble.

Less than three minutes later, she had a reply:

NEW Message, StarveilBrian1981@StarveilRebellion.com: 4:41 p.m. EST
Priority: HIGH
Subject: RE: Need your HELP

Madi,

Consider it done.

I'll contact a couple of my other friends and get them involved, too. BTW, have you asked Ava to do some checking? The girl is one of the better hackers out there.

—Brian

Madi chewed the side of her thumbnail as she reread the e-mail. Could she trust Ava with this? Did she have a choice anymore? After a long moment, she wrote Brian a reply.

Reply to Message from StarveilBrian1981@StarveilRebellion. com: 4:45 p.m. EST
Priority: HIGH
Subject: RE: RE: Need your HELP

You are AMAZING, Brian. Thank you. I'll contact Ava and get her help, too. Let me know what you and your friends find. :)
—Madi

After sending off twelve more requests to MadLibbers far and wide, Madi spent her evening sifting through years of comments and posts across various platforms, hoping for a glimpse of the troll. There were angry comments, but they seemed random: individual readers who came and went, never staying. The problem was, she'd *deleted* the worst of them.

"Goddamnit!" Madi sighed. "I messed it up when I got rid of the comments."

Near midnight, she headed downstairs to eat. Afterward, she filled the dishwasher and washed the counters, needing something to distract her. When she finally came back upstairs, it was nearly one in the morning. Madi's breath caught as she logged into her laptop.

Four messages waited in her inbox.

The first was from her mother, telling her that she and Madi's father had spoken at length about Madi's plan to take a year off from school, and that she supported the decision. The second was a random e-mail inviting Madi to do a talk at New York Comic Con, as part of their online ventures community. The third was from Ava. Madi clicked OPEN with trembling fingers.

NEW Message, ArtWithAttitude@Buffyverse.com: 12:08 a.m. EST
Priority: HIGH
Subject: RE: Need your HELP

Hey Madi,

Ran a few years of MadLibs comments and posts through the Wayback online database. (Figured you'd probably deleted the comments, but they might be there.) Turns out they were. Got a pile of them, then filtered it through a metadata collator my friend C used for his grad research. Here are a few interesting phrases that popped up:

It just pisses me off that fandom doesn't welcome men the way they do women . . . Believe me, Millburn's in the middle of nowhere! . . . It's the fault of all those feminazi campaigners! . . . I hate it! Can't wait to get out! . . . And that's where I have to call bullshit. Absolutely NO. Stories like this are half the problem with society. All lies! . . . Screw friends falling in love. Keith deserved better . . . As one of "those guys" hanging out and watching from the sidelines, I'm just saying this movie SUCKED . . . It's the fault of those damned SJWs! Hate them!

No idea who your troll is. The names he uses are random, but metadata says it's the same source. (I just sent the data to Brian, too. He might be able to track down your poster.) Hope that helps. I attached the link with the full document HERE.

—Ava

Shaky with adrenaline, Madi opened the next e-mail, from Brian.

NEW Message, StarveilBrian1981@StarveilRebellion.com:
12:21 a.m. EST
Priority: HIGH
Subject: RE: Need your HELP

Madi,

Just got some information from Ava, which I collated with the data sources I'd located. I've got your troll. It's @fandometric. He's been hiding in plain sight:

Tweet from a few weeks ago: *@fandometric: @MadLib Feel free to vent. We're all here for you.*

Tweet from the last post: *@fandometric: @ArtWithAttitude It's the fault of those damned SJWs! Hate them!*

"SJW!" Madi gasped. "That's what the troll called me in his e-mails." She tried to imagine all the people who'd gone to school with her through the years. She wasn't close friends with anyone, but she couldn't think of anyone who'd have reason to hate her, either. No clear enemies. An image of a black-haired boy with angry eyes floated to mind.

"Except for Robbie's rude friend Gavin . . ."

Worried, she returned to Brian's e-mail.

I ran the flagged posts through a couple tracking programs. No go. The troll's using Tor (or something like it) to block his IP address. But then I sent the info to a buddy of mine who uses Tor and a few other *special* programming tools. (Please don't ask, all right? And you can't tell the police who sent you this.) My friend was able to use a couple of his sources to locate the origin. You've got two main suspects:

1) *Gavin Alhorn, Millburn, NJ.*

2) *Robert Sullivan, Millburn, NJ.*

There's no way I can tell you *how* I got those names, so you'll need to catch them in the act.

Let me know if I can help.

—Brian

Madi stared at the screen. *Robbie or Gavin.* All she needed was proof and she could go to the police.

It was time to lure the troll out of his cave.

"Gavin Alhorn?" Sarah repeated.

"Yes, Gavin. He's Robbie's friend," Madi said. "Black hair. Angry. I've seen him around the school a couple times. He pushed between us the day you went to the library for the study group."

"What *about* Gavin?"

"I think he's the troll, but I'm not certain. I need to double-check before I confront him about it."

Sarah frowned. "So what're you going to do?"

"I need to talk to him. But it can't be too obvious." Madi ran her fingers through her hair. "God! Why is it always so much easier to be a detective in the movies?"

"I know how you can talk to him."

Madi dropped her hands to her side. "How?"

"He games with Robbie. I can invite us along."

"You think Robbie will say yes? I mean, if Gavin's his friend and all."

Sarah gave her a level stare. "Robbie likes you, Madi. I'm sure he'll say yes the second I tell him you're coming."

Madi rubbed her sweating hands on the sides of her jeans. "Yeah . . . I guess that'll work. I just need to talk to Gavin, that's all."

Sarah nodded. "Give me a minute. I'll text Robbie."

Robbie's house wasn't just a house—it was the upper floor of the ancestral Colonial Inn where Madi and Sarah had played as children. Robbie's parents, Mr. and Mrs. Sullivan, were the proprietors. Arriving, the memories of walking along the beach with Laurent flashed to mind. For a second, Madi considered sending Laurent a Snapsed of the ruins where he'd tried to convince her to climb to the top, but she held back. She'd screwed the relationship up by her own actions; the least she could do was respect his decision to move on.

"You coming, Madi?" Sarah called from the front door.

She slipped her phone back in her pocket without taking a photo.

Robbie's mother was bubbly and smiling, the perfect made-for-TV mother if Madi had ever seen one. She bustled the two of them upstairs to the family's suite with a shout of "Come on down for cookies in half an hour, kids!"

Madi glanced over at Sarah and raised her eyebrows.

"Parents are weird," Sarah grumbled.

The door opened before Madi could answer. Robbie was there—his damp hair looking more brown than red. Madi wished that he liked her sister rather than her. He genuinely seemed nice, and Sarah had so few friends.

"C'mon in," he said, heading inside. "I've got the gaming system in my room."

Sarah followed, Madi two steps behind as she drew in details from the cozy apartment. There were bowls of potpourri on tables, an open "look book" of Robbie as a baby next to the couch. The furniture was antique but polished to a sheen, and black-and-white photographs of the ruins in matching frames covered the walls. It all looked like it had been taken out of a design magazine.

"You coming?" Robbie called.

"Right, sorry! Just looking around," Madi said, embarrassed. "It's a beautiful home, Robbie."

"It's all right, I guess." He swung the door open and stepped inside. "Just sucks having guests around all the time."

Robbie's room was the antithesis of his mother's homey decorating style. Clothes lay in piles in the corners, the bed unmade. The distinct scent of body odor hung heavy in the air, choking Madi.

"You are a slob, Robbie," Sarah announced. "This room is filthy."

"Sarah!" Madi gasped.

Robbie just laughed. "My room, my rules." Sarah took a seat on the floor at the end of the bed, and Robbie tossed a controller into her hands. "Here, let's play."

Madi tried to find a clean place to sit, but the options were limited. She finally opted for the chair next to Robbie's computer desk. The laptop was chugging away on a download, and she slid it carefully out of her way.

"Here you go, Madi," he said, handing her a controller with a grin and settling himself down in front of the TV.

"Um . . . wasn't your friend supposed to be joining us?" Madi asked.

"Who, Gavin? Nah. He canceled at the last second."

Madi's face fell in disappointment. "He did?"

"Uh-huh. His computer got hacked last night. He's reprogramming his firewall and trying to recover the files he lost." Robbie turned on the game, and the basement of an underground lab appeared. "All right, then—let's play!"

The home screen started up with a roar of music.

"What're we playing?" Madi asked, getting herself into position.

"*Zombie Death Squad 3*," Sarah said.

Madi shrugged. "Never heard of it."

Robbie took position at the front. "The premise is that we're stuck in an abandoned fallout shelter far below the surface of Earth, a year after a biological war. There are air shafts that reach the ground, but they're a maze."

"The point of the game is to get out," Sarah explained. "Just keep moving up."

"Except when you have to move down to avoid certain death," Robbie added.

On-screen, the characters inside one of the white-walled rooms began to scream, their eyes turning black, skin sinking corpselike around their eyes. The roar of the music grew louder.

Madi gave a nervous laugh. "Well, that's not good."

"Nope," Robbie said. "Because some of the air vents are laced with the zombie virus, and that means . . ." On-screen, the countdown began. "We've got to get moving. There are other teams playing the undead. We're survivors. Move!"

For the next ten minutes, the trio dodged and moved through the maze, Madi's admittedly poor gaming skills left Robbie and Sarah in several compromised positions. Madi's giggles grew into panicked laughter as she lodged her character in the corner of a storage room.

"Wait!" she shouted. "I'm stuck! I can't get out!"

Sarah disengaged from the zombie she'd been fighting to help her sister. Madi's avatar moved in the same direction over and over again, slamming its face into the metal cupboards.

"Back up!" Robbie ordered. "You're going the wrong way."

Another undead lurched into view.

"HOW?! I can't seem to move my legs."

"You deal with Madi," Sarah said. "I'll take out the trash." She headed into the engagement.

"The green button," Robbie snapped. "No, not that one. The other one!"

"Hurry up, guys," Sarah warned. "I can't keep this up all day."

"C'mon, Madi! Get with it! You're killing us here!"

But Madi was laughing so hard she could barely breathe. She finally spun her character around. "I'm out!" she shouted. "We need to—"

The cupboard burst open, two zombies appearing out of nowhere.

"Run!" Madi screamed. "Save yourself! I will sacrifice myself for you!" And she awkwardly two-stepped her avatar directly into the path of the attackers.

Robbie made a hissing sound. "Fuck! I'm out." He dropped the controller to the floor and stood. "Don't think I've ever gotten a score so low."

"Relax," Madi said. "It's just a game."

"You made me lose!"

Madi's laughter faded uncertainly. "Geez, Robbie. I didn't think you were so—"

"I should've known better than to let you play!"

"Leave her alone," Sarah said. Her face had gone white except for two bright red blotches of color on her cheeks.

"So what? You're gonna defend her?"

"Madi's never played this game before; she didn't know how to—"

"Figures you'd take her side. SJWs are all the same!"

Madi's heart began to pound so fast she felt dizzy. *SJW. That was the troll's taunt.*

"I'm outta here," Robbie said as he stalked from the room.

Madi stared at the closed door. She knew Robbie. He'd been in her freshman classes. He was smart, nice . . . funny, even. He tutored for Wattley's class and had invited her to hang out at the library when he'd been helping Sarah. He always seemed nice . . . *until he didn't.*

Sarah's words rose in Madi's mind: *"Robbie only asked me to go to the movie because he likes you. . . ."*

The realization slammed into the center of Madi's chest. Robbie's interest had developed in the background of her all-too-stressful real life the last few weeks. His attraction to her had been a fact Madi had grown aware of, but ignored. She'd never once considered that he might be there—*online*—too. Under the guise of @fandometric, Robbie could have watched her for months! He would have seen Madi's online romance with Laurent, and when his offline attentions had been rejected, his frustration would have turned into anger.

Robbie had trolled Madi out of jealousy, punishing her for choosing Laurent rather than him.

She swallowed hard, other details falling into place. The troll's knowledge of Madi's New York trip was the one element that had never made complete sense, but now did. His words ran through her mind: *"It's a small group, mostly one-on-one review. . . ."* Robbie and Sarah talked during the tutoring sessions he ran. He easily could have found out about Madi's comings and goings since Sarah was known to overshare. And since Robbie lived at the Colonial Inn, it would have been easy enough for him to take photos from the veranda without being seen. He'd probably heard Laurent call her *minette*.

"H-he's the one," Madi whispered.

"He's what?"

"Robbie's the troll. He's fandometric! He's the person who's been harassing me."

"He is?"

"Yes!"

Sarah's eyes widened until they looked like they were going to pop from her head. "What do we do?"

"The police need proof," Madi said. "I . . ." She turned to the laptop on the desk next to her. "I need to check to be sure."

"But you can't just go on his computer! That's illegal!"

"I have to, Sarah!"

Her sister began to pace the clothes-strewn room. "I don't know, Madi. It's wrong. I don't think you should."

"I'll only look and see if I can find something. You keep him out of here."

Sarah stumbled to a stop. "But how?!"

"I dunno. Stall him or something. Hurry, Sarah! Keep him out of here."

Her sister staggered to the door. She looked like she was going to be sick. "You have five minutes. That's it."

"I need more!"

"Five," she repeated. "And if I start screaming, you'd better get out."

"Five minutes." Maddi nodded. "Got it."

The first step was easy. Robbie's computer was in the middle of downloading a torrent, and when Madi had tapped the keyboard, she didn't need a password to get in. That was the first, and only, break she got.

Her fingers blurred over the keyboard as she searched for evidence of his trolling. Madi couldn't breathe. If he caught her, she'd have to explain what she was doing. *I was wrong about Laurent! What if I'm wrong about Robbie, too?!* Her gut said she wasn't.

On the other side of the door, she could hear Sarah speaking too loudly.

". . . but I thought your mom said she was making cookies. Can't you go get us some?" And then Robbie's reply, too low to be heard. "Please, Robbie," Sarah pleaded. "I really want those cookies." More grumbling. "Oh no. Madi never eats cookies. She's—she's—She just doesn't."

The door stayed closed.

"Please," Madi gasped. "All I need is proof." If she could find an account with "fandometric" or a draft of his trolling, she'd have all the evidence she needed.

Madi tried to open his e-mail, but the password stumped her. Then she looked through draft documents. All blank. She went to his browser history— completely clean.

"No!" As Brian had warned her, the troll was good at covering his tracks.

The voices in the hallway grew closer.

Madi closed her eyes, trying to dredge up all the details of the troll she could imagine. But in her panic, she couldn't find the right words, and without e-mail access she couldn't search his outgoing mail.

"If I only had a good IP address to—" A single word came to mind, and she typed it into the computer's search: *Tor.* The program that hides your IP address. The program appeared in the task manager just as Sarah began to scream.

"Madi! MADI!" Sarah wailed. "Robbie won't get me any COOKIES!!!"

Madi right-clicked on Tor and hit END TASK. Tor was off! She closed the task manager and bolted for the door, but Robbie was standing on the other side.

The door banged into his shoulder. "Ouch! What the hell?" he yelped.

"Sorry!"

"Your sister's freaking out. You'd better go—"

But Madi was already past him and sprinting down the stairs two at a time. "Let's go, Sarah!" she shouted. "We've got to GO!"

20

Madi knocked on the office door, waiting until she heard her father mutter, "It's open." He looked up as she stepped inside. "What's up?"

"Dad, we need to talk."

Her father dropped the papers in his hand on the desk and came around to Madi's side. "That sounds serious. What's happened?"

"I found him."

"Found who?"

"The person who sent those photographs to the papers. The same person who turned me in to Mrs. Preet. It's a troll. A troll from the MadLibs site."

"Madi, this is a lot of information to throw at me at once." Her father sat down and patted the chair next to him. "I need you to start at the beginning."

"Well," Madi said, "I guess it started when I finished up reviewing the *Starveil* series. There was a reader who . . ." Her words faded. "No, wait. It was before then. This actually goes back further."

"Back to what?"

"In the months before I decided to do online school, I got really active in a couple fandoms."

"Fandoms?"

"Groups of online people who like the same thing."

Her father's expression glazed over. "I don't—"

"Like Internet communities," Madi explained. "People talking on the net, chatting and posting art and writing stories and stuff. And one of the websites I used to hang out on was Redux."

"Madison, is this story bad? Are you mixed up in something illegal?"

"No," Madi said tiredly. "It's nothing like that. God, Dad, you have got to stop being so scared of the Internet. Redux was a great place at first. And I was really happy to have people to talk to, since I'd sort of lost those connections to people at school. And for the most part, the people online were cool. Most of them, at least."

Her father tapped the armrests on his chair, scowling. "And those who weren't cool?"

"It was one person, mainly. And he started to bully me—troll me, is what it's called—until I finally left."

Her father's brow crumpled. "But, sweetie, why didn't you tell me any of this?"

"I dunno. It seemed like dumb kid stuff. And you and Mom were busy with getting Sarah diagnosed." She shrugged. "I didn't want to bother you guys."

"Oh, Madi."

"So I left Redux and found some new communities—nicer ones. And then eventually I started working on the idea of creating my own blog. That's what I did with MadLibs, and everything went well for almost two years. Really well, actually! But then I finished reviewing *Starveil* and all of a sudden, I had this anonymous poster heckling me."

"But why?"

"Bullies are bullies. It doesn't matter to them why." Madi glared out the window as she spoke. The words were easy to say, but they bothered her more than she could explain. She'd spent her whole life trying to protect Sarah from the cruel taunts of classmates who didn't understand her otherness. She'd considered herself immune to bullies, but it seemed one had found exactly the right way to push her. It exhausted her.

"At first it wasn't so bad," Madi continued. "I blocked the poster. I tried to find the IP address. I switched off anonymous commenting. But nothing seemed to lead back to him. Whoever was doing the trolling was smarter than most. He hid his address. He changed his usernames." She looked up, catching her father watching her, slack-jawed. "I'm pretty sure the troll was the one who turned me in for breaking the school code and for plagiarizing. I think he sent the pictures of me and Laurent."

"Bastard!"

"Yeah, that name kind of fits," Madi said with a tired laugh. "When I went offline to finish my project, the troll disappeared again."

"Because you weren't posting?"

"Maybe," she said. "But I had other people posting, friends who were helping out. Laurent even took a turn. And then the troll came back. He told me he'd start causing trouble." Madi winced. "And then those pictures showed up. When I reported what happened to the police, they told me it could take months to catch him."

"Months?!"

"The troll's smart. He hid his tracks really, really well. And since there was no solid proof it was him, the police said the cyber-harassment charges probably wouldn't stick. They've been looking into it, but I decided to get evidence on my own."

Her father ran his hand over his mustache, frowning. "So how do you find someone like that? Can you go back to the police? Can we ask them to—"

"I already know who it is."

Her father made a sound like he'd been punched, and all the air had rushed out of him. He leaned forward. "Who?" he growled. "Who's doing this?!"

"It's Robbie."

"Who?"

"Robbie Sullivan, a guy I used to go to school with. He's a senior at Millburn Academy. He runs Sarah's study group, actually."

Charles blinked. "But isn't that the person you two were gaming with today?"

Madi nodded. "That's when I found the program on his computer that prevents his IP address from being logged." She smiled grimly. "I turned it off. If he trolls me again, I'll be able to see him. Catch him. That'll be all the evidence the police need."

Her father sat back against his chair and pulled off his glasses. His face was pale. "So what now?"

"I need you to drive me to the police station. I'm ending this."

"How?"

"I'm going to lure Robbie out so the police can catch him."

Madi glanced over at Sarah sitting next to her on the couch. They'd opted for a rerun of some movie Madi could barely remember about a guy who died, but stayed on Earth, haunting his wife as he searched for his killer. Sarah had dozed off halfway through it, but Madi's nerves had kept her awake. She'd written the MadLibs post in record time. Now it was time to post it.

"You think it's okay?" Madi asked.

Her sister yawned and stretched, still half asleep.

"Sarah?"

"What?"

"Do you really think the post is okay?"

Sarah looked over as she reached for the game controller. "Yes. Have you posted yet?"

"I will in a second." Madi chewed her lower lip as she scanned through the opening paragraph. "I just want to make sure it's right. This has to work."

Blog Post 219, Friday 3:41 p.m.:

The Ghosts of Movies Past

I wasn't planning on doing a rewatch, but after one of the worst weeks in my life, I found I couldn't sleep. I flicked through late-night television, hoping it would drown out the voices in my head, the ones telling me I wasn't good enough, not smart enough, not cool enough for this blog. What I found was *Ghost*, an iconic movie. It's a little past my '80s theme—since it was released in 1990—but it captures so much of the same hope the other movies have, I decided to do a post about it anyhow. . . .

The cursor hovered over the POST button. Madi tried to catch Sarah's eye, but she was already gaming. "You think Robbie will take the bait and troll the post?"

"Probably."

Madi glanced down at the bottom of the laptop screen, rereading the ending.

Her fingers tightened into fists as she read the last few lines.

> And that brings us to what—after long consideration—will be the final post of the '80s Extravaganza. Starting tomorrow, I'll open up a new post for possible MadLibs rereads. (I've already had one request for a comic series!) I look forward to seeing what you suggest. Check in for that tomorrow.
>
> Thanks to everyone who has given me support over the last difficult weeks. So many of you have taught me the strength of online friendships. I can't thank you enough.
>
> *exit, pursued by a bear*
>
> **MadLib**
>
> ---
>
> Comments enabled.
>
> Tags: #MadLibs #Ghost #Special shout out to all my readers and supporters—you rock! #80sMovies #Madi watches things and then blogs about them #Funemployment

"Here goes nothing," Madi said. She pressed POST and the MadLib went live. "Let's just hope it works."

"It will," Sarah said.

"But how do you know?"

On-screen, Sarah was in a complicated dance of punches and rolls as she fought her way through a group of soldiers. "Action and reaction," she said. "It's physics. Things have to balance out at some point."

For the next two hours, Madi fought the urge to text Laurent and tell him that she found the troll and was working with the police to catch him red-handed.

She wanted to beg forgiveness. (Again.) Madi wondered what Laurent would think of her latest post, but he didn't appear to have seen it. No comments from @laurentabelard appeared. Meanwhile, all her other online friends—oblivious to the ongoing drama—played their part, commenting enthusiastically on the blog and her surprise post of a 1990 classic.

Then the troll appeared.

This is the worst goddamned post I've ever SEEN! You had a bad week, huh, @MadLib? Then why don't you crawl back into your hole and CRY about it! Fucking BABY!

Madi knew that the police wanted her to keep Robbie online as long as possible, but she was shocked by the level of his attack. With no face-to-face consequences, the lowest level of depravity flowed onto her post. Strangely, the more vitriolic his taunts, the less she felt the barbs. He was a kid—*an angry little boy*—not a monster. Knowing his identity changed everything. He no longer frightened her.

By dinnertime, the attack had slowed, the comments dwindling until they stopped altogether. One final message appeared in her MadLibs e-mail.

> **NEW Message, @YouveBeenPwned:** 5:18 p.m. EST
> **Subject:** Here, Piggy, Piggy, Piggy
> You scared, little girl? GOOD. I like that. But don't go hiding on
> me just when things are starting to get fun! IT'S TIME TO PLAY.

Madi's anger was gone. The barrage had deadened her emotions. Icily controlled, she composed one final reply.

> **Reply to Message from @YouveBeenPwned:** 5:29 p.m. EST
> **Subject:** RE: Here, Piggy, Piggy, Piggy
> No. I'm not scared of you.
> Know why? I know the kind of person you are. Hiding in your
> room. Sulking about life. Wishing you were someone—anyone—

else. Yeah, I know all about you. You're weak. Sad. Scared. Even
this message terrifies you. (Because you KNOW I'm right.) And
you know what else? I feel bad for you. I really do.

I pity you.

You're sick, and you need help. I hope you find it.

She sent it off without a second thought, then blocked the server. The
deleted replies came in a frenzied rush.

Automated response to *all users*@hackster.com: 5:31 p.m. EST
Messages from this server have been rejected by the e-mail
client. Please contact the system administrator.
Automated response to *all users*@hackster.com: 5:32 p.m. EST
Messages from this server have been rejected by the e-mail
client. Please contact the system administrator.
Automated response to *all users*@hackster.com: 5:34 p.m. EST
Messages from this server have been rejected by the e-mail
client. Please contact the system administrator.

Sick to her stomach, Madi closed the laptop and pushed it off her lap.
She slumped down on the couch, breathing hard. *I'm not scared anymore.* She wasn't even certain when that had happened, but she knew it
was true.

The house phone rang.

"Madi?" her father called from the kitchen. "Can you grab that? Pretty sure
it's for you."

For a split second, she wondered if it was Laurent, but it was the police. "We've got him," a gravelly voiced officer announced. "Thanks to you,
they had a warrant ready and were able to take Robbie's computer. He's
only eighteen, so he'll get the lesser, fourth-degree charges, but he *will* be
charged."

"Th-thank you."

"Thank *you*, Ms. Nakama. You did a great job tracking him down. I can't say what the verdict will be. It may still be a fine, but the harassment will stop."

"Good." She wanted to say more, but her throat closed.

"We'll be in contact with you again to finish the paperwork. For now, you can relax. It's over."

For some reason the word *over* was the final crack in the armor she'd built around herself in the days since Laurent had disappeared from her life. Hearing it, Madi's adrenaline-fueled energy finally waned. Her head fell back against the couch's pillows, and she closed her eyes, tears rolling down the side of her face.

"Over," she whispered. "It's over. . . ."

Saturday felt like the aftermath of a tornado. The MadLibs post lay in ruins, the mess of the page a layer of commenting carnage Madi didn't know how to clean up. After one or two attempts at appropriate replies to her fans, she gave up. With a sigh, she selected PRIVATE and updated last night's post. The screen of the laptop flickered and reloaded, the destruction of the troll battle pushed aside for the police to deal with.

Madi pulled her laptop closer and cracked her knuckles.

"That's gross," Sarah grumbled.

"It helps me think."

"Still gross." Across from her, her sister lounged in their father's chair, her feet bumping Madi's every once in a while. "You want to go do something? It's a nice day. We could go down to the park or walk to the pond."

"Maybe later, okay?"

"Okay."

Madi looked back at the open document. The goal of this new post was rebuilding. *A fresh start.*

Blog Post 220, Saturday 1:19 p.m.:
And Now Back to Your Regularly Scheduled Programming

As I'm sure many of you noticed, yesterday's post was . . . *insert Inception horn blare* . . . an epically BAD day on the MadLibs blog. Things got out of hand and a lot of people got hurt in the process. I tried to wade through the comments this morning and respond to each of you personally, but in the end, it was too much. Sorry, guys. You're getting one LOOOOOOONG reply addressed to all of you. There was more going on than you realized. . . .

Half an hour later, Madi was almost finished typing, Sarah waiting patiently. Madi stretched her back, putting a hand on her laptop so it didn't tumble from her knees.

"You want to go now?" Sarah asked.

"In a bit, okay? I just want to finish this up."

"What're you writing?"

"A new post. I need to let the MadLibbers know what happened."

Sarah groaned.

"I *will* go to the park with you. Promise. I just need to do this first."

"Fine . . ." Her sister sighed as Madi scanned through the final paragraphs.

The first thing I want to do is explain *why* I let things play out as I did. Many of you AMAZING MadLibbers tried to come to my rescue yesterday, and I need you to know how much I appreciate that. THANK YOU. But I didn't need rescuing. With the help of a number of you, I was able to locate the troll. I can't talk about what's going on with him (since it's an active investigation), but I can promise you that he won't be coming back to MadLibs to spew his hate. And that's the really important detail I want to end on: what this blog means to me and how it needs to go forward from now on . . .

Madi gnawed at the edge of her nail, trying to figure out how to bring it all together. It was important that her readers knew what had happened. To know she cared about their emotions, too. Once MadLibs was back in working order, she could start the funemployment future she wanted.

Her sister bumped her toe, jarring Madi from her thoughts.

"Now?" Sarah asked.

"Just about . . ."

You can comment here on the blog. You are welcome to disagree with my posts. In fact, I WANT that kind of discussion, but I need it to stay positive. All right? I'm taking things a step at a time. I'm going to start vlogging, too (something that still kind of scares me)! And with all of that, we need to work together. I'm really PROUD of the positive, safe space that MadLibs was . . . and will be again. Let's keep it that way. To quote *Bill and Ted's Excellent Adventure*: "Be excellent to one another."

And that ends my latest (and not-at-all-on-the-topic-of-pop-culture) MadLib. Thank you to everyone who stood by my side. Online and off, you are my friends. *My REAL friends!* And I'm grateful for each and every one of you!

musical accompaniment rises

*Madi spins the *Inception* top on her desk*

exeunt

MadLib

Comments enabled.

Tags: #MadLibs #RL #Madi blogs about things and sometimes gets off topic #Funemployment

"Almost ready, Sarah," Madi said, the cursor clicking on the POST button. "I'm just posting this now." She looked up and smiled. "Thanks for waiting for me. Actually, thanks for everything you did the last while. I don't know what I'd do without you."

Her sister didn't answer.

"You ready to go, Sarah?"

Her sister slumped lower in the easy chair, a magazine blocking the view of her face. "In a minute," she muttered. "I'm finishing something."

293

Madi's phone buzzed and she looked down in surprise. In the last seconds, a new comment had been posted.

Comments on Blog Post 220: And Now Back to Your Regularly Scheduled Programming

Comment 1.1, @TheNewestMadLibberAround: Thanks for posting this, @MadLib. I think it's important that commenters realize there's a difference between intelligent debate and attacking a person for their opinions or beliefs. I know it's sometimes difficult to know what people are thinking or feeling, but a textual format can help with that. What you write is what you mean. That goes both ways. When trolls post, they want to hurt people. That's not acceptable in any situation. Anyhow, I'm very proud of how you handled the situation. Good work.

Madi glanced up, confused. Her sister's hair was just visible above the pages of the magazine she held. That was the first clue. It was one of their father's magazines about fly fishing, something Sarah and Madi rarely, if ever, picked up.

"Sarah?" Madi said.

Her sister's face appeared over the top of the pages. "Uh-huh?"

"Are you . . . ?"

"Am I what?"

Madi glanced at her phone's screen and back again. Other comments had begun to arrive, but it was the first one that caught and held her attention: *Sometimes it's difficult to know what people are thinking or feeling, but a textual format can help with that.* Hadn't Madi said almost the same thing to her sister about texting?

"Did you comment on my post?"

For the briefest moment, a smile flitted over Sarah's mouth before the magazine popped back up in front of her, blocking Madi's view.

"Maybe."

"Maybe?"

"And maybe not."

Madi smiled. "Well, if you did, I'm glad. It's about time you joined the MadLibbers."

Sarah tossed the magazine beside the chair, pocketing her phone. "Oh, I've been there for a while," she said. "Just lurking in the background."

Madi giggled. "Well, I'm glad you finally spoke up."

"Me, too."

It was after dinner and Madi was in her bedroom when she heard her father's footsteps come down the hall. He popped his head in the door. "Sarah and I are going to watch a movie tonight. You want to join us?"

"No thanks."

"Everything all right? You disappeared right after dinner."

Madi sighed and set her phone down. She'd finished replying to everyone's comments on her post, but now that it was done, she felt emptier than ever. "It's nothing, Dad. Just tired."

"Tired, huh?"

"Mm-hmm." She put her arm over her eyes, wondering at the weight in her chest. One username had been conspicuously absent from today's postings: @laurentabelard. She hadn't meant to search for him, but hadn't been able to stop herself.

Her father's footsteps crossed the floor. "Madi, are you sure you're okay?"

Her throat ached as she answered: "No. No, I'm not."

She felt rather than saw him sit on the bed next to her. "What's wrong? I thought catching this guy would be a relief. The whole trolling thing is over."

Madi made a choking sound. "That's not what this is about."

"It's not?"

Madi swallowed hard, but the lump in her throat wouldn't go away. She dropped her hands to her sides, staring up at the ceiling until her father touched her arm.

"Talk to me, Madi."

"I—I thought it was Laurent."

"What?"

"Wh-when I figured out it was a MadLibber, I thought for a while it might be Laurent. When I told him, he was so upset he cut me out of his life. I—I—"

"Is this why you guys haven't been hanging out lately?"

"Yes." She sat up and wiped her eyes. "I—I tried to explain, but he was hurt, and now I've wrecked everything."

"It can't be that bad."

"But it is! He's never going to talk to me again."

"So go to him and explain."

Madi stared at him. "But Laurent's in New York."

Charles took off his glasses and cleaned them with the corner of his shirt. "So's your aunt."

"But I can't just take off."

"Why not?"

"What if Laurent doesn't want to see me?"

Her father perched his glasses back on his nose and smiled. "Then you'll have to convince him otherwise."

It was almost nine thirty by the time Madi navigated the subway and found her way to the apartment Laurent had shown her when she'd visited New York. The sky was a cloudless black dotted with faint stars, and the streetlights cast halos of green where they rose into the foliage. Traffic hummed in the distance. It was a picture-perfect New York night, and if Madi weren't so terrified of what she was doing, she'd almost find it exciting to be back in the city.

She walked up the steps of the building to the foyer, fighting the urge to throw up. What would she say to Laurent? How could she make him understand? On the top step, she scanned through the numbers until she found Laurent's: 305. Woozy with nerves, Madi pressed the button.

No one answered.

She pressed it again. Still nothing. Madi shifted foot to foot, embarrassed. Maybe the buzzer was broken. She pushed it again, waiting for the count of ten.

Nothing.

"Oh, for God's sake!" she snapped. "He's not even home."

She pulled her phone out of her pocket, meaning to tell her aunt Lisa that she'd be showing up early. A message from her father waited for her on-screen.

> Tell Laurent I said hello.

"Kinda hard when he's not even here," she muttered.

She headed down the steps and peered up at the apartment, a looming brick building from the turn of the century, dotted with a gridwork of yellow squares. Madi's gaze caught on the third floor. The lights were on.

Excited, she pulled up her texts from Laurent, spinning back through weeks of flirting all the way to the night they'd been texting and her mother had interrupted.

> i'll be terribly careful with strange women hanging out under the fire escape. 😄 but if it was YOU under my window, i'd invite you up.

"The fire escape!"

Madi headed around the side of the building to the nearby alley. Her hands tightened into fists as she scanned the shadows. New York didn't seem nearly as nice from this perspective, definitely more *Gangs of New York* and less *When Harry Met Sally*. Her eyes rose to the third floor. Sure enough, there was a narrow window facing the fire escape. It glowed brightly, a tall figure passing in front of the glass every once in a while.

"Laurent."

Madi walked to the bottom of the fire escape. It hung well above her head, and even the thought of trying to climb it made her legs turn to water.

"Why does it have to be so high up?" she moaned. "I hate heights!"

But when she looked up again, Laurent paused near the window, his face in profile. It was definitely him. Seeing him redoubled her resolve. She climbed atop the nearby garbage bin, balancing on the lid.

"Heaven help me, I'm going to die in a Dumpster!" She stretched farther, farther, almost there, fingers reaching. . . . "Sweet baby Jesus, get me through this!" She leaned out toward the bottom rung of the ladder.

"Damnit!" There was absolutely no way she could reach.

Resigned, Madi climbed down from the Dumpster and headed back to the foyer. She buzzed again and again. Still no answer.

"May I help you?"

Madi yelped in surprise. She turned to discover an elderly woman waiting behind her.

"Sorry," Madi said. "I'm a friend of Laurent's. I need to talk to him. But he won't answer the door."

The woman leaned closer. "You sure he's home?"

"He's definitely home," Madi said. "I saw him through the window, but he's got his headphones on. He can't hear the buzzer."

"Oh dear. That's too bad."

Madi's eyebrows rose. "Wait! Could you walk up to his apartment and ask him to come down? He's in three-oh-five."

"I don't know, dear. My arthritis makes stairs difficult. Laurent helps me with my groceries sometimes, you know."

Groceries! With that, Madi realized she had a name. "You're Mrs. Marcioni, aren't you? Laurent told me about you."

She grinned. "He did?"

"Yes, he did. And I'm so sorry to ask you to help, but it's so important that I talk to Laurent." Her voice wavered. "Please," she begged. "If you could just get Laurent for me, Mrs. Marcioni, I'd really appreciate it."

"But if he can't hear the buzzer, he won't hear me knocking."

Madi groaned. She hadn't considered that. "I just really need to talk to him. I even tried the alley."

"The alley?"

"I was going to climb up the fire escape, but I'm too short." Madi hung her head, close to tears. "This is stupid. It's not going to work. I should just leave."

The old woman patted Madi's hand. "Hush, now. Come with me." She unlocked the door and waved Madi inside. "Any friend of Laurent's is a friend of mine," she said, then dropped her voice. "Just don't tell anyone in the building that I let you through the door."

"Thank you."

The two of them walked slowly up to the first floor, where Mrs. Marcioni's apartment was located.

"Go up to the third floor and knock," Mrs. Marcioni said. "I'll wait here a minute, in case he doesn't hear you."

Minutes later, Madi was back on the first floor, sweaty and frustrated. "He didn't hear me."

Mrs. Marcioni nodded at the window at the end of the hall. "There's the fire escape"—her eyes twinkled—"if you were serious about that."

"I—I was," Madi said. "I am."

"Good," Mrs. Marcioni said, grinning. "Then you'd better get going."

The window opened easily, and Madi stepped out onto the fire escape. Her stomach dropped as she made the mistake of looking down. She spent half a minute hyperventilating. This had been a *terrible* idea.

"Don't. Look. Down."

She climbed the first ladder.

The next.

By the time she made it to the third floor, she was shaking from exertion, her fingers claws where they wrapped the rusting bars. She scrambled onto the metal-gridded balcony, pressing herself as close to the building as possible. She couldn't look down. If she did, she'd die.

"L-L-Laurent," Madi said through chattering teeth.

She could see him on the other side of the glass. He sat on his bed, headphones on, a book of Ansel Adams's black-and-white photography open on his lap.

Madi unclenched one hand and lifted it to the window, knocking. "L-Laurent!" she called again.

He turned the page.

Madi slid over so that her entire body was pressed up against the glass. The wind tugged at her hair, her fear escalating into pure terror. There was no way she was going to be able to climb down. If Laurent didn't let her in, she'd have to stay here on the balcony forever. She'd grow old here. Die here. Her body decomposing on the grill. Mrs. Marcioni would never know what had happened!

Madi banged hard on the glass. "LAURENT!" she shrieked.

He looked up. Their eyes locked.

For several long seconds he didn't move. Madi pressed her face until her whole cheek and nose were squished against the glass. "Please!" she begged. "I'm scared of heights, Laurent! Let me IN!"

That seemed to release him from his trance. He jumped up from the bed, sprinted to the window, and pulled it open so fast he banged Madi's chin on the bottom frame as the window rose.

"Madi!" he gasped, dragging her bodily inside. "What are—How are— *Comment es-tu arrivé ici?*"

She wrapped her arms around him, terrified of how far up she'd climbed. "I'm sorry for just showing up, but I had to see you again," she said. "I was wrong about you, Laurent. I'm so sorry! The troll was making me crazy, and I didn't know what to believe."

"I . . . I don't know what to say. I can't believe you're here."

"I had to talk to you."

His shock passing, Laurent's expression cooled. "Please, Madi," he said, removing himself from her grip. "You need to let me go."

Embarrassed, she stepped back. "I'm sorry, I just needed to talk to you."

He crossed his arms. "So talk."

"I'm sorry," she croaked. "I'm sorry for everything."

Laurent didn't reply. Madi could feel everything coming apart at the seams. Her stunt on the fire escape hadn't fixed a thing.

"Look, I know you're leaving in a couple weeks," she said, voice breaking. "And I know nothing's ever going to be the same. But I can't let you go back to France thinking that you hate me. I just can't."

Laurent's expression grew pained. "Madi, I don't know what you think is going to happen with us, but—"

"I'm so sorry for what I said. What I thought. And I understand if you never want anything to do with me. I deserve that!"

"You do."

"But I'm hoping that we can at least say good-bye as friends." She offered her hand. "Please? Just friends. Nothing else."

Laurent took her icy fingers in his.

"I'm sorry," she whispered. "And I understand why you're angry at me, but please . . . *please* don't hate me."

He closed his eyes, but didn't let go of her hand. The next words seemed to hurt him. "I don't hate you. I don't think I *could* hate you."

"Can we be friends again? Please?"

"Friends?"

Madi's fingers tightened. "Yes, friends. Nothing else. Just friends, so that when you go—" Her voice broke. "When you go back to France I can still be your friend."

Laurent's thumb ran over the back of her knuckles. He nodded to the window. "That was a very dramatic entrance for a friend."

"I—I thought so."

"You had it planned out?"

"Not really. I tried ringing the buzzer first. Then knocking on the door." Madi swallowed hard. His fingers were still wrapped around hers, and her brain wouldn't translate that properly. "The whole up-the-fire-escape thing was kind of a last-ditch effort."

"I had headphones on."

"I know," she said with a nervous laugh. "That's why I climbed up."

"It was very Lloyd Dobler of you." The corner of Laurent's mouth twitched. "So what would you have done if I hadn't let you in, hmmm?"

"I guess I would've waited outside until . . ."

"Until I felt sorry and let you in?"

Madi cringed. "Yeah. Something like that." For a moment neither of them spoke. Madi could feel something balanced between them, and somehow she knew it had to do with the spots where their palms touched. He'd taken her hand and hadn't let go. *That mattered.*

"Laurent, I . . ." Both of them started talking at once.

"You go ahead," he said quietly. "I'll listen."

"I'm so sorry, Laurent. I hope you can forgive me for ever doubting—"

All her thoughts disappeared as Laurent pulled her into his arms and kissed her. The weeks of longing surged as Madi slid her arms around his neck, standing on tiptoe to reach his mouth. Where their other kisses had started out hesitantly, this one burned with passion from the second their lips met. Minutes passed, and it was only the sound of a door opening—somewhere in the distant apartment—that broke them apart, panting.

Laurent stepped back, though he didn't let go of Madi's hand. "Was it okay that I kissed you?"

She blinked, resurfacing. She was in Laurent's bedroom. *Oh right, I ran off to New York to win him back like in some cheesy movie.*

"Better than okay," she said. "It was perfect. . . . *You're* perfect."

She caught Laurent's eyes and he smiled. *"Quand je t'ai vu pour la première fois,"* he murmured, his lips a breath away from hers, *"c'était le coup de foudre."*

This time she didn't laugh at his words. Breathless, her hands slid up his chest, resting there. "What does that mean, Laurent? Tell me what you just said."

He reached out, cupping her face between his palms. "It means yes, I forgive you. How could I not? I'm in love with you, *minette. Je t'adore."*

And like that, everything in Madi Nakama's life changed once again.

21

"You look good wearing my future."
(Some Kind of Wonderful, 1987)

When Laurent thought of that summer, the last two weeks of June seemed brighter than all those that followed. He'd spent half of it crashing in the Nakamas' spare bedroom, his host family growing so concerned that Madi begged her father to call and intervene. Charles Nakama's assurances put them at ease, but the days rushed by faster than either he or Madi wanted.

With his student visa ending, Laurent needed to leave for France. The College d'Arts in Paris had been his dream for years, but now he fought its arrival. He couldn't stay in the States. But his heart couldn't move on. Not with Madi standing on the other side of the glass at the airport. A year apart felt like a lifetime. And Laurent had no assurance Madi would feel the same come next summer, when he hoped to visit.

He lifted his phone and took one final photograph, then sent it to her.

Counting the days 'til I see you.

Summer flew past, Laurent's days filled with preparations for college, his sleepless nights with memories of Madi. Their Snapsed dates took place every few days. Occasionally, he could tell where Madi was from the images she sent him.

Coffee for one. Missing you.

Other times, it was someplace new. The thought of Madi making her way through life without him at her side left Laurent smiling through heartache. She had started her real life. With the inclusion of her new vlog section, MadLibs's popularity had skyrocketed yet again, success followed by success.

Laurent and Madi shared long conversations via text, but their schedules were thrown off enough that the talks felt stilted, their answers too many hours apart. He occasionally woke up to discover rambling late-night e-mails.

NEW Message, MNakama@MadLibs.com: 2:39 a.m. EST
Priority: Normal
Subject: Missing You

Laurent,

Had another awful night. Miss you so much. I can't sleep these days. You're too far away, and I'm too awake. (Maybe it's time I cut out the caffeine.) I stayed up late watching reruns and trying to do another video for MadLibs, but nothing would click. Deleted all my footage and will start over today. (I need my favorite cameraman behind the lens.) So lonely the last few days. So sad.

Can't go on like this. Don't want you to worry, though. I'll get through. I will.

Love you.

—Madi

He sent his replies any moment he was able, but they often went unanswered.

> just got your e-mail, madi! so sorry i missed it. just leaving school now.

> are you okay? do you have time to talk? i'm on the metro, but we could text.

> you online yet? i'm home now

> 🙁 write me. call me. anything.

Laurent knew it would get worse as school began. He was right. Hours passed without replies. Phone calls disappeared entirely. Across an ocean, Madi was falling into bed at the same time Laurent was heading to class. He knew it was only a matter of time before the hours stretched to days and weeks, and their relationship would end through forgetfulness, not anger.

With this in his mind, Laurent sprawled on his bed, a book of photography techniques open before him. *Rule of thirds . . . neutral space . . . perspective lines . . .* He'd already reread the same page twice, but the concepts weren't making their way to his brain. Madi hadn't answered the last two texts he'd sent her, and though Laurent knew she was likely just busy—MadLibs was booming—he couldn't help wondering if the inevitable "end" he'd been waiting for had happened while he was sitting in his Introduction to Photography class.

Laurent's phone buzzed, and he scrambled to grab it from the nightstand.

u feel like going on a date tonight?
(i have snapsed open and ready!) 😘

"Madi!" he breathed, then typed in his reply.

of course! where are we going?

i'm thinking coffee would be a good start

Laurent grinned as he tapped in an answer.

coffee is ALWAYS in order! where to?

well, i don't have a license (or car), so i'm
putting on my shoes. u ready to walk?

Rocking the sneakers.

ha-ha! love it. those are magnifique!
oh, how I've missed you, madi!

i've missed u too 💔 but we're together again. that's what matters.

how i wish we were.

take my hand, laurent. this is our time

i won't let go. 💕

good, because i'm not that great with directions & i've only been told this coffee shop is good

we're going to a new one?

yes! all right. i'm on the street. let's go

Braving the crowds.

Laurent stared down at the screen, hands tightening around his phone. *4...3...* He knew that street. And the text was—*2...* He leaned closer, squinting at the menu board. *1...* It was in French!

The image blinked out before he could figure out where it was. *"Merde!"* Laurent scrambled to reply.

> OMG wait! WAIT!
> where are you, madi???

> i'm on my way to meet u for coffee. ur holding
> my hand. we're walking. aren't we?

> no, really. WHERE are you?!

> i'm getting closer to u with each step 😄

Getting closer.

Laurent jumped from the bed, his chest heaving. There was no mistaking that sign. Madi was definitely in Paris!

> TELL ME WHERE TO MEET YOU!!!!!!!

> i'm certain you can find me, if you keep
> your eyes open . . . 😃

Another Snapsed appeared.

This place looks nice.

Laurent's fingers were shaking so hard he could barely type.

I KNOW LES DEUX MAGOTS!

thought u might

can't type. on my way!

 i just ordered our coffees. i'm getting something a little fancy this time. pretty sure u will approve of the taste!

One for you, one for me.

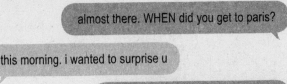

almost there. WHEN did you get to paris?

this morning. i wanted to surprise u

you did! YOU'RE ACTUALLY HERE!

LOL i am! i've been dying to tell u!

hold on. i see the café!

Do you see me???

YES!!!!! 😄

Madi's phone buzzed at the same time a figure came through the door. For the briefest moment her gaze caught on the Snapsed that had appeared on her screen. *Is that me?* Before she could decide, a familiar voice interrupted.

"*Madi?*"

Madi's head bobbed up, and she surged to her feet. "Laurent!"

The Parisian café faded as she focused on the man standing before her. Every detail that had dimmed in the last months of separation jumped back into focus: His lashes were black at the base but pale brown at the tips, his lips a perfect curving bow, the skin of his jaw stubbled dark, and his nose dotted with freckles, too light to be seen at a distance.

Laurent was beautiful, yes, but more than that, he was good and kind.

"I've missed you, *minette*."

Madi smiled through happy tears. "Missed you, too, Laurent."

"How are you here in Paris?" he murmured as he brushed a tear away with his thumb. "I don't understand."

"It was time to start living my own life." She smiled up at him, laughing. "And that meant moving on."

"But you have a life in the States. A family."

310

"I do, but I've always wanted to travel. Besides, there's no reason I *can't* do MadLibs from Paris. Sarah and I text every day. My being in France won't change that."

"You came."

"I'll always come back to you, Laurent. I love you."

"Love you, too."

And as he leaned in to kiss her, the *rest* of Madi Nakama's shining future began.

Author's Note

I have two jobs: the first is my Superman job as a writer of YA and contemporary fiction; the second is a Clark Kent job as a high school teacher. I'm also a mom to three boys, one of whom has special needs. Every once in a while, these divergent paths converge.

I teach a technology program specifically designed for students with mental, emotional, and physical challenges, the goal being to give them technical skills that will help them in both their academic and personal pursuits. Spending three hours a day with these incredible students has given me a valuable perspective into their lives. They have tremendous gifts, skills, and—yes—challenges, too. But their differences are far less important than their similarities. They are a part of the school community. They live important lives. Yet too often in literature, these special individuals are ignored and overlooked.

Why is that?

In the school where I teach, approximately one in every ten students has some kind of special need (including every single child in my specialized technology class). In my mind, that ten percent of students should be visible in #YA literature. This book tries to do that.

While *Internet Famous* isn't Sarah's story, her inclusion is a powerful statement. It's important that she's there. And to all the students who inspired me to create her, I want to say: *Thank you.* You are amazing.

FEELING BOOKISH?

Turn the page for some

Swoonworthy EXTRAS

Blog Post 418, Saturday 11:02 p.m.:

The Force Awakens!

With a blast of John Williams's music, I launched into *The Force Awakens*, the ONLY movie in the *Star Wars* franchise I've never seen, and the movie that @StarveilBrian1981 has been promoting for more than a year. How did I miss this film? I moved to France last summer and was a little distracted with settling into my new MadLibbing life. ;) With the hubbub of RL settled, I'm watching—FOR THE FIRST TIME—the movie that's launched a thousand new ships.

Williams's music is only surpassed by the perfectly 1970s receding text. *mad screaming* The classic *Star Wars* intro is the best thing about any movie series EVER (and I'll fight anyone who says differently). I must admit, though, the title always throws me. *THE FORCE AWAKENS.* Was the force asleep before this? Did it miss the alarm? IDEK.

And from that epic intro, the newest *Star Wars* movie starts in the midst of some kind of get-together with a cutie-pie rebel dude and—wait!—is that the three-eyed raven from *Game of Thrones*? Yes, I think it is. So raven and rebel are chilling when a whole lot of bad guys show up. And just like that, the fight's on!

Pew! Pew! Swchwomp! Pew! Pew! Pew! (Is it wrong to love sound effects this much? Don't answer that. 'Cause I totally do).

The guy with the fabulous hair—who we find out is Poe *Damn*-eron!—gets separated from his cute little robot, BB-8. There's a whole lotta fighting going on. Now, I'm not a huge fan of stormtroopers in general, but these guys seem even less "with it" than usual. Meanwhile, the epic bad dude shows up. How do I know?

    A) He's in Darth Vader cosplay.

    B) He's super tall, and that is a prerequisite in this franchise: smol versus tol. (Check Tumblr for details. If you're over six feet, you're a baddie. More on that later!)

Back to the planet where one stormtrooper's having a panic attack. And—oh crap!—the old guy just bit it. Poe shoots, but—WHOA!—Did evil Jedi guy just stop a laser blast midair? Yes, he did. We've got an epic J. J. Abrams lens flare to show how important this event is. I'm pretty sure this is an homage to the original series, when Obi-Wan was killed, but I kind of feel bad because we know so little about this guy (other than he's also dead on *Game of Thrones*. RIP). Meanwhile, there's a whole lot of banter and sass between Poe and bad dude, and for whatever reason, Darth Cosplay decides not to kill him.

Aaaaaaaand the stormtrooper with the conscience isn't shooting, but his superior (who is also a tol) has taken note. He's definitely getting written up for this one. Hold on. I've got to search who plays Captain Phasma, because she sounds REALLY familiar.

disappears onto the Internet

Aha! Knew it! It's Brienne of Tarth. She's six three, and the smol/tol Internet theory holds. (Aside: The *GOT* rewatch starts in two weeks. Woot! Check in for that later.)

All right. Back to business: The new scene begins, and we are introduced to an adorable scavenger, Rey, who has paired up with BB-8. She understands the blips and beeps, and is fabulously awesome. Her apocalyptic steampunk garb is ah-MAZE-ing. She's had literally less than a minute of screen time, and I'm already under Rey's spell. (Note to self: Must buy a Rey action figure!)

OMG OMG OMG! Cheesy transitions FTW!

All right, so we know a few things about this scavenger girl:

A) She's living on her own by scavenging tech.
B) She can talk robot. (Is she a robot herself? Oh! I like that idea, but this isn't Battlestar Galactica, so it's doubtful.)
C) She insists her family will come back someday. Curiouser and curiouser!

There's an awesome escape with Poe and Finn, the boy-next-door-stormtrooper, who appears to have missed the class on how to suppress your emotions.

(Offscreen: Finn talking to himself made me snork out loud and Laurent can't stop laughing.) Is it just me or is there a level of romantic tension between Finn and Poe? Uh-huh. You bet there is! And I'm all in for Finn-and-Poe shenanigans!

The two steal a TIE-fighter. *squeals* Could this be the start of a road-trip fic? Unfortunately, they end up crashing on the surface of the planet, and Finn isn't able to get Poe out before the craft gets sucked underground. Noooooooo! : (Finn heads off, hugging Poe's jacket like some sad little prize of what could have been. *sobs* My shipper heart is breaking! Why are you making me FEEL these things, *The Force Awakens*? WHY???

Dying from thirst, Finn heads to the village, where Rey is taking no shit from anyone. (Question: How difficult is it for the stormtroopers to get to the surface? I mean, it seems like Finn's been down there for hours). Anyhow—back on the planet, Rey is beating up two guys at once. Let there be no question: I LOVE REY. I want to BE her. And it appears that Finn does, too. Unfortunately, she doesn't see it that way. She chases Finn down, starts kicking his ass, but luckily they end up bonding over. . . . *insert epic music*

THE MYTH OF SKYWALKER.

Then, Finn's horrible-terrible-no-good-first-day-as-a-nontrooper gets worse when the rest of his onetime colleagues show up to catch him, and Rey won't let him play the part of the hero. "Stop taking my hand!" now ties for my favorite line in this film. Off they go! Cardio time! And they end up taking off with . . . garbage!

scratch that

IT'S THE FREAKING MILLENNIUM FALCON!!!

But even once they get off the planet, things aren't quite going the way they should be, but troubled or not, our fabulous BFFs are off and running. Incidentally, I love that Finn lies about his origin and makes it seem like he's in the resistance . . . and BB-8 totally covers for him. Woot! Meanwhile, Kylo Ren discovers his plan didn't work out and channels his inner man-child so he can destroy an entire room.

That poor First Order assistant. Kylo Ren is the boss from HELL. I imagine the guy is probably thinking: *But my personal e-mails were on that computer.* They must have a full-time repair crew. LOL

After another bout of epic music . . . Han Solo arrives! You heard me right. HAN freaking SOLO! Now, I'm totally up for the new adventures of Finn and Rey, but the retro-stylings of Han and Rey are a close second. I could totally go for a spin-off. These two are literally finishing each other's sentences. She's fixing his bucket-of-junk ship in ways even Han can't imagine! Is it wrong I want a buddy ~~cop~~ smuggler movie? They'd be amazing together! The old curmudgeon smuggler and his scavenger apprentice. I imagine Chewie roaring as he rolls his eyes at the camera. LOL

Okay—those rathtars in the ship are freaking me out, but . . . but . . . is that a reference to *Raiders of the Lost Ark* I see? That rolling thingie definitely looks like a ball rolling down the hall. Yup. This show is *full* of references! It's like an homage to film homage. A FILMOMAGE!

Along the way, we discover Han Solo is Ren's father. AAAAAHHHHH! WHAT IS MY LIFE?!? (Also, I now need *another* spin-off prequel. Would that be Episode 6.1? I could totally go for 6.1, 6.2, 6.3 . . . If Flash updates every two weeks, why can't *Star Wars*???)

rewinds to find out what I missed while flailing

Oh! And it appears there's a map (which fills us in on what Poe was carrying). Also—can I ask the obvious? Like, *why* did Luke leave? Going full-hermit seems like an extreme reaction to an apprenticeship program gone awry. Though I really love Finn and Rey together, the second-mate offer is golden. TAKE THE JOB OFFER, REY!!! (She doesn't). So, with a lot of could-have-beens, the band of rebels—Finn, Rey, Han, and Chewie—head off to a thousand-year-old party palace.

As an aside: The Darth Helmet is hella creepy. Can you imagine keeping your grandpa's head on your coffee table? Nope. Me neither. First Order or not, that's just weird.

Okay. Here's where we are with the plot:

A) Finn wants to run away.
B) Rey wants to go home.
C) Kylo wants BB-8.

D) BB-8 wants to deliver the message.

E) Han Solo wants a drink and his ship.

And finally . . .

F) Maz Kanata seems to know EVERYTHING about EVERYONE, but won't explain why or how.

Things get a little LSD trippy when Rey has a flashback/flash-forward after she stumbles down into the inexplicably creepy basement. I'm no scavenger, and I'm certainly nowhere near as badass as Rey, but if I started hallucinating, a basement in a dance club would be the LAST place I'd go. There's SO much going on at this point that I had to pause and rewind to catch up. I'm pretty sure we've got a flash of Luke's creepy robot hand on R2-D2, Kylo and his First Order posse killing some random dude, and then some kind of forest scene. Rey realizes—*WHOA! I shouldn't have done that!* (No kidding, Rey.) And then, just to twist the knife, Maz Kanata tells Rey that the person she's waiting for *isn't* coming back. Niiiiiiiice.

But the bad day isn't over. (C'mon, it's *Star Wars*.) Kylo Ren and henchmen show up and the whole place gets trashed. Meanwhile, Rey has a lot of FEELS and runs off into the forest with BB-8. Side note: It's pretty convenient that stormtroopers can't actually aim. You'd think that the Empire would look into that design flaw.

Kylo heads into the forest to get Rey, where it becomes completely clear Rey's out of her depth. Kylo Ren Force-kicks her ass. Meanwhile, Finn freaks out when he realizes that Rey has been taken, and there's the reunion with Han and Leia. The feeeeels!!! But that's only the start.

Wait for it. . . .

WAIT. FOR. IT. . . .

The big reveal is that Kylo Ren is Han AND LEIA'S son. (But of *course* he is, because who else could Han love *other* than Leia? I mean, really!) The one small part of their chat that made me giggle is Han hinting that there's *"too much Vader"* in Kylo, which seems to be the equivalent of *"that's your side of the family's fault."* Leia doesn't seem to mind. Maybe—like me—she's been missing Han, too.

(Please tell me you've seen the adventures of Emo Kylo Ren on Tumblr. If not—GO LOOK IT UP.)

And then the moment. THE. MOMENT. Oh God, you guys. I can't tell you how I've been waiting for this. Poe and Finn reunite, but Finn's wearing his jacket like some YA novel with the quarterback and his best friend/soon-to-be-boyfriend. THIS IS ADORKABLE! Holy crap, did Poe just do a lip bite??? In case you missed it, I rewound, and YES, he actually did. I seriously love this movie!!! #StormpilotFTW

Now, amidst the family bonding and Poe/Finn feels, Rey is locked up with Kylo Ren. And as much as he claims she's there as his guest, Kylo, dude, I'm pretty sure this isn't the definition of "guest behavior," unless you're using *12 Cloverfield Lane* as the benchmark. (Aside: If you missed my MadLib on that, you can find it <u>HERE.</u>) So Kylo monologues a bit like any good James Bond villain, but then the mask seems to bug him, so he pulls it off, and oooooooh! He's actually really good-looking under that mask. Not scarred or creepy or disfigured. Halp! I'm suddenly conflicted about Kylo. Damn, son. You have L'Oréal hair!

ahem

Okay, so Kylo does the Jedi mind-reading trick as he tells Rey he'll take whatever he wants, but Rey's not some weakling. She repels his attempts. Stranger yet, she CAN fight off his Force attack. Kylo's face—when he realizes he can't get into her head—is FANTASTIC! OMG I love Rey!!! Because now she's in *his* head. And that changes everything.

Change scene to Snoke, Kylo, and tol number three, whose name I'm too lazy to look up, but who was in the *Ex Machina* movie. (ETA: Laurent tells me it's Bill Weasley aka Domhnall Gleeson, son of Brendan Gleeson aka Mad Eye Moody.) Seems this is all a 3-D Skype meeting of some kind, and Snoke says he wants the girl. *shudders* Snoke is creepy AF, but I'm glad that Andy Serkis is getting work.

Meanwhile, Rey pulls an Obi-Wan. Wait! NEW THOUGHT! *hyperventilates* OMG—could Obi Wan be her dad??? I mean, she was abandoned, right? Could that be why? He's not coming back because he's actually dead. She does almost the same thing as Obi-Wan did when he and Luke met up with the stormtroopers.

Cut to . . . Temper tantrum number two. EPIC! I kind of love that the two nearby stormtroopers run away because CLEARLY they have seen this happen before. No one wants to be around Kylo when he loses a prisoner or his popcorn burns in the microwave. (God! He must have been a JOY when he was a teenager.) Somewhere the plant manager for this place must be face-palming. *What?! Sector seven's trashed AGAIN?!*

In other galaxy news . . . the rebellion creates a plan, and the plan seems to be . . . almost the *same plan* as the way they destroyed the Death Star thirty years before. (WTF???) Serious question here: It's been, like, a full generation since the Death Star was destroyed. Isn't the oscillator design flaw something the Empire should have addressed in that time? Anyhow. I don't care about blow-ing things up because POE AND FINN ARE TOGETHER AGAIN! *swoons* They have another moment, and though they don't kiss, there's lots of hot and heavy *looking*. Yes. I'm definitely invested in that ship. I totally want them to make it! They are bbs, while Leia and Han are all sorts of adorbs.

So at this point, there's lots of action and fighting and running around. And then Finn, Han, and Rey reunite! We just need to throw Poe in here for one big family picture. Man—I love this movie so much! They're just about to leave when Han decides they need to blow this place up, and dude, I *really* have a bad feel-ing about the plan. This is the equivalent of stepping over the dead body in the doorway. You're out! DO NOT go back in! (Han Solo isn't listening, though.) And, of course, this gets worse because Kylo is *also* here. Han calls out to his son. (Another TERRIBLE idea.) Ugh! I need everyone to run away! RUN AWAY!!!!

turns off TV

gets a snack

checks e-mail again

comes back

turns on TV

Crap. Nothing's changed. Kylo and Han are having what seems to be two dif-ferent conversations about what's going on, and I'm hiding under Laurent's arm so I don't have to watch the scene. Oh God, oh God, oh God. Shit's about to go down, I can totally *feel it*! The moment the helmet dropped and the sun's light went out, I knew something BAD would happen.

Me (shouting at the screen): *Ben has turned evil, Han!!! RUN AWAY.*

Laurent (laughing): *He can't hear you.*

Me: *Don't listen to Laurent. Run! RUUUUUUNNN!*

So, apparently I don't have the Force, because—despite all my shouting—Han gets skewered. OMG OMG OMG OMG NOOOOOOOOOOOOOOOOOOO!!!!!!!!!! I can't believe what I just watched! Side note: The Empire needs better building codes. I mean, what's with all the massive drops and no side-rails?!) Leia's moment of realization tore my heart out, too. Ugh. She KNOWS Han is dead and their son is to blame.

Aaaaaaahhhhh! Everything hurts and it's raining on my face. :(

Chewie going badass on the remaining stormtroopers made me feel a tiny bit better. And then Finn and Kylo fight. Got to admit I was a little bummed Rey was out for the count at this point. The girl doesn't need someone to save her. She's got the Force, damnit! But then . . . (wait for it) REY IS BACK!!!

The theme song swells and I'm ALL IN! No e-mail checking! Kylo is weirdly awesome at this moment with the *You need a teacher* claim. (Why does that sound like he means something else?) But I just want Rey to kick his ass from here to Alderaan. Then Rey closes her eyes and brings it. The girl has SERIOUS Jedi moves. I love how she terrifies Kylo, because she's completely untrained but still kicking it.

When the dust settles, everyone (minus Han) comes together. Oh, my HEART! Finn, my poor space-bb is hurt, but dear, sweet Poe—*gasps* Poe is RIGHT THERE as Chewie carries Finn off the Millennium Falcon. *Be still, my shipper heart!* Yes, of course I'm worried about Finn (I actually am) but—but—this moment between the two of them is EVERYTHING. Poe doesn't leave Finn's side. He doesn't hide his emotions. LOOK AT THE EXPRESION ON HIS FACE! <3 This is the #Stormpilot reunion I have been waiting for! *dies*

Act three is closing fast as R2-D2 wakes up and the map is complete. HOORAY! When Leia says good-bye to Rey, my heart broke a little. I do kind of wish we'd had a moment like this: *My father had the Force, my twin has the Force, my son has the Force . . . and I'm feeling a little ripped off here.* Leia, of course, is perfect, so she doesn't say it. But I'm allowed to think it.

So Rey takes charge of the Millennium Falcon and my FEELS ARE BACK IN FULL. Chewie has a new sidekick. Since Han is gone, can we just have adventures of Rey and Chewie now for, like, three more movies? Please? PLEASE???

But Rey's got a plan. She heads to the map's source. *MASSIVE MUSICAL

MOMENT* A figure turns around and we see . . . LUKE!!! (Who has been AWOL up to this point.) Rey and grumpy Luke have a very tiny moment on the island, and the credits roll. With that, the MadLib on *The Force Awakens* comes to an end.

Wow! What a ride! One of the things I loved the MOST about this movie were the references to the original trilogy. There's a sense of passing the torch on to a new generation and the general consensus that everyone should just forget the prequels happened at all. There were endless perfect moments, and the inclusion of a nonhet ship. *draws hearts around Finn and Poe* And Rey . . . REY. My girl. I can't say enough about her and how amazing she is! It makes me so happy that she's finally moving forward with her life, rather than waiting around, a message we could all learn from.

Here are my final stats.

Series Rating: 8/10 Mad!Cows, with ALL the Mad!Love going out to the original *Star Wars* trilogy, and *The Force Awakens* in particular. Those were amazing films! (I'm just not going to mention Episodes I through III.)

Movie Rating: 11/10 Mad!Cows for *The Force Awakens*, which has put my fangirl bat-signal into overdrive. If you've got any Finn/Poe fic to suggest, please comment below!

Would I rewatch it? YES! (In fact, I'm doing that tonight.)

Thank you again to @StarveilBrian1981 for suggesting the *Star Wars* re-watch! It's been quite the ride. And if you've got something I should be reading/viewing/playing, please message me at: MNakama@MadLibs.com. I'm always open to more.

musical accompaniment rises

exeunt

MadLib

Comments Enabled.

Tags: #MadLibs #The Force Awakens #Madi watches things and then blogs about them #Funemployment

A Coffee Date

between author Danika Stone and her editor, Holly West

Holly West (HW): What book is on your nightstand now?

Danika Stone (DS): I hope you mean *books* [laughs] because I always have a pile going. Right now that includes: *If I Was Your Girl*, by Meredith Russo, *Carry On*, by Rainbow Rowell, and *The Kick-Ass Writer* by Chuck Wendig. I've been reading that one for months, a few pages at a time, whenever I need a little boost to get my writing game on track.

HW: If you could travel in time, where would you go and what would you do?

DS: As boring as it sounds, I'd probably go hang out with my dad, who passed away almost a decade ago. It's strange how many things I see and think, *I should tell Dad about that,* only to remember I can't anymore. There's this growing pile of life events that I'd want to tell him about. Becoming a writer is one of them.

HW: Madi talks about a lot of different rewatches for her blog. What is on your rewatch list?

DS: Right now I've been feeling the urge to watch *Deadwood*, and maybe *Rome*. I'm a sucker for historical fiction, no matter how much license they take! I'm waiting for more *Sherlock* and the next season of *The 100*, since I fangirl both. And I really want to catch up on *Supernatural*, too, since I only got through season one and then got caught up in editing a book!

HW: Where did you get the inspiration for *Internet Famous*?

DS: When I was a junior in high school, I did an exchange to Quebec, to work on my French language skills, and later, in my second year of university, I went on a full-year student exchange to the States. Both of these times away from home were amazing-slash-terrifying. [laughs] I was alone and had to find my own way to get around, to make new friends, to force myself out in the world. It's hard! That was the inspiration for Laurent's experiences.

Madi's inspiration came from Mark Oshiro (from MarkDoesStuff), who is an amazing blogger, and [a] genuinely kind person. His approach to blogging and fun-employment show how people can use their passions to keep themselves employed and reach like-minded fans.

The inspiration for the actual plot is a little darker: the problem of Internet trolling. It isn't one specific event that caught my eye, but around the time of the Gamergate scandal, I started thinking about how differently people [behave] based on whether they are anonymous or not. *Internet Famous* is a fun book, but it also addresses some very serious social issues that occur online.

HW: What's your process? Are you an outliner or do you just start at the beginning and make it up as you go?
DS: I'm a little bit of both. I start with an idea and it tends to poke at me for a few months (or years). Then I do some prewriting to discover which characters are waiting around in the wings, begging to be included. Once I have the voices for the mains down pat, I start a brief plot-plan. It's in point form and gives me a general idea of what I'm going to cover.

None of this planning is carved in stone—and a lot of the later ideas get thrown away partway through the first draft. Once I have that very rough road map, I start writing. And once I'm writing, I don't stop. Period. Until it's done. Because you can always edit a terrible first draft, but a blank page is just a page with no words on it.

HW: What do you want readers to remember about your books?
DS: My books are about teen culture and a digitally connected world, but beyond that, I hope readers remember the heart the stories carry. There's *goodness* and *friendship* and *hope* in them. Madi saves herself. If readers remember that, I'm happy.

ALL IS FAIR
IN LOVE AND
FANDOM

*W*hen überfan Liv's favorite character is killed off, she and her best friend, Xander, an aspiring actor and steampunk enthusiast, decide to fight back—and end up changing everything!

*L*iv had spent her entire life feeling like a nerd. The social outcast. The freak. In middle school, she'd tried to hide her differentness, keeping her online activities completely anonymous and wandering through fandom as a lurker. But no matter how hard she tried to appear normal, there was some invisible mark that kept her apart from her real-life peers, like they could sense she wasn't one of them. Liv wasn't invited to football parties or asked out on dates. She hovered at the edges of social events, looking in and wishing she could join. By high school, she'd made the jump to visibility— at least online—creating vids, reading fic voraciously, and even wearing the occasional *Starveil* T-shirt to school. But living in Boulder, a city of mountain climbers, sports fans, and activists, she'd always known she was an outsider.

Arriving to drop off their bags at the Marriott, the feeling disappeared.

While Dragon Con took place in a number of downtown Atlanta buildings, the Marriott hotel was the epicenter of the event. The entire atrium floor of the gigantic building swarmed with a melting pot of nerd culture. Stormtroopers chatted amicably with aging television stars while waiting in line at Starbucks. Bewigged anime cosplayers posed alongside pro wrestlers and *Game of Thrones* characters, the lines for panels filled with teenagers and seniors alike. At least ten variations of Captain Matt Spartan had spied Liv's Spartan "Only One Man Calls Me Darlin'" T-shirt and had made a point of shouting out a "Hello, darlin'!" to her. She stared wide-eyed as glass-walled elevators shot up fifty-two floors like pods in a launch tube. Everything—from the glaringly bright carpet swirling with psychedelic lines; to the hotel's open ceiling ringed by story after story of balconies, the distant roof so high it made her head spin; to the people decked out in cosplay—was torn from a science-fiction novel. It seemed Liv had spent the last eighteen years in search of her people, and in one sudden explosion of fate, they'd all been brought together in this place in time. Her eyes filled with tears as a sudden awareness hit her.

They were all nerds.

danika stone

is an author, artist, and educator who discovered a passion for writing fiction while in the throes of her master's thesis. A self-declared bibliophile, Danika now writes novels for both adults (*Edge of Wild*, the Intaglio series, and *Ctrl Z*) and teens (*All the Feels*). When not writing, Danika can be found hiking in the Rockies, planning grand adventures, and spending far too much time online. She lives with her husband, three sons, and a houseful of imaginary characters in a windy corner of Alberta, Canada.

danikastone.com